# ASSASSINS

FORGE BOOKS BY MUKUL DEVA

*Weapon of Vengeance*

# ASSASSINS

## MUKUL DEVA

A TOM DOHERTY ASSOCIATES BOOK | NEW YORK

This is a work of fiction. All of the characters, organizations, and events portrayed in this novel are either products of the author's imagination or are used fictitiously.

ASSASSINS

A Forge Book
Published by Tom Doherty Associates, LLC
175 Fifth Avenue
New York, NY 10010

www.tor-forge.com

Forge® is a registered trademark of Tom Doherty Associates, LLC.

The Library of Congress Cataloging-in-Publication Data is available upon request.

ISBN 978-0-7653-3772-6 (hardcover)
ISBN 978-1-4668-3571-9 (e-book)

Forge books may be purchased for educational, business, or promotional use. For information on bulk purchases, please contact the Macmillan Corporate and Premium Sales Department at 1-800-221-7945, extension 5442, or write to specialmarkets@macmillan.com.

First Edition: July 2015

Printed in the United States of America

0  9  8  7  6  5  4  3  2  1

*This book is dedicated to Dhirendra Saxena.*

Each of us has a Krishna in our lives, a charioteer
who guides us and supports us, no matter what
the circumstances or how severe the odds.
That is what Dhirendra has always been for me:
a bulwark of support.

# ACKNOWLEDGMENTS

This book would never have been possible if it had not been for certain people who came into my life at the right time. My editor, Bob Gleason of Tom Doherty Associates, and his assistants, Kelly Quinn and Elayne Becker, for their consistent support and for putting together this book so well. My agent, Al Zuckerman of Writers House, who was invaluable in helping to give the story shape. And, considering the chain of synchronicity, Fran Lebowitz, who brought us together. Also, the dozens of other people I interviewed to get a handle on the technical aspects, who prefer to stay anonymous.

A very special vote of thanks to Meher, my favorite younger daughter, who went through every draft of this book and helped with several creative suggestions.

Thanks also to the National Arts Council of Singapore for their perennial support. Singapore has been a fantastic breeding ground for me, freed me from so many worries, and enabled me to focus single-mindedly on writing.

Any errors, factual or technical, that still exist in this book are solely my fault or have been deliberately left in there by me to prevent any misuse of a technology or an idea.

# AUTHOR'S NOTE

This book is a work of fiction, although some of the events mentioned here may have actually taken place.

All the characters, countries, places, and organizations described or mentioned in this book are fictitious or have been fictitiously used, and any resemblance to any place, organization, country, or person, living or dead, is absolutely unintentional.

In several cases, artistic license has been taken with the places mentioned in the book, distances between places, and the general topography.

In order to prevent an actual attack from being carried out on any monument or building, the location and layouts of all monuments and hotels mentioned in this book have been suitably altered. Similarly, the security arrangements of all places have been fictitiously described.

The technical details of the various weapon systems, the specifications and methodologies of bomb making and weaponry, as well as the tactics and security procedures employed by any police, military, intelligence organization, and/or militant organization, as also all criminal, forensic, and investigative procedures, have been deliberately kept slightly vague, inaccurate, and/or incomplete, once again to prevent any misuse, accidental or otherwise.

There is no slur or malice intended against any religion, race, caste, creed, nation, organization, or people.

*Harry was left to ponder in silence the depths to which girls would sink to get revenge.*

—J. K. Rowling
*Harry Potter and the Half-Blood Prince*

# DECEMBER
## 22

# ONE

Leon Binder needed to quickly secure at least two safe houses in Delhi and get on with the critical aspects of his mission. However, doubts kept hammering at him. Never had he taken on a twin-target assignment at such short notice.

*Five measly weeks to eliminate Pakistani Prime Minister Abid Zardosi and the ex-dictator General Pervaiz Masharrat . . . it was not enough.*

Leon rationalized his skittishness.

*Two heavily protected targets . . . each had survived a dozen assassination attempts.*

It was no secret that the people who wanted to see Zardosi dead would easily fill the twenty-eight thousand capacity Lord's Cricket Ground without much effort. Equally numerous were those who wanted the deceitful Masharrat pushing up daisies.

*That's why their security staff takes things so seriously. I should have had more time for planning this.*

Leon valued his careful, meticulous planning; rightly so, it had helped him succeed each time *and* kept him alive.

This time, to make things worse, both targets were reaching Delhi on the same day. Leon felt certain that in the wake of the 2008 Mumbai terror strike and the more recent attack on the Israeli-Palestinian Peace Summit held at Delhi, the Indian authorities would pull out all stops to ensure no further embarrassment.

There was no denying the complexity of the tasks. Equally undeniable was that he could retire in comfort if . . . *when* . . . Leon auto-corrected himself . . . he had terminated these two targets.

But he needed more time to study their routines and routes, evaluate their quirks, then decide who to hit first, where and how.

There was much to be done and now just six days left. His stomach clenched tighter.

And knowing how much his white skin made him stand out added to his turbulence. Yes, he *had* operated a couple of times on the Indian subcontinent, but that did not make it any easier.

The klaxons in his head had not yet started blaring, but soon they would.

Leon thought he had put away these doubts during his six-day weapon procurement sojourn in Seoul. Now he realized they had been overshadowed by his apprehension of betrayal by Ri Yong Ho, the rogue weapons dealer from Pyongyang. Betrayal was a possibility Leon could not ignore. And that fear had submerged his worry that Ri Yong Ho would be unable to get hold of the Sarin-AXR aerosol he so desperately needed to complete this mission. Ri Yong Ho had once worked in the North Korean industrial complex at Sinuiju and was possibly the only one known to Leon who could come up with the deadly sarin at such short notice.

Then the monotony of life intervened.

"Isn't it a lovely apartment?" The landlord's English was fluent, but the accent unmistakably Indian. Six feet tall in slippered feet, the powerfully built, jeans- and kurta-clad Om Chandra was smiling. The crisp white, freshly laundered kurta gave him a scholarly look, but he made Leon uneasy. Perhaps his constantly darting eyes, which evaded making contact. Perhaps his alert posture, which was in marked contrast to his silken, over-friendly tone. Possibly both. They gave Leon the impression of a man with a violent disposition or a deceitful temperament. Again, possibly both.

*Someone to watch out for.*

"It is perfect." Checking the impulse to walk out as fast as possible, Leon lied, pitching his voice several octaves higher. A lopsided smile accompanied his practiced American accent. Both went well with his current cover; the one Leon referred to as his benign American hippie look. Padding around his waist and an extra pullover added the required inches to his girth. His almost shoulder-length hair, liberally showing lots of gray, had been left loose and unkempt. His slumped posture and shuffling gait reduced his height and added years to his age, giving Leon the appearance of an aging out-of-shape hippie; useful to lower the guard of an opponent.

Leon maintained his lopsided smile as he surveyed the serviced apartment. It was a seedy, run-down place: peeling paint, faded curtains, and furniture that would have been more at home in a scrapyard. If the pictures advertising it on the RoomsToShare website were of this same apartment, they had been taken ages ago. And that's possibly why there were no endorsements from previous users.

Barring the exquisitely crafted ivory chess set on a side table in the living room, Leon saw nothing that appealed to him. Yet it had some obvious advantages; located in the last row of the four-story, eight apartments per block, government-built colony of Sarita Vihar, it was a corner house with no external signboards that it was being run as a serviced apartment. Inside a middle-class residential colony, it was not likely to attract attention.

More important, this landlord had not asked Leon for any identification: a given in this terror-infested day and age. That reinforced his suspicions about Om Chandra, but it also made the apartment eminently desirable. Cautioning himself to watch his back, Leon pushed aside his misgivings.

"I will be taking it for two weeks as I had requested in my email. My wife will only join me later." There was no wife; however, Leon knew that mention of a wife invariably lulled suspicions.

"Good, good." Pleased, and now visibly relieved, Om Chandra shifted gears. "Is there anything else you need me to help you with, sir? A chauffeured car? A maid to cook for you? Or even . . ." —he allowed a sly smile to complete that sentence—"any other kind of *entertainment* . . . till the wife comes along. You just need to tell me."

Leon had no doubt what kind of entertainment. *Drugs, girls, boys, and perhaps even weapons . . . this man would be wary of getting the cops involved.* Leon decided it was an opportunity worth capitalizing on. "A car would be great, though I don't want a driver. I assume the car would be auto-transmission."

"It'll be what you wish it to be, Mr. Berman." That's the name Leon had given him, David Berman. "Though the rental for automatic gears is a little higher."

"How much higher?" Leon sensed it would be a mistake not to bargain. Om was the kind who would take it as a sign of stupidity or worse, weakness. And Leon had no desire to set himself up as a mark. He negotiated.

Ten minutes later, ensuring Om Chandra left feeling good, Leon had the two-bedroom apartment to himself and the assurance that a suitable car would be delivered within the hour; auto-transmission but Indian make, nothing that would make him stand out; his white skin did that already.

Once Om Chandra left, Leon's thoughts returned to his targets. He was sure the conference Masharrat was speaking at would be easier for him to penetrate, so Masharrat was tactically the first choice. However, strategically he should be targeting Zardosi first.

*The Paki prime minister would be far less protected here in Delhi than in Pakistan.*

Taking out Zardosi now would also save him a high-risk journey into Pakistan. Plus there would be more opportunities to hit Masharrat, who was based in Dubai and prone to shuttling around the world on speaking gigs.

*On the other hand, the minute I take down the first target they pay me half the remaining seventy-five percent. Then I can carry out the second strike with detailed planning and preparation.*

Feeling the pressure, Leon decided to focus on the tactically easier target first. That sorted, he then got down to the next item on his agenda.

# TWO

Suresh Kurup, the recently appointed director of India's National Intelligence Agency, the NIA, gave Sir Edward Kingsley a worried look. "I don't see how you can convince Gill to take on this assignment." Kurup's thick eyebrows, which stood out prominently on his long, thin face, were beetled up. He was in a well-tailored midnight-blue business suit. However, right now the suit looked as rumpled and worried as his expression—both evidence of a long, sleepless night. "I'm not even sure if he will meet with us, considering he declined to come to the office yesterday."

"Perhaps because he assumed it was to do with your inquiry on the Israeli-Palestinian Peace Summit fiasco." Kingsley rationalized, but Kurup could see the MI6 director was worried, too.

"Whatever." Kurup felt a surge of irritation. "I have only been doing my job. The fact is Gill *did* screw up and now has to face the consequences. Bloody hell! How on earth did he fail to pick up that his daughter was going to attack the peace summit?" Kurup nearly succumbed to the need to share the intense pressure he was under, from his political masters *and* the media. That blatant attack and murder of several foreign delegates had shamed India on every possible international platform. Compounding the nation's shame was the fact that the daughter of the Indian Anti-Terrorist Task Force commander had carried out the attack. Yet to settle into his new assignment, Kurup could not forget the merciless hounding he had been subjected to; finding a scapegoat had become a national imperative. "I doubt Gill will meet us . . . much less agree to take on this assignment. Why should he?"

"He *will* meet us." Scrunched up beside him in the rear seat of the cream-colored Škoda Yeti, Kingsley replied doggedly. "And he *has to* take it on. Gill is our only hope."

But Kurup knew he was not imagining the tendrils of doubt in the MI6 director's clipped British tone.

Though the Škoda Yeti was a spacious SUV, both men were tall; their heads impacted the roof with every bump in the road. And bumps there were in plenty on the road from central Delhi to the outlying suburb of Chhatarpur. Since the NIA director offered a high value target to terrorists, the Yeti was sandwiched between two escort cars with four heavily armed agents in each. Courtesy of the lead car's siren they maintained a brisk pace despite the rush-hour traffic. The mini-cavalcade swept past the Chhatarpur temple complex: a beautiful collection of buildings that drew the devout and the tourist with equal fervor. But today, wrapped up in their worries, neither man noticed it.

"Let's hope he does." Pondering the consequences if Gill refused to accept this assignment, Kurup worriedly surveyed the ruddy-faced Englishman. Even the Savile Row, steel-gray suit was unable to hide Kingsley's bulk. His tiny goatee looked incongruous on so massive a man. "Though, to be honest with you, I am still not convinced we need Gill . . . or that he is the best man for this."

"Trust me. No one knows Leon Binder better." Kingsley replied. "Like I told you, Suresh, the three of us were not only classmates at Imperial College, we also shared the same apartment in London. We were close . . . especially the two of them. Ravinder knows how Binder's mind works." After a pause, he added. "If anyone can stop Leon Binder, he can."

"If we *have* to stop Binder. I cannot imagine the consequences if Binder manages to assassinate either Zardosi or Masharrat on Indian soil." Both men *had* already discussed that several times, but it did not stop Kurup from repeating himself. "Those morons in Pakistan will go apeshit. India has always been the favorite red rag for the Paki generals; the only reason they keep harping on the plight of Muslims in Kashmir and other parts of India is to distract the attention of their people from the sorry state of affairs in Pakistan. That's why the low literacy levels and shitty state of their economy suits the generals; it ensures people are too busy struggling to survive and so the generals get away with draining their country's resources." Realizing he was launching into a diatribe, Suresh checked himself. "The assassination of any Pakistani on Indian soil will give them the best possible excuse to raise the India bogey, throw out democracy in Pakistan, and it could easily lead to another Indo-Pak war."

Kingsley knew Suresh was not overstating things; in the sixty years of its existence Pakistan had left no stone unturned to ensure Indo-Pak relations remained on a precipice; that gave them the perfect reason to divert most of the Pakistani budget toward the army. "Not to mention what would happen to global peace if the fundamentalists seize power in Pakistan." he muttered darkly.

"I just don't get it. What *are* your people doing?" Kurup was plainly bitter. "First one of your agents shoots up delegates in the Israeli-Palestinian Peace Summit right in the heart of Delhi. And now we have London-based terror groups sponsoring assassinations here." His tone turned plaintive. "How on earth do you allow obviously criminal groups like the Sisters of Benazir to function so openly in England?" He gave the upholstery a frustrated thump. "Seriously . . . how the hell did you guys ever manage to colonize half the world?"

"Dumb luck, I guess, old chap." Kingsley returned his smile. But, like Kurup's, his smile was brittle, too.


Edward Kingsley knew the NIA director was right. That a Palestinian terrorist like Ruby Gill had managed to penetrate *and* survive undetected in MI6 for so many years had dealt a serious blow to the agency's credibility. Her attack on the Delhi peace summit had left a lot of red faces in England.

And now this . . . *if the assassinations sponsored by the London-based SOB succeeded*, it would make life seriously hairy for MI6, and Kingsley in particular. Ten Downing Street had been brutally unambiguous: with elections around the corner, if MI6 got any more egg on its face, Kingsley would be put to pasture. And *that* could well be the least of his worries.

*I have to stop Binder. Rather,* help *the Indians stop him . . . and considering how things are done here, that is going to be a bitch.*

Kingsley bit back the scowl before it hit his face. His lack of direct operational control had never galled him so much. But control over operatives of another agency on foreign soil was beyond the realms of possibility.

*I must convince Ravinder to take this on. He, at least, has the same motivation I do to bring that bastard Binder down.*

That made him feel better. Marginally.

*But poor Ravinder. With the death of his daughter and the peace summit fiasco, he must be a total mess. Would he be able to cope? Stopping an accomplished assassin like Binder would be no mean task . . . Binder had successfully stayed ahead of the police in several dozen countries for well nigh three decades.*

Kingsley's anxiety counterattacked with renewed vigor.

Suresh saw Kingsley's ruddy face turn redder still and sensed his discomfiture.

Before more talk could develop, their convoy pulled up at a black metallic gate. Inset into a twelve-foot-high boundary wall, the gate was shut. A guard peered out from a grilled window to the right. Both spymasters watched one of the agents in the lead vehicle lean out and parlay.

"Do you think he will let us in?" Kurup's fingers nervously tap-danced on the car seat as he saw the guard reach for a phone.

"He has to." But again, there was more hope than certainty in Kingsley's reply. As if to substantiate that, he added, "Did you know, back in college the three of us were called KGB?"

"KGB?"

"Kingsley, Gill, and Binder." The MI6 man elaborated with a vague half smile, but his attention was on the gate guard. "We were apartment mates and very good friends . . . really close. Inseparable. Till . . ." Kingsley broke off as the huge gates swung open. Soundlessly. "He *is* going to meet us. I told you he would." He was unable to keep the triumphant note out of his voice. But his relief was far more evident.

The opened gate revealed a six-hundred-foot-long graveled drive, which led to a sparkling white farmhouse, standing in a lush, well-manicured garden.

As they drove down, to the right was a swimming pool, over which hovered the mist of a chilly December morning. To the left, a tennis court, but the missing net gave it a desolate look. Between that and the porch was a garage large enough for three, perhaps four, cars, but it was empty.

Except for the guard at the gate and a gardener puttering in the distance everything was silent. Graveyard silent.

Even Suresh, a Delhi-ite, found it hard to imagine that the non-stop cacophonous hustle-bustle of Delhi lay within reach. He felt a twinge of envy as he took in the surroundings. The place reeked of money. Old money.

*No wonder this guy is so snooty.*

Then, on the stairs to the porch, Suresh spied the man they had come to meet. Though on the uphill side of fifty, the tall Sikh with a black, tautly bound turban stood ramrod straight. His chin jutted forward. Unblinking eyes tracked the inbound cars. He looked agitated.

As they drew closer Kurup noticed the grief lines that had aged his face. But from his demeanor and carriage it was easy to deduce he had spent the better part of his life in uniform.

Then the cars halted. Steeling themselves, the spymaster duo got ready to alight. Kurup knew Kingsley was equally eager to get to the business at hand.

# THREE

Ravinder Singh Gill stood on the stairs dominating the porch and watched the trio of cars come up the drive, their heavy tires crunching the gravel. He could not decide what he was feeling more, anger or curiosity.

Kurup was the last man on earth he expected to play host to.

*What the heck is he doing here? Didn't the blighter get the hint when I declined his invitation yesterday?*

In light of Kurup's shoddy behavior as chairperson of the inquiry investigating the disastrous Israeli-Palestinian Peace Summit and his attempt to pin the blame on Ravinder, the NIA chief was not someone Ravinder wished to see, and certainly not at his house. Shocked at the Kurup's audacity, Ravinder had been about to order the guard not to open the gate when he mentioned that Sir Edward Kingsley was accompanying Kurup.

That had taken him by surprise. Ravinder liked Edward, though he mistrusted the spymaster's motives. Above all, Ravinder could not walk away from the fact that, though it ended badly, Edward *had* been helpful during the Ruby investigation. That obligation and Ravinder's curiosity had led to the gates being opened.

*But what could he possibly want? MI6 directors don't go around paying impromptu visits to old college mates . . . even those they were close to.*

*They* had *been close to* . . . Ravinder corrected. They had kept in touch, but never regained that magical camaraderie they had once shared.

*Farah's death had extinguished that.*

Ravinder pushed away the memory of Farah Fairfowler, Edward's long-dead fiancée; it was ugly and unsettling, the first time he had confronted death. It had been up close and gruesome. Though the incident happened three decades ago, the recollection was painful still. Farah's bloodied face, contorted in fear, still haunted him. Those memories left him with mixed feelings concerning Kingsley; a part of him missed the friendship they had once shared, and yet another part wished they would never have to meet again.

The lead car pulled past and the Škoda Yeti slid to a halt beside him. Ravinder picked up Kurup's sheepishness the minute the NIA chief alighted. Making little effort to conceal his distaste he shook Kurup's hand, but a brief, perfunctory shake. Ravinder then turned to greet Kingsley; the bulkier man was a bit slower in alighting.

*What on earth could they want from me? Cannot be anything straightforward . . . it never is with these intelligence types . . . devious blighters.*

"It's great to see you again, Edward." Ravinder's curiosity was aching to burst free. "A long way from your usual beat, aren't you?"

"You haven't changed a bit, Ravinder. Well, perhaps a couple more wrinkles since we last met." Kingsley bypassed the question as they shook. "How long has it been? And how are you, old boy?"

Ravinder examined the Englishman, keen to spot the changes the last thirty years had inflicted on him. Barring the gray hair and a dozen more kilograms, Ravinder could not spot any.

*He has fared well. Good.* Ravinder smiled. "The years have been kind to you, Edward."

"I'm not complaining, old chap." Edward grinned, patting his girth. Ravinder sensed Kingsley, too, was happy to see him, but also uneasy. Then Edward's grip tightened and his smile faded. "Terribly sorry about what happened with Ruby," he murmured.

With a thud Ravinder was back in the present. Suddenly he felt that awkwardness again, akin to what Farah's death had unleashed. Ravinder could sense Edward's anxiety, mirroring his own. It persisted as Ravinder led the way to a patio adjacent to the living room, overlooking the pool. Six garden chairs circling an oval center table were arranged in the patio. Despite a weak sun fighting to make its presence felt through the heavy December fog, it was a pleasant place. Peaceful.

However, the peace did not last long.

"We have a problem, Mr. Gill," Suresh said without preamble; both spies sat on one side and Ravinder across, facing Kingsley.

Kurup's tone again reminded Ravinder that these two men wanted something from him. Badly.

*And that something would probably not be good for me.*

"Don't we all have problems?" Ravinder quipped, swiveling his chair to keep an eye on both opponents.

*Opponents?* The word stuck in his head.

Why had he chosen it?

It *felt* appropriate.

*Wonder which of the two I need to watch out for? Kurup? Aggressive and demanding. Or Kingsley? The friend and hence harder to refuse.*

Unsure, Ravinder perched on the edge of his chair, eying both warily. "I certainly have enough, so I'm not sure if I even want to listen to your problems."

"Ravinder, we need your help," Edward chipped in, trying to keep his tone collegial. "Have you heard of the SOB . . . the Sisters of Benazir?"

"Sounds like a corny soap opera," Ravinder quipped. "Has it something to do with Benazir Basheer, the Pakistani politician who was assassinated at Rawalpindi some years ago?"

"That's right. The SOB is a group of her supporters. Based in London . . . a rabid bunch. *Very* fanatic lot and loaded to boot. Hence capable of tremendous damage."

"Aren't they all?" Ravinder tried to show he didn't care. But he was intrigued. "And what about this SOB is disturbing your sleep, Edward?"

"Not his alone," Suresh interjected, "they are about to disturb everyone's."

Ravinder's eyebrows hiked one notch up. "How so?"

Suresh elaborated. "Benazir's people believe three men were behind her murder. Pervaiz Masharrat, then the military dictator, Abid Zardosi, the current Pakistani prime minister, and Beitullah Mehsud, then the commander of the Tehreek-e-Taliban Pakistan."

"Masharrat and Mehsud I can understand; they definitely had it in for her. But Zardosi?" Ravinder's eyebrow hiked higher. "Her *husband*? Seriously?"

"That's what they *believe*," Suresh stressed.

"I guess we're all entitled to our beliefs." Ravinder shrugged.

However, his curiosity had been aroused and Edward picked that up. "The problem is the SOB have decided to act on this belief."

Ravinder noticed his worried tone. "They've already taken out Beitullah Mehsud and have now decided to assassinate the other two."

Ravinder tutted. "I thought it was the Americans that got Mehsud."

"The missile that took out Mehsud was certainly American, as
was the drone it was fired from, but it was an SOB operative who
guided it there," Kurup responded.

"Right." Ravinder's snort communicated his disbelief.

"It is no laughing matter, Mr. Gill."

Ignoring Kurup's irritated frown, Ravinder grilled Kingsley.
"Let's get real, Edward. This is assassination we are talking about.
Of two people who take their security obsessively. Not a public rally
in Hyde Park. Also, I must confess that, considering the two gentlemen you say they are targeting, the lethal little sisters have my
best wishes. Someone should have done this a *long* time ago. By
actively aiding and abetting the jihadis these two gentlemen have
done more damage to global security than a dozen Osamas."

"That's what many in London believe, too"—Kingsley gave a rueful
smile—"but the problem is the SOB are planning to hit one or both
of them in Delhi. *That* would create a grave problem, Ravinder."

The NIA director again made to speak, but Ravinder cut him
off. "Let me get this straight, Edward. We have a bunch of political activists . . . people who have never wielded anything deadlier
than a fork and knife . . . planning to assassinate an ex-dictator
who has survived a dozen such attempts *and* the prime minister of
Pakistan . . . a banana republic, I grant you . . . or should I say a
*mango* republic"—Ravinder could not help the sarcastic reference to
the exploding mangoes that had allegedly been used to murder an
earlier dictator of Pakistan—"but a country nonetheless."

Conversation stalled as a maid emerged with a laden tea service,
an assortment of biscuits, and some savory sandwiches.

"Our intelligence confirms they are doing just that," Suresh said
after the maid had gone inside. "Either Masharrat when he speaks
at the New India Times Summit, or Zardosi when he comes to Delhi
for the Indo-Pak T20 cricket match."

"Your *intelligence*?" Ravinder threw him a withering look.

The gibe made Kurup go red.

"We infiltrated the SOB a long time ago." Kingsley preempted
Kurup's angry outburst. "The intel is positive, Ravinder. They have
already launched the operation."

"Either way I see no problem." Ravinder was still not sure what they wanted from him, but was determined to steer clear. "Just tell both those buggers to stay the hell out of India. Cricket diplomacy has never achieved a damn thing. Besides, given the state of affairs in Pakistan, who the hell listens to Zardosi, anyway? He cannot even buy toilet paper without an approval from his army chief." Suresh made to speak, but Ravinder headed him off. "And Masharrat! Why should we even allow him in India? That fork-tongued bastard was planning the attack on Kargil even when he was sitting here in Agra, allegedly talking peace with our prime minister."

"Come on, Ravinder. You know things don't work like that," Suresh responded. "Diplomacy must go on."

"Not from where I am looking at things. Pakistan never has and never will stop attacking India, and since they don't have the balls to do so openly, they will continue using terrorist groups to fight their proxy war. Nothing has changed in the last sixty years, so why should we kid ourselves that it will be any different this time?" Ravinder countered. "And in any case, I'm sure MI6 and NIA are more than a match for a ragtag bunch of political activists. At least, I hope to God they are."

"They are not the problem." Kingsley sounded grimmer now. "The big worry is that the SOB leader Fatima Basheer has hired one of the world's deadliest assassins for this job."

Claustrophobia clutched Ravinder. He sensed something sinister straining to be unleashed, and desperately hoped the Englishman would stop.

But Kingsley leaned in closer, intruding on his air space, denying that hope. "They have hired Binder. Leon Binder."

His words struck like hammer blows. Ravinder started violently. "Leon Binder? *Our* Leon?"

"Yes. *Our* Leon." Edward spat out the name as though it were an epithet. "And once again, he brings nothing but death and ugliness into our lives."

Ravinder was blown away. This unexpected blast from the past had taken the wind out of his sails.

Kingsley saw he had scored and drove home the advantage. "Please help us stop him, Ravinder. You're the only one who can."

"Why me, Edward?" A strangled croak. Ravinder was struggling to cope with this sudden ghost from a long-dead past. Never had he imagined life would again deliver all three of them to the same crossroads at the same time.

"Who knows him better?" Kingsley countered. "And Ravinder . . ."

"This could be the ideal opportunity to prove your loyalty and redeem yourself," Kurup arrowed in.

Ravinder blanched as the words jabbed him, barbs of cancerous pain.

*How dare he? After three decades in uniform and everything that I have done, do I still need to prove my loyalty?*

Suppressing the urge to slap Kurup, Ravinder focused on Kingsley, searching for words to explain why he could not take on this assignment . . . to share the self-doubt threatening to submerge him . . . of not knowing whether he could successfully complete this mission. And, *even worse*, of knowing that *when* he failed, he would not survive the failure.

Ravinder thought the MI6 man sensed it too, Kurup's insensitivity and his self-doubts. He felt Edward's hand on his shoulder. "Don't sell yourself short, my friend. I can think of no one better to watch my six."

That unexpected touch felt like balm to Ravinder. It unleashed memories of the camaraderie they'd once shared. With that also came thoughts of Leon and the accompanying guilt those memories invoked. Right from the day Farah had died.

*How can I explain my guilt about Leon? Especially to Edward . . . he will never understand. But I need to know if . . .*

"That's your *only* reason for wanting to go after Binder?" Ravinder pinned Edward with a questioning look, aware how badly the MI6 man had taken his fiancée's, Farah's, death.

*Has he gotten over it even now?* Ravinder reflected.

*Perhaps not.* Ravinder knew Edward was still a bachelor.

Silence gripped the patio. The sun had strengthened and it was a beautiful day. However, this was lost on the three men. Like the tea service lying untouched on the center table.

"Are you sure what happened back then . . ."—Ravinder did not take his gaze off the Britisher—"between Leon and Farah has nothing to do with it?"

Taken aback by his directness, Edward blinked. Finally shook his head. "No. You know that's not true, Ravinder."

"Do I?" Neither man broke eye contact.

Edward pulled his hand back from Ravinder's shoulder. Hurt. Perhaps also angry. Ravinder felt the chasm between them widen. It saddened him, but he *needed* to know.

Kurup was watching both, riveted. Head swiveling like a Wimbledon fanatic.

"Come on, man. That was . . ." Kingsley faltered, broke eye contact. Ravinder noticed he was trying hard to stay calm.

Kingsley sought eye contact again. "That's not fair, Ravinder."

And Ravinder knew it wasn't. The Edward he had known was a fair man. He *wanted* to give Kingsley the benefit of the doubt. Simultaneously, his instincts were screaming at him to walk away.

Intellect clashed with emotion as Ravinder tried to rationalize. He was aware Edward was right; there was no one who knew Leon better. And Ravinder could easily visualize the consequences if Leon succeeded in killing either Zardosi or Masharrat on Indian soil; the severity was an undisputed nine on the Richter scale. Indo-Pak relations were always precariously teetering on the edge of a deadly cliff; the slightest push could unleash the dogs of war. The thought of a war between the two nuclear-armed neighbors was terrifying. However, Ravinder's emotional flux and insecurity maxed even that.

"No, Edward. Perhaps it is not. I'm sorry." Ravinder stood up and moved away, suddenly eager to distance himself from the spymasters. Though unable to suppress a twinge of guilt, Ravinder was firm, hardened as much by his mistrust of Kurup as by his desire to steer clear of anything to do with Binder. "I *do* understand the magnitude of the problem, but I want nothing to do with it."

Kingsley opened his mouth to protest. And Kurup looked as though he were about to explode. That's when Kurup's mobile began to ring.

# FOUR

Fatima Basheer could appreciate neither the luxurious fourth-floor suite of Delhi's Maurya Sheraton hotel she'd checked into on arrival from London fifteen minutes ago, nor the beautifully landscaped garden outside her window. She was hyperventilating; her worst fear, that Binder would refuse to proceed with the mission, was coming alive. She'd been dreading that since she had discovered Cherry Rehmat, the SOB financial controller, had leaked information to MI6 about their hiring Binder.

"If there is a leak at your end I will call it off *and* keep the retainer." She remembered Leon's warning when he had taken on the assignment.

"What exactly did he say, Mr. Verma?" She tiredly rubbed her well-sculpted face, for once unmindful of the makeup. "Tell me again." Worry lines creased her peachy skin. Even her lush black waist-length and usually immaculately coiffured hair were disheveled. Right now she was showing every one of her forty-four years.

Mindful of the huge sum of money Fatima had promised him, and aware he was already in too deep, Ashok Verma, deputy director NIA and one of Kurup's principal aides, stifled his exasperation and repeated, "Very little actually . . . once I told him you were reaching Delhi today."

"Oh?"

"Yes. He was livid about the security leak at your end."

"Did you tell him that we have . . ." Fatima floundered, searching for palatable words. She hesitated to say it out loud, though she had felt great satisfaction in having Cherry killed. ". . . ensured there would be no further leaks?"

"I tried. I did everything you asked me to, but he did not seem inclined to listen." Uncomfortable with such a dangerous conversation on his office phone, Ashok was in a hurry to end the call. "He said the damage had already been done."

Fatima sensed his reluctance to talk. Exhausted by the long flight from London and already freaking out at this latest setback, she snapped out of control. "Tell me *exactly* what he said," she hissed coldly, wanting to remind Ashok she was in charge.

It did.

Now regretting that he had allowed himself to be talked into this thankless task of being the conduit between Binder and Basheer, Ashok elaborated. "He said that since MI6 *and* the NIA have been alerted, it would be too risky to even make an attempt. Not to mention the Special Task Force hunting for him."

"But did you remind him that there are only five days left and now that we have eliminated Goel, the task force chief, they are completely disorganized . . . hardly in a position to stop him?" But Fatima realized the futility of this conversation; it was Leon, not Ashok Verma, she needed to convince.

"I did. That proved to be the last straw. He blew up when he I told him what had happened to Goel." Ashok had been reluctant to get involved with *that*. He had agreed only when Fatima doubled his payout *and* because Vishal had carried out Goel's kidnapping and interrogation.

"Why?" Fatima was perplexed; she had hoped that would appease Leon.

But Ashok's nervousness had reached the end of its tether. "You can ask him yourself. He wants you to meet him at the Qutb Minar at three p.m."

"The Qutb Minar? Did he mention how I am to find him?"

"He said he'd find you."

Swamped by a sea of gloom Fatima ended the call and tossed her mobile on the bed. She had no idea how she was going to convince Leon to continue with the mission, but knew she had to do it. Finding and making contact with the right man had taken her seven months. Convincing the SOB council to agree to the huge payout demanded by Leon had taken almost as long.

*And in one stroke that double-crossing bitch Cherry shafted us. All for the sake of a few pounds.*

Fatima's grimace deepened.

*Well, not really. A lot more than a few.*

Fatima remembered how stunned they had been to learn Cherry had siphoned off most of the fifty-million-pound SOB war chest, hard-earned money donated by the thousands of Pakistani sisters who had sworn allegiance to Benazir. After paying Leon his first instalment of five million pounds, and the five million now due to him on reaching Delhi, there was barely enough left to buy toilet paper.

The thought of telling Leon she did not have money to pay his last two installments of five million each, after he terminated both targets, petrified her.

*But I cannot let him know right now. Not till he has done the job.*

Deciding she would worry about it later, she focused on the immediate problem—convincing Leon to keep going.

*I have to make this work. I've waited too long for this revenge. I cannot fail. Not with the end in sight.*

She checked her watch. There were still a couple of hours before she needed to start out for her meeting with Leon. Pacing the hotel room she began to rack her brains, trying to figure out how best to counter the impact of Cherry's betrayal and convince Leon.

Once again, anger at Cherry for placing her in this dangerous dilemma gripped Fatima. Her hands clenched in tight, hate-filled balls. She regretted not having driven the knife into Cherry's throat herself.

*Treacherous bitches like her need to die slowly and painfully. And to think she almost got away with it. She would have, too, if I had not taken Zaki to the zoo that day.*

Using the stub Fatima lit another cigarette and took a long drag, trying to calm herself down. But she was unable to prevent her thoughts from turning to the past.

Like all eight-year-olds, her son Zaki had the energy of a dozen men and the enthusiasm of twice that many. By time they reached the monkey enclosure of London Zoo, Fatima was ready to have him placed with them.

"Don't go too far, Zaki. Mommy needs a break." Dying to take the weight off her feet, Fatima collapsed on the bench by the bushes. The bench was not too clean, but it was the only unoccupied one in shade. Pausing long enough to pull a packet of salted peanuts and a Coke mini from her bag, Zaki joined the crowd of kids making faces at the monkeys. Left to her own devices, Fatima nodded off.

Voices from the other side of the bush woke her. More probably it was that one of them was familiar; Fatima would have recognized Cherry Rehmat's high-pitched voice anywhere. It was raised even higher in disagreement.

"But that's not what we agreed upon," she heard Cherry say. "It's too dangerous for you to call me. Let me . . ."

"Pipe down." The man she was with cut her off, but he was speaking in a low tone and Fatima could not make out what he said subsequently. Intrigued, she peered through the bush. Cherry's back was to her. There was nothing exceptional about the man Cherry was talking to, but he may as well have had the word SPOOK branded on his forehead. One glance and Fatima knew; the daughter of a man who'd spent his life steeped in Pakistani politics and served twice as the governor of Sindh, Fatima had grown up seeing him surrounded by such security and intelligence types. Her skin was tingling as she watched them converse, their voices now too low for her to overhear.

A moment later Cherry said, "Give me five minutes to get clear." And walked away. By now every nerve ending in Fatima's body was on fire.

Brushing aside Zaki's protests she rushed him out to her car and was ready by time the man emerged, found his car in the packed parking lot, and drove out. Fatima followed him all the way to the Vauxhall Cross SIS building, MI6 headquarters. There she sat, parked at a safe distance from even the prying cameras she knew would be watching everything around, but with a clear view of the building. Her heart sank with every passing minute. An hour later she could deny it no longer; Cherry Rehmat, the SOB financial controller, was cavorting with MI6. It did not bode well even in the best of times. Right now, with the Binder mission recently launched and a special diktat in place for all of them to lie low, the implications left Fatima breathless. Then anger arrived. It was raging by time she dropped Zaki home and arrived outside Cherry's house. Zeenat, a loyalist whom she had called from outside the MI6 office, was already there, parked three houses away. And Zeenat was equally furious when Fatima briefed her.

"You watch the back of the house in case Cherry tries to run." Fatima waited till Zeenat called to confirm she was in position and then headed for Cherry's front door; gripped tightly in her right hand was an Electric Shock 3.8 Million Volt Tactical Security Stun

Gun. A cute little thing, just two inches by four inches, and pink to match her outfit, it was part of every woman's accessory kit in these insecure days.

Fatima was a raging inferno when she rang the doorbell. In the minute or so it took for Cherry to get the door, her anger had peaked. By time Cherry opened the door, Fatima's grand plan to deal with this in a collected, masterful manner was a faint memory.

Cherry blanched when she saw Fatima on her doorstep. And Fatima *knew*. As certainly as though Cherry had delivered a signed statement: guilt danced naked in her eyes.

"You bitch!" Fatima hissed, suppressing the urge to shove the stun gun in Cherry's face. "You told them about Binder?" It was hardly a question. But Cherry nodded, unable to take her eyes off Fatima.

"Everything?" Fatima grilled her. "They know about his targets? And Delhi?"

Another dazed nod.

"MI6?"

Yet another nod.

"*Why?*" That erupted as a despairing sigh.

Cherry's mouth fell open, but only a useless flurry of words emerged. And the last vestiges of Fatima's control snapped. "You fucking bitch." She pulled out the stun gun. Cherry's eyes widened. Her panic shattered her inertia. Slamming the door in Fatima's face, Cherry turned and ran toward the rear of the house.

Fatima's hand, extended out to stun Cherry, took the brunt of the door slam. It hurt like hell, but prevented the door from closing. Cursing, she pushed it open again and ran behind Cherry. Straight into the umbrella stand by the door.

By the time she got up and reached the back door, Cherry was on the kitchen floor. Her chopping knife was trapped awkwardly in her throat. Bright red blood pulsed out in a thick, rich stream from the punctured jugular artery. Zeenat stood over her, horror and satisfaction fighting for dominance on her face.

"What the hell?" Fatima flipped. "I needed to question her . . . find out how much she told MI6. Why the hell did you have to . . ."

"She attacked me." Zeenat pouted, defensive.

Fatima sensed Zeenat was lying. "Fuck!" She wanted to slap her. Instead she knelt and checked if Cherry was alive. No chance. Now Fatima was in a hurry to get away. Already the smell of fresh blood was filling up the room.

*Wonder where Cherry's husband and kids are?*

But it was only curiosity. Not fear. Right now if they had chanced upon her, Fatima would have done them in herself; her anger at Cherry had not yet found release. Aloud, Fatima said, "Wipe your prints from everything you've touched, Zeenat. And make damn sure you lay low till this blows over."

And there was regret in Fatima's heart that it had ended so quickly for Cherry. That feeling escalated when she decided to take her own advice and get out of the country. Parking Zaki with his cousins in Canterbury, Fatima decided to convert her trip to Delhi into an extended holiday to Dubai; always a good place to shop.

Fatima was arranging the second-stage payment for Leon when she realized Cherry had embezzled the bulk of their funds. And she wished it had been she, not Zeenat, who had driven the knife into Cherry.

F atima started as the cigarette stub seared her fingers. Using it to light another, she tried to soothe her jangling nerves.

*Now the important thing is to ensure Leon doesn't pull out. But how?*

Fatima resumed pacing the hotel room as she wrapped her head around that.

*The money! That should be a good starting point.*

She checked the banking app on her mobile. The five million payable to Leon was ready for transfer. But she worried money alone would not be enough to keep Leon in the game.

*What else can I do?*

*I need to make him see how important this is. How much it means to me . . . to all of us?*

*But why should he care about that?*

Nervous fingers lit another cigarette.

# FIVE

Vishal Bhardwaj grimaced as he surveyed Goel's mangled remains, surprised how quickly the body had decayed. And dismayed it had been discovered so fast. When Vishal had dumped it under this culvert, in the midst of an abandoned field near Najafgarh on the Delhi border, he'd been confident it would not be discovered anytime soon. And it wouldn't have been, if it had not been for a bunch of village kids who had picked this very field to play in. Vishal could see them clustered in the distance, gawking.

*Fucking hicks.* He wanted to strangle the lot. But right now he needed to muddy the waters, to ensure his involvement was not discovered and the Special Task Force (STF) was kept so busy chasing its tail they had no time to worry about Binder. That's what Fatima Basheer was paying him for, and he had every intention of collecting that payment. Vishal shivered, rubbing his hands to keep away the cold. It didn't help; a brisk wind was sweeping the open field, and neither his brown woolen trousers nor the matching jacket were adequate to combat it. And the damp was seeping into his thin-soled loafers. He contemplated getting back into their car, but was reluctant in case he missed something the crime team came across.

*Would they?*

Vishal was pretty certain he'd left no clues, yet he couldn't stop worrying.

"Damn!" Beside him Philip Cherian, the heavyset, graying STF second-in-command, dressed in his trademark black suit, white shirt, and thin black tie, was shaking with anger. "No one deserves to die like that." Goel's body was riddled with marks of torture: cigarette burns on his face, several nails pulled, and an eyeball gouged out.

"I agree." Vishal's reply was muffled by the handkerchief he'd pressed to his nose, vainly trying to keep out the stench of decaying flesh.

"Poor bugger." Philip looked tearful. Understandably so, as Philip had served with Goel for several years, most recently as the second-in-command of this task force. "I wonder how they got him. Goel was always very cautious."

"Obviously, not cautious enough." Vishal turned away from the body, which had been removed from under the culvert and was now being examined by the Crime Scene Team. Watching from the road were three paramedics, waiting for the CST to finish. One of them was leaning against the ambulance, smoking. The other two squatted beside it, looking bored. For them death was an everyday occurrence.

*Until it comes for them.*

The thought dropped into Vishal's head, randomly.

*And it does, for all of us.*

*Strange how often we forget that.*

*Wonder if they will scream as loudly as Goel had.*

Vishal remembered how easily he had broken the Special Task Force commander.

*Fucking girl. He had squealed like a bitch.*

He realized Philip was giving him a strange look. "What?"

"Are you okay, Vishal?"

"Of course. Why?"

"I asked you a question. You seemed . . ." Philip jerked a thumb at the body. "Sometimes they get to you."

"I'm okay." Vishal stepped away and removed the rumpled hand-kerchief from his nose. "What did you ask?"

"Tell me again, what did Goel say when he left the office that afternoon?"

"He said he'd received a tip about Binder and was going to meet his source." Vishal had thought through the story and was confident it would stick.

"Any names, places . . ."

Vishal shook his head.

Cherian persisted. *"Anything* else?"

"No. Nothing. I offered to go with him, but Goel refused, saying he didn't want to spook the source." Vishal, a clear six inches taller than the second-in-command, gave him a defiant glare. "Haven't we

been through this already? Don't you think you should be informing the director we've found Goel, instead of wasting time playing
twenty questions?"

Philip's eyes narrowed into angry slits. Vishal realized he'd gone
too far; the man *was* his superior officer, and now with Goel dead
possibly the new STF commander. As it was, their relationship was
not the rosiest. Knowing he could not afford to be kicked out of the
task force, especially if he wanted to continue two-timing for Fatima,
Vishal made a sorry face. "I apologize. That was uncalled for." He
looked at the body, which the paramedics were now wrestling onto
a gurney, and added. "I guess all this is getting to me . . . more than
I realized."

The irritation on Philip's face receded; death was always a great
alibi. He backed off.

Retrieving Kurup's number from his mobile's address book,
Philip hit dial.

# SIX

Ravinder gathered from Kurup's stunned expression something was seriously amiss.

"*What?*" Kurup sounded shell-shocked. "Where did they find the body?"

That got Edward's undivided attention, too.

"No. Don't call her, Philip. Go to Goel's house and speak to his wife." Ravinder saw the NIA director's expression harden. "Actually, let *me* do that. I'm the one who ordered Goel to take charge of the Special Task Force, so I should be the one to break the news to his wife. Text me the address and meet me there in, say, two hours."

Putting down his mobile, Suresh turned to the two men; both were watching him closely. "They've found Goel's body." Noticing Ravinder's unspoken query, he added, "Goel was one of my officers . . . one of the best. I had put him in charge of the Special Task Force we have deployed to stop Binder."

"Must have gotten too close." Kingsley looked grave.

"Apparently, but no one knows whom he was going to meet or why. Even the last call to his mobile was from a public booth. We have no idea what he was onto."

Ravinder felt Kurup's frustration *and* his distress. Despite his dislike for the NIA director, Ravinder felt for him; the loss of a man is not something that goes down well with any commander. And Kurup's willingness to be the one to bring the terrible news to Goel's widow earned him Ravinder's grudging respect.

*Perhaps he is not a total arsehole.*

Aloud, Ravinder asked, "Was he working on anything other than the Binder case?"

"No. This task force was set up specifically to find and stop Binder."

"Then obviously Binder is behind this," Ravinder pointed out.

"Obviously!" Kurup slapped his thigh angrily. "And they have taken him down at the worst possible moment. There is no time to bring in a new man."

"Let the 2IC take charge." Ravinder sensed what was coming and was desperate to deflect it. "That's what seconds-in-command are for."

Ravinder saw an unseen signal pass between the two spooks. Kurup replied, "The problem is, we suspect a mole . . . someone on the inside who is passing information to Binder."

"What makes you suspect that?"

"Too many coincidences." Kurup looked sheepish. "Only a handful of people knew MI6 had tipped us off about this assassination attempt . . . or attempts. Yet Binder came to know. And now this." He sensed Ravinder's unspoken query. "Why else would Goel have been taken out? We had not publicized either his taking over the STF or even that a task force had been deployed to hunt down Binder. Everything was being kept under wraps."

"Why? Why not publicize the hunt and keep Leon under pressure?" Ravinder challenged.

"Politics mostly." Suresh looked exasperated. "The PM wants it kept quiet." He gave a defeatist shrug. "We have no idea who the mole is, but it has to be someone in either the National Intelligence Agency or the Special Task Force. No one else is in the loop."

Taking the cue, Kingsley arrowed in on Ravinder. "You have to do this, Ravinder. Please. You're our best bet."

"Ravinder." Kurup added to the pressure. "I know it is going to be tough, but you know how it is when it's anything to do with Pakistan, especially after the Mumbai attack. PMO doesn't want a word of this Binder assassination attempt to leak because the Pakis will use it to raise a hue and cry, and divert international attention from their own involvement in funding terror activities across the globe."

Ravinder felt claustrophobic. He wanted to back off, tell them to go away, but couldn't. *Not now.* Not with a fellow cop down. Even the thought felt disloyal. Though riddled with conflict, he reluctantly nodded. "But I need to speak with my family first."

"That's the spirit." Suresh jumped to his feet. He looked as though he'd spotted light at the end of a long, gloomy tunnel.

"Thank you, old chap," Kingsley added, with an understated half smile. But Ravinder sensed his relief.

"We shall give you every possible support." Kurup again reached for his mobile. "Let me instruct my deputy, Ashok Verma, to get the STF officers together. When would you like to meet your team?"

"Tomorrow morning. First I need to talk with my wife and daughter," Ravinder repeated. "They're not going to be . . ."

"But why waste the whole—" Kurup began.

"Tomorrow morning would be fine." Kingsley cut him off. Kurup's agitation was evident. He was about to speak, but Kingsley again preempted him. "And if you want, I can make Chance available to you for this assignment."

"Chance?" Ravinder was surprised. "Chance Spillman? He's still in India? I thought he'd be back in London, convalescing."

"He's okay now. I brought him back." Kingsley shrugged. "He could be a useful liaison between our agencies."

"I see." Ravinder eyed him narrowly. "You were sure I'd agree?"

"You're not the kind to back off, Ravinder. Not when the cause is right." Kingsley murmured, again with that half smile. "You never were."

*Isn't that what you said when I was feeling bad about testifying against Leon?*

Ravinder was unable to block that thought. Unsure how he felt about that, Ravinder changed the topic. "Having Chance on the team would be great." And he was surprised how light that made him feel. He *had* developed a good rapport with Chance during the peace summit and respected the MI6 man's professionalism. They had come within a whisker of stopping Ruby's attack on the Israeli-Palestinian summit.

*This time we will succeed. We* will *stop Binder.* Ravinder made a silent promise. *No cop killer could go unpunished.* "When do the targets reach Delhi?"

"The cricket match and the summit, both are on the twenty-seventh of December." Kurup replied. "Both Zardosi and Masharrat arrive early that morning."

*Damn!* Dismay swept through Ravinder. "But that gives me only five days."

"Six." Suresh gave what he believed was an encouraging smile. "If you count today."

"Yeah, right." Ravinder's sarcasm was pungent enough to strip paint. Then another thought struck him. "Since both events are on the same day, can you at least ensure both targets are onstage at the same time?"

It took only a second for Suresh's brow to unfurrow. "Ah! I see. That will halve our problems, since Leon can only go for one target at a time." Then he frowned again. "Unless he uses someone else for one of them."

"That's not Leon." Edward and Ravinder spoke simultaneously.

"That's not how Leon operates. He's a loner," Kingsley elaborated. "He never uses an accomplice for a hit. For support tasks, yes, but never for the hit. Hasn't ever done it."

"Good thinking, then," Suresh acknowledged, but grudgingly, as though wishing he'd thought of that. "Of course an exact overlap is not going to be possible. Much as Masharrat *mian* loves the sound of his voice, the cricket match will obviously last longer."

"Place his speech in the middle of the match, then," Ravinder suggested.

"That shouldn't be a problem." Kurup nodded. "I will do my best."

"That's all anyone can do." Ravinder gave him a penetrating look, as though to say, *I also tried my best to stop Ruby. Remember that. Remember that when you judge me.*

If that registered with Kurup he showed no sign of it, or perhaps he was too caught up in the worrisome situation. "This time we *have to* succeed. Benazir's vendetta could rip the already fragile Indo-Pak peace to pieces. Let's not forget, hell hath no fury like . . ."

"Women squabbling." Edward completed with a chuckle, trying to lighten up the tense atmosphere.

All three laughed. However, the laughter was forced and the lightness fleeting. Doubt and conflict were already swirling through Ravinder as he saw the spymasters to their car and watched them depart.

The wind picked up suddenly. A shiver traced its way up Ravinder's spine as the chill sliced through the reluctant recruit's blazer. Apprehension flailed him, about what he had allowed himself to be talked into, as well as the disastrous consequences, if he failed . . . *again.*

The sour taste of his failure to stop the attack on the Israeli-Palestinian Peace Summit still lingered in his mouth.

"I cannot . . . *will not* . . . . . fail this time," Ravinder vowed. Then louder. And then a third time, louder still. "And you will not escape this time, Leon Binder."

He was still lost in thought when the gates swung open again and a gleaming BMW 750Li drove in. Ravinder could see the white-liveried Jagjit Singh at the wheel. In the rear was Simran, returning from the gurudwara sahib. Always a deeply religious lady, Simran had dived deeper into religion ever since the Ruby incident.

*I hope she is feeling calm, full of peace and divine love.*

Another wry smile fleetingly creased his lips. Ravinder knew his wife would blow a gasket when he told her what he had agreed to do. Totally fed up with his police life, she had compelled him to resign after Ruby's attack on the Israeli-Palestinian Peace Summit. Not that Ravinder blamed her. He knew his job and his past had brought far too much grief to the two people he cared for the most, Simran and their daughter Jasmine. The thought that he was going to cause them more worry tore at him.

*But I have to do this.*

Ravinder girded himself for the coming battle.

The Bimmer halted and Simran, clad in a light pink sari, alighted. She was a few pounds overweight, but very feminine and elegant. Her black waist-length hair was braided in a thick plait. A well-maintained, wrinkle-free skin hid her years well. She looked at least five years younger than her age.

Ravinder did not need to do the math; with Jasmine planning a *surprise* party for the past few weeks, it was impossible to forget that Simran's fiftieth birthday was three days away, on the twenty-fifth of December.

Despite his apprehensions, he was unable to bottle up the smile that the sight of her brought. That elicited an equally fond smile from Simran.

Ravinder sighed. He sensed he would not be at the receiving end of such smiles for much longer.

# SEVEN

Leon was finding it tough to reconcile the fact that he had decided to expose himself to a client; and that too, so close to ground zero. It was a big first, and it was weirding him out.

*Nothing about this mission makes sense. Why the heck did I take it on?*

The thought troubled him again.

*The money, of course. Twenty million pounds is enough to retire in style.*

Five was already collecting interest in his bank.

*Well, not really. When do the damn Swiss ever pay interest?*

And Fatima was to hand over another five today.

His mind idled, wondering what she was like. So far his contact with her, or anyone from SOB, had been in his usual ultra-cautious manner; first through a cutout, then electronic, and eventually telephonic. Seldom had he met a client face-to-face.

*But never has a client exposed me like this.*

Leon needed to know if he'd been betrayed or SOB had simply fucked up. Just the thought he could have been set up enraged him.

"Sir, would you like me to show you around?" A tap on his arm brought Leon back to earth. "Authorized guide, sir." The man who had accosted him held up a metallic badge, simultaneously exposing a set of tobacco-brown teeth. He was swathed in a bulky blue jacket, ideal to conceal several weapons.

"No, thank you. I'm good." Leon waved him off, instinctively checking if his wallet was still there. It was.

*Not for long if you keep daydreaming,* Leon admonished himself. But he was glad he'd chosen the Qutb Minar for this meeting. There were plenty of tourists around, mostly Asians, common enough these days, but a fair number of Caucasians, too. Leon was confident he blended in.

Using his camera for surveillance, Leon sectored and scanned the area. The Qutb Minar, the main monument, a 72.5-meter-high red sandstone and marble minar, was to his right. To his left the Ashoka Pillar: a massive iron pillar. Around both were lush green gardens: immaculately tended grass, ringed by flowerbeds and neatly trimmed thigh-high hedges. To the right of the main gate, stretching away in the distance, were a row of low sandstone buildings, possibly as old as the minar. A few score people, mostly foreigners, thronged the area. Cameras, Cokes, chips, and water bottles were visible in abundance.

*But nothing else.* Leon could detect no cause for alarm.

*Yet.* He reminded himself.

Ever cautious, he retraced his steps and rechecked. Finally, crossing over to the other side of the Ashoka Pillar he settled down in the grass, making sure he had a clear view of the entrance. Though it was only half past three, the weak winter sun had already begun to wane. Waves of people moved in and out, the last-minute rush before closing time.

His mobile chirruped, an incoming text. Fatima confirming she was outside. Leon asked her to describe what she was wearing and told her to come toward the minar. He read her reply and then settled his attention on the entrance.

A moment later, Leon made her out immediately. It was not only the attire she had described, but also the way she was gawking around, obviously trying to spot him. Fatima was dressed very Indian: bright red kameez, black salwar, contrasted with a black thigh-long cardigan, and bandhani dupatta.

Leon brought the Canon EOS 5D Mark III camera up to his eye. It was a professional model. The 22.3 megapixel full-frame sensor with a 61-point autofocus instantly brought the woman at the gate to life in vivid Technicolor glory.

Leon felt he had been body-slammed. He could have sworn he was looking at Farah.

*Farah. Freaking. Fairfowler.*

*Quirky as her Brit dad and sexy as her Paki mother. Edward Kingsley's fiancée, but apparently always willing to get some on the side. Isn't that why she . . .*

Stunned, Leon double-checked.

*But Farah is dead.*

Her blood-smeared face, with that shocked expression etched on it, swam before his eyes.

*What the hell?*

The coincidence shocked him. Realizing he was holding his breath only when his mind began to scream for oxygen, Leon forced himself to relax.

"There are always six other people in the world who look exactly like you and a nine percent chance you will meet one of them." He remembered his mother telling him. Apparently there was something to that old wives' tale after all.

*Why the hell does another Farah have to land up in my life?*

Leon grimaced.

*Hadn't one screwed up my life already?*

The woman in the camera drew closer. Leon sharpened his scrutiny; now on the people around Fatima.

Minutes passed.

*Nothing.*

Fatima appeared to be alone.

But he kept watching.

*Niks.* Leon lapsed into Afrikaans subconsciously.

*She seems to be alone.*

He allowed a few more minutes to reconfirm that. Finally, satisfied, he rose and began to close in, from her left. His pace measured, but his mind still whirling with a potpourri of thoughts.

He was looking forward to this conversation, as eager to collect his payment as he was to find out if she was the one who'd betrayed him.

*If she had, she would die.*

Betrayal was not something Leon could allow to go unpunished; he wouldn't last long in this trade if people did not fear the consequences of betrayal.

*And now this . . . this uncanny resemblance to Edward Kingsley's fiancée, the long-dead Farah.*

His head fuzzy with these thoughts, Leon was halfway to her when he spotted her pursuers. They were fifty feet away, which is why he'd missed them earlier, but closing fast now. There were two of them, both in their mid-thirties. The shorter one was bulkier, but both were swarthy, with slicked-back hair.

*Like Puerto Rican pimps.*

*Or cops playing undercover?*

Leon could make out they were either trailing Fatima or tracking her.

*Amateurs. Should know better than to stare at their mark.*

Without breaking stride Leon continued past Fatima. Once past the two men he circled back.

By now the duo had split up and were moving to outflank Fatima. Leon kept a steady pace behind them, mingling with passing groups of people to ensure he did not stand out. He realized both men had eyes for no one other than Fatima.

*Has she brought them with her or led them here?*

Leon pondered that.

*Is she the bait or the target?*

Either way he knew he had to get rid of them.

*And her. If she is the bait.*

The thought that she could be setting him up angered Leon further.

*Betrayal could not go unpunished.*

If Leon determined she had shafted him, he planned to make her an example people would remember.

*Besides, she owes me money.*

The gun in his jacket pocket felt reassuring.

*And if she is the target, then I need to find out who else is in the game. More important, why?*

By now Fatima had halted in the middle of the lawn to the right of the Ashoka Pillar. She looked bewildered, gawking at people passing by.

The taller man closed in and accosted her, pulling out a badge and showing it to her.

*Tourist guides.* Leon realized it was like the badge the other tourist guide had flashed at him earlier. *Or at least pretending to be.*

He almost laughed with relief, realizing they were likely setting her up. Leon was now certain she was the target, not the bait to unearth him. It was a timeless drill: approach solitary women as tourist guides, get them in a lonely corner, rob them, and, if the opportunity arose, rape them. Fatima would not even see the second guy till it was too late; first the taller one would lull her with sweet talk and tourist-guide stuff. From the ruins of Rome to the pyramids of Cairo and the monuments of Delhi, the same deadly game was played out a dozen times daily.

Making up his mind with a snap, Leon accelerated. He *needed* to talk to her, and was confident that Laurel and Hardy would evaporate when they realized their mark was not alone.

"*There* you are." Leon pitched his voice higher, again emphasizing the American accent. "I've been looking for you everywhere."

A frisson of frustration crossed the taller crook's face before his guileless smile slid back in place. For a minute Leon thought he would continue his tourist-guide spiel; then without another word he backed off. Leon noticed the other one falter in midstride and also change direction.

In quick succession Fatima looked startled, confused, and then relieved.

Continuing with the small talk, Leon casually took her elbow and led her away, toward the base of the monument where the crowd was thickest; there is always safety in numbers.

# EIGHT

Fatima could not decide whether she was relieved Leon had made contact or more stressed at the difficult conversation that lay ahead.

Before she could settle that question Leon arrowed in. "Care to explain what your people are playing at? Didn't I make it clear I'd abort if your lot could not keep their mouths shut?" Mindful of the crowd, Leon kept his voice low; however, Fatima did not need to tap into her female intuition to feel his anger.

"You did. But it wasn't my fault. I swear," she pleaded. "We had no idea Cherry Rehmat would turn traitor . . . and I'm sure Ashok Verma explained it to you. We have already taken care of her."

"Too bad. That's not my problem." Still that same bland undertone. Fatima hated it. "Doesn't change a thing. I'm pulling out. All I need from you is the five million due to me on reaching Delhi."

Fatima now sensed steel in his tone, as though warning her not to renege. Her heart plummeted; she didn't care about the money, she just wanted him back on track.

*I cannot fail. Not when the end is so near.*

"Please," she appealed, "please don't stop now. You *have* to do this."

"*Have to?* I don't have to do any such thing."

"But you do." Fatima was almost begging now. "This is not just about money, power, or any such thing. These two men snatched away from me everything that anyone could hold dear." Fatima saw she wasn't making any impression; her desperation mounted. "Just hear my side of the story and then decide." She tugged at his arm. "Please."

Something in her tone caught Leon's attention. Also, perhaps her uncanny likeness to Farah, which drew him and repelled him in equal measure. He'd always found Farah attractive; that she'd been another man's fiancée, forbidden fruit as it were, had added to the attraction. Yet the sight of her bloodied face scorched his memories even now. Her death had altered the course of his life. It was the only reason he was here today.

Fatima felt a hiss of relief as he nodded. By now they had reached the end of the garden. A well-painted wooden bench beckoned. "Could we sit for a moment?" She felt suddenly drained.

He didn't say a word as she sat. Then, a moment later, with another quick look around, he sat beside her. "I'm waiting." There was a curious expression on his face, inquisitive yet aloof.

Fatima sensed this was her last chance to convince Leon. *If I fail . . . I cannot.* She pulled herself together. *Failure is not an option.*

"That day when they killed Benazir I was right there by her side. She died in my arms." Her outspread hands held her attention. "And it wasn't just the death of my aunt . . . or a dream for my country; that day I lost everything I cherished." Her voice was now merely a heartbreaking whisper.

Then everything around her dissolved. Leon. The wooden bench. The neatly trimmed garden skirted by flowerbeds. The plethora of tourists, milling around in the fading light of another chilly December evening.

Fatima felt herself being sucked into the hailstorm of bloody memories. Back to that fateful day, the twenty-seventh of December in 2007, when kismet had torn her life apart and cut her adrift.

She had traveled this road often, but it never got any better. The voices were still as loud. The screams even louder. The blood, slimier and redder than ever. And the smell, that sticky, peculiar smell of death. Like cottony wisps of cloud it clung to her. Filling up her senses. She knew these memories would leave her in peace only when the vendetta was over. When both the murderers, Zardosi and Masharrat, had paid for their crimes with their lives.

"Isn't it ironic that both these murderers are coming to Delhi on the twenty-seventh of December, the very day they killed Benazir? Is that not a sign from Allah?" Fatima watched him closely.

Leon stayed silent; signs from Allah obviously held little appeal for him. But she could see he was intrigued.

"A bunch of her supporters, including my husband, had gone from London to be with Benazir. We'd been in Pakistan about a week, and on the twenty-seventh Benazir was to preside at an election rally at Rawalpindi."

Fatima marshaled her thoughts, evaluating what and how much she needed to share with Leon to get him back on track.

"Rawalpindi was an important constituency. It had always been so, for our party and our family. We needed to make a fabulous impression. And we knew we would. The atmosphere in the city was so . . . so electric . . . right from the moment we landed. They cheered her every inch of the way, to Liaquat National Bagh, the park where the rally was to be held."

*P*akistan Paindabad! Pakistan Paindabad! (Long live Pakistan.)
Fatima could see the grounds of Liaquat National Bagh as clearly as she'd been able to that day; sweaty, heady excitement lay heavy in the air, which reverberated with coordinated, throaty cries of *Long Live Pakistan*.

The head cheerleader was a young, heavily bearded man in his late twenties, hired for his stentorian voice and theatrical vocabulary. She saw him pace the dais, dominating the crowd of five thousand strong with missionary zeal.

And there were a large number of women in the crowd; surprisingly, they were the more vocal ones. Surprising because woman moving so freely in public was no longer a common sight in Pakistan. Not since the Islamists had become the dominant voice in Pakistan. Even those who condemned their views no longer dared speak openly. Such dissent generally resulted in death.

But that day women were out in full force. Perhaps because it was a woman they had gathered to greet. And not just *any* woman. This was *Benazir Basheer*, their savior, the Hope of Democracy, returning after eight years of exile.

Fatima remembered how they had fled Pakistan, the entire Basheer clan, in the dead of the night. And those eight long years of self-imposed exile; to ensure Benazir or her husband were not imprisoned for any of the dozens of charges of corruption and embezzlement of public money that lay pending in various Pakistani courts. But Fatima knew she would not share that with Leon. Or mention that Benazir had not just allowed the Islamists to rise but had actively encouraged them.

*The same Islamists who were now gunning for her.*

"Benazir was returning as the messiah. The one who would set the country free from the military yoke that had held Pakistan in an iron grip for most of its sixty-year existence." Fatima's pride was evident. "A star was being reborn."

So enthused was Fatima and so powerful her narrative, the story came alive for Leon—part memory, part hearsay, and part reconstruction.

Flame-colored banners of the Sisters of Benazir rubbed shoulders with the vibrant green ones of the Pakistan Peoples Party. Adding to the merriment and the energy pulsing through the jam-packed grounds were brightly colored canopies and little boys running through the crowd, passing out the packets of biscuits, savories, and water bottles that enticed people to attend such political rallies.

The atmosphere was almost festive.

It would have been completely so had it not been for squads of heavily armed police ringing the grounds. Or the dozens of sullen, steely-eyed men mingling with the crowds. They held themselves aloof from the fervent sloganeering. Their eyes held nothing but disdain as they continually swept the crowds . . . watching and waiting. And wherever they moved, little bubbles of tense suspicion followed. Reaching out and touching those around. Ensuring people swayed out of their way and even avoided eye contact. Whether they were spooks of the ISI or goons of the Pak Army, no one could be sure. But both merited a wide berth. And it was given to them.

Easily mistaken for these spooky goons were four young men, two on either side of the crowds. Nothing in their clothing or demeanor distinguished them or attracted attention. Perhaps the only remarkable thing was that there were no security personnel within twenty meters of either pair. But given the turbulent atmosphere, this was unlikely to be noticed by anyone. It was not.

The four stood silently alert. Tense. In the crowd, yet not a part of it.

The duo nicknamed Bomber 1 and Bomber 2 for this mission stood toward the left, away from the red-carpeted entrance to the park. As close to the dais as the zealous and overly protective Sisters of Benazir would allow anyone.

The second pair, Bomber 3 and Shooter, had deployed on the fringe of the crowd, at the entrance, where the red carpet began its journey to the dais.

All four watched. And waited. For their target. For martyrdom. And the promised allotment of seventy-two celestial virgins.

If any of the four was afflicted by doubt or second thoughts, it did not show on their faces. They had no reason to. The man who had sent them here, the *Ustad-e-Fidayeen*, the Master of the Fidayeen who ran the suicide bombers school, had made that clear. If their target walked out from here alive the four of them would die a far more horrible death than they could countenance.

This was the day they had been groomed and trained for; to deliver death to the target assigned to them. Their own lives had little consequence. Nor did the lives those who happened to be in the way, purposely or by chance. Inshallah. That would be as God willed it.

Pity. Fear. Remorse. All these had been hammered out from them during the years they had spent with the *Ustad-e-Fidayeen*. Right from the day he had purchased them from their parents; and all for the princely sum of twenty dollars each. They had been impressionable five- to seven-year-old kids, their minds merely blank sheets of paper waiting to be written upon. Now all they could do was kill. That had been indelibly inked into their fate.

So they watched and waited.

And then the wait was over; a seven-car cavalcade swept around the corner and came to a halt near the gates. All seven were Toyota Land Cruisers; all black except for the white one in the middle.


The energy was electrifying." Fatima spoke as though she was sleepwalking. It seemed as though she was not really aware of Leon's presence anymore. And there was a tremor in her voice; fears of that day still lingered. "I can never forget what it was like when the car doors opened." She drew a long breath. "The sound, the sights, the smells . . . everything is embedded here." She tapped her forehead.

*Jeay Benazir.* (Long live Benazir.)

*Pakistan Paindabad.*

As the fourth Land Cruiser came to a halt at the park entrance, where the red carpet began its run, all the way to the dais, the cry of the crowds mutated from *Long Live Benazir* to *Long Live Pakistan.*

"Everything seemed so . . . so . . . larger than life . . . perfect . . . but I was unable to shake the feeling that something was terribly wrong." Fatima didn't realize she was clutching Leon's arms, her nails digging in, almost breaking skin. "I *knew* something bad was about to happen. I tried to stop Aunt Benazir from getting out of the car, but she just laughed. Even Zunaid, my husband, who was sitting up front, told me not to be silly." Her nails dug in even harder now. "They both laughed at me and got out of the car."

The chanting of the crowds escalated. Dramatically. Hitting fever pitch as Benazir alighted from the white Land Cruiser and began to make her way toward the dais: a short, thickset woman clad in an ornate traditional regal purple-colored Sindhi *ajrak* and white headscarf. Benazir was smiling broadly and waving continually. Basking in the orchestrated, short-lived adoration of all such political gatherings.

In a tight ring around Benazir were four women, each younger and bulkier than her; the body armor jackets worn by all five women contributed to their bulk. Necessitated by the threat to her life, especially since her arrival in Pakistan, their custom-designed Kevlar vests were so integral a part of their attire they now scarcely noticed it. The four women comprising the innermost security cordon, dedicated, long-standing Sisters of Benazir, were grim-faced. Their tension was visible in the way they gripped each other's hands and in their rigidly alert postures. They edged forward slowly, like a Roman beetle pushing its way through a barbarian horde.

A few feet ahead was yet another ring of people; this comprised eight men. They looked equally alert and harried; aware of the threat Benazir faced, incensed at the lack of cooperation from the government and the lack of support from the security forces. Appalled they were not even allowed to hire professional security contractors to combat this threat. And fearful they were inadequate to counter it. Yet ready to die trying.

On the last two counts the dozen praetorians guarding Benazir were right.

They *were* grossly inadequate to blunt the weapons that had been launched against her today. And die they *would*, before the sun set on another smoggy Rawalpindi afternoon. As would the woman they were trying to protect.

I'm sure she was aware of it, but at an emotional level Benazir refused to acknowledge that no one wanted us . . . *her* . . . back. Her return was a threat to General Masharrat, whose dictatorship was encountering increasing public resistance. Despite the amnesty Masharrat had granted her, Benazir's return signified the loss of his presidency and exile or even possible imprisonment for offenses ranging from corruption to murder to fostering global jihad."

Trapped in the middle distance of memories, Fatima turned to Leon, desperately eager to help him see the complete picture.

"Neither the ISI, nor the army, which has ruled Pakistan for so many decades, wanted Benazir back. They stood to lose a substantial amount of power and a lot of money. Since 1970, they had not only enjoyed close ties with the Islamists, but also allowed themselves to be used by successive Pakistani leaders to suppress political opposition. Like the jihadis, they were opposed to her on principle. They saw her as a foreign-bred Anglicized woman . . . a heretic and an American stooge." Fatima looked fiercely angry. "Mind you, this is despite the support Benazir had given them over the years. Now this same lot was baying for her blood."

Fatima was oozing bitterness. "And none of us realized that the real danger was from our own family. Isn't it strange how many enemies we make when power and money are at stake?"

Leon neither moved nor replied. Only his eyes, constantly alive, watching her and the area around, showed he was listening. Fatima felt a wave of despair. For a moment she almost gave up. Then, all those years of hate and anger came broiling back. They steeled her resolve.

"The chanting of the crowd hit fever pitch as Benazir mounted the dais."

*Jeeeaaaay Benazir.*
A consummate politician, Benazir raised her hands above her head and began to clap. The crowd clapped with her, caught up in the hysteria of the moment.

"*Nara-i-Takbeer, Allah O Akbar.*"

"*Nara-i-Haidri, Ya Ali.*"

"*Awam Hero Hero, Baqi Sab Zero Zero.*" (The people are heroes. Everyone else is zero.)

These slogans currently popular in Pakistan erupted from her. Echoed sonorously by the cheerleader. And repeated thunderously by the crowd. The hysteria was sky high now.

No one noticed Bombers 1 and 2 inch toward her, about eight feet apart. And they were still twenty feet from the dais.

Finally holding up her hands for silence, Benazir began to speak. "These are the slogans that greeted me when I arrived in Rawalpindi. I know this is the city of brave and sacrificing people."

An appreciative roar from the crowd.

Bombers 1 and 2 covered yet another couple of feet to the dais.

"Rawalpindi is my second home. When my father was a minister, I used to live here. I used to go to school here. It is here I lived many moments of joy and sorrow. And always the brave people of Rawalpindi stood by me, in moments of happiness and in my hours of sorrow. You have *never* let me down."

The roar of the crowd was like a continual roll of thunder.

The distance between the two assassins and the dais receded by another foot. But still not close enough. Not enough to penetrate the living bulletproof shield guarding the woman on the dais.

Blissfully unaware of her death creeping closer, Benazir resumed her rhetoric. "This is the same city which thronged to Liaquat Bagh when the dictator Yahya Khan refused to leave and forced him to step down."

The crowd responded with another defiant roar.

"This is the same city where the government of the Pakistan Peoples Party was established. Rawalpindi is the same city from where my father started his struggle against the dictatorship of General Ayub Khan and young Abdul Hameed sacrificed his life for democracy. This is the city which has defeated all dictators and Inshallah will once again inflict a crushing defeat on another dictator and usher in an era of democracy."

"*Allah O Akbar.*"

Five thousand lusty throats roared out their support.

"*Awam Hero Hero, Baqi Sab Zero Zero.*"

Bomber 2 was now within fifteen feet of the dais. However, Bomber 1 was stuck a few feet farther away. So dense was the crowd that now neither could move.

"The sun of democracy will rise again on the horizon of Rawalpindi." Benazir ramped up the rhetoric. "The people of Rawalpindi love democracy and will never bow their heads before an autocratic regime."

From eight feet away Bomber 2 turned to look at his running

mate. On cue, as though intuitively signaled, Bomber 1 also looked at him.

Nods of confirmation; faces still devoid of expression.

Lips moved in silent prayer.

Nerves steeled themselves.

Their hands reached inside their coats. Seeking fingers expertly found the cold plastic knobs they sought.

*"Allah O Akbar."* Bomber 1 was unable to stop the war cry that tore loose from him. It was lost in the thunder of the chanting crowd.

Fingers depressed the knobs. Powered by tiny cells, electric sparks leaped forward and completed the circuit. The clicks, if any, were drowned in the roar reverberating around the park.

Just a fraction of a second apart the bombs lashed to their waists exploded. Bombers 1 and 2 both vanished in a burst of bloody graffiti. As did those hapless men and women around them. Mostly women. A ghastly foul-smelling red mist enveloped the area.

In one horrifying second we lost twenty-three members of the Sisters of Benazir. Thirty-one other citizens of Rawalpindi also died. Another eleven of those wounded succumbed later." Fatima's voice broke, shattered by an admixture of anger and sorrow. "But they collectively absorbed the blast, ensuring Benazir remained unscathed."

However, the frail cocoon of illusionary security Benazir was living in now lay in tatters. Benazir looked pulverized. Suddenly shrunk. As though the bravado that died within her had had physical form.

There was a long moment of stunned silence.

Then the screams of the dying rose through the crowd, throwing it in tumultuous confusion.

We knew we had to get Aunt Benazir out of there." Fatima's tone and expression were now frenetic, as though she was back on the stage, in the thick of the blasts again. "Two of the security guards in the inner cordon had not survived, but two others took their places, enclosed Benazir in a protective pincer, and we began rushing her toward the safety of the bulletproof Land Cruiser."

But moving through the panicked crowd was tough. Everyone was headed for the gate, and the illusion of safety that lay beyond. Surprisingly, not a single policeman ventured close to Benazir. Or perhaps, given the dynamics and vagaries of Pakistani politics, not so surprising after all.

The confidence of Benazir's protectors increased as they drew closer to the convoy. The drivers of all seven vehicles had powered their engines; totally spooked, they were raring to go, to get away from the madness of death that now gripped the crowd.

As the entrance loomed larger, the rising confidence of Benazir's guards was visible on their faces. None of them were aware that this feeling of relief was very similar to the relief that hits inexperienced soldiers when their camps or defenses first become visible; the closer they get to the camp, the stronger the feeling of relief. Perhaps it is the security of knowing that the guns of their sentries could now cover them. Perhaps it is the sight of their barbed wire and defenses. Either way, like horses heading back to their stables they tend to speed up and also lower their guard. Sight, sound, smell, grips on rifles, and the tension in alert limbs—everything starts to lose that vital edge, that hair-trigger response, which keeps men alive in battle.

This is something every commander worth his salt is aware of. That is why the smart warrior struck at these times. The smart terrorist certainly did. And the *Ustad-e-Fidayeen*, who had tasked this killer cohort, was definitely smart. Brutal, evil, unscrupulous, but also a shrewd, tactically savvy planner.

The visibly escalating confidence of her guards did not go unnoticed by their protectee. Transference took place and Benazir's bravado also began to stir. Assuming she had cheated death, yet again. Not realizing she had not.

The first two bombers had done only what they were meant to. Either take out Benazir or drive her toward the other two who waited outside."

Fatima was unable to keep the pain of retrospective wisdom off her face.

In the ensuing pandemonium no one noticed Bomber 3 and Shooter halt a few feet from the white Toyota Land Cruiser, which was parked nearest the gate. They reached it at the same time as Benazir and her protective ring.

The powerful Toyota engine was revving madly. The driver itched to get Benazir inside and hurtle away. One of the Sisters of Benazir pushed her forward and Zunaid held the door open for her.

Benazir had one foot raised to enter the car when Shooter pulled out a 7.62mm Tokarev semiautomatic pistol. Though designed in the 1930s to replace the Nagant M1895 service pistol, the TT-30 is a solid, reliable weapon that fires a steel-cased bottlenecked cartridge. It was a used, but well-maintained weapon, more than adequate for the job at hand.

Shooter fired. Thrice. He was seven feet from her and unlikely to miss.

How many times he hit her will remain buried in the vaults of history, since it is unlikely the real medical records will ever see the light of day. Masharrat ensured that." Tears were now trickling down Fatima's cheeks. "However, whether he hit her once or thrice is a moot issue, since by now Bomber 3 was within definite kill radius."

Leon was fascinated by this eyewitness account. But it was the curiosity of a specialist. Nothing more.

"The third bomber detonated his belt bomb barely four feet from Benazir."

There was little left of the solitary Sister of Benazir standing between Bomber 3 and his target. Along with Bomber 3 she absorbed most of the blast. But there was enough explosive power in the bomb to get past her and cut down the target, too.

The blast picked up Benazir and hurled her into the bulletproof car. En route her head struck the metallic lever of the sunroof.

Benazir collapsed in a welter of blood.

Zunaid, who'd been helping aunt Benazir into the car, was . . . we barely found anything. I would've died too, but six months pregnant and unable to keep up, I'd fallen behind and so was at a safe distance."

Fatima was silent and still for a very long time; her face like an Arctic dawn.

"Safe enough for me, but not the baby." Her eyes were dry. She had cried over this too often. Grief was long gone. Replaced by an unquenchable thirst for revenge. "My baby, my husband, my aunt, my dreams for our country . . . they killed *everything*. This vendetta is all I have to live for." Her fingers dug deeper into Leon's forearm, now drawing blood. "You must not refuse. *Please*. They *have* to pay . . ."

"How are you so sure of all this?" Leon asked, freeing his arm. "That these are the men behind Benazir's death?"

Fatima examined him closely, trying to determine if she had managed to convince him. Unsure, she resolved to try harder.

"Because of Ashfaque Kayani, the ISI operative Masharrat had used to communicate and coordinate with his accomplices. Kayani was privy to every single detail of their operation to eliminate Benazir. Mehsud provided the killers. Masharrat ensured the crime scene was washed clean, Benazir's medical records vanished, and no impartial inquiry was conducted. And Zardosi . . ."—Fatima's anguish visibly increased—"Zardosi was the worst. That . . . that . . . horrid man ensured no autopsy was held . . . as Benazir's husband he had the legal right to deny one . . . *and* he used the sympathy wave that followed her death to become the prime minister."

"You're sure of all this?"

"Of course. Kayani put together the strike on Masharrat's orders. He ensured the assassins got into the ground with bombs and guns, and the crime scene was washed clean of all evidence. Perhaps that's why, *because* he knew too much, Mehsud's men came gunning for him the day after her murder. However, Kayani got lucky . . . they left him for dead, but he pulled through. However, he knew he wouldn't last long if he stayed on in Pakistan," Fatima elaborated. "That's why he came to me . . . to us, the Sisters of Benazir . . . for money so that he could escape from Pakistan with his family."

"Why you of all the people?"

"Because he had nowhere else to go," Fatima retorted grimly. "And he knew our people were trying to find out who'd ordered Benazir's assassination." Pause. "Kayani thought he could sell us the truth." The change in her tone made it clear Kayani had erred, fatally.

"And you can trust him?"

"By the time we were done with him, he could not have lied even if he'd wanted to," Fatima responded softly. "Besides, he had no reason to lie."

# NINE

L eon checked his laugh with an effort.

*People seldom need a reason to lie.*

He had enjoyed the story, in the way any professional hearing about another in the same trade would. Not that he considered Mehsud's men professional by any yardstick.

*Any fool can kill if they are not worried about dying. The art is to get away with it. That is what denotes a professional. But then, these attackers were only the weapons. The real killers were the men who had sent them.*

That thought discomfited him, starkly bringing home his own reality. Before he could dwell on it, the ringing of a mobile distracted him. Leon saw Fatima reach into her bag. His ever-simmering suspicions flared and suddenly his senses were on DEFCON ONE. His hand was on his weapon as hawk eyes swept the area.

*Nothing unusual.*

However, his hand stayed within his jacket. The cold butt of the pistol reassured him. He saw Fatima falter and then slowly draw out a mobile from her bag. She looked at him, seeking permission to answer. He nodded, but tense now.

"What? Yes. He is with me." Leon heard her say. His sense of danger flared brighter. He was now on the edge of his seat. But everything around still seemed normal. "I will tell him that, Mr. Verma. Hold on." Leon saw her look at him; she seemed uncomfortable again. As though aware the news would not please Leon. "That's Ashok Verma, my man inside the the NIA. They found Goel's body and have appointed someone else as the STF commander."

"Ask him . . ." Leon broke off and held out his hand. Fatima passed him the mobile. "Tell me more," Leon queried Verma crisply.

He had already made up his mind to exit this mission, but still needed to remain in the loop till he had collected the money the SOB owed him and was safely out of India.

"They have brought in an ex-cop. A senior guy . . . and apparently at the behest of the MI6 director."

Leon found that strange. "What has MI6 got to do with this?"

"Apparently Sir Edward Kingsley managed to convince our director that this guy is the best man for the job. It appears they both know you well."

Leon went still. He was aware Kingsley was the MI6 director. Also that MI6 was onto this operation due to the leak at SOB end. However, he was not aware Kingsley was in town. Leon felt a painful tightness across his chest, the same angry, choking sensation the memory of Kingsley always ignited.

*And . . .*

"Who is this new guy?"

"Like I said, an ex-cop. He retired a few weeks ago as the head of our Anti-Terrorist Task Force. Ravinder Singh Gill. I've never met him, but going by his record he seems to be one hell of a cop."

Leon felt he had entered the eye of the hurricane. Everything went still. And eerily silent. Even the march of memories halted. Anger. Disbelief at this coincidence . . . everything was immobile.

*Edward Kingsley and Ravinder Gill. The two men who . . . No!*

Leon allowed the stillness to ferment . . . to coalesce into a decision.

*This cannot be coincidence. It is Destiny. It must be . . . Life, giving me the chance to make those two bastards pay for everything they have done to me. For all the pain . . .*

His decision clicked into place. Leon *knew* he would now do this. *I have to.*

He'd thought of this . . . of taking revenge . . . so often. Nearly set out to do so twice, but both times something had gotten in the way.

*Third time lucky.*

Leon was suddenly light-headed.

*How can I walk away from such a golden opportunity to strike back at both these bastards?*

That the SOB would be paying him to do so only made the deal so much sweeter.

Thoughts and feelings began playing again, but a discordant orchestra. Memories began to push forward—old, but bloody and still painful. He remembered how . . .

*Not now!* Leon halted them. *I have to keep all the emotional crap out of the way and ensure I walk out of this alive. That would be the sweetest revenge.*

Leon reminded himself to focus on the practicalities.

*Painstaking planning and innovative implementation. That's what has kept me alive all these years.*

Leon became aware that Fatima was staring at him strangely. And he heard a squawking coming from the mobile still in his hand. He refocused.

"You are right, Mr. Verma," he said into the phone. "We will need to be more careful now. I know them both well. Gill is a smart cookie. So is Kingsley. Neither is to be underestimated."

"I agree. If there is nothing else . . ."

"Wait." Leon paused to marshal his thoughts. That's when he noticed the relief on Fatima's face and realized she had sensed he'd changed his mind. He didn't care. No more games. His complete being was focused on Ravinder and Edward, on hurting them. Nothing else mattered.

"Mr. Verma, how good is this Vishal Bhardwaj? This guy you have planted in the Special Task Force to work for us?" Leon decided to first get that end under control.

*Know your enemy. Classic Sun Tzu. Knowing what the enemy is doing is always a good and logical first step.*

"I handpicked him." Leon was amused at the way Verma appropriated credit. "Vishal is perfect for this job. He is sharp, experienced, and . . . completely ruthless." Leon thought he detected something in that brief pause; however, he couldn't quite put a finger on it and then got distracted as Verma spoke again. "Vishal pulled off the Goel thing on his own. Got him out of the office, took him down, *and* got all the information we wanted from him."

"And you can trust him?" Leon remembered this was the exact same thing he'd asked Fatima a moment ago. The irony made him smile.

"Trust him? How do you mean?"

"What could I mean, Mr. Verma?" Leon countered. "I don't plan to marry him. I just need to know if I can trust Vishal to give us the right information and in time. And not to crack under pressure if things go wrong."

"Of course. That's why I chose Vishal. He's solid. He will ensure we know everything the task force looking for you is up to so that we're always one step ahead."

"Good. Text me his number and tell Vishal I want to meet him tonight."

"*You* want to meet him?"

Leon heard Verma's surprise. He guessed the reason—Leon rarely allowed an accomplice to see him.

*This time it's different. Not just my final mission, but also possibly my last opportunity to take revenge.*

The need to hurt Edward and Ravinder was so overpowering that Leon brushed aside operational caution. "Yes, Mr. Verma, I think it's best I brief him personally and explain how important his task has become now."

"I see." But Verma sounded doubtful. "Okay. I'll tell him and text you his number so you can coordinate the meet."

"Excellent. And please touch base with me every day . . . or whenever something important happens. Keep me up to speed." Leon ended the call and handed the mobile back to Fatima. "Fine. I will complete this mission, but one more screw-up at your end and I'm out of here."

"Oh! *Thank you!*" Leon saw Fatima's cheeks were wet. "Thank you so much."

Uncomfortable with her tears Leon hardened his tone. "You will do nothing, and I mean *nothing*, without checking with me first. Is that clear?"

"Crystal. I promise. I will do what you say."

"Transfer the money to my account." He held out a piece of paper with his account details.

She pulled out her mobile, launched the mobile banking app, completed the two-factor authentication, and transferred the money. When it was done, she showed him the screen. He nodded, only half attentive. "Good. Now stay out of sight till this is over."

"I will," she promised. "And I will be here if you need me for anything."

However, Leon was no longer listening and missed that last part. His mind had already donned combat gear and begun to break down the operation into a tactical checklist. And he felt acutely alive; he couldn't remember the last time he had felt like this.

# TEN

Fatima watched Leon walk away with mixed feelings. She wished she could figure out what had made him change his mind. She was sure it was something that had come up whilst he was talking to Ashok Verma, but try as she might, Fatima could not put a finger on it.

Knowing he was back on track thrilled her. Not knowing what had made him change his mind irked her.

Caught on that uncomfortable crossroads she decided to stick around Delhi for a few days more and not go ahead to Dubai to lie low, as she'd planned earlier.

*Just to keep an eye on things.*

And, she had no qualms admitting to herself, to gloat when Masharrat or Zardosi bit the dust. That thought made her smile.

*Wonder which of them Leon will take out first?*

*I hope it's that awful man, Zardosi.*

She mulled over that, not sure if Masharrat's death would give her as much satisfaction. Lost in thought, she headed back to her hotel.

Fatima was exiting the Qutb Minar complex when she again remembered that with Cherry's having cleaned out the SOB accounts, she was in no position to pay Leon the last two installments any time soon. The thought of reneging on a deal with a man like Leon drove a shard of fear through her. But she allowed her insatiable craving for revenge to smother the fear.

*I will cross that bridge when I come to it. I first need to see this through.*

Unable to resist the sudden urge for contact, pulling out her mobile she called her cousin to check on Zaki.

"He misses you, Fatima. Almost every hour he asks when you will be back."

"Aww." She felt her heart lurch. "Put my baby on." And everything faded into insignificance the minute she heard Zaki's excited yell. "When are you coming back, Mommy? Where are you? What are you getting for me?"

She was glowing when she finished answering his questions and finally ended the call, reluctantly. And the pain in her heart was physical, as strong as the urge to hold her boy close.

*No more. Once this is over I will not leave him alone.*

Fatima grimaced as she realized how much of her life had been sucked away by this vendetta.

*But I have to do this. For Zaki . . . his father, and the sister he never got to see . . . and for Aunt Benazir.*

Anger swept aside everything else.

*Just a few more days.*

Gritting her teeth she called Vishal and told him to meet her after he had met Leon.

"But that is going to be very late." Vishal was speaking in a hushed tone; she sensed he was with people.

"I don't care how late it is." Like Leon, Fatima had decided information signified power and control. She was determined to keep an eye on things. On the hunter *and* the hunted.

# ELEVEN

Jasmine sensed something was amiss when she walked into the living room. The atmosphere in the stable-size room was like half-melted ice cream, thick and cold.

Simran had planned the room as a display window for their royal heritage. And she had spared no expense, compensating for the relative frugality she had been forced to show in the officially allotted houses they had lived in whilst Ravinder had been in police service.

The ceiling was twenty-four feet high, with a pristine white marble floor and ice blue, nearly white walls. The room was massive, like a royal audience hall. Huge sofa sets, adequate to seat twenty people, occupied three sides of the room. The fourth side had two elegant mahogany doors, one on either side. The outer one that led to the porch was the guest entrance. The second led to the kitchen and service area. Centered on the wall, between the two doors, was the life-size portrait of a grim-looking Sikh gentleman, Ravinder's grandfather and the last maharaja. Arrayed around this were dozens of photographs of both arms of the family in all their regal finery. The family vanity wall, as Ravinder referred to it, was Simran's pride and joy. A well-coordinated array of Persian carpets, large brass flowerpots, and other knickknacks were tastefully distributed around the room.

Jasmine, who'd been bursting to share with them news of her acceptance for the Master of Laws program by three American law schools groaned inwardly when she spotted Simran's stiff posture and icy glare. Ravinder, looking equally distressed, was tiredly pacing the room. He stopped in mid-sentence when he saw Jasmine.

"What's going on, Dad? Mom?" Jasmine gave them a questioning look.

"Your father is losing his marbles." Simran threw Ravinder an angry look. "Why don't you tell her what you've agreed to do? Let's see what she has to say."

Jasmine noticed Ravinder's face was bright red. In light of the doctor's warning a fortnight ago, that alarmed her. "I think that can wait, Mom." Taking Ravinder's arm she led him to a sofa. "Why don't you sit down, Dad? Looks like your blood pressure is acting up again. Didn't the doctor tell you to take it easy?"

"That is *precisely* the point," Simran raged. "Despite that, your father has decided to take on another case . . . to stop some assassinations . . . and that too he is going to be working with that rascal Kurup from the NIA."

*What the hell?*

Jasmine was stunned. Kurup and his accusations against Ravinder for failing to protect the Peace Summit was a hot topic in the Gill house. There were no points for guessing that Suresh Kurup was not high on their dinner invitation list. Jasmine's instincts screamed at her to ally with her mother. But worry about Ravinder's health and their collective peace of mind trumped that. She knew this wasn't the time to allow her emotions to take charge.

"And the worst is, he refuses to even tell me what he's going to do." Simran's anger had spiraled out of control. "That's why I know it's dangerous . . . he always . . ."

"Guys, guys." Jasmine mustered her most soothing tone. "Could we take a moment? Have a cup of tea . . . and calm down a bit."

"Calm down?" Jasmine saw Simran's lips thin out and knew she was on the verge of going thermonuclear. "How can . . ."

"*Mom!*" Jasmine realized that came out a lot sharper than she had intended. Both Ravinder and Simran looked startled. And Simran looked offended, too; no one spoke to her like that.

Realizing she'd gone too far, Jasmine took a deep breath. Contrite. Softened. "Mom. *Please*. I'm sorry. I didn't mean to raise my voice, but getting worked up is not going to help anyone." Her mind whirling, she rang for the maid and ordered tea.

It came and was consumed in uncomfortable silence. But the stress in the room had abated, enough to permit a nearly civil conversation.

Half an hour later, the facts lay bare before Jasmine. She felt strange; having to arbitrate between her parents was a new and quite nerve-racking experience. As a lawyer in training, she now got a sense of what it was like to be a judge; to make decisions with the pressure of getting it right, every time. It discomfited her.

*Glad that's not going to happen to me any time soon.*

Realizing she was procrastinating, Jasmine focused. Ravinder's decision to reenter the fray dismayed her. Jasmine was aware Ruby's death had been a tremendous shock for him. That she'd died at his hands had all but killed Ravinder. She had seen how hard he'd struggled to hold it together, especially during the inquiry that followed. Though Ravinder never spoke about it, Jasmine sensed his self-esteem and confidence had both taken a massive beating.

*Yet* . . . Jasmine could see the change; now his shoulders were level and, though he looked worried and stressed, that familiar, determined gleam was back in his eyes. Jasmine sensed Ravinder needed to do this. Badly. She decided to help. If he succeeded, the father she hero-worshiped and doted on would be back.

*If he fails* . . . Jasmine pushed away that awful thought and turned to her mother.

"Mom, I understand where you are coming from." Simran, sitting straight as a soldier, shimmered with righteous anger. "I know it's only concern for Dad's health, which is upsetting you. But let's look at it from his point of view, too."

"*What. Point. Of. View.*" Each word was delivered explosively. "Are you *supporting* him?" Jasmine saw her fighting for control, incredulous. "What do *you* know? You're just a child."

"I am *not* a child, mom." Jasmine kept a tight leash on her anger, but was firm. "And I worry for *both* of you." Simran made to speak, but Jasmine headed her off. "No, Mom, please allow me to finish." A shocked Simran subsided in her chair. "We've all gone through so much in the past few months. Especially Dad . . . we've both seen what he has been through. And yes, we are both worried about his health, *but* . . ."

"No buts, Jasmine," Simran interrupted coldly. "I will *not* sit back and allow my husband to self-destruct. He has done enough and given enough for his precious uniform. And it has gotten him nothing . . . *nothing* but trouble and hurt."

"Mom, do you remember when I was learning to ride and fell off the horse on the very first day?" Jasmine was not sure where the words came from. But she sensed that if she did not get the situation in check, it would spiral out of control. And without knowing why, she knew she had it in her to do so. "You remember how badly my leg had been hurt?"

Simran nodded, puzzled. "So?"

"I still remember what you did the next day. You told me to get back on the horse. *Don't let your fears stop you from doing what you need to.* That's what you told me, Mom. Likewise, today if Dad needs to do this, we must support him."

Jasmine saw her parents staring at her. Despite the tension-ridden atmosphere, there was, as always, love in their eyes. Today, along with the surprise, there was something else, too.

*Respect?*

A wave of warmth swamped Jasmine. Her bubble of self-confidence and poise burst. Knowing she was about to tear up, she left the room hurriedly.

# TWELVE

Ravinder was unable to keep the pride out of his voice. "Simran, our baby has grown up."

Simran could not look away from the door slowly swinging shut behind Jasmine. "Yes, she has." She sounded subdued.

Ravinder sensed her confusion; knowing Jasmine was right, and yet disliking the implications. "Jasmine is right." He added gently, "I *need* to do this, Simran. Please." Simran stiffened. "I need your support, Simran." He was barely audible now. "I need to find myself again. *Please.*"

Ravinder saw her look away. Torn. But she was silent. Finally, in a low, hesitant tone, as though not sure if she should voice the fear at all, she said, "I have always supported you, but . . . what if you . . ." Simran was unable to complete the sentence.

For a very long moment that fear hung between them. Dark and heavy, like a rain-laden cloud.

"I will not fail," Ravinder said firmly. "I *cannot.*" That last word was expelled forcefully. "If I pull back now . . . if I don't finish this, I will not be able to live with myself."

Silence returned.

When Simran finally looked up, Ravinder saw desperation in her eyes, and a compelling need to leave this moment behind.

"You are right. Our baby has grown up," Simran said loudly. Much louder than usual, as though keen to drown out the thoughts plaguing her. "This is the first time I have seen her like this."

Relief hissed through him. He knew Simran well enough to know he had just received her support, though she would not say it out loud. Not just yet, anyway. He smiled, grateful for that, and the diversion. "I know what you mean. For a moment there, I could have sworn that was you talking."

Simran gave a wan smile. "Haven't I been telling you that we need to find a boy for her and get her married?"

"There you go again." Ravinder was relieved to see her smile. "But I hear you. And between the two of us I think you're the best person to do so. You obviously have much better taste in spouses than I do."

They both laughed. The laughter submerged the tension. But not too deep. Ravinder sensed it lay just beneath a wafer-thin layer. And would linger there, just waiting to break surface, till this whole thing was over.

As if to reinforce that, Simran said, "I still think it's a lousy idea, Ravinder." Then, after a longer pause. "I have a really bad feeling about this mission of yours."

Ravinder didn't know how to respond; he was feeling lousy, too, but he knew he couldn't *not* do it.

*So be it.*

Ravinder knew his best bet was to wrap up this messy operation *fast.*

*Where are you, Leon Binder?*

Knowing Leon, he was aware the hunt would be hard. And deadly.

*Cross-country, chess, shooting, boxing . . . no matter what . . .* Ravinder remembered Leon had always bested him. *Except fencing . . .* but even that had been a close thing; Leon had won as often as he had lost.

*Yet there is no way but forward. Damned if I don't. Maybe even if I do. But at least there is a chance if I try. I must. I have to.*

Ravinder steeled himself for the hunt.

# THIRTEEN

Leon knew he needed to find another, safer place to stay. The Sarita Vihar serviced apartment did not give him good vibes. Though, when he broke it down, he could not find any specific problem with it. Located in a middle-class residential complex, the apartment was secluded, was safe from prying eyes and, most important, in addition to the main entrance, had two possible exit points, which would be invaluable in case of an emergency.

*It's that damn landlord.*

Om Chandra gave him the creeps. Leon had learned to trust his instincts. That's what had saved him so many times.

*Especially that day in Istanbul.*

Suddenly Leon realized why Om Chandra was making him so uneasy; he closely resembled the owner of the service apartment Leon had hired in Istanbul when he had been engaged to take out that diamond merchant.

*What* was *his name?*

Leon tried hard, but twenty-six years had rolled by and the names had been eradicated from his memory: of the diamond merchant he had terminated and of the landlord he'd hired the safe house from.

*Funny! Both of them almost got me killed and now I can't even remember their names.*

An ironic laugh escaped him.

Luckily he had been alert that day. The landlord's shiftiness had first alerted Leon. That's when he began to notice all the telltale signs: the landlord was sweating profusely, exhibiting a twitch on his right side, repeatedly checking his watch, and constantly peering out the window. When Leon heard cars screech to a halt outside, he'd been sure. By time the cops broke in, the snitch was dead and Leon gone. Vanished in the byways of Istanbul.

That was the last time Leon had operated from a single safe house. Since then, having one secure base per tactical identity was an essential part of his SOP. For this mission Leon needed at least two. And, if he managed to find time, three.

*Backups are always good.*

From that day he had also ensured that every safe house he selected had at least two entries and exits, the more the merrier.

Leon pulled out his mobile. It was a brand-new Samsung Galaxy S Duos. A dual-SIM phone and perfect for his purpose. Both lines were hooked onto Hotspot Shield, a commercial VPN service, which he used to effectively mask his current location by switching server countries randomly. Launching the Notes app, Leon tapped open the list of six serviced apartments he had culled from the Internet before coming to India. The two he had checked out before Sarita Vihar had not made the cut; both had only one way in and out; absolute deal breakers for Leon.

The next serviced apartment on his list was in Jorbagh, which Google informed him was a posh residential colony located in central Delhi.

This apartment listing had four photos, all of which appeared promising. However, Leon had by now realized that Kodak and reality rarely ever saw eye to eye.

Tapping the address on Google maps, Leon instructed his phone to chart out the route and began to follow it.

Half an hour later he drove past a quiet old but primly maintained bungalow located beside Jorbagh market. Slowing down, he surveyed the house. By now last light was almost upon him, but it was still bright enough to give him a fair idea of the layout.

*Worth exploring.*

He drove on till he found an isolated side lane to park in. Surrounded by the gloom, after twenty minutes in the backseat, the aging American hippie had been replaced by a much more staid-looking British travel writer. The well-worn tweed jacket, turtleneck pullover, fashionable horn-rimmed spectacles, and neatly tied ponytail went well with the new persona of Noel Rednib.

Life had also taught Leon Binder the wisdom of keeping every operational identity apart and sheltered from the others. That way he would run out of options only when all his identities got blown.

For *that* to happen the cops needed a lot of resources, even more luck, and tons of time. By then Leon would be long gone.

Parking on the other side of the market, he walked back to the bungalow with the serviced apartment and rang the doorbell. The stocky, sixty-plus lady who came to the door had a pleasant, motherly feel. And, from the way she peered at him through thick bifocals, Leon sensed she was half blind.

*This is getting better and better.*

"Good evening, ma'am." Leon reverted to the clipped London accent he had grown up with. "I would like to have a look at the service apartment you have advertised."

She seemed delighted and, chattering incessantly, led him up to the right portion of the house, the part looking out on the road in front and the market across from it.

"What do you do, young man?"

"Not so young, ma'am." Leon laughed. "I'm a travel writer. Here to do a piece on the Golden Triangle." Leon knew that is how most tourists referred to the Delhi-Agra-Rajasthan circuit.

"Ah, but isn't that what everyone does? There is a lot more to write about. Every bit of India reeks with so much history." She bestowed a benign smile on him. "We used to travel so much when Mr. Kapoor was alive. He was a civil servant, you see . . . so life was good. Now, of course." She sighed. "But I shouldn't be complaining . . . life could be so much worse."

From that and the general condition of the house, Leon guessed money was now tight; the furniture and fitments were neat and clean, but had seen better days.

"Well, here we are." She showed Leon in.

"This is just what I need." Leon did not need to fake enthusiasm. The one-bedroom suite was as warm and cozy as its pictures on the website.

The absent-minded Mrs. Kapoor sealed the deal by forgetting to ask Leon for identification. Leon liked even more that the bungalow had no other occupants, barring her and the equally geriatric couple who worked there. But it was the treadmill in the garage that clinched the deal; Leon hadn't exercised for ten days and could feel his body, used to a five-mile run every day, stiffening.

A half hour later, Leon was alone in the apartment. He felt strangely at peace for the first time since he had reached Delhi. Aware he had caught a break with this house.

*Don't get complacent.*

He cautioned himself, aware complacency was his deadliest foe. But the bed looked inviting and Leon was unable to resist the temptation to take a load off his feet. Lying there, looking through the large French windows, he could see the colony market across the road.

THE MEAT LOCKER. The neon sign above the corner shop beckoned, reminding him it had been a while since he had eaten.

*I'll grab a bite when I step out to meet Vishal.*

Unwilling to expose this safe house to anyone, he had already decided to meet Vishal at Sarita Vihar.

As if on cue his mobile rang. Vishal.

Giving him the Sarita Vihar address, Leon got ready to leave. Though he still had an hour and a half, Leon factored in the time to change back to the American hippie persona, a spot of food, and the drive across town.

The mission was back to the forefront of his thoughts by the time he put down the phone. The knot of tension inside drew tauter as his mind sifted through the operational details and began to work out the outcomes he wanted from his meeting with Vishal.

Though he knew meeting Vishal was important, the risk of additional exposure made him uneasy. It reminded him that there were too many firsts on this mission, and most of them not the good sort.

*I need to be more careful.*

Opening his laptop, Leon retrieved the file Fatima had emailed him on Vishal Bhardwaj and went through it.

Within minutes, Leon realized Vishal's dossier was what people in service call a *steady* record. Peppered with a string of small but regular successes. None individually earthshaking, but collectively enough to show a steady worker. The best way to justify regular promotions, yet not to expose himself to any major risk or controversy. Leon knew this was how most cops on the take survived and flourished.

*Interesting.*

Leon then mulled over everything Verma had shared with him.

Vishal's handling of the kidnapping, interrogation, and elimination of his boss, Goel, was ample testimony of his ruthlessness and the precision with which he planned and operated. The fact that he had gotten away with it, from right under the noses of his STF colleagues, confirmed he was smart, too.

The photograph with Vishal's dossier drew Leon's attention. It showed a well-built clean-cut man crossing the road and getting into a maroon Ford Fiesta. The date stamp showed it was recent. The man's demeanor showed he had been aware of the camera. Leon studied him: tall, dark and . . . *hungry looking?*

*And such men are dangerous.*

*But if he were not, what use would he be to me?* Leon rationalized. But he knew he'd need to be on his toes; accomplices such as this could be as deadly as the cops hunting him down.

*And what could be more dangerous than a cop gone rogue?*

That reminded him of Edward and Ravinder. Both had been hovering just below the radar ever since his conversation with Ashok Verma. So far Leon had kept them at bay. He pushed them away again, aware they would unleash memories and emotions he did not wish to deal with.

*Not now.*

Not whilst in the thick of such a crucial operation.

# FOURTEEN

Vishal was excited. Since he had learned he would be working with Leon Binder, he'd pored over Binder's file with the enthusiasm of an evangelist, absorbing every detail of the thirty-six operations executed by him.

*Allegedly executed by him*, Vishal corrected. Barring the first few, possibly when he had been perfecting his tradecraft, Binder had seldom left any traces. *The man is a fucking ghost. But a rich one, if he's carried out even half the hits attributed to him.* Just the one Binder client the cops managed to arrest had confessed to paying Leon a million dollars to take out a business rival. *And that was over seventeen years ago. And here I am, content with pocketing a few measly thousand rupees in weekly kickbacks.*

The more Vishal thought about it, the more the idea of doing something big appealed to him.

*Why not? But not like Binder. He's a bit of a wimp. I'd like my hits to be spectacular: high-decibel affairs, so people sit up and take notice. The kind the media will rave about for years.*

What had started as a random thought when Verma had approached him on Fatima's behalf, to join the Special Task Force and help the Binder mission, grew into an obsession with every passing hour. His success at kidnapping, interrogating, and then terminating Goel boosted the idea.

That's why he was so turned on by the prospect of meeting Leon. *I could learn a lot.*

However, he didn't need a doctorate in logic to understand that when such dangerous men, wanted on every continent, allowed you to see and thus identify them, the implications were seldom good and often fatal. That fear had gnawed at him ever since he had gotten the message from Verma. However, eventually the excitement and his aspirations to be an international and famous gun for hire won the day.

As instructed by Leon, once outside the apartment in Sarita Vihar, Vishal texted him. He thought he saw the curtain of one of the front windows move, but the movement was so slight he was not sure he hadn't imagined it.

Then the door cracked open.

Vishal felt another pulse of anxiety, as though life was warning him not to enter. He almost succumbed. But his unquenchable thirst for excitement and his aspirations again won the day, propelling him forward.

*Why worry? What's the worst that can happen?*

Settling his jumpy nerves he pushed open the door and entered.

Brightly lit, clean but sparsely furnished room. No trace of any personal belongings anywhere. A half-empty half-liter bottle of Coke Zero and the debris of a Subway sandwich littered one end of an otherwise bare dining table. Vishal assimilated the room and analyzed the implications.

*Safe house. Recently acquired.*

Vishal sensed Leon did not live here. He respected the professional precaution. Admiration for the long-haired and unkempt man seated by a coffee table at the far end of the room climbed a notch. Though Vishal was surprised how bulky the man was, almost overweight; he'd expected a lean mean fighting machine. Then he realized most of the bulk appeared to be layers of clothing. Vishal also noticed that Leon's right hand stayed out of sight. He was certain it held a gun. That was disconcerting, but Vishal had not expected otherwise. He pushed away the spike of fear that jabbed him and forced a smile, trying to play it cool. "Hi."

"Hey there. How are you doing, Mr. Vishal? Come right in." Leon called out. Not even a hint of a smile, though.

The fact he did not rise to greet him irked Vishal. It made him want to create an impact that would command respect. He was trying to think of something when he spied the chessboard on the coffee table beside Leon. The board was in play. Studying the pieces Vishal noted it was a recently started game.

"That's an unusual opening gambit . . . the Torre Attack? Isn't it?"

"You're familiar with it?" Leon was impressed. "Not many people are."

"I try to catch a game whenever I can," Vishal replied, his ego somewhat appeased. "I love chess. You?"

"I like it, too." Leon now smiled. "Fancy a game?"

"Why not?" Vishal returned his smile. He realized how smoothly Leon was building rapport. Being acknowledged made him feel good. The challenge also was too obvious to ignore. He was determined to beat Leon.

"Ever tried the Goring Gambit?" Leon asked as they reset the pieces.

"I don't much care for it." Vishal shrugged. "It is not very advantageous if you are playing white."

"Depends how you develop the play." Vishal noticed Leon was watching him closely. "White or black?"

"White." Vishal replied immediately.

"Sure." Leon swiveled the board around. "Any particular reason why you prefer white?"

"I like to go first," Vishal said shortly, brows knitted, his attention now focused on the board. Making up his mind, Vishal played.

# FIFTEEN

Leon personally preferred black; he liked to make his move only after his opponent had committed himself. Changing stride midway is seldom easy for an attacker and invariably gave Leon the advantage.

He could not help smiling as he saw Vishal's opening moves: e4 e5; advancing the King's pawn two spaces forward.

*So . . . impatient, eager to commit* and *a risk taker . . . had gone for the Goring Gambit, though he had just communicated his belief that it was not the most useful for the player going first.*

Leon filed away these nuggets of information. Experience had taught him that sooner or later they would come in handy; either to control Vishal or to eliminate him, whichever way the cookie crumbled.

*Interesting bloke.*

Leon took up the gambit by responding with an Nf3, moving out the King's Knight; risky, but he wanted to push Vishal and see how he would respond. And, though he wanted to focus on the game, it struck him that Vishal's perspective and his experience as a cop could provide valuable insights into how Indian security would protect both targets.

*I could also use him to ascertain other options for launching my attack.*

Lost in thought, Leon was taken by surprise when Vishal suddenly changed tack. He realized Vishal had lulled him. It was done expertly, and suddenly the situation developing on the board had become far more dangerous than Leon had supposed. Realizing he could lose . . .

*That is so not happening.*

Leon's innate competitiveness asserted itself.

*Not on my watch.*

He wasn't sure what had happened or when, but he sensed from Vishal's demeanour it was no longer just a game. More a joust for psychological dominance.

Suddenly Leon felt alive again after a very long time.

Then Vishal caught his eye; the cop was leaning over the board, his stance aggressive, deep in concentration, and he also seemed to be brimming with joie de vivre. Leon was surprised how closely Vishal's feelings seemed to mirror his.

*Is that what I am like?*

The thought discomfited Leon. It had been years since he'd paid attention to such things. To himself.

*Why? What am I scared of finding?*

Leon did not like the direction his thoughts were progressing in. But was unable to stop them.

*Who am I?*

Vishal moved again.

And Leon realized he would lose if he didn't respond strongly and smartly.

Pushing away all distraction, Leon got down to playing both the games—the one on the board and the one being fought in their minds.

# SIXTEEN

Vishal forced a smile as Leon checkmated him. "Damn!" He felt like kicking himself. "I almost had you."

"Perhaps. Perhaps not." Leon's expression was noncommittal. "I think you were way too focused on my queen and bishop."

"I didn't realize the knight was the real threat till it was too late," Vishal admitted grudgingly. "You're good."

"Chess is fascinating. A lot like life." He was still speaking softly, but Vishal sensed the change; Leon had become businesslike. His next words confirmed that. "And also what we are going to do. No?" Leon didn't wait for an answer. "It is seldom the obvious threat that one should worry about."

"I'm not sure I understand," Vishal responded. "Do you mind if I ask, which target are you planning to take out?"

"No, I don't mind." But, much to Vishal's irritation, Leon didn't answer. Instead he countered with "If I gave you the option, which target would you pick and how would you bring it down?"

Vishal guessed he was being tested. "I have been thinking about that." He drew out a notebook and pen from his jacket pocket. "Let's take them one at a time. Masharrat first." Flipping open to a blank page, he began to plot. "The general arrives by private jet the evening before his talk. He lands at the VIP terminal of Palam airport. Rather appropriate, given he is a Paki." Vishal looked up expectantly.

Leon looked puzzled. "I didn't get that. Why is it appropriate?"

"It's a joke. Masharrat landing at the VIP terminal, I mean." Vishal grinned. "Since we often refer to those buggers as Vile Ignorant Pakis."

"Right. I get it." Leon looked amused. "Please go on."

"The jet is owned by a holding company registered in Ras Al

Khaimah, which is allegedly owned by a gangster known to have worked closely with the general in making the nuke-for-missile-technology deal with the North Koreans." Vishal flipped open his iPhone and checked some notes. "Masharrat's ETA is 1745 hours on 26 December. He is taken to the US embassy for a dinner being hosted by the American ambassador and then spends the night at his hotel, the Hyatt Regency. The next morning he reaches the Siri Fort auditorium by 0900 hours, has breakfast with a select group of delegates, addresses the keynote session post lunch, returns to the airport, and flies back to Dubai."

"So?"

Vishal was unable to read anything from Leon's expression. He continued. "So, we can bring down the jet provided we have access to a Stinger or a similar surface-to-air missile." Leon responded with a headshake. "Right. I figured as much. We can also strike at the Palam airport. However, this is heavily guarded by the Indian Air Force and will require a huge task force *unless* we are able to subvert a couple of key people in the air force. Very difficult, but given time, doable. However, in either case, it is unlikely the hit team will get away alive."

All Vishal got was an inscrutable nod from Leon. The lack of response irritated Vishal.

"We could also take Masharrat out during the move from the airport to the embassy, from there to the hotel, or the next morning from the hotel to Siri Fort, or from there to the airport. He will be in a bulletproof limo, escorted by the usual complement of eight security vehicles, including an ambulance and electronics vehicle. The security has been put in place by the conference organizers, using elements of Delhi Police and a private security agency. In addition, the general is bringing along six of his own men. They are keeping route info secret and security is well-planned and heavy. However, it is doable and getting away would be relatively easy."

By now, Leon's lack of response was agitating Vishal but he forced himself to stay calm.

"Lastly, of course, would be to strike at the conference venue itself, the Siri Fort auditorium. This also is well protected, especially considering he is not the only VIP present. However, given that it's a paid event and anyone can buy their way in, this venue could provide several opportunities." Vishal knew he had given a succinct analysis. He did not, however, get a chance to relish it.

"So," Leon asked piercingly. "What would you do, where, and with what weapon?"

Vishal was glad he had given this thought. He answered decisively, "I'd give it a go at the summit, probably when Masharrat is mingling with people."

"Weapon?"

"I need to think that through." Vishal faltered; he had tried hard, but been unable to come up with a definite action plan. "Offhand, a sniper rifle might be best."

"Sounds good." Again, Leon's bland smile irked Vishal.

"There are many possibilities," he added aggressively. "A lot would depend on how long I have been planning this and the budget available, of course."

# SEVENTEEN

Leon gave a broad smile, reverting to the bluff American persona effortlessly. "But of course. That's a brilliant analysis, Vishal." The germ of an idea had taken root. He evaluated it rapidly.

*It would bring down the risk to me considerably and enhance my chances of success.*

Deciding to develop it *and* test Vishal's value to the plan, he asked, "And Prime Minister Zardosi? What's your take on him?"

Vishal ran through Zardosi's routine, and as before, analyzed the pros and cons. Again, a concise and thorough analysis.

Leon could see Vishal was feeling good about himself. He decided to bring him down a notch.

"Would you help me understand *why* you have given so much thought to this?" His bonhomie had evaporated; now there was an edge in Leon's tone.

# EIGHTEEN

Vishal picked up the change in tone instantly. That and the sudden change in topic discomfited him; he was certain he did not want Leon to find out about his aspirations of joining this profession.

*No one likes competition.*

Refusing to be daunted, he pushed back gamely. "That's obvious. As part of the task force deployed to stop you, that's what I am supposed to be doing. Aren't I?"

"Is that all?"

"What else could it be?" Vishal countered.

"I don't know. You tell me."

Leon's unblinking gaze was unsettling. Perhaps that was why Vishal blurted it out. "Well, I've often wondered what it would be like, to do the work you do."

"You did, did you?" To his surprise, Leon laughed. "I thought as much."

Lulled by the deviousness of the man across the chessboard, Vishal relaxed. "Yes. I've been thinking about it for a while." He admitted, now not so sheepish. "Tell me, what is it like?"

Ignoring that, Leon queried, "Let us assume you had to execute this mission. What would you do?"

This time Vishal deliberated longer, organizing his thoughts before he spoke. "If I were you, I would plan to strike both targets simultaneously. I'd lead the primary strike personally and let another team handle the second target. However, I would let the second team strike moments before I did."

"Why?" Vishal sensed Leon already knew the answer and was still testing him.

"A diversion is useful only if it draws attention away from the primary attack," Vishal retorted, now irritated by Leon's supercilious attitude. "But I would not treat it purely as a diversionary attack, because I think it *is* possible to bring down both targets."

"That's impressive. Very impressive." The sudden warmth in Leon's tone surprised Vishal; he didn't realize how expertly Leon was keeping him off-balance. "I like the way you think, Vishal. You have a good head on your shoulders. And I was wondering whether you'd like to play a bigger role in this mission?"

"You mean as a diversion?" Vishal bristled.

"Come on, Vishal." Leon gave him a disarming smile. "We are talking as equals here. You already know I have the mandate for both targets, and I like your idea of taking out both simultaneously."

Vishal's gut reaction was to walk away; instinct warned him it would be dumb to trust Binder. But greed and his personal aspirations weighed in; Vishal badly wanted to believe Leon needed him. "In that case I'd be delighted." He replied. "What would you like me to do?" Vishal was embarrassed by his eager schoolboy tone. To compensate for that he added, "Assuming I will be adequately paid, of course."

"Of course." Leon's smile made Vishal uncomfortable; he couldn't help feeling that he had walked into a trap. "You've given me a lot of fresh ideas, Vishal. Give me a little time to think things through and we can work out the money then."

"You certainly are a careful man." Vishal forced a laugh, still trying to get rid of his uneasiness. He was dying to know what Leon wanted him to do and how much he was planning to pay, but thought it tactically unwise to push any more.

"Isn't that nice?" Leon commented evenly. "Let me call you. Soon." His tone communicated the meeting was over.

Vishal exited the way he had entered, with mixed feelings: excited at the prospect of new challenges, yet worried for his safety and happy to be out of the room.

There was something about Leon he had not been able to put a finger on. And that unsettled him. As did the prospect of a closer working relationship with Leon, thrilling though it was. Vishal was aware proximity to such men could have fatal repercussions. But he so wanted to walk down this road that he could not bring himself to ignore the opportunity.

# NINETEEN

Leon was thrilled that, as thorough as it was, Vishal's analysis of the targets had not unearthed his attack plan. He was now even more confident he would succeed.

However, the ideas ignited by Vishal had struck a chord. A diversion could reduce his risk greatly and increase the chances of success. Even better, he could see it coming together without much additional effort and wanted to wrap his head around it while their discussion was still fresh.

*I should have thought of this myself.* Leon massaged his face tiredly. *I'm getting old . . . too old for this crap.*

And it had been a long day. Coming as it did in the wake of the stressful encounter with Ri Yong and the eleven-hour flight from Seoul, he was feeling drained. Leon knew he should return to the Jorbagh apartment and get some rest; the coming days would be no less taxing. But the urge to capture and think through the new idea thrown up by Vishal proved irresistible.

He began to make notes, working out the finer details of how both targets could be attacked simultaneously. The only difference was that his diversionary attack would be only that, not a parallel attempt to take out both targets, as Vishal had suggested.

*But that's for me to know and him to figure out.*

Despite his tiredness, Leon grinned.

*By the time he does, it will be too late.*

Then the grin faded.

*Vishal is a devious one. Must watch my back.*

*And will it be sufficient to decoy Ravinder? Underestimating him would be a mistake; the cloth head is as sharp as they come.*

Leon did not realize when exhaustion overtook him. He nodded off.

# TWENTY

Ravinder tarried as long as he could. Despite Simran's acquiescence, he was reluctant to call Kurup. Finally, when the clock stuck ten, aware he could not put it off any longer, Ravinder called Kurup.

"I will be at the task force office at nine tomorrow morning. Could you please have all the officers there so I can meet them?"

"Of course. I will text you the office address and also email you the personnel files of all STF officers . . . and everything we have on Binder." Kurup seemed eager to please. "Is there anything else you need?"

"Not that I can think of."

Kurup picked up his unease, so he added reassuringly. "You've made the right decision, Mr. Gill. We really appreciate your help in this."

But Ravinder was still uneasy when he put down the phone and made his way up to their bedroom. The sense of foreboding that had gripped him since he had learned of Benazir's vendetta refused to leave him alone.

# TWENTY-ONE

Vishal was exhausted, too. And his uneasiness about Leon refused to dissipate. He was a couple of miles away from Sarita Vihar, crossing Escorts hospital, when he remembered he had to meet Fatima. The thought of the long drive to the Maurya Sheraton, all the way across town, was vexing. But he knew he would have to go; she *was* the one paying the bills. That irritated him further, making him feel like a lackey. It was in this mood that he turned left on the flyover and headed down Outer Ring Road. Traffic was bad and every passing mile made him pricklier.

By time he rang the doorbell of Fatima's hotel room, exhaustion and edginess held him in a tight vise. Then Fatima opened the door and Vishal felt someone had injected a large dose of Viagra straight to his heart.

Freshly bathed, rested, happy she'd gotten Leon back on track, in a white cotton T-shirt and knee-length denim skirt, Fatima looked *good*. Despite the late hour, expecting company, she had done her hair and her makeup was in place.

"Come on in, Mr. Bhardwaj." She stepped aside with a smile, waving him toward the sofa. "Would you like something to drink?"

"Vishal is good enough for me."

"Vishal it is."

Whether because he was tired or because he wanted to, Vishal misread the signals: he thought Fatima was giving him a come-on. He felt something within stir as he headed for the sofa. "I'd love a whiskey, thank you. A little soda and some ice." Throwing himself on the sofa he loosened his tie.

If Fatima found that strange, she kept it to herself. Handing over a drink, she said, "I thought it best to let you know what I expect from you."

"Sure." Vishal eyed her over the rim of his glass. He was only half listening.

# TWENTY-TWO

Leon jolted awake. For a moment the brightly lit unfamiliar room confused him. Then he saw the chessboard, his notebook beside it, and his brow cleared. Realizing he had dozed off and how tired he was, he dreaded the drive back to Jorbagh, but knew he could not stay on here. His operational instincts, suspicion of Om Chandra, and recent meeting with Vishal made that idea unacceptable.

*Perhaps a few moments more.*

Picking up the Coke Zero that had come with the Subway meal, he took a sip. Grimaced. The Coke was by now flat and lukewarm. He was putting it down when the chessboard caught his eye. The thought of the recently played game with Vishal made him smile; Leon took pride in the quality of his game. Chess had been one of his most enduring memories. It was also the one thing he associated most closely with his mother; they'd played almost daily, right through his childhood.

*The chessboard Dad gave me had been bigger. And the pieces so much better . . . solid marble.*

He remembered his mother's smile whenever he'd told her, "I'm going to be a grand master one day."

His smile turned bittersweet; he might have been one, too, if it hadn't been for Edward and Ravinder.

*They stole all my dreams.*

The smile mutated into an angry scowl. Unfeeling fingers began to toy with the sand timer kept by the chessboard to mark time for the players. Flipping it. Unseeing eyes watched the sand slither down, with grim finality. Then the sand ran out. Flip. Out. Flip. Out.

As the sand ran through the hourglass, again and again, three decades slipped away.

Leon could not decide what was worse. Being shackled and frog-marched by two bland-faced, sweaty bobbies down a crowded corridor at the Old Bailey, with everyone turning to stare at him. Or that he would soon be confronting his mother. The stricken look he knew she would give him seared his heart, making him wish he, not Farah, were dead.

The sight of Farah's dead face hammered at him again.

*She didn't deserve to die.*

Leon again wondered why Farah had screamed rape. The last he remembered, they had been sitting by the fireplace playing chess. Farah wasn't in his league, but decent nevertheless. And they had been drinking. Not heavily, but steadily. Then Farah had pulled out some weed and started smoking. She'd offered him a toke.

*Why the hell did I have to smoke it, too?* Leon lamented. Drugs of any kind were not something the freakishly health conscious Leon indulged in. But that day he had. And he still didn't understand why.

*Kismet. Or perhaps just the compulsion to impress Farah.*

The weed multiplied the effect of the whiskey. On both of them.

Leon's next coherent memory was of Ravinder at the door, staring at them. Farah and Leon were still by the fireside, but now naked. And he was mounted on her.

Ravinder looked stunned, the amazement of a man who walks in on his best friend making out with their other best friend's fiancée.

Then Farah had screamed, *"No! Help me."*

Leon had not been able to figure out why she had done so. But he did remember she'd done so *after* seeing Ravinder. He remembered that clearly.

Her ear-shattering scream jolted all three of them out of the frozen tableau.

Then everything got blurred and bloody. He vaguely recalled Ravinder running forward, pulling him off Farah, and hitting him. Leon *could* remember hitting back. But he could not recollect who had brought the poker into the fight. He thought it was Ravinder, but . . .

*Was that wishful thinking?*

*Denial?*

*Damn! Why can't I remember?*

The next hot flash of memory was Farah lying on the floor. Still stark naked. But now in a tight fetal ball. And blood was pulsing out of a gash on her forehead. And dripping off the tip of the poker in his hand.

*But I didn't hit her. I know I didn't. I just snatched the poker from Ravinder to save myself.*

Now Ravinder was screaming. And there was blood everywhere.

Then the door burst open and a sea of blue flowed into the room.

*Bobbies. So many of them.*

Leon hadn't ever seen so many cops in one place.

Keep moving." The cop on Leon's left tugged his elbow, shattering his memories of that gruesome day.

Leon gulped a deep breath, trying to inject oxygen into his brain; it was suffocating.

He knew his case had drawn considerable press; it is not often an Imperial College senior is arrested and tried for the rape and murder of a fellow student, especially not one who regularly made the Dean's List and the local press for his prowess as an athlete: boxing, rowing, cycling, javelin, shooting. Leon was a natural.

The accusatory glares and *oh-my-God-look-there-is-that-monster* whispers as the cops thread their way down the packed corridor, with Leon sandwiched between them.

"I'm innocent," Leon wanted to scream. "Don't judge me without hearing my side of the story. I did not rape her. And I did not kill her."

But no words emerged. He could not feel his tongue. Or even reach his thoughts. As though he was suspended in a vacuum.

*Ravinder will set it all right. He will tell them what happened.*

Leon felt hope bubbling under his skin, threatening to break free. Unaware he was suffering the same delusion all those under trial do—that they would be miraculously found innocent and exonerated. He knew Edward, completely besotted by Farah, would never believe it had been anything other than rape. But Leon was certain Ravinder would tell the truth.

*Ravinder is a stand-up guy, and we have always been close. Much closer than Edward, whose strange, somewhat prissy upper-class mannerisms surface every so often. But Ravinder is like us, one of the blokes . . . he is a good man.*

Then Hope, always a fickle mistress, did a somersault.

*What if Ravinder didn't?*

Despair came sweeping out of the darkness. Leon felt his heart plummet.

"Keep moving." The policeman on the left yanked his arm again, harder this time. Leon sensed his tension; the crowds jamming the corridors of Old Bailey were making the policemen nervous. There were so many people, the numbers increasing every moment, and they looked really angry.

As though handed a cue, someone shouted, "Lynch the sod!"

"Cut his nuts off!" The cry was taken up and grew louder.

The cop's grip on his arm tightened and they got moving again. The corridor seemed endless, but the onward motion felt good. Leon could feel his despair trickling away. He was suddenly eager to reach the courtroom.

*They* will *believe me. More important, Mom will understand. Once Ravinder explains what actually happened, she will understand. She has* to.

They hit a security barrier. Considering the publicity and angst Farah's rape and murder had thrown up, the cops had barricaded this part of the courthouse. They were checking identity and purpose before letting anyone in.

Of course, Leon and his escorts were hustled through. And immediately they sped up. Past the barrier, the crowd was sparser. Soon they turned the final corner to the courtroom.

Leon started as he saw all three of them. His mother was to his left, facing Edward and Ravinder. Edward had his back toward Leon. Ravinder and his mother were also facing away from him, at an angle. None of the three saw him.

Excited, Leon made to call out.

But a roar went up from the picket line across the road, beyond the trio, distracting him. It was a robust crowd, mostly female. The sight of Leon had incensed them. Their words were drowned out by the incessantly flowing traffic. The placards they were waving were not.

*Hang Binder.*

Leon's heart plummeted.

*Castrate the rapist.*

Despair skyrocketed.

He turned hungrily to the trio ahead. *Ravinder can save me.*

Before he could speak, Leon heard his mother say, "My Leon is a good boy. Both of you know him. Help him. *Please!* He would never hurt a fly."

"Neither would Farah," Ravinder shot back brusquely. "And she's dead. How could he have done this? Farah was Edward's fiancée."

That Ravinder, not Edward, had uttered those words struck Leon like a body blow. His mind reeled. He almost blacked out. Hope flamed and charred. Then from those smoldering remains arose rage. Phoenix-like. A dark and dangerous rage. The likes of which Leon had never experienced before.

The rage blocked everything out, smothering Leon in a dark, dank cocoon as he swept past them into the courthouse. They had seen him now and were looking at him. His mother was calling out to him, but Leon had nothing for her. Blindsiding them, he surged ahead, pulling along the surprised cops. Ignoring even his lawyer, Leon walled himself off from everyone and everything.

That rage stayed with him as he watched the courtroom drama play out. Only when they asked him to stand for the verdict did he look at his mother, cringing in the corner. Her stricken expression said it all, a confused cacophony of hope and despair. Leon could tell she didn't want to be there, was ashamed to be there, and yet would not have missed it for anything, in the hope that they would find her beloved son innocent.

Leon saw her hopes being dashed one by one. Inch by inch he saw her die.

Though his ears did not hear his being pronounced guilty or his mind assimilate its implications thereafter, not once did his eyes leave his mother's face. Every wrinkle of pain on it was etched on his heart. Even today.

And the pain was only to get worse.

The judicial system inside the jail was far swifter and infinitely less merciful than the one practiced at Old Bailey.

*Child molesters deserve death by castration. And rapists get raped.*

That was the law. And it was delivered in Leon's case, too. Mercilessly.

They came for him the very first night. Six of them. Lifers who no longer feared the law. They held him down and raped him again and again. Through that endless night Leon suffered more pain and humiliation than he had believed possible. No one heard his screams, stifled by the stinking sock stuffed into his mouth.

Even if they did, no one cared. Neither the other inmates nor the prison guards patrolling the corridor. Not even the security cameras, which usually missed nothing.

It was only as dawn broke, as Leon lay crying on the cold prison floor, mind and body mangled, that the last memory flash burst in on him.

*Ravinder was rushing toward him, the poker raised in the air, when his foot caught on the rug, sending him and the poker crashing down. Ravinder hit the floor and the poker thudded on Farah's head, hard. The blow hammered her down. And blood began to trickle from a gash in her forehead.*

The flash of memory was brief. So fleeting Leon was not sure he had seen it at all. Then it strengthened, whether because Leon's memory had refreshed it or due to cognitive dissonance, he could not be sure.

*But I am. I remember now. I am sure. Ravinder killed Farah.*

Doubt counterattacked.

*How is that possible? I'd been through this with my lawyer a dozen times. How could I not have remembered earlier?*

The fog of confusion refused to lift.

*But I know. I didn't kill Farah. Ravinder did.*

Conflicted, Leon sat up on the cold prison floor, his pain and humiliation forgotten. Swamped by this bigger and bitter one.

*That's why Ravinder refused to meet me. In fact, even refused to meet my eye all this while.*

Leon swore.

*That is why the bastard had been in such a hurry to crucify me.*

"I will make him pay." Leon realized he'd shouted only when his cellmate told him to shut up. He lapsed into a listless sleep, itching for morning so that he could speak to his lawyer. There was hope in his heart. Again.

But when he woke the next morning, he was no longer so sure.

*Did it really happen like that? Was Ravinder the real killer?*

Doubts plagued Leon, tormenting him.

*Had he imagined it? What was it, hope or reality?*

For a long time, Hope and Despair seesawed madly, driving him to the brink. In the end, it was Despair that seized the day.

*Even if it was true, would anyone believe me?*

As it turned out, no one did. Not even his lawyer; he didn't say so, but it was written all over his face.

*But I will get even. I will find Ravinder and kill him. If it takes a lifetime, so be it. But he will pay for what he has done to me.*

Leon lashed out. His arm angrily scattered the wooden chessmen across the living room of the Sarita Vihar service apartment. The rage jabbing at Leon was as sharp as it had been thirty years ago. No! Nurtured by the years, sharper.

*You bastards made my mom beg. You made her grovel. You drove her to the grave.*

Yet again her grief-stricken face swam before his eyes, and her sob-soaked pleas echoed painfully in Leon's head.

*You crucified me . . . for your own misdeeds . . . just because Farah was a slut.*

Leon's face tightened in rage.

*Now I will show you . . . you and that arrogant prick, Edward.*

He bounded to his feet, his tiredness now swept aside.

*One way or the other I will make you suffer the same pain and humiliation.*

Mechanically retrieving and replacing the fallen chessmen on the board, Leon switched off the lights and left the apartment. Soon he was in his car, heading for Jorbagh, now eager to get a good night's rest and looking forward to the morrow.

*No matter what the cost, I will bring down at least one of the targets . . . right under their bloody noses.*

In the darkness of the car Leon grimaced, as though in physical pain.

*It will be so much fun to hurt Ravinder. To make him squirm. And that bloody Edward, too. The arrogant prick.*

The irony brought a smile to his lips. A cold, cold smile. That the same men who had been responsible for setting him on this deadly path now stood between him and his targets.

*I was always better than the both of you. Definitely better than you, Ravinder Gill . . . you fucking cloth head.*

Leon hammered the steering wheel with an angry fist. The horn blared out in the dark night, like a battle cry.

# TWENTY-THREE

Fatima swung instinctively when Vishal placed his hand on her thigh. In the close confines of the hotel room, the slap rang out like a pistol shot. Equally shocked, she watched his expression change; stunned disbelief swept aside by a blinding rage. Fatima felt a rush of fear.

*This man had shown no compunction in kidnapping, torturing, and killing his own boss.*

Her fear escalated into panic, but she fought to keep it off her face.

"You bitch." Vishal's face suffused with rage. He made to rise.

The venom with which the words were expelled unleashed something in Fatima. She *knew* if she showed the slightest fear, he would . . .

"*How dare you!*" Clamping a lid on her terror, Fatima put as much force into her tone as she could muster, ensuring she did not break eye contact. "Do you think I'm one of your floozies?"

That hit home. She saw Vishal sink back into the sofa, but he was glaring at her angrily.

"Don't *ever* forget who is paying the bills around here." Fatima forced herself to match him glare for glare. "Now get out." She pointed at the door, willing her finger not to shake. "*Out!*"

But the danger was far from over. Vishal maintained eye contact. His rage was now replaced by a cold, calculating look, which made Fatima more fearful. Then he rose, towering over her. She almost shrank back instinctively, but forced herself not to cower.

"This is not over." Vishal leaned over her. "You horny cougar." Fatima suppressed the urge to scream. "Not by a long shot." The hand he wagged in her face seemed like a chopping knife. "I will get you for this. *Bitch! Just you wait!*"

Her finger, still pointing at the door, had now begun to tremble. But Fatima did not break eye contact. "Get out. And make sure you give me daily updates on everything happening in the task force and between Leon and you. Otherwise you can kiss your money good-bye."

Still glaring at her, but fighting the urge to smack her, Vishal headed for the door. Then he was gone.

Fatima sat stunned as the door clicked shut behind him. When she was sure he would not be back, she ran to the door, slipped on the security chain, and rushing to the toilet, threw up. Only then did she start crying.

*How much worse will it get?*

She felt drained and awfully alone. Another bout of vomiting racked her.

*Perhaps I should leave for Dubai and let Leon handle it. That's what I am paying him for.*

Then her need for revenge asserted itself. She knew she did not want to leave anything to chance; she'd given too many years of her life to this. She wanted to be here and keep things on track, just in case some new complications arose.

*No.* She stiffened her spine. *I will see this through.*

Her eyes took in the time on the wall clock. Almost midnight.

*Just four days more. On the fifth day one of the monsters would die. Zardosi or Masharrat. I want to be here to see it happen. I have earned that right.*

Her thirst for vengeance steeled her resolve.

# TWENTY-FOUR

Vishal strode angrily through the Maurya Sheraton lobby, sure everyone could see Fatima's hand imprinted on his cheek. It fueled his rage. Face burning with humiliation he retrieved his car from the valet, furiously engaged gears, and headed home.

*That fucking cocktease; I know she wanted it.*

He rubbed his cheek angrily.

*Just four days more. The day I get my money I will nail this Paki cunt . . . fucking high-and-mighty Fatima Basheer.*

The decision came to him instantly. Soon as this mission was over he would let her have it, then clear out of the country and start off as an independent contractor, like Leon Binder, but bigger.

*Bigger than anything this world has seen.*

No more working for the chickenshit government. He grinned.

*This Paki bitch is going to be my first one.*

Grin widening, he floored the accelerator, hurtling through the semi-deserted Delhi roads. He again felt energized and good about himself. And the future seemed bright.

*Soon as I get my hands on this money . . . no more penny-pinching . . . no more measly Marutis and fucking Fords . . . I'm going to get me a Merc or a BMW . . . something swish.*

Vishal's grin broadened.

*And I'm so done with this shit-kicking country. Puerto Rico. Mexico. Spain . . . or perhaps Greece. Or maybe check them all out . . . travel for a year and see which one I like the most.*

Exploring all these pent-up dreams filled him with excitement.

*And I'm going to find me a sexy Sheila . . . big ass, big tits . . . someone hot and willing to spice up my nights.*

He contemplated changing direction and heading for a pickup place. It had been a fortnight since he'd gotten laid.

*It's not as though someone's waiting for me at home.*

*Home? Which fucking home?*

An orphan, Vishal had no recollection of his parents. He had no idea who he was or where he'd come from: rich, poor, Hindu, Muslim, Christian, Jew, or . . .

Vishal shrugged.

*What fucking difference does it make? Whoever they were, my parents didn't want me. And home had been . . . what?*

His earliest memories were of the dingy state-run orphanage in Daryaganj. High ceilings, peeling paint, crumbling walls, the perpetual stink of decay, and food that tasted like uncured leather. And of course the lanky warden and his two fat, sweaty matrons, who ran the place. Who loved making the kids go down on them, when they were not busy humping each other.

*The Holy Trinity.*

Vishal laughed, a cold, hate-filled half laugh, half cry.

Without realizing he was doing so, Vishal began wiping his mouth, trying to get rid of that nauseating taste, which had been a part of his life since he was five. For seven horrid years.

Vishal's emerging hard-on of a moment ago had vanished; now he was tearful. And filled with rage. A cold, limitless fury, which the very thought of the Holy Trinity always unleashed in him. Even today. Three decades had gone by, but that disgusting taste, the foul smell, and his burning rage were stronger than ever.

Vishal realized he was gripping the steering wheel so hard his hands were hurting. Rolling down the window he lit a cigarette and took a deep drag.

*Why bitch about it? At least I got out.*

As the consequence of a Delhi Police CSR project, a thirteen-year-old Vishal had found himself first in a Delhi Police boarding school and eventually in the Police Academy. Both had been strict, the discipline harsh, even impersonal, but that's the only time in his life Vishal felt safe. And he blossomed, excelling both in academics and sports.

*Otherwise where would I be now? Perhaps still in a police station, but on the wrong side of the bars.*

By now Vishal's mood had swung; all thoughts of picking up a whore had melted into the night. And the darkness within had grown deeper. He could feel the viciousness grow, stronger and wilder.

Vishal was parking outside his apartment in K-Block Green Park when a clock in one of the houses began to chime. Twelve tinny strikes echoed out in the otherwise silent night. And just like that, the twenty-second of December mutated into the twenty-third.

It was with a heavy, angry tread that Vishal went up the narrow flight of steps to the third-floor one-bedroom studio apartment he called home these days, ever since he'd been posted to Delhi. It was nearly identical to the ones he'd occupied in the various cities that police life had taken him.

*And same as the ones that would come . . . unless I follow the Binder model and build a new life.*

The idea was growing more appealing by the minute. Vishal *knew* he could not . . . *would not* . . . live out his days in such sur-roundings.

*Just a few days more . . .* then a new country, swanky house, sleek car, money in the bank, and of course a hot dame.

For the moment, everything else faded. Vishal smiled.

# DECEMBER
# 23

# ONE

Ravinder awoke to the bonging of the grandfather clock kept in the dining room. Imported by one of his ancestors, a mahogany long-case from the house of William Whipp, dating back to the 1700s, its chimes were loud enough to liven up a graveyard. Ravinder would have gladly given the damn thing away, but Simran loved it.

He tried to go back to sleep, but his restless mind refused to co-operate. And memory lane seemed like a street he didn't want to go down. Not right now. He was already feeling awfully muddled.

Kurup and Kingsley suddenly landing up at his house. Leon re-surfacing in his life, bringing back memories of Farah and that hor-rific evening when he'd walked in on Leon raping her. Then her horrible death at Leon's hands. And what followed—that had been even worse: his being forced to choose between his two best friends. Even though Leon had broken their trust by sleeping with Edward's fiancée, taking Edward's side to testify against Leon had been hard; all three had been so close, Ravinder was not certain he would have done so if Leon hadn't killed Farah.

And now this, his agreeing to lead the manhunt for Leon. The grave implications if he failed. And of course, Simran's surprisingly strong resistance to his decision.

*But I understand where she's coming from.*

Ravinder was aware Simran had never fully reconciled to his past, either his first marriage to Rehana, or Ruby, his daughter from that marriage. Nor had she liked his decision to join the In-dian Police Service. As a royal, albeit from a minor Punjab princi-pality, and a bright one at that, Ravinder had been expected to join the more glamorous Indian Foreign Service.

*Why on earth would you want to be a chowkidar?* That had been

Simran's derisive comment when he'd shared his decision to join the police after their betrothal.

His *to protect and serve* quip had so enraged Simran that Ravinder had been surprised she'd not broken off their engagement. He guessed only the dread of embarrassment had stayed her hand. The memory made him smile, but it was a fleeting, rueful one. Replaced soon by the troublesome thoughts besieging him.

*Damn strange! The way those years in London keep coming back to haunt me. First Ruby, and now Leon . . . like the bloody fog in London, never ending.*

Guilt and anger swamped him. But Ravinder pushed them aside, determined not to get bogged down. With his confidence already at low ebb Ravinder knew he needed to focus on the mission. It was tough enough to stop one of the world's deadliest assassins, one whose career had lasted longer than the life-span of most people in this bloody profession.

*I* have *to ensure I get off to a good start with the task force officers. No other way. With just four days left I cannot afford to dilly-dally.*

Another twinge of apprehension.

*I wonder what they have heard about me?*

*It doesn't matter.*

*I will have to earn their respect . . . and fast.*

Shelving his apprehension, Ravinder attacked the tasks confronting him.

*First, understand the strengths and weaknesses of the team.*

He had gone over their dossiers, but Ravinder knew documents could tell you who had done what but *not* why. People are people; dossiers and annual performance appraisals cannot capture their essence. To lead them effectively, Ravinder had to find out what made them tick.

*Second, go through the routes and routines of both targets, identify the most vulnerable points, and secure these against an attack by Leon or his henchmen. Not that Leon used many, and seldom for anything important, if his past hits were any indication.*

Isolating Leon was critical; it would put him under pressure.

*Men under pressure are more prone to making mistakes.*

That reminded him, he again needed to go through everything they had on Leon: earlier targets, hits, misses, and similarities in the MO; the whole nine yards. He had been through them once, but he felt the need to do so again. More thoroughly.

*Third, and most important, find Leon.*

That made him pause.

*How? He wouldn't exactly be advertising his presence. On the contrary, if his history and basic tradecraft were any yardstick, Leon would use several operational identities and muddy the trail at every step.*

Ravinder knew guesswork was pointless; the possibilities were endless.

*There* has *to be another way.*

More thought.

*The mole. Find the mole and he . . . or she . . . would lead us to Leon. So how do I find the mole?*

Ravinder realized his thoughts were spiraling into a loop.

*Counterproductive.*

He hauled them back, deciding it was best to know his team first. Then evaluate the options available. Only then, act.

Realizing he was too keyed up to sleep, Ravinder went down to the study and spent the next hour going through the dossiers of the STF officers. Then he began to study Leon's previous hits again.

*Even the smartest criminal has a pattern. The trick is to find it. That is the only way I can stay one step ahead and bring him down.*

It was a thick file, but more conjecture than hard evidence. As he turned the pages, the last three decades of Leon's life came alive. Ravinder jotted down the key points.

- *1983. Istanbul. Target diamond merchant named Namik Kemal. Weapon used, poison.*
- *1983. Cairo. Target Salah Abdel Sabour. Chemically induced heart attack.*
- *1984. Ottawa. Atilla Altikat, Turkish diplomat. Drive-by shooting.*
- *1986. Bangladesh. Sheikh Usman, prime minister designate. Sniper rifle.*
- *1987. Colombia. Jaime Pardo Leal, leader of the Patriotic Union Party. Poison.*
- *1989. Germany. Alfred Herrhausen, chairman of Deutsche Bank. Knifed.*
- *1990. Kenya. Seth Sendashonga, former interior minister of Rwanda. Poison.*
- *1991. Enrique Bermudez, founder of Nicaraguan Contras. Sniper rifle.*

- *1993. Algeria. Kasdi Merbah, former prime minister of Algeria. Bomb.*
- *1994. Azerbaijan. Shamsi Rahimov, intelligence and security chief. Bomb.*
- *1999. Paraguay. Luis María Argana, vice president of Paraguay. Knife.*
- *2000. Ofra, Israel. Binyamin Ze'ev Kahane, leader of Kahane Chai. Poison.*
- *2001. Seattle. Thomas Wales, federal prosecutor and gun control activist. Poison.*
- *2001. São Paulo, Brazil. Antonio da Costa Santos, mayor of Campinas. Bullet.*
- *2004. Iraq. Ezzedine Salim, acting chairman of Iraqi Governing Council. Poison.*
- *2007. Japan. Iccho Itoh, mayor of Nagasaki. Bullet.*
- *2008. Syria. General Muhammad Suleiman, security adviser to president. Poison.*
- *2010. Bangkok, Thailand. General Khattiya Sawasdipol. Sniper rifle.*
- *2010. Mexico. Robert Torre Cantu, politician. Bomb.*
- *2011. Libya. Abdul Fatah Younis, commander in chief of the Libyan armed forces. Bomb.*
- *2013. Guatemala. Carlos Castillo Medrano, mayor of Jutiapa. Sniper rifle.*

By the time he turned the last page Ravinder was feeling overwhelmed. Leon had cut a broad and bloody swath across the globe. The sheer ingenuity of his hits amazed Ravinder. Putting aside the file, he turned to the notes he had made. Soon some points became obvious.

- *Leon innovates constantly and rarely repeats an MO.*
- *No known accomplices. Even operationally, none used for any major task.*
- *Negligible collateral damage; even when a bomb had been used, barring the target, few people had been killed.*
- *In most cases it was hard to attribute the hit to Leon; he was seldom present by the time it was discovered the victim had been murdered. Most cases remained unsolved, attributed to*

*him more on the basis of hearsay and rumors than on any con-crete evidence.*

- *No photos, barring the thirty-year-old mug shot taken by the London Police at the time of his incarceration.*
- *No identified permanent place of residence.*

He stared at his notes, trying to see if he'd missed something . . . to spot a new clue or pattern.

Nothing.

The feeling of being overwhelmed was stronger now. Ravinder took a deep breath and stilled his thoughts, seeking coherence.

*The man is a ghost . . . a whisper in the wind. So much paper, yet so little to go on. But that's not possible . . . there have to be some traces . . . there always are . . . especially these days . . . digital foot-prints always remain. I'm missing something.*

Clearing his head, Ravinder reexamined his notes, trying to match the emerging picture with the man he'd once known so well . . . had shared an apartment with . . . laughter, tears, and beers . . . so much.

*Who are you, Leon Binder? What on earth have you become?*

An arrow of guilt pricked him. Unwilling to get distracted he pushed it away.

*What are you planning this time?*

*Where are you right now?*

*How do I find you?*

Ravinder knew *those* were the questions he needed to focus on. He was lost in thought when the grandfather clock boomed out again, five ponderous strokes.

# TWO

Leon had set the alarm for five. Bursting with energy when it triggered, he sprang out of bed. Even at this early hour, despite the bone-chilling cold, Delhi was alive. Milkmen, newspaper boys, and a host of other morning merchants could be heard going about their business: ghostly figures shrouded in the dense early-morning winter fog.

Wanting to ensure his battle plan was bug-free, Leon decided to go through it again, first on paper and then on ground.

Using the Hotspot Shield Elite VPN he was subscribed to, which secured his data traffic and made it virtually impossible for his location to be tracked, Leon logged into the Google account he created at the start of every mission and accessed the Google drive. All operational notes and data for this mission had been stored on this drive, ensuring he would never be caught with any incriminating evidence on his person. As an added precaution, in case the account got hacked, Leon had set up alerts to let him know whenever any of the files were accessed.

Immersed in a virtual walk-through of the operation, he began to factor in the diversionary attack Vishal had suggested.

Leon was lost in data and details when the first pain struck. A few minutes later, the second. It was only when the third, even bigger, wave of pain hit that Leon realized it was not something he could wish away or ignore.

Another hour and four visits to the washroom later Leon realized Delhi Belly would stop him dead even if the cops did not.

*Damn! I need to recon both venues, collect the sarin . . . Ri Yong Ho had promised delivery today.* And *hand it over to Nitin so he can fabricate the weapon.*

But the pain was now too strong to ignore. Unwilling to draw attention to himself by going to a doctor, Leon tried Jorbagh market. The sole pharmacy provided the required Norflox-TZ tablets and hydrating salts. From the general store adjacent to it, Leon procured the curds, bananas, and honey that the pharmacist advised would be good for him.

By now in acute discomfort, Leon returned to the serviced apartment, dosed himself, and waited impatiently for the medicine to take effect. He had lost several valuable hours. There was much to be done and already half the day had been wasted. His anxiety ratcheted up.

# THREE

Vishal was in a foul mood when he drove his Ford Fiesta into the STF office parking, still seething at Fatima's rebuff and apprehensive about their new chief.

The STF office was an ugly single-story block with a dozen rooms surrounded by a ten-foot-high unpainted brick wall topped by four strands of rusting barbed wire. On the other hand, it was conveniently located opposite Nehru Place, accessible by public transport, with an abundance of shops and eateries around.

His immediate concern was not the investigation of Goel's kidnapping and murder; common sense told him the hunt for Binder and stopping the assassinations would be everyone's first priority. However, though it was not the first time he'd killed a man, it was definitely the first time he'd tortured anyone and killed in cold blood, and his anxiety level was high.

Vishal was parking when he noticed an unfamiliar black BMW 750Li at the end of the lot and guessed it was Ravinder's.

*Our new chief travels in style.*

His lips pursed enviously. The high-end Bimmer was the kind of car he coveted.

*Soon.*

He promised himself.

*No more shitty hatchbacks.*

That made him feel better. Then he spotted Philip Cherian's silver Fiat Linea, parked on the other side of the Bimmer. His smile vanished.

*That ass-licker must be trying to weasel his way into Ravinder's good books right from the get-go.*

Dismissing Philip, he turned his thoughts back to Ravinder.

*Is Gill really that good?*

Though loath to admit it, Vishal *was* apprehensive about Ravinder. Their new commander had been the topic of discussion at the STF since they had been informed Ravinder was taking charge. Like the others, Vishal, too, had read up on Ravinder; and there was no denying he had one heck of a record, barring the disastrous Israeli-Palestinian Peace Summit during his final stint as chief of the Indian Anti-Terrorist Task Force.

"Don't make the mistake of underestimating Ravinder Gill." He remembered Leon's warning of the previous night. "He's very quick on the uptake and doesn't miss a thing."

"Sounds as though you know him well." Vishal had not missed the familiarity with which Leon had spoken.

Ignoring that, as he did most of Vishal's questions, Leon had countered, "You'd better know him, too. The faster the better."

Despite this, or perhaps *because* of this, a thrill shot through Vishal. Living on the edge, where he could smell the danger, taste it, almost touch it, made him feel alive. Riding high on that, he pushed open the office door.

# FOUR

Ravinder turned as Philip Cherian, the task force second-in-command, tapped his arm. "And this, sir, is Vishal Bhardwaj."

Ravinder took in the tall, dark, and lean man who had entered; Vishal carried himself well and was sharply dressed, in navy trousers and a sky-blue shirt, topped with a deep blue corduroy blazer.

*He doesn't much look like the photo in his file.*

*Perhaps because that had been in uniform.*

Ravinder noticed Vishal's scrutiny as they shook.

*Wary. The usual apprehension of meeting a new boss? Or something else?*

Ravinder realized Kurup's warning about a mole was making him inordinately suspicious.

*Not good. I'll never get them all on the same page with such an attitude.*

Reminding himself to relax, he smiled. "Good to meet you, Vishal."

"Good to have you on board, sir." Vishal's grip was firm and his return smile formal. "Welcome to the Special Task Force."

"I believe you were also with the Anti-Terrorist Task Force." Ravinder wanted to let them know he'd done his homework.

"That's right, sir." He seemed jovial enough to Ravinder, though he could sense some strain between Philip and Vishal. "Almost seven years, but I was based in Hyderabad till the NIA director mobilized me for this task force."

"Ah, that's possibly why we never met."

The door opened again, short-circuiting their conversation. A woman entered: mid-thirties, about five and a half feet, sparse frame. Her startlingly fair complexion contrasted with her staid gray kameez, black salwar, dupatta, and thigh-high sweater. The indifferently tailored dress was worn like a military uniform. Her solemn, humorless demeanor gave impetus to that impression.

"Sir, this is Saina Khan." Cherian beckoned her forward. "She's from Delhi Police. Very experienced investigator and our primary liaison with the local police."

Ravinder sensed Cherian respected her ability but did not much like her; the enthusiasm in his tone was not mirrored by his noncommittal expression.

"Good morning, sir." Saina stiffened to attention a few feet away. Polite but unsmiling. Making it clear she respected her space. Barring a cursory nod, she acknowledged neither Philip nor Vishal.

Ravinder had no idea how effective she was at networking with and influencing the local police, but it seemed obvious Saina made no effort to do so with the rest of the team.

"All well with her, Philip?" he asked in an undertone when Saina had moved—more like marched—off to her cubicle at the far end.

"Yes, why?"

"Just wondering . . . she seems very quiet."

"She's always quiet." Philip gave a brief smile. "Keeps to herself, but she's very competent. Don't worry about her, sir."

"Saina is Saina." Vishal chipped in from behind; Ravinder had not realized he'd been listening in. He noticed the look Vishal was giving Saina; it wasn't pleasant.

*Why the bad blood between them?* Ravinder made a mental note to find out.

The door blew open yet again and another woman trooped in; she was also in her mid-thirties and about the same height, but in marked contrast to Saina, she had a very pleasant demeanor and a lot of energy. She had in tow a tall, well-built, blue-eyed Caucasian man with close-cropped blond hair and a bewildered look.

"Hey, guys! He was wandering around looking for our office." The newcomer called out cheerfully. "This is Chance Spillman from MI6." Then she noticed Ravinder and stiffened to attention. "Good morning, sir, I'm Archana Singh."

As Ravinder returned her salute he noticed the change in Vishal and Philip. Both had straightened up. Vishal ran an unconscious hand over his hair. One look at the pert, smiling Archana, with shoulder-length hair framing a decidedly lovely face, made it easy to see why. Her brown business suit set off by a beige top was formal

enough, but showcased a well-endowed and well-maintained figure. However, it was the warm, captivating smile that set her apart.

"Archana is from NIA's Cyber Cell. She handles our communica-
tion, electronic intelligence, and cyber needs." Philip's attention,
like Vishal's, was on Archana. "She is a whiz with computers."

Though she reined it in really fast, Ravinder also noticed the look
Saina threw at Archana; it was full of contempt. On her part, Archana too avoided eye contact with Saina. Again, Ravinder wondered
whether it was just a woman-to-woman thing, or if the two ladies
had any history together.

*Damn!* Ravinder's heart sank; he could see clearly that the people
arrayed around him were anything but a team, still in the storming
phase. *This is what I have to find Leon and bring him down. Crap!* It
was a shitty feeling.

Had he had time, Ravinder would have preferred to bring in a
new team of people he knew and trusted. *Alas!* Ravinder's anxiety
hiked north several notches.

By now Chance had shaken hands with the others and come up
to him. He looked a bit off-kilter. Ravinder felt a twinge of awkwardness too; he liked the man, but couldn't forget that a few weeks
ago Ruby had tried to kill him.

*How does one greet a man who has been shot at by his daughter?
And who has shot back at her!*

"Good morning, Mr. Gill," Chance said politely. "How's it going for
you?"

"As well as it could, Chance." Ravinder smiled, extending his
hand. "How have *you* been doing?" Ravinder tapped his collarbone
lightly; that's where Ruby's bullet had struck Chance. "The wound
better?"

"Almost good as new, thank you."

"You two know each other?" Vishal seemed surprised.

Ravinder exchanged a quick glance with Chance. Both smiled.
And just like that the awkwardness between them dissipated. Surprisingly, with that lightness, Ravinder felt his confidence climb.

"Yes, we do," Ravinder replied. Vishal was obviously expecting
more, but Ravinder refrained from further comment. Instead he said,
"Now that we're all here, let's get cracking on the case." When he saw
the others nod, he added, "What does one do for tea around here?"

"One rings the bell." With a smile Archana did just that. Moments
later a huge, familiar man, with an even bigger grin, hove into view.

"Gyan? You?" Ravinder was delighted; ignoring Gyan's salute he went closer and shook hands. Gyan had served as his office runner for many years. Though lacking Einstein's mental agility, Gyan was a solid man to have in one's corner and was devoted to Ravinder.

"I asked to be sent here when I learnt you're back, sir." Gyan's gentle voice was at stark variance with his Hulk-like proportions.

"How's your son doing?" Ravinder had ensured Gyan was given relatively light assignments when his son was diagnosed with cancer a couple of years ago.

"By God's grace he is responding well to the treatment, sir."

"That's wonderful."

# FIVE

Philip Cherian watched the interplay between Ravinder and Gyan; one can tell a lot about a man from the way he interacts with his subordinates, and how they respond to him. So far Philip liked what he saw.

*This is what we need.*

Like Goel, the previous STF chief, Philip was a Bomb Disposal Squad veteran. They had also served together in the NIA for five years. Goel's death and the horrid manner of it had left him with a burning desire to ensure the new STF succeeded; at least his friend wouldn't have died in vain.

*Ravinder is obviously good with people, but let us see what he does next . . . operationally.*

Philip made up his mind to do everything he could to help Ravinder succeed. He was aware that with only four days left, Ravinder would need all the help he could get.

*Four days!*

Philip wondered if ninety-six hours were enough to find and stop one of the deadliest assassins in the world.

*We have already lost a man . . . a good man. Who else?*

Philip surveyed the others in the room. And much as he hated it, his tension grew.

# SIX

Ravinder, keenly aware of the clock's counting down, wasted no time getting down to business.

"First things first, guys." Having spent the better part of the night planning, Ravinder had worked out what he wanted done. He took charge as soon as they were seated around the conference table with an assortment of tea, coffee, and cookies. "In light of what happened to Mr. Goel, all of us will ensure we keep the others informed about our movements at *all* times. No lone ranger stuff *at all*," Ravinder emphasized. "Move in pairs whenever possible. If none of the others is free, take one of the local cops with you. Saina, please ensure we always have a couple of Delhi police guys on standby."

Saina made a note on her iPad mini.

"Secondly, our priority is to ensure both targets are safe as long as they are on Indian soil. So, Philip, I want you to go over Zardosi's agenda with a fine-tooth comb. Imagine you are a hit man and root out every single point at which he is vulnerable and how best he could be got at. Chance, you back him up. Play devil's advocate."

From Philip's expression Ravinder knew he had struck the right chord with his 2IC.

"Vishal, I want you to do the same for Masharrat." Ravinder was surprised at Vishal's sudden, though fleeting grin. However, focused on giving directions, he didn't dwell on it. "Saina, you team up with him."

Vishal's smile vanished. Saina nodded, but the look she threw at Vishal screamed *nasty*.

Ravinder again noticed, but decided he didn't have the time to deal with their personal peeves and idiosyncrasies right now. There *was* no time; they would have to deal with their interpersonal issues as best as they could. "Philip and Vishal, both of you will give detailed presentations on your targets first thing tomorrow. The rest of us will critique them. *Then* we will evaluate the protection plans to ensure we have covered all bases and the targets are secure."

With the defensive part of his plan addressed, Ravinder now went on the offensive. "Archana, I want you to collate a list of everyone who was privy to the intelligence inputs given to NIA by MI6. *Everyone,*" Ravinder stressed, "in NIA *and* in our task force. Someone is feeding information to Binder. We have to find him. Or her. *They* will lead us to Binder."

Everyone turned to stare at him. But they knew he was spot-on.

Ravinder noticed the looks they exchanged were fraught with suspicion. He wished he could have done without this disruption to his team, but knew it was unavoidable; the traitor had to be unearthed. Aware this was a rocky and pointless road to traverse, Ravinder tried to banish his anxiety. But it clung to him, weighing him down.

Once again, he wished he'd had more time to bring in a new team: people he knew and trusted. But he also knew it was not an option and he had to manage with what was available.

*I have to get them pulling in the same direction.*

To enable that and highlight the importance of their task he added, "And guys, I cannot stress this enough. Come what may, we have to stop Leon Binder. Don't forget that Pakistan retains its importance on the world stage only by keeping its so-called enmity with India alive and fermenting. As long as they can dangle the threat of an Indo-Pak nuclear war they will continue getting economic support from the Americans. That's also why they keep the specter of terrorism alive, even though they always pretend they are helping the world to fight it." He gave them all a solemn look. "I personally have no love lost for either Zardosi or Masharrat, but God forbid one of these two idiots is killed in India; their loony generals will play that card forever . . . it may well lead to an Indo-Pak war."

The expressions of his team made it clear that he was not alone in his dislike for the two Pakistanis.

# SEVEN

Vishal felt his delight at being given the same task he'd done with Leon considerably dampened at being paired with Saina. Her holier-than-thou attitude bothered him. That she sensed it and ignored him aggravated Vishal even further.

Whatever little of his happiness was left evaporated when he heard Ravinder's final command to Archana.

*So he suspects there is an informer.*

It was only logical, and Vishal had figured it would happen sooner rather than later. However, hoping the new chief would need time to settle in, he had not expected the mole hunt to start so soon.

*Leon was right; this bugger is sharp.*

He was still absorbing that when Philip added to his stress.

"Sir, why aren't we issuing an APB for Binder? That will put him under pressure and curtail his freedom of movement."

"Fair question, Philip," Ravinder conceded. "There are two problems. The first is that we have no idea what name or nationality Leon has used to enter India. Considering approximately seven million foreigners visit India annually . . . that's approximately twenty thousand people per day . . . looking for a man with no name or nationality would be worse than hunting for a needle in a haystack." Ravinder allowed that to sink in. "To add to that, we don't have any recent photos of Leon. So what APB do we put out?"

Before Vishal's delight at that could take hold, Archana delivered it a knockout punch.

"Do we have any photographs, sir?" she asked.

"Yes, we do." Ravinder accessed on his laptop the photo taken when Leon was arrested after Farah's death. "But, like I said, the most recent one we have is about thirty years old."

"That is a decent enough start, sir." Archana replied, leaning across and examining the photo on his laptop. "It's best to share such things on the task force's O-drive, sir. Then we can all access it."

"Tell me how and I will." Ravinder gave his laptop a helpless look; computers were definitely *not* his thing.

"Sure." Archana began pounding her laptop keys. Paused, eyes riveted to her screen, thought, and then launched another furious burst of keyboard pounding. She was smiling broadly when she looked up this time. "I've done that, sir."

"Done what?"

"Copied the photo on your computer to the task force's O-drive." Archana looked as pleased as Punch.

"You have?" Ravinder looked confused. "How on earth did you do that?"

"Your initials and date of birth is *not* a very good password, sir." Archana grinned.

Ravinder's befuddled expression made Vishal laugh. The others, too. Even Saina smiled, albeit sourly.

"Didn't I tell you, sir? Archana is amazing." Philip grinned. "No computer is safe from her."

Ravinder joined the laughter. "I must change my password."

"You should. Often." Vishal heard Archana say. "And do avoid the names of your parents, wife, children, or pets. Best to jumble it up." When Ravinder looked even more confused, she added. "Use a combination of alphabets and numbers and include at least one special character randomly."

Ravinder sighed sheepishly. "Then how on earth will I remember it?"

"There are apps for that, too. Or you could do something simple . . . write it down." Archana grinned.

Vishal noted how the incident had created camaraderie in the team; and he was dismayed. Since Goel's kidnapping the team had been in disarray; everyone had been walking around on eggshells. Then when Goel's body was found, work had ground to a complete halt, despite Philip's best efforts.

And now Ravinder was undoing all the damage and bringing them up to speed real fast.

*This needs to be stopped.*

Vishal decided that putting Ravinder out of commission would make the task force dysfunctional again.

*I need to talk to Leon and figure out the best way to do that.*

Vishal saw Ravinder begin pecking at his keyboard, the two-fingered peck of someone not comfortable with computers.

"Computers and smartphones," Ravinder muttered. "They make me feel so dumb."

"As for the photo," Archana continued when everyone stopped laughing, "let me get the task you've given me out of the way first and I will then age the photo." She noticed Ravinder's puzzled look and explained. "I created an app that allows me to age a photo." A shrug. "It is not foolproof, but it might give us some reasonable options of what Binder *could* look like now."

"Sounds good to me, Archana. Let us see what you come up with and then get the APB out." Ravinder looked impressed. And Cherian pleased.

Vishal's dismay increased as he saw the others now seemed charged up. Cursing inwardly, he too started working. Rather, he pretended to, since his discussion with Leon was still fresh and he could have given his presentation right away.

*And that, too, straight from the horse's mouth.*

# EIGHT

Leon was feeling drained and queasy, but knew he could not avoid stepping out any longer; a recon of both venues, collection of the sarin, *and* handing it over to Nitin *had* to be done.

A couple of bananas, a bowl of curds, and another dose of Norflox steeled his resolve. However, it was past noon by the time he felt stable enough to leave Jorbagh. The GPS suggested that, of the two venues, Siri Fort auditorium was closer, so he headed there.

NEW INDIA TIMES SUMMIT

Red and white banners on both sides of the road and progressively larger billboards guided him to the auditorium as effectively as the GPS.

With the summit just four days away, the auditorium was a hive of activity. From painters prettying up the walls, men erecting shamianas, trolleys bustling around with an assortment of furniture, security men installing metal detectors, and electricians stringing up lights, everything seemed to be happening simultaneously. And chaos ruled. To the untrained eye, it would have seemed the venue would never be ready in time for the conference, but from past experience Leon knew this is how things happened in India; everything would fall miraculously in place at the eleventh hour.

The chaos was familiar to Leon, who had cased many such venues. Aware that confusion invariably favored the attacker, he found it reassuring.

Behind the auditorium was a restaurant complex with a huge car park. Leaving his car there, Leon ambled back to the auditorium, again in his American hippie avatar—a camera slung around his neck, a water bottle, and a tourist map in hand. He was coming up to the gate when he saw Fatima waving at him from across the road.

*What the hell!* Leon froze, furious. *Didn't I tell her to go back to London?*

"Where do you think you are going?" The policeman accosting him looked irritated; he had been turning away tourists since morning.

Leon switched on his happy hippie smile. "I was just . . ."

*"There* you are." Smiling broadly, Fatima sashayed up and took his arm. "I have been looking for you everywhere." Then turning to the surly policeman, she switched to Punjabi—heavily accented, but passable enough for someone who was obviously a foreigner. "We are here on our honeymoon, Inspector. Do you mind if we look around for a few minutes?" She ramped up the charm. "We only have a couple of days in Delhi and are trying to see as many places as we can."

The constable looked them over. But Leon saw his surliness replaced by a hint of amusement. "Okay. Go ahead. But don't go inside. The auditorium is presently closed to the public."

"Oh, really." Fatima did her dumb bimbo thing again. "Is something going on?"

"That conference in a few days." The cop waved at the banner overhead. He had now lost interest in them and wandered off to shout at another furniture-laden lorry blocking the gate.

"What did you tell him in Indian?" Leon asked as Fatima led him away, still clutching his arm.

"Indian? There is no such language. That was Punjabi."

"Whatever."

"Just that we are here on our honeymoon."

"Very funny," Leon said dryly. "And what exactly are you doing here? I thought I'd made it clear you were to leave Delhi."

"I'm not going anywhere till this is over," Fatima said firmly. "And aren't you glad I came by when I did." She gestured at the cop.

"Seriously?" Leon freed his arm. Making no attempt to curb his sarcasm he quipped, "I can take care of myself, thank you."

"But you will admit a couple is less likely to draw attention," Fatima pointed out.

Leon began to reply, then did not.

*Why not? I don't need to take her everywhere . . . only where it suits me.*

However, Leon had been on his own too long and the thought of having someone around unsettled him. It made him feel like a goldfish in a bowl. Especially when that someone was an emotional and easily excitable woman. Not to mention that freaky likeness to Farah Fairfowler.

*Yet . . . what the hell?*

"You will do *exactly* what I tell you to. No questions," he said firmly. "At no time must you draw attention to us. Clear?"

Delighted at his capitulation, Fatima agreed. She followed him as he circled around the auditorium.

Leon didn't need much time here; he needed only to see the layout, especially possible entry and exit points, and the security arrangements at both. That did not take very long. However, not wanting Fatima to notice any difference in the time and effort he expended at either venue, he poked around a bit more before leaving for Ferozeshah Kotla stadium, where the cricket match would be held.

By now they had been together for over an hour, but having her around still felt strange to Leon. He had operated on his own so long that he'd even forgotten what it was like to have company. And, loath though he was to admit it, Leon liked the change, especially that she was so easy on the eyes. But he was still uncertain how much, if at all, this excitable client of his would listen to him.

Aware how important this reconnaissance was, Leon tried to blank everything else out and focus, but Fatima was making him nervous. He also worried she would draw attention to him.

# NINE

Fatima could sense Leon's unease, but her fascination at being able to see the mission actually being implemented overshadowed everything. This vendetta had occupied a large part of her life and now, being here with Leon, the man who would bring it to fruition, seeing it come alive, suddenly made it so tangible. She was excited beyond words.

"Did you find what you wanted?" she asked as they exited Siri Fort.

"Yes."

"What?" She looked perplexed. "I didn't notice . . . err . . . you didn't take any notes or anything?" Less than an accusation, more of a question. It earned her an exasperated look. But that only enhanced her curiosity. "What exactly are we looking for?"

Leon did not bother with a reply, just a cold glare.

Fatima wasn't sure what she had expected, but she had expected *something*. So far she had seen him do nothing except wander around and occasionally take photos, apparently of nothing in particular. At least, nothing she could discern. Yet she was fascinated, as much by what they were doing as by the man; Leon intrigued her. His broody aloofness was so refreshing; men usually tried their best to endear themselves. Not Leon.

*How can anyone be so remote . . . so detached?*

Fatima was puzzled. And, for the first time since she had hit puberty, she found herself jockeying for attention. It excited her, making her nervous and even more talkative.

"Have you decided which of the two you are going to . . . attend to first?" she asked as they entered Ferozeshah Kotla stadium, for the tenth time since morning.

"I'll let you know when I do." Also on tenterhooks, Leon snapped testily.

"Oh." Fatima was crushed by his tone. She felt the urge to appease him. "Is there anything I can do to help?"

"As a matter of fact you can. By not asking so many questions and allowing me to focus."

Fatima was speechless, unable to handle the sudden rush of emotions. She didn't realize he was equally conflicted: enjoying her attention, but not liking that fact. Tears sprang to her eyes. Fatima saw him flush, sensed he was embarrassed.

*Or is he just worried I'm drawing attention to him?*

Suddenly angry, Fatima wiped away her tears. "I don't have to put up with this shit. I'm surprised how easily everyone forgets who is paying the bills around here," she muttered bitterly. "First that bastard Vishal and now you."

"And don't *you* forget, I told you to stay away and let me handle this," Leon retorted, but she had his attention; the comment about Vishal intrigued him. "What is that about Vishal?"

"The son of a . . . he tried to hit on me last night." Fatima realized she would be in a mess if Leon asked why she had called Vishal to her hotel late at night. She couldn't handle all this anymore. "To hell with it. I don't need to take this, from you or anyone else. Just make sure you do the job." She walked away, leaving him surprised.

A moment later Fatima was regretting her outburst, worried how Leon would take it. But by the time she turned, Leon had crossed the parking lot and was entering the stadium. She contemplated going back and then decided against it.

Feeling more confused and lonelier than ever, she headed back to her hotel.

# TEΠ

Leon was surprised at the churn of feelings as he watched Fatima walk away: dismay at his churlishness, intrigued by her comment on Vishal, relief he could get on with his tasks, and yet, for some strange reason he couldn't fully fathom, sorry to see her go. Fatima intrigued him; especially the way she'd shared her story so openly. Leon couldn't even imagine making himself so vulnerable to anyone. The very thought terrified him.

*Is that why I've been pushing her away? Because she is getting to me?*

Leon was so surprised he halted.

*Who are you, Leon Binder?*

This question, which had been nagging him more and more, especially recently, hung heavily before him.

*Where are you going next? Yes, twenty million pounds is a lot of money and will allow you to stop running. But from what? And for what?*

As before, Leon hit a blank wall.

*What are you living for?*

Leon tried to visualize what life would be like when this mission was over. But all he could see were sterile safe houses. A never-ending line of them. Luxurious houses, but not homes. Impersonal. Bereft of personality. Barren walls. With none of the photos, paintings, and knickknacks that made a house a home . . . and had been such an integral part of his childhood . . . his only abiding memories of that place people called *home.*

Leon tried harder.

*Niks.* Still nothing.

He tried to look for a face other than his own. Someone to talk to.

*Anyone.* But still only blackness.

*Fatima? Is that why* . . . Leon was seized by the urge to turn around and go looking for her. The urge was so strong it stunned him. But he couldn't turn. Rooted to the ground by the deepest, darkest fear he had ever experienced. He tried hard, but was unable to understand the crippling fear. Let alone overcome it.

Waves of sadness overwhelmed him. He felt so tired he wanted to lie down right there by the road. Lie down and just let go. Of everything.

*What's happening to me?*

*You're getting old, that's what's happening.*

Leon tried to laugh it off. Couldn't. He felt even more dismal.

*No! Really . . . where did it all go? When did life pass me by?*

But he was too tired to even think.

Then from that blankness arose a deep dark fury.

*If Gill and Kingsley hadn't crucified me, I also would have had a life . . . a* normal *life.* Leon was shaking with anger now. It rejuvenated him. *I would have also had a home. A family. And someone to . . .*

A shout from behind jolted him back into the present. A bunch of workers were setting up barricades to funnel the flow of people into the stadium. Their supervisor seemed upset at the pace of work.

"What are you? A bunch of old women?" the portly supervisor yelled. "Get moving, girls! We don't have all day."

It reminded Leon he would draw attention if he didn't get moving. He threw a quick look around to check if anyone was watching him. No one was.

*Why should they?*

Leon realized he'd spent the last thirty years of his life blending in, ensuring no one saw him or noticed him.

*Now no one does.*

The need to be acknowledged suddenly seized him, shockingly strong. But no one was looking at him. Life and people swirled all around him, but no one seemed to even notice him. As though he didn't exist. As though he were trapped in an opaque bubble. He reached for his mobile, unable to resist the urge to call Fatima.

"Hullo! Sahib!" He looked up, startled; the supervisor was giving him an exasperated look. "Could you move to one side, we are trying to finish up here."

With an almost grateful nod Leon moved on, returning the mobile to his pocket. Even that slight interaction was enough to appease his need.

*I have to stop allowing these things to bother me.*

*Not now!*

*Not ever, actually!*

Leon did what he was best at and had been doing so well the past three decades: pushed away these draining emotions and got on with the job.

Though his eyes didn't miss a single detail and his camera captured everything he deemed relevant, Leon was unable to keep his mind from wandering back to Fatima and his own life. This was the first time he had been thrown in such close quarters with the emotions and motives of any client, or such an attractive client, who dared to feel *and show it, too*, so blatantly. Consequently, the long-bottled emotions that had been unleashed unsettled him.

His mind was still muddled with these thoughts when he finished with the recon of the stadium and went to collect the sarin.

Perhaps that is why he missed the man at the far end of the alley when he walked up to the address given to him by Ri Yong Ho in Seoul.

The Sanjay Gandhi Transport Nagar, as the name suggests, houses the offices and warehouses of dozens of transport companies. The Batra Transport Company, which was located in the seedier part of it, was one such company. It was in the center building. The office-cum-warehouses on either side were unoccupied, in a state of disrepair.

It was a fair drive from Ferozeshah Kotla and Leon might not have found it had it not been for the GPS-equipped Honda City that Om Chandra had provided him. Even then it took over an hour, and his stomach was acting up again by the time he reached there.

Alerted by Leon's call, Batra, the company owner, who moonlighted in many dubious areas, had been expecting him; he had deployed a man at either end of the alley.

Leon picked the one at the end from where he entered. It would have been hard not to; over six feet tall, with a build that would make a Mack truck feel small, the watcher stood out like a sore thumb. His clumsy attempt to maintain a low profile made him even more conspicuous.

The one at the other end was smarter and blended in with the trio of men working on a truck parked near the mouth of the alley. Loud metallic clangs rang out as they worked on the truck's body.

They allowed him to enter before following him to Batra's office.

Leon had a bad feeling; hijackers were a constant worry whenever collections were to be made or payments delivered. Leon had encountered them several times at this stage of an operation and come to accept them as yet another challenge to be dealt with. But that didn't make it any easier. In fact, to bypass that danger, he would not have come here if he hadn't been worried that transit damage might have made the sarin containers fatal. Leon needed to ensure the sarin was still safe to handle before he came near the damn thing. He could not do that in a public place and hadn't wanted Batra to come to his; people dropping dead at a public place was the last thing Leon wanted.

Having identified himself, Leon asked Batra, a fifty-something man who had obviously never seen the inside of a gym or walked more than a dozen feet in any direction, "You have my items?"

"Of course," Batra replied in passable English, indicating the cardboard carton kept on his table, about a meter long and half as wide. Despite the winter chill, Batra was sweating profusely.

Later Leon realized that should have forewarned him. And he cursed himself for not being more aware.

"Open it and show me."

It took Batra a while to cut through the layers of duct tape and open the container. From inside the carton emerged a large, wide-mouthed vacuum flask, blue with a two-liter capacity.

Leon held his breath as Batra unscrewed it. Out came another, smaller vacuum flask, also with a wide mouth, but red in color and half a liter capacity. Leon had to force himself not to step back when Batra began to open that. But he did pull out a handkerchief and hold it to his nose. Aware that the next few seconds could be Batra's last. Also his own, if Ri Yong Ho had screwed up the packaging.

Leon's tension must have shown because Batra now looked taut, almost fearful. "What is in this flask?" He stopped unscrewing the second flask and held it out to Leon, "Here you are. Open it yourself."

Simultaneously, the large man Leon had spotted at the mouth of the alley emerged from the shadows, closing in on Leon. He looked grim and menacing.

Aware that if the man got in close, his size would give him a deadly advantage, Leon reacted rapidly. Pulling out a .22-caliber pistol from his waistband he fired. Twice. The small caliber weapon made little noise, which is why Leon preferred it to a more lethal, bigger caliber handgun. Aware the weapon load was lighter, Leon had gone for definite kill shots, head and heart. He did not miss. The first bullet took the giant in the left eye. He was already dead when his heart stopped from the second. Dust billowed as he hit the floor heavily. Swirling in the air long after the echoes of the shots had bounced off the warehouse walls.

That distracted Leon. Long enough for the second man to close in. There was a violent blow to his right arm; a sharp shard of pain shot through his elbow. The pistol went flying out of Leon's hand. There was a grunt to his immediate rear and Leon sensed the second attacker, behind him, was priming for another strike.

His mind in overdrive, ignoring the pain in his elbow, Leon dropped straight down, simultaneously swiveling to face the new threat. The second man was luckily not so large, but was armed with a thick bamboo stick. Having smashed the pistol out of Leon's hand, the thug was raising the bamboo to deliver a final killing blow on his head. The bamboo was already at the highest point of its trajectory.

By now Leon was on the ground, his weight distributed evenly on both hands. Using them to pivot, Leon kicked hard, straight at the attacker's balls.

The bamboo man's eyes bulged and he uttered a strangled scream as Leon's kick landed. Delivered with the full force of desperation by a man who had scant respect for the Marquis of Queensberry, the kick doubled him up in agony.

But Leon was not resting on his laurels. Again using his hands, Leon jackknifed to his feet and smashed the man's nose with his knee. Two more rapid blows to his exposed neck and the second attacker went out like a light.

Snatching up his pistol with his left hand Leon spun around on Batra, aware the danger was not yet over.

Flask in hand Batra stood frozen, petrified; his goons had never failed him before.

"You stupid pig! Weren't you already being paid well enough?" Leon's tone was low and all the more menacing for that. "Open it."

Batra felt his fury. Hands shaking with fear, he complied immediately.

Leon only allowed himself to breath a minute after Batra had pulled out two 100-milliliter deodorant sprays from the smaller flask. He held them up for Leon, one in either hand. The fact Batra was still alive made it obvious the aerosol had not leaked.

Leon checked the signed paper seals he had placed on both cans at Seoul; they were intact. He shook them; both cans seemed full. Then he made Batra put them back into the flask before relieving him of it. Only then, placing the pistol against Batra's forehead, Leon relieved him of his life.

Batra sank to the floor like a beached whale as the low-caliber bullet, lacking the power to push through and exit at the other end, mashed his brains.

Leon headed for the door, stopping only to put one more bullet in the head of the second attacker, who was by now showing signs of life. Whether they had meant to hijack his shipment or just rob him, Leon knew he could not let them live.

*Dead men tell no tales and seek no revenge.*

Leon was relieved, aware he was lucky to still be alive. Cursing his carelessness he headed back to his car. He was confident the sounds of repair work ringing through the alley had masked the gunfire, but knew the bodies would be discovered sooner rather than later.

*Dead bodies always get the cops worked up. Not good!*

He rapidly replayed the sequence of events in his head to check he was leaving behind nothing that could lead the cops to him.

*Clear.*

Transferring the pistol to his left hand and flask to his right, Leon got moving.

Yet his unsettled feeling was mounting, putting him on the edge. Leon did not mind that. He knew the edge would prevent him from any more slipups and keep him alive. But it was draining him fast. By now the pain in his right elbow was bad, rendering his right hand almost immobile. And his stomach was acting up again. Half a mile out he pulled over and popped a couple of Norflox.

Another mile, driving past Babu Jagjivan Ram hospital, Leon wondered if he should go in and look for a doctor; the pain in his right hand was too much to ignore. It worried him. The bamboo stick had landed hard. Leon hoped there were no broken bones. With the strike just four days away, a broken arm was the last thing he could afford.

Not for the first time he contemplated aborting. It wasn't the first time he was going up against alert security forces, but it was definitely the first time they were specifically expecting him. Also it was his first twin target assignment, and that too at such short notice. And now this. Flexing his fingers, Leon wondered if the bamboo had cracked any bones; the pain was terrific.

*Bad enough to forgo the last ten million pounds?*

Despite the pain, Leon laughed.

*Not bloody likely. And not half as bad as what I suffered due to Edward and Ravinder. They stole my life.*

Leon knew this was his best and possibly his last opportunity to get back at them.

*I'm getting too old for this shit.*

And the twenty million pounds from this assignment would be more than enough to afford a peaceful and luxurious life. Enough to wipe out all traces of Leon Binder and begin life with a clean slate.

*No way I'm sitting this one out.*

Steeling himself he drove on. But the pain in his arm soon left him no choice. Reluctant to draw attention by going to a doctor he stopped at the first pharmacy he spotted on Bahadur Shah Zafar Marg and picked up a crepe bandage, a can of Relispray, and a strip of painkillers.

The pain spray warmed his arm and the tightly bound bandage offered some support but also made driving more tedious. By time he arrived at Jorbagh it was already dark.

# ELEVEN

Vishal was certain he needed to do something to send Ravinder back to the pavilion. And *fast*. It had taken the man hardly any time to take charge and press all the right buttons.

Right through the day, Vishal had watched with dismay as the room buzzed with energy. Barring a brief break for a surprise pizza lunch that Ravinder had called in, they had worked relentlessly.

Ravinder spent the day either working the phone or on his laptop. Archana seemed to have gone into deep dive mode and was lost in her computer; barring fingers flying across the keyboard, once in a while pushing her hair out of her eyes, and an occasional sightless gaze heavenward, she showed no signs of life. The other three shredded the routines of both targets over and over again. Even the usually dour and taciturn Saina had thrown herself into the discussion, helping analyze weak points in Zardosi's and Masharrat's routines and how best they could be attacked.

Vishal's anxiety mounted as everything he'd gone through with Leon came up for discussion.

*I need to get word to Leon. We need a serious rethink.*

"Sir, I think I have the list." Archana spoke up suddenly. Her excitement touched the others. The room went silent.

"You mean the list of people who knew about the MI6 inputs?" Ravinder jumped to his feet. Archana nodded.

Vishal immediately spotted the change; Ravinder had started looking tired as evening bore down, but now looked energized again.

"There are a total of seven people who knew everything." By now all of them had stopped working and were hanging on her every word.

Ravinder's mobile rang. "One second." He interrupted Archana and took the call. "Yes?"

"Dad, it's me, Jasmine. Wanted to ask if you'd like me to pick you up. Jagjit Singh is driving me today. He can take your car back and we can ride together in mine."

"I will be a while."

"That's fine. I have just started back from Rekha's house in NOIDA. I will call you when I reach your office. If you are free by then I will pick you up. Otherwise I will leave Jagjit there to drive you back."

Ravinder was happy; he was tired and not looking forward to the long drive home. Eager to get back to Archana, he agreed and ended the call.

"Yes, Archana, you were saying?"

"Sir, there are a total of seven people who knew about the inputs provided to NIA by MI6," Archana repeated. "There are three at the NIA. One is obviously Mr. Kurup the director."

"I think we can safely rule him out." Ravinder waved her on.

"Then are his two deputies, Ashok Verma and Sikander Ali."

Vishal felt he had been suddenly thrown on an ice slab. It took all his willpower to contain his shock.

*That pansy Verma will go down like a ton of bricks at the first sign of trouble.*

Vishal felt Saina, beside him, also stiffen. But he was so engrossed in his worries, it didn't really register.

"Okay." Ravinder absorbed that. "No one else at the NIA?"

"No." Archana sounded confident. "I have checked every single paper trail. There are obviously others who knew bits and pieces, but only those three had complete access."

"I see." But Vishal sensed Ravinder's uncertainty. "You said seven. Who else?" Ravinder finally asked.

"Four more." Archana replied. "Here." She wordlessly pointed at Philip, Vishal, Saina, and then herself. "Logically it had to be one of these seven . . . who not only had all the intel inputs from MI6, but also knew Goel had been given charge of the STF."

The room was still now. Cold and silent. Like the eye of a hurricane.

"If anyone betrayed Goel, it had to be one of these seven," Archana repeated.

The temperature in the room dropped even lower.

Vishal shivered as cold tendrils of fear slowly made their way up his spine.

# TWELVE

Ravinder could feel every eye in the room on him. Knowing his leadership was now being tested, he felt the pressure. And the anxiety that every commander leading a new team faces; still unsure of their capability *and* reliability, and yet having to be mindful of the team's need to be trusted. Adding to the pressure was his awareness of the rapidly ticking clock; there was much to be done and too little time to do it in. Also, Ravinder could not ignore the fact that his relationship with Kurup was still fragile.

*Kurup will freak out if I point fingers at his senior officers without hard evidence.*

The worry that Archana may have missed something assailed him. Also that she could be right about one of the STF officers being the mole. Or both. Ravinder was not sure which he dreaded more.

He drew a long, deep breath, forcing himself to stand down; aware pressure and worry would help no one . . . except the mole and Leon, of course.

*But I have to find the rat. Otherwise we are screwed before we get started. Also, that is possibly the fastest way to get to Leon.*

"I hope you are sure, Archana," Vishal spoke up. "The director is going to come down on us like a ton of bricks if there is any mistake."

Hearing Vishal state his fear out loud made it even more real for Ravinder.

"That's true." Ravinder gave Archana an elevated eyebrow.

"I am sure." She repeated, but now sounded a little uncertain.

"Philip . . ."—unwilling to take a chance, Ravinder made up his mind—"may I request that you help Archana double-check?"

It was the right call. Even Archana appeared relieved. "That would be best."

"Excellent." Ravinder was glad Philip concurred.

His mobile chirruped: an incoming text. Jasmine telling him she would be at his office in five or six minutes. Ravinder noted it was almost seven.

"Why don't you guys do that and we can decide on next steps first thing tomorrow."

That got a series of relieved nods.

"It's running late, let's wrap up for the day."

The nods were more vehement now; everyone was looking tired.

Ravinder also noticed that Vishal and Saina both looked troubled. Saina, head down, eyes trapped by intertwined fingers, seemed lost somewhere deep in her head. Vishal, brow knitted in fierce concentration, was sitting on the edge of his seat, looking ready to bolt.

However, because Ravinder was now tired and also eager not to make Jasmine wait, neither of them fully registered on him. Wrapped in thought, gathering up his laptop and mobile, Ravinder headed for the door.

The day had not gone so badly after all.

*But one more day is gone and we're no closer to finding Leon.*

And the grim reminder that one of his team could be working for the other side was disconcerting. Unwilling to allow anything to dampen his excitement, Ravinder reminded himself that he had known it was never going to be easy. At least he had laid the foundation properly; hopefully they would get a break tomorrow.

*As for the mole in the task force, let me worry about that later, if the NIA guys are in the clear.*

That consolation lasted only till he reached the gate.

*What if there is a mole at both ends, the NIA and the STF?*

*That* shook him. He was pondering over it when Jasmine's car, a silver Maruti SX4, pulled up beside him. Powering down the rear window, Jasmine grinned up at him. As always, he felt a tug in his heart and a loving smile creased his face. Instantly he felt his accumulated tension and worry recede, a bit, at least for the moment.

"Hello, Princess. Good to see you."

"Hey, Dad. You look tired." She displayed a set of perfect, even teeth. "Come on in."

Handing over the keys of his BMW to Jagjit Singh, the driver, Ravinder got into the front passenger seat. Jasmine took the wheel and they drove away.

# THIRTEEN

Vishal was now in a mad rush. He was aching to talk to Leon and find a way out of this predicament.

*Verma is a wimp. He wouldn't last long if* . . . when *they got to him.*

Vishal knew it was only a matter of time before the net closed in on Verma.

*And then me.*

He forced himself to hold on till he saw Ravinder's driver maneuver the BMW out of the gate. A quick look into the office showed him that Philip and Chance were clustered around Archana, one on either side of her, engrossed in whatever she was sharing. Saina was at her desk; she seemed tense and lost in thought.

Deciding he wouldn't be missed, Vishal headed for his car, keen to call Leon. He was aching to warn him and discuss how best to deal with Verma.

# FOURTEEN

Jasmine sensed her father's tiredness. Also, his face looked too red. "Your blood pressure okay?" she asked worriedly.

"Just tired." Ravinder sank back into the seat. "It has been a long day."

Jasmine's mobile rang. "Yes, Mom." She clicked on the Bluetooth headset. "Dad is with me. Yes. We should be home in an hour. I need to stop at Jorbagh to pick up my dress from the tailor. . . . Of course I can do that. Please text me the list." She ended the call quickly, knowing Ravinder hated it when anyone used the mobile while driving. "Mom wants me to pick up some cold cuts," she explained.

Ravinder, relishing the opportunity to rest, had closed his eyes. He nodded. Then nodded off. A couple of times Jasmine heard him mutter. Then he moaned as though in tremendous pain. She realized he was again in the throes of the same nightmare that had been plaguing him since Ruby's death.

By the time Jasmine pulled into the parking lot of Jorbagh Market he was moaning loudly, again and again.

"Ruby. Don't do it. There need not be any more killing." Jasmine heard him plead. She felt tears prick at her eyes; she knew how much pain he had been in since he had had to shoot her half sister.

Wanting to relieve him from the nightmare, she shook him awake. Ravinder woke up with a start, looking befuddled and tearful.

Pretending she had not noticed anything amiss, Jasmine said brightly, "Come with me, Dad." For a moment she thought he would refuse, but then he silently followed her out.

Ravinder was still logy as he accompanied her to the tailor and then toward The Meat Locker a few shops farther down. They were almost there when the gunshot-like sound rang out; a passing motorcycle engine had backfired.

It shocked Ravinder. Electrified, he spun around, his hand racing for the shoulder holster that should have been there but was not.

"Dad," she began, and then broke off, horrified.

Ravinder stood frozen, staring at his hand. It was clawed, as though holding a pistol. He looked shell-shocked. Stricken.

"Dad. *Please.*"

But Ravinder was lost to her. His gaze riveted on his right hand. "I shot her with this hand." A strident whisper.

His expression was so dark and pain-ridden that Jasmine was terrified he would do himself harm. "Dad, don't do this to yourself." She shook him. "Please!"

Ravinder looked at her then, but still befuddled. He seemed to be in tremendous pain. "I will never carry a gun again." He shook his head slowly, tentatively, like a prizefighter regaining his feet after being knocked down. "*Never.*"

"That's fine." Jasmine realized she needed to be firm. "*Don't* carry a gun if you don't want to. But snap out of this. You did what you had to."

"That's what your mother says, too," Ravinder said hollowly.

"And she's right." Needing to break his melancholy mood, Jasmine tugged at his arm. "Come. Help me, Dad. Let us get the meat and go home. Mom is waiting for dinner."

He followed her into the shop.

"I will never carry a gun again." She heard him mutter as they entered The Meat Locker. And she noticed his right hand was still clawed.

Worry filled her. Jasmine knew she could not allow anything to happen to her father; it was impossible to contemplate life without him.

Ravinder's mobile began to ring. Jasmine saw him reach for it eagerly; he seemed desperate for any distraction.

"Yes, Archana. *What?*" Jasmine saw his face turn white. Then crumple. He looked thunderstruck as he tiredly put the mobile away.

"What happened, Dad?" Jasmine was now deeply worried.

"Goel's wife tried to commit suicide," he whispered brokenly, barely audible.

"Oh!" Jasmine was shocked. "Who is Goel? Someone at your office?"

"The Special Task Force commander I replaced." She saw the desolate look on his face. "They found his body yesterday . . . he'd been tortured and murdered."

Jasmine was speechless. And now petrified, suddenly realizing how dangerous this assignment could be.

*Perhaps Mom had been right to get upset at him for taking on this assignment.*

Reluctant to take that road, she asked, "Do I need to take you back to your office . . . or the hospital?"

"No." Ravinder looked befuddled. "Archana said she's okay now. And the doctors have sedated her and placed her on suicide watch. No visitors for now." He didn't feel like telling her what Archana had really said: *neither Goel's wife nor their sixteen-year-old daughter wanted to even see a cop, especially not one from the Special Task Force.*

But his despondency reached out to Jasmine. Taking his arm she walked him back to the car. Ravinder seemed to be sleepwalking; she realized his condition was a lot more fragile than she'd thought.

*Or he had, for that matter.*

And she again wondered if she had made the right call in supporting his decision to go back to police work.

# FIFTEEN

Leon was coming out of the washroom when the gunshot-like sound rang out. He peered out of the window, but it was dark. He saw neither the errant motorcycle nor Ravinder and Jasmine. Then he realized his mobile was glowing; he had put it on silent when entering Batra's place and forgotten to turn the ringer back on.

"I've been trying to reach you for such a long time." Vishal sounded worried.

Leon ignored that. "What happened? All well?"

"No, all is not well." Tersely, Vishal brought him up to speed. "If they get their hands on Ashok Verma, I am screwed; he's a spineless ninny. *And* they are likely to put out an APB for you tomorrow." Vishal explained how Archana was going to use a computer program to age the old photo of his, which they had.

Leon was not surprised about the APB; ever since he had learned about the leak to MI6, he had known it was only a matter of time. He was confident his disguises would hold. But their tumbling upon Ashok Verma so fast dismayed him; with Verma out of the loop their advance intel from NIA was gone. However, he kept his apprehension on a leash, unwilling to agitate Vishal any more. "What do you suggest we do?"

"There are no options," Vishal fired back immediately. "We need to get Verma and Ravinder out of the way."

"You cannot keep killing everyone, Vishal."

"But this will buy us the time we need . . . just a few days more. Verma is a wimp. I know him; no way he will stand up to any interrogation. The minute he opens his mouth, I'm screwed."

"What if you take out the other deputy?"

"The other deputy? Sikander Ali?" Vishal sounded thoroughly confused. "What good would that do?"

"It could muddy the waters. Ravinder may get the idea that Ali was the mole and *that* could get Verma off their radar . . . for now, at least." Leon let that sink in. "Verma could still be useful, you know."

From the change in his tone, Leon sensed Vishal liked the idea. "That's devious. A good double bluff. Definitely worth a shot. It could buy us the time we need."

"So do it."

"You want me to do it?"

Leon held his silence, letting Vishal know he was not into rhetorical questions.

"Okay," Vishal said after a long pause. "I will do it tonight."

"Keep me posted."

"And what about Ravinder?"

"What about him? You can't knock off everyone. What do you think will happen if two STF chiefs die in as many days?"

"But we have to do *something*. He is too bloody smart for his own good. We have to stop him." Leon kept quiet. The silence worked because Vishal then added, "At the very least we need to do something that will get him off this investigation for now."

"Such as?"

"What if something happened to someone in his family? That should get him off our backs for a couple of days. And that's all we need."

*I need to watch this bugger carefully. Vishal is too ready to kill.*

In Leon's book violence was a last resort, when nothing else would suffice. Violence attracted too much attention, which was never desirable. At the same time, Leon liked the idea of hurting Ravinder. "You have something in mind?" he asked.

"How about"—Leon sensed Vishal was winging it, modifying as he went along—"an accident involving either his wife or his daughter?" The sight of Jasmine picking up Ravinder from the office was still fresh in Vishal's mind.

"You can set it up?"

"Why not?"

"Then do it." The more he thought about it, the more Leon relished the idea of causing pain to Ravinder. But he was careful to keep his emotions in check; conscious he did not want to show anything that either fed Vishal's fears or made his own visible to him. "But make sure nothing happens to Ravinder."

*I want that bastard to feel every possible pain . . . to suffer the way he made me suffer.*

Long after the call ended, Leon lay awake. Now it wasn't just his stomach that kept him up. It was also the pain in his elbow. Even more, it was the whirl of painful memories. Inch by inch his mind retraced those two years he had spent in jail.

*Over seven hundred days.*

Of rape. Humiliation. And beatings. Of pounding away the pain in the gym, letting it all out on the punching bag.

In the end those hours paid off. That and the humiliation, which not only kicked all compassion out of him but also helped him realize he was very resilient. In the days after he escaped from jail, it was that physical fitness that kept him going. Got him across the globe to the Congo. And put him on the path he trod today.

Leon remembered the first time he had been engaged to terminate a target. That was the only time he had been to Cairo.

Anwar Sadat had already paid the price for pandering to the Israelis. But Salah Abdel Sabour, the man who had worked out every single detail for Sadat, was still alive. And that was not acceptable to many zealots in the Arab world.

Leon again wondered if they had known he was a Jew when they hired him. *Probably not.* He found the irony amusing.

His smile matched the darkness of the room, which was complete, barring the flickering light from the Meat Locker's sign across the street, which intruded, but intermittently.

# SIXTEEN

Vishal was not sure which was stronger, his anger at Leon's cool response to the possible threat he was facing if Verma talked, or his relief that he now had a free hand to address that threat *and* also put Ravinder out of action.

*I'm going to do such a spectacular job that Leon will . . . But why the hell am I so keen to impress him? In a couple of years no one will even remember him.*

Vishal promised himself yet again. *I'll show the world. And by God, my operations will be gloriously spectacular. Not quiet pussy affairs like Leon's, where people did not even come to know a hit had gone down.*

Realizing he needed to plan both jobs, he headed for the Vikram Hotel. Its 24-hour café and lounge, aptly called 1440, for the number of minutes in a day, was one of his favorite hangouts. Not something a cop could afford.

*But what the fuck . . . what's the point of being a cop if one has to pay?*

His sardonic laugh momentarily drowned the music of the car stereo. "Is it true that you want it? Then act like you mean it." Shakira's FIFA World Cup song for 2014, "Dare (La La La)," filled the car.

*I'm earning enough from this mission . . . and this is just the beginning. Once I start out on my own, money will never be a problem.*

Half an hour later, seated in a cozy corner of 1440 with a Bloody Mary, a kebab platter, and roasted cashews before him, Vishal was busy doodling in his notebook.

Another half an hour and one more Bloody Mary later, he had figured it out. Deciding to attend to the Ravinder situation first, he went to work on his laptop.

Like all cops, Vishal had access to all criminal databases countrywide. As an STF man his access was virtually unlimited. Within fifteen minutes he had culled out three candidates who met his three criteria, which were straightforward: based in or near Delhi, a willingness to maim or even murder for money, *and* they should not know him.

Pulling out a mobile phone with a fresh, anonymously procured SIM card, he called the first man on his list.

"No women, no children. For no amount of money," the hit man replied, surprising Vishal.

*Now we have killers with a fucking moral high ground. What next?*

A woman answered the second hitter's phone, said he was laid up with a broken leg. Grimacing, Vishal cut the call without another word and dialed the last number. Kapil Choudhary, a trucker with a penchant for peddling drugs, had been tried five times for murder but never convicted.

*Third time lucky.*

"I charge more for women," Kapil pointed out when he described the assignment.

"How much more?"

"I just have to hit and run? Right? Whether she lives or dies doesn't matter. Right?"

"Right."

"And she is not someone famous or anything. Right?"

"Nope. Wife or daughter of a retired cop. You decide which."

"Cop? You didn't say anything about cops."

"I just did." Vishal was irritated. "And he's a *retired* cop. Not the same thing."

"Once a cop, always a cop," the trucker retorted. "Never a good idea to mess with them."

"What's so special about cops? We are people, too." Vishal bit his tongue, realizing he had slipped. The silence at the other end confirmed Kapil had picked up on that. Flustered, Vishal asked, "How much more?"

"One million. Total." Kapil sounded cautious now, subdued. "In five-hundred-rupee notes. Nothing new, nothing in series."

Vishal knew he could have brought down the price, but letting slip he was a cop had shaken him. And the Bloody Marys were making him magnanimous.

*What should I care? It's not my money. And it is not so much when you think in dollars. The fucking Indian rupee is heading south faster than Sherman . . . it will soon be like the Vietnamese dong; I'd need a carton to buy a condom.*

"No problem. But it has to be done tomorrow."

They finalized how the payment would be made—deposited in Kapil's bank account.

"Half first thing in the morning and the balance when the job's done." Vishal's tone brooked no discussion. It didn't get any.

Vishal took his account details, then texted him Ravinder's address, photos of his wife and daughter, and the numbers of all three cars the Gill family used.

"Make sure you are outside his house first thing tomorrow. Follow whichever woman comes out first. Hit her when you get the chance and run. *Don't* fucking get caught." Satisfied he had that in control, Vishal wrapped up the call. "And keep me posted. You can send a message to this number. I'll call you back if we need to talk."

*Now to take care of Sikander Ali.*

Using the laptop, Vishal accessed the file of Kurup's second deputy.

In his mid-forties, Ali was also an ex-ATTF man and had been Vishal's superior in the Anti-Terrorist Task Force; several years ago and only briefly. But Vishal remembered him: a kindly, soft-spoken man. Ali now lived with his wife in a DDA apartment in Munirka.

Vishal grimaced; middle-class colonies like Munirka were the worst. The apartments were crowded together and lacked privacy, and there was generally someone about, even late at night.

*On the other hand, they have little or no security.*

Vishal checked the time again; it was only nine.

*Best to wait till two, maybe three in the morning. Safer. Would also give me time to catch a nap.*

It had been a long day. And it was yet not over. Also, seeing how hyped-up Ravinder was, Vishal guessed tomorrow would probably be worse. Draining his glass he headed home. The taste of the Bloody Marys lingered in his mouth.

As he waited for the traffic light to turn green, Ali and his wife came to mind again. Ali had been a good boss, one of the rare decent types, always keen to develop and showcase his subordinates. Uncomfortable, Vishal tried to push away the thought, but it lingered, bothering him a lot more than it should have.

*I just took care of Goel. How different or difficult could this be? Ali is also in the way.*

That made him feel marginally better.

*But his wife? What's she got to with this?*

Vishal had met her just once, but he could remember her face.

The taste of the Bloody Mary turned sour. Grimacing, Vishal accelerated as the light turned green, trying to leave these unwanted thoughts behind.

# SEVENTEEN

Simran was frantic with worry when Jasmine told her what had transpired in the market. She was also contrite, realizing she should have been more supportive, especially over the past two months since Ruby's death.

*Perhaps that's why he is so withdrawn.*

"Sometimes just sharing a problem helps to lessen the burden," she said to Ravinder as gently she could when they were retiring to bed.

He nodded, grateful, and she could see, wanting to lighten up. But something held him back.

"You know you are very important to me . . . to Jasmine *and* me." Simran caressed his face. "We both worry for you."

"Yes. I know." He looked really tired and preoccupied. "And you two are all I have."

"I am here if you wish to talk . . . about anything."

"I know." He cuddled closer to her, almost like a child seeking the sanctuary of a womb. "Tonight I just want to rest."

"That's nice. Do that. You worry too much." She drew him closer. "Don't forget, it doesn't matter if we succeed or fail, as long as we try our best."

"I *am* trying my best." Ravinder looked grim.

"I know you are," Simran whispered reassuringly. "You always have. And that's all that counts."

"Goel . . . the officer I replaced at the STF. His wife tried to commit suicide."

"Oh!" Simran was shocked.

The silence stretched endlessly.

"Goel has a sixteen-year-old daughter."

Simran couldn't think of anything to say; a big slice of fear lodged in her chest.

"Just hold me, Simran," he said after a long silence. "I want to sleep."

She did. Almost instantly he was asleep.

Equally soon, with the sleep, came the nightmare. Simran and Jasmine referred to it as "The Ruby Nightmare."

Ravinder moaned. Then again, louder.

Simran watched helplessly, wanting to wake him up and scare away the nightmare, but knowing he needed the sleep, too. Once again she wondered when the ghosts of his first wife, Rehana, and their daughter, Ruby, would leave him alone.

*If ever.*

Simran was stunned when she heard him call out in his fractured sleep. Several times. He was yelling for Leon and Farah. And she wondered which new ghosts from the past had returned to haunt him.

He yelled again, a pain-soaked cry. Unable to bear it, Simran clicked on the bedside light and shook him awake. She was shocked by the look in his eyes when he woke up. Uneasy, she gave him a glass of water. He drained it in one go. Then, a few minutes later, when he looked more settled, she asked, "Who are Leon and Farah?"

"Why?" He looked guilty.

"You were calling for them in your sleep. No other reason."

Simran could see in his eyes that something was bothering him. Badly. She sensed Ravinder wanted to talk. He went so far as to open his mouth, but then didn't say anything. And then the moment passed. With a tired sigh Ravinder lay back.

Unwilling to push him, Simran stayed silent. But she was worried. She sensed he was right on the edge; whatever was bothering him was big. She prayed he would find the courage to talk about it.

"You know you can talk to me about anything?"

Ravinder nodded.

"Whatever it is, we can deal with it together."

He nodded again and then, clicking off the light, lay still.

But Simran could sense he was still awake.

# EIGHTEEN

Leon jerked upright, unsure what had waked him up. It was an eerie feeling. As though someone had walked over his grave.

*What the hell have I gotten myself into?*

The crappy feeling, which had persisted since he had taken on this mission, strengthened. Trying to will it away, he lay back again. Then he remembered.

*Shit! I forgot to call Hakon and Baxter and get details of Naug.*

Professor Thorbjorn Naug was the man who would be speaking at the conference before General Masharrat's keynote. A Norwegian scientist who had been delving into cosmic dark matter, Naug was a professional terminator's ultimate wet dream. He was till recently an unknown. The facial similarity between Naug and Leon was enough to ensure that some clever makeup would complete the illusion. Naug was a little heavier, but nothing an extra layer of clothing would not resolve. The two had matching heights *and*, most critically, as the speaker immediately before Masharrat, Naug provided Leon with the perfect way to get close to the target.

Picking up his mobile Leon first called Hakon, his man on ground in Oslo, whom he'd tasked to get the lowdown on Naug.

"How is Oslo?"

"Freezing," Hakon replied cheerfully. "Like always."

"Did you get the info I wanted?"

"Pretty much. Some bits and pieces left, which I'll have tonight. You will find them in your mailbox by morning." Hakon sounded a little high. "Everything you wanted to know about Professor Thorbjorn Naug, but didn't know whom to ask."

"Yeah, right." Leon laughed as he ended the call. Hakon was a good man; bit of a drunk, but solid when sober and hadn't let him down.

*Yet.*

Satisfied that was under control, he then dialed Baxter in London, where Naug was right now, attending another nerdie conference before coming to Delhi.

*I hope Baxter has gotten the details of Naug's hotel and flight to Delhi.*

The phone rang for a long time, not going to a machine or voice mail.

*Where the hell are you, Baxter?*

Leon knew it was only around nine in London; Baxter couldn't be asleep.

*I hope he has not done something stupid.*

He tried a couple more times. Same result. Fretting, he lay down to sleep, but luck was not favoring him today; his stomach started spasming again. Also, despite the crepe bandage, the pain in his elbow was back with a vengeance. Though not overly fond of medicines, Leon popped another painkiller, hoping it would help him sleep.

# NINETEEN

Vishal had just fallen asleep when his mobile tugged him awake. Irritated, he reached for it. His irritation escalated when he saw the caller's identity glowing on the screen.

*What the hell does that bitch want now?*

"I specifically told you to brief me every day," Fatima fired into the phone without preamble. "Didn't I? What happened today?" Still perturbed by his crude pass, she was a lot more aggressive.

Vishal resented her tone; it added to his anger at her earlier rebuff. Wanting to lash back, but aware the shoe was on the other foot and if he messed with her any more, he could end up without another dime, other than the measly advance.

"I've been busy," he muttered.

"With what?" Fatima shot back rudely. *"That* is precisely what I want to know."

Now even more irritated, Vishal gave her a watered-down version of the day's proceedings. Out of spite, he mentioned neither the plan to get Ravinder out of the game nor Sikander.

The call ended as it had begun, badly.

Hating her for banging the phone down on him, Vishal rechecked that his alarm was set for two a.m. and lay down again. He carried his irritation as he went back to sleep.

# TWENTY

Fatima was as incensed by Vishal's attitude as she was by the lack of any tangible news. And she could not push away the feeling that Vishal was not giving her the full story. For a long moment she contemplated calling Leon and asking him for an update, but realized she didn't want to aggravate him. And the lousy aftertaste of their last meeting, especially the abrupt parting, still lingered.

*Tomorrow!* she promised herself. *Tomorrow I will touch base with him in person and find out what's happening.*

But her uneasiness stayed with her late into the night. It was only after she had demolished all four of the miniature bottles of whiskey in the minibar that sleep finally found her.

# TWENTY-ONE

Ravinder thought he was dreaming when he heard Kingsley's voice. Only when Edward called out his name for the third time did Ravinder realize it was the phone; he'd picked up the call half asleep.

"Ravinder? That you?"

Ravinder was surprised; Edward was slurring.

*Is he drunk?*

*Edward?*

*No!*

The idea seemed ludicrous. "Are you all right, Edward?" Ravinder was wide-awake.

"Why wouldn't I be?"

*He's* definitely *slurring.*

"You realize what time it is, Edward?" The clock on his bedside table glowed in the dark: almost midnight.

"I have to leave for the airport now." Edward seemed oblivious Ravinder had spoken. "I wanted to say bye." A long bout of crackling followed; Ravinder sensed Edward had switched the phone to his other hand. "Promise me you will get him." Only now Ravinder noticed the sogginess in the MI6 man's voice; he was stunned when he realized Edward was not drunk, he was either crying or had been recently. "Don't let that bastard get away this time, Ravinder." There was a distinct sniff. "I have waited a long, long time for this . . . to avenge Farah's murder."

"I will, Edward," Ravinder reassured him, unprepared for this situation and struggling for the best way to deal with it. "I *will* give it my best shot."

"You do that, old chap. I'm banking on you." The silence that followed was so long Ravinder thought Edward had hung up. But he suddenly spoke again, a broken whisper. "It wasn't the first time."

Ravinder felt a dark foreboding surround him. "What wasn't the first time?"

"Farah was Farah."

"What wasn't the first time?" Ravinder repeated, his bewilderment mounting.

But Edward didn't seem to be listening. "Farah was Farah," he continued hollowly.

"Why are you telling me all this *now*?" Ravinder could barely croak; the feeling he might have wronged Leon scalded him. "Are you trying to say Leon and Farah . . ."

"But Leon?" Another horribly long pause, but now Ravinder was afraid to speak; he was desperate to understand what Edward meant, yet not sure he wanted to know. "I trusted Leon . . . we *both* did . . . we were best friends, weren't we? Anyone else would not have hurt so much . . . but *Leon*? He had no business breaking my trust . . . he blindsided me."

"Edward, why didn't you tell me all this then?"

"He murdered her, Ravinder. You were there . . . he took my Farah away from me." Suddenly Edward's voice hardened; Ravinder felt his resurgent rage. "Watch out for him, Ravinder. He will come at you from your blind side . . . from where you least expect him. You know Leon does that . . ."—and then Edward was suddenly tired and weepy again—"Leon *always* does that . . . be careful, Ravinder."

This time Edward did hang up. But it was only when the irritating drone had blasted his ear for a long time Ravinder realized he'd still not cradled the phone.

Ravinder lay in bed, deeply troubled; from the start he'd been unsure of Edward's motives and . . .

*Now this . . . what did Edward mean? Had Leon and Farah . . .* naah . . . but Ravinder was no longer sure . . . of anything. *Had he been wrong in testifying against Leon?* Ravinder remembered his unease even at that time. *Had Edward lulled him by appealing to his sense of honor?*

Now more than ever he regretted having accepted this assignment.

*K.G.B.*

*Kingsley. Gill. Binder.*

The brotherhood had not fared well the last time around. It had brought nothing but death, destruction, and pain . . . for all three of them.

*And the people around them.*

Ravinder was seized by a bottomless sense of foreboding. Then, he realized he could not deal with this also, on top of everything else that was happening.

*Not if I want to retain my sanity!*

Employing all his willpower, Ravinder pushed away all doubts.

*I need to focus on the task . . . there is so little time.*

But Edward's last remark kept returning to haunt him.

*What was his blind side? What would Leon be planning?*

Ravinder floundered in the dark, worried he would disturb Simran's sleep and struggling to again find some of his own.

# TWENTY-TWO

Simran sensed Ravinder's unease: it lay between them like a rotting corpse. But unsure how to deal with it and unwilling to trouble him further, Simran lay still, pretending to be asleep.

*I should not have listened to Jasmine. Or allowed Ravinder to take on this mission.*

She could not push away the feeling that they had all gone wrong: Ravinder in taking on this assignment, and Jasmine and she in supporting him.

As the night grew darker, the feeling of doom grew deeper. And down in the hall the grandfather clock began bonging. It did what it had done every day, every hour on the hour, since it had rolled out from the factory some three hundred years ago; with twelve resonant gongs it ushered in yet another day.

Simran, unaware of the operational details, did not know that now only four days were left for Benazir's vendetta. For one of her killers to pay the price. Perhaps both, if Vishal had his way and Leon his wish.

# DECEMBER
## 24

# ONE

Vishal was not feeling even slightly rested when the alarm roused him. His tiredness, coupled with his irritation at Fatima and the tension of the long drive down fog-laden roads, ballooned into a cold rage. Stopping at a cash deposit machine at the SDA complex market he deposited fifty thousand rupees, from the advance he'd received from Fatima, into Kapil Choudhary's Union Bank of India account. After being closeted in the heated car for so long, he was shocked by the cold outside.

His mood was killingly foul by time he jogged into the Munirka DDA residential complex. An ugly cluster of yellow-colored four-story blocks packed tighter than sardines in a can. Cars were lined bumper to bumper on both sides of the road, leaving barely enough space in between for traffic to squeeze through.

At three in the morning the complex was deserted. Enveloped in a thick, wet fog and an eerie silence, barring the guard, whom he could hear patrolling between the adjacent blocks. The periodic thump of the wooden stick all such guards carried, striking the road, marked his passage around the apartment blocks.

Dressed in a dark brown jogging suit, hood pulled up against the brisk winter breeze, Vishal had entered the colony across the rear boundary wall, a badly cemented eight-foot-high brick affair, with three strands of barbed wire on top. He had chosen a section where the wall had partly crumbled and vagrants had stolen the barbed wire.

Once inside, Vishal was confident he would pass muster even if someone spotted him; there were not too many people crazy enough to be out at this unearthly hour, in this bone-chilling cold, but it was not an implausible sight. Even if someone thought it bizarre, the couldn't-care-less detachment bred into big-city dwellers would keep him safe.

Slowing down to check the house numbers, Vishal identified the block in which Sikander Ali's apartment was located and jogged around it. Each block had two wings, separated by a flight of stairs going all the way to the top. Sikander's apartment was on top, on the fourth floor of the wing to his right.

Barring the solitary security light atop the apartment's iron grill door, the house was asleep. Even that light failed to make much of an impression on the notorious Delhi fog.

Vishal light-footed up the four flights of stairs, his Puma sneakers making no sound. Taking pride in staying fit, he was delighted his breathing had scarcely escalated.

The iron grill door barely resisted his picklock for a minute. The wooden door behind it, not even that long. Easing both doors shut soundlessly Vishal came to a halt in the Ali living room. The faint scent of a room freshener greeted him, probably aloe and green tea. But Vishal couldn't be sure. He stood stock-still, waiting for his eyes to adjust to the darkness. It took all of three minutes. But Vishal knew that patience, like physical fitness, was essential for his deadly aspirations. He used the time to slip on long surgical gloves, elbow length. Soon the room began to take shape in front of him.

*The sofas—one two-seater and two single-seaters.*
*Side table on both ends of all three sofas.*
*A rocking chair to the extreme right.*
*Carpet.*
*An oval coffee table in the middle of the carpet.*

Like a soldier, using the corner of his eyes, Vishal absorbed the placement of each item as his night vision sharpened. The tables, with the ever-present knickknacks on them, were the most dangerous. If displaced they would generate sound. And right now sound was his worst enemy.

The corridor leading away from the living room now caught his attention. Three doors opened out on this corridor. The first was immediately at the mouth of the corridor, to his right. The second was a little ahead, to the left. Vishal knew both of these would lead to bedrooms; the typical layout of DDA apartments. The third door, straight ahead, led to the bathroom for the second bedroom.

Confirming the silencer was screwed on tight, Vishal hefted the 10mm N99 pistol in his right hand, allowing it to settle in. A prewar weapon, it had been liberated by Vishal from a police evidence room. Though the gun was famous for its ruggedness, Vishal was aware that even fully restored it would not be good for use beyond a few rounds.

*As long as it holds together for two shots, I'm good.*

Now confident about his night vision, Vishal ghost-stepped forward.

The bedroom door had been left ajar; Vishal guessed this was to trap the warmth of the heating and allow in fresh air. The Alis were asleep, both facing to the right, away from the bedroom door. And now the scent of room freshener was stronger. But Vishal still couldn't place it. For some reason that bothered him.

Vishal halted by their bed. Barring the loss of most of his hair, Sikander looked just as Vishal remembered him. Even in sleep, gentle and fatherly. A flicker of emotion stalled Vishal. For a long moment, he paused, wondering if there was any other way. Realized there wasn't. Then the moment passed. His finger took in the trigger slack as he positioned the pistol.

Sikander Ali must have felt the press of cold metal against his temple because he stirred. Vishal completed the trigger squeeze and the 10mm slug slammed into Ali's brains, mushing them. It is certain Ali did not know when and how he died.

Though silenced, the sound of the shot seemed surprisingly loud to Vishal. He had already shifted his focus to Ali's wife. She stirred. Her eyes flickered open. Befuddled. Then they spotted Vishal and shot open. As did her mouth, to scream.

That was as far as she got. Vishal's second round, again fired at point-blank range, bludgeoned the life out of her. Now moving faster, Vishal removed the silencer and pocketed it.

Placing the pistol in Sikander's right hand he ensured his prints were on the N99 at all the right places, including the trigger.

One final check.

*Murder and then suicide.*

That is how Vishal wanted the script to read.

*If that doesn't muddy the waters, I have no idea what will.*

Five minutes later, both front doors were locked behind him. Vishal took another minute to ensure neither door showed signs of forced entry; that would blow the suicide theory out the window.

Satisfied, he headed down the stairs.

Nineteen minutes had expired since the time he'd come over the boundary wall. And two lives.

Forty-five minutes later Vishal was back in his apartment. He took a stingingly hot shower, but it did not make him feel clean. Then he went to bed, but with the adrenaline hangover yet to die down, he was unable to sleep.

The clock was showing half past four by the time he dozed off. But Vishal realized his anger with Fatima had still not abated. Neither had his fear of being exposed; traces lingered, like artillery shell splinters lodged against a vein, making their painful presence felt every now and then.

# TWO

Ravinder was feeling rested when he awoke. Despite everything, after a long time he felt *almost* at peace. He was about to get up when he caught sight of Simran sleeping beside him. She looked tranquil. A sense of guilt and longing seized him: guilt at having upset her and an overpowering longing to ensure nothing disturbed her tranquility again.

*When push comes to shove, she has always stood by me.*

His eyes moistened. He succumbed to the longing.

"What?" Simran murmured, half opening her eyes as she felt his lips on hers.

"Nothing." He kissed her again, tenderly. "Go back to sleep."

It was only moments later, while brushing his teeth, that he regretted not telling her how much he loved her. He wished he'd woken her up and made love to her. Then, like the hot water screaming out of the shower, reality returned as he remembered Goel's wife had attempted suicide.

*I have to ensure his death is not in vain.*

Thoughts of Leon swamped him again.

*Where could he be? And what's he planning?*

Edward's ominous phone call and warning reverberated in his head. "Watch out for him, Ravinder. He will come at you from your blind side . . . from where you least expect him."

*What is Leon planning? And what had Edward been trying to tell me?*

Ravinder's confusion escalated. And his emotional turmoil. He wanted to pick up the phone and call Edward. But he didn't . . . couldn't . . . something held him back . . . Perhaps not knowing or even wanting to know the truth was safer.

*What truth?*

*Does it matter?*

*I've taken this on and now I have to finish it. There is too much at stake.*

Unwilling to get bogged down, Ravinder pushed away those troubling thoughts. But he could not push away the feeling he'd missed something in Leon's file. Some pattern or something in his MO that he could use to second-guess Leon and find him before Leon found his targets.

Keen to put that worry to bed, Ravinder got ready and went down to his study. Soon he was again lost in the three-decade long bloody trail Leon had left across the world.

*June 1983. Cairo. Salah Abdel Sabour. If ever a man had lived below the radar, Salah had, despite the critical role he had played in Anwar Sadat's administration. But he had been protected. Heavily protected. However, not enough to stop Leon Binder.*

Considering this was only Binder's second professional assignment, Ravinder marveled at the ingenuity of Leon's attack plan and his meticulous implementation.

*They had not even come to know Salah had been murdered till the autopsy several hours later. By then Leon was long gone.*

The hit would never have been traced back to Leon if it had not been for the inadvertent capture of one of the men who had hired him, and *his* spilling the beans. The snitch, willing or unwilling, had paid the price; and his death had been swift and spectacular. The bomb that took him out not just ended his life; it also rendered his body into bloody shreds. An unambiguous statement from the assassin; any breach of faith would not be tolerated.

*Nineteen eighty-three. Over three decades ago. Two deadly strikes within the space of a few weeks. Wonder how much more sophisticated and efficient Leon has become since?*

Anxiety that he would fail tugged at Ravinder. *Again.*

Steeling himself, he returned to the laptop and forced himself to concentrate.

*June 1983. Just months after Leon's escape from prison.*

This time it was not fear that tugged at Ravinder, but guilt. About Farah. A large dose of it. Multiplied by Edward's recent phone call. It gnawed at his peace of mind. Sapping the restful energy he had woken up with.

He was delighted when Jasmine sailed in, balancing a tray with steaming hot tea and the digestive biscuits he loved.

"It's Christmas, Dad," she complained jokingly. "Don't tell me you are working today."

"Unfortunately Santa stuffed Masharrat and Zardosi in my stocking." Ravinder laughed. "I'd chill, too, if only those two morons would stay away from India." But shutting the laptop, he joined her on the sofa overlooking the garden. "Are you now going to tell me what you have planned for Simran's birthday?"

"No, Dad. *No way.*" Jasmine grinned. "That is going to be a *complete* surprise."

Then they sat. Mostly in silence, father and daughter, and watched the sun struggle to pierce the morning fog.

By the time they got up to join Simran for breakfast, most of Ravinder's earlier equanimity had been restored. The easy banter between the women in his life as they planned a relaxed day at the spa reinforced it. Ravinder found it reassuring; the realization that, despite the turmoil caused by Leon's return in his life, some parts of it remained so mundane and ordinary. He cherished the sheer, everyday monotony; it grounded him and brought some semblance of normalcy.

"Why don't you join us at the spa, Dad. You could do with a massage," Jasmine suggested.

"That I would love." Ravinder smiled. "But not today. Next week. Soon as this is over."

"That's a date." Simran wagged a finger at him, but smiling. "I'm going to hold you to that."

"Done." Ravinder felt his heart smile as he caressed her cheek. "You have yourself a date, my dear."

"Get a room, guys." But Jasmine looked delighted. "And, Dad, don't forget we have dinner with Rekha's family today," Jasmine added as Ravinder headed out for office.

"I will be back in time, Princess." Ravinder thought Rekha's parents were overbearing and pompous. He was not overly fond of them, but he knew the girls were close; both were planning to go to the same law school in America for their Master of Laws program. Also, right now this was another bit of normalcy Ravinder craved.

"Don't bother, Dad. Your office is en route to NOIDA. We will pick you up."

Then he was in the car, comfortably settled in the plush rear seat, with Jagjit Singh at the wheel. His mobile beeped as the BMW navigated out of the gate.

"How is it going, Ravinder?" Edward sounded excited; no awkward traces of the last time they'd spoken. Ravinder realized he must have been really drunk then. "There is something you should know. Fatima Basheer is not in London. Neither are the other top three SOB people."

"And?"

"We have traced the other three; they have gone to ground in Dubai . . . which means we don't have a hope in hell of extraditing them. Anyway, the point is that Fatima is not with them."

"You think she is here?" Ravinder felt a tingle of anticipation. "In India?"

"We cannot be sure, Ravinder. There is no record of her leaving the UK on her official passport, so wherever she has gone, she is using a false passport. But if she is in India . . ."

"And we find her," Ravinder completed, "there's a good chance she can lead us to Leon."

"Perhaps. If Leon lets her know where he is."

"Will he be that dumb?" Ravinder felt some of his excitement abate; it seemed improbable that Leon would do something that stupid.

"Not likely, old chap, but we have nothing to lose. If we can get our hands on her . . ."

"*If!*" Ravinder laughed. "A Paki in India on a false passport! That's like Christmas come early. The cops here will . . . just send me a photo, Edward, and let me pass it to them."

The call left Ravinder in a thoughtful mood. But energized; he felt more hopeful.

A few minutes later his mobile beeped again; an incoming WhatsApp message. Clicking it open he was shocked to find Farah Fairfowler staring at him. Only when he read Edward's message did he realize it was Fatima Basheer. Suddenly there wasn't enough air in the car; Ravinder felt winded—the similarity to Farah stunned him. He felt a wave of nausea as Farah's bloodied face swam before his eyes; the way he had seen her the last time. With a massive effort he pushed away that memory. Several deep breaths later he felt control return. That is when he remembered that Farah's mother had been a Pakistani, too.

*Could there be a link between Farah and Fatima? And the Sisters of Benazir?*

He pondered that as he watched the dense Delhi traffic crawl past with sightless eyes.

*Nah! That would be too much of a stretch.*

But the thought would not go away. He was about to call Edward and ask him how the MI6 man felt about the similarity. Remembering how besotted Edward had been with Farah, he could not bring himself to pick up the phone.

*In any case, what difference does it make?*

Shelving these thoughts he forwarded the picture to Archana, with instructions for an alert to go out: *Top Priority. Locate and follow, but do not apprehend unless subject is attempting to flee the country. If so, must be taken alive at all costs.*

Ravinder needed Fatima to lead him to Leon. He was confident Archana would have the APB out before he reached office. So intent was he on having that done, Ravinder forgot to copy the other task force officers on the message.

# THREE

Leon was not having a good Christmas, either. His rumbling stomach had kept him awake most of the night. And the large red welt on his elbow did not look good. Leon flexed his fingers and his arm; they were mobile, but the pain was awful. Leon hoped it was only the stiffness caused by a night of immobility, but wondered if he should get an x-ray. The thought of going to a doctor lacked appeal.

*Perhaps later . . . if it doesn't improve.*

Applying Tiger Balm, again recommended by the friendly neighborhood pharmacist, he retied the crepe bandage and then checked his mail to ensure Hakon had sent the dossier he'd compiled on Naug. He had.

*But nothing from Baxter yet.*

Worried, he reached for his mobile and dialed Baxter.

It rang and rang, but again there was no response from Baxter. Leon's worry escalated; he needed Professor Naug's flight details from London. He didn't want to take any unnecessary chances by going to Naug's Delhi hotel any earlier than required.

*Where the hell are you, Baxter, you prat! Christmas or no Christmas, I'll kill you if you are on a binge.*

But Leon knew Baxter would not have done that; they had operated together before and Baxter had never let him down. *That* is what was worrying Leon. Perhaps the SOB leak was worse than he'd envisaged. Perhaps the cops had gotten their hands on Baxter.

*But how would they know about him? No one at SOB knew about him.*

*Have I missed something?*

He fretted over that, his mind examining possibilities. Despite his growing uneasiness, Leon was not yet able to spot any new, mission-abort signals.

*Other than the fact that this bloody mission seems to be jinxed.*

Downing another Norflox to settle his stomach and a Combiflam to dull the pain in his elbow, Leon got dressed. The idea of a decoy attack was clear in his head, but he had yet to work out the details on the ground.

*I must do that today, during my final recon.*

He decided to start with the stadium.

# FOUR

Vishal saw Ravinder emerge from his BMW as he drove into the office parking lot. To his dismay Ravinder looked spry and seemed to be bubbling with energy.

*But not for long. Kapil Choudhary would soon attend to that.*

Vishal wondered where Kapil was.

*Had he taken up position at Ravinder's house?*

Keen to check, he was reaching for his backup mobile with the untraceable SIM card when another car pulled up and a couple of cops got out. Greeting Vishal, they kept pace with him all the way to the office. No way he could call.

That added to Vishal's irritation; unable to sleep and with the effects of the adrenaline hangover still lingering, he was in a foul mood. The energy he encountered when he entered the office only made him feel worse.

"Did you guys pull an all-nighter?" Ravinder was asking.

"Almost." Philip had that smug look, which Vishal hated. Though, like Archana and Chance, he looked haggard. All three were clustered around her table.

"These two guys wimped out by midnight." Archana laughed. "But we double-checked every single thing."

"And?"

"And it is rock solid, Boss." Philip replied. "No room for ambiguity."

Chance nodded concurrence. Archana looked pleased and relieved.

"So it is either of the two deputy directors from NIA, or one of you four?" Ravinder gave each of them a long look.

Vishal's heart plummeted, but he stayed poker-faced, meeting Ravinder's eyes like the others.

Then things went from bad to worse.

"Let's do this." Ravinder commanded decisively. "Archana, find out where both those guys are right now, Ashok Verma and Sikander Ali. Meanwhile, I will bring their director up to speed. After that Philip, Vishal, and I will bring them in. Chance, you and Saina will be the backups. Be ready to move."

"Sure. But where is Saina?" Chance queried.

"Not in yet." Philip responded. "Must be on her way."

"What do you want me to do, sir?" Archana was looking left out.

Before Ravinder could respond, Philip did. "Why don't you start work on Binder's photograph?"

Ravinder nodded approvingly, delighted to see his team coming together. "It would be great to have that APB out ASAP. Only you can do that."

That made Archana happy.

Vishal saw Philip draw his weapon, check it, and return it to his shoulder holster. Then he drew a pair of plastic handcuffs and tossed one across to Vishal. "I don't think they will be required, but just in case."

Pocketing the cuffs Vishal also went through the motions of checking his weapon and spare mag. But his mind was in a whirl, full of apprehension.

*Damn! I should never have listened to Leon. It would have been better to get rid of Ashok.*

Vishal knew he could not let Verma be taken alive.

"Ali has still not reached the office, but Verma is already in." Archana replaced her phone and called out.

Vishal fretted, wondering when they would discover Sikander's death and if it would provide the required diversion. He realized things could get sticky really fast if it did not throw Ravinder off Verma's trail.

*Where the hell is Kapil Choudhary?*

Vishal wished he could call him and find out, but with the team huddle still in progress it would have looked strange; attention was the last thing he wanted right now.

# FIVE

Ravinder, midway through dialing Kurup's number, replaced the handset when he heard Archana call out that Ali had still not reached the office. "It *is* still a bit early. Perhaps we should wait for Ali to get in and then bring both in simultaneously."

"I agree, sir," Philip chipped in. "It would be best to bring both in at the same time. If we take the wrong man in first, the right one would get away."

"You mean if we took the right one in first, the wrong one would escape." Chance's tongue-in-cheek humor broke the tension.

Not looking forward to the conversation with Kurup, Ravinder was happy to defer it. However, aware time was at a premium he did not wish to waste a moment. "Guys, while we are waiting, I suggest you two present your plans on the targets." He looked at Vishal and Philip.

Ravinder was confident they would find something of value, either a weakness in the security umbrella or some method of attack, which NIA had not thought of yet.

*That should mollify Kurup.*

Ravinder joined the others at the conference table.

Philip took the initiative. Flicking open his iPad he accessed his notes and crisply narrated Zardosi's program, from his arrival at Palam airport till his departure two days later. "On twenty-seven December, the bulk of his time will be spent at the Ferozeshah Kotla stadium witnessing the T20 Indo-Pak cricket match. However, the next day there is a meeting and joint press conference with the Indian PM prior to his return to Pakistan."

"I doubt Binder will try anything when the two prime ministers are together," Chance commented.

"Logical. Double the security." Philip moved on to the second part of his presentation. "While considering how best an attack could be mounted on Zardosi I kept in mind the one basic thing that distinguishes a professional assassin from an amateur or a suicide attacker: the imperative to escape. That's why I think Leon is most likely to use a rifle or remotely detonated bomb."

Watching him, Ravinder felt his confidence soar; the team *had* started performing. Much better than he had expected when he met them yesterday.

"That is also why," Philip continued, "I think Leon will attempt a strike at the stadium. Either on the VIP box or when Zardosi comes out for the prize distribution."

"I have requested the director to ensure Zardosi does not give away prizes." Ravinder made a note to check if his suggestion had been accepted. "It will be almost impossible to keep him secure if he comes out in the middle of the ground. That bloody stadium can hold seventy thousand people and Zardosi would be completely exposed."

"*Seventy thousand.*" Even Chance, a cricket buff like most Britishers, was impressed.

"Precisely. And given that we are playing Pakistan, you can bet every single seat will be taken. Impossible to keep an eye on such a crowd." Ravinder's concern showed. "There are scores of possible sniper positions in any stadium . . . and a dozen other ways to get at Zardosi once he is out in the open."

"Agreed. That's why their routes are being kept secret and will be heavily guarded," Philip conceded. "The primary concern is during the cricket match. It is a public event, after all. We *have* to ensure Zardosi stays in the VIP box."

"I've already spoken to the NIA director about this and I *will* do so again," Ravinder promised.

"In that case, Leon's best option would be to go for Zardosi with a sniper rifle, either in the VIP box or when he is en route to or from it," Philip concluded. "Bombs are possible, but chancy from the assassin's point of view, since they may or may not get the target."

"What about poison?" Archana asked.

"True. Binder has used poison several times, but for both these targets I don't see how he can get close enough."

"In the VIP box, the hotel, or even at any other event . . . even prime ministers have to eat," Archana pointed out.

"*Everything* they eat or drink is going to be closely monitored." Philip had clearly thought this through. "Also, if the killer is to be certain, he has to ensure his target is the first to take the poisoned food or drink."

That, too, was logical. If someone else took a fast-acting poison, their demise would give away the game. Conversely, if the poison did not act fast enough or acted first on someone else, there was the possibility of medical attention reaching them in time.

"What about something exotic?" Chance asked. "Soluble thallium salts, ricin . . . darts fired from something innocuous like an umbrella or pen?"

"Yes, those have been used effectively many times and are possible," Philip admitted, though a bit skeptically. "They would require Binder to get close to the target. Also, if we are to go by the MI6 intel, then Binder has just been given this assignment. I'm not sure he would have time to put together anything too elaborate."

# SIX

Vishal was unable to decide what upset him more: Philip's impeccable analysis, Ashok Verma's imminent capture, or the fact that Ravinder had gotten the team together and energized so fast.

"Well done, Philip. That was good. Vishal, what about you?" Vishal realized Ravinder had addressed him only when he heard his name. "Let us see what you've got."

Perhaps it was the praise given to Philip, perhaps the choice of Ravinder's words, or perhaps it was merely Vishal's need to win, but he was seized by a compelling urge to outshine Philip. Instinct warned him it was a childish idea and dangerous, but he was unable to help himself. In fact, a part of him *wanted* to flirt with the danger.

"I'm ready, sir, but let me first highlight that I don't fully agree with Philip. From everything I have read about Binder, we should not rule anything out. The man has been in this trade for thirty years. It's safe to assume he can get hold of whatever he needs—no matter how fancy—shortage of time notwithstanding."

"I agree with that," Ravinder acknowledged. "It would be best if we planned for that, too."

"I was just expressing my views." Philip's discomfiture delighted Vishal.

"That's cool." Ravinder must have sensed it, too, and moved to smooth things over. "What about your presentation, Vishal? You ready?"

"Of course." Keen to show he was a cut above, Vishal referred to neither his notebook nor his tablet. Quickly detailing the thirty hours Masharrat would spend on Indian soil, he concluded, "My analysis is that, if the general is the target, Binder will strike during the conference. They are expecting two thousand people to attend. Two thousand people who have *not* been security vetted . . . basically it's open house to anyone who can cough up the delegate fees. And the Siri Fort auditorium is not the easiest of venues to secure." He paused, expecting questions. There were none. The lack of reaction irritated him. Spurred on by that and wanting to sow some confusion, he added, "In fact, if I had to do this, I would attack both targets simultaneously."

"How?" Philip challenged. "Both targets are on stage almost simultaneously. Masharrat is speaking bang in the middle of the cricket match."

"So what? Masharrat's speech is only ninety minutes." Vishal's need to show Philip up mounted. "If I were Binder I'd use a second team to go for my secondary target."

"I see. Which would be your primary?" Vishal was so pissed with Philip that he failed to realize the STF second-in-command was not being deliberately difficult; Philip was genuinely exploring the option Vishal had tabled.

"Obviously, Zardosi would be my first choice," Vishal shot back, his chin jutting out aggressively.

"Why is that obvious?" Chance leaned into the conversation.

"Because Zardosi, being the prime minister, would be better protected at home." Vishal sensed his emotions were getting the better of him, but seemed unable to harness them. "Also, keeping in view the current political climate in Pakistan, which white man in his right mind would want to take a trip there? You more than anyone else should realize that white is not the flavor of the month with the Pakis."

Vishal's aggressive tone irritated Chance, and he made no bones about letting it show. Realizing the situation was escalating, Ravinder stepped in.

"Guys." Ravinder's pacifying tone made Vishal realize he had almost lost it. "All of you have valid points."

Vishal was seething, but now had the worst of his emotions in hand. He fell silent. But the room was uncomfortable.

"Also, I would like to point out that not once in all his years as an assassin has Binder ever used an accomplice for anything other than support tasks." Ravinder let that sink in. "Even the few he used never saw him. The ones that laid eyes on him never lived to tell any tales. At least no one the cops in any country could lay their hands on."

The silence this time was longer. Vishal felt as though someone had shoved ice cubes in his shorts; he shivered. Luckily Ravinder had everyone's attention and no one noticed.

"Thirty-six hits that can be safely attributed to Binder, in almost as many countries, and not once has he used an accomplice for anything other than logistics, admin, surveillance, or intel support." Ravinder paused again. "Or as red herrings."

"That does not mean he never will," Vishal murmured, aching to have the last word. But Ravinder's words kept ringing in his head; they filled him with dread. He again wondered why Kapil Choudhary had not done the job on Ravinder's wife or daughter. By now Ravinder should have gotten a call from some hospital.

# SEVEN

Ravinder sensed they had gone the distance with this exercise. "Right, guys, now check the security plans and ensure the threat perception has been fully covered."

Philip nodded. And Ravinder could see that Vishal was still glowering. Vishal opened his mouth to speak, but Archana preempted him. "Sikander Ali has still not reached the office."

Ravinder checked the time, almost ten.

*Ali should have reached office by now.*

"Check if he has applied for leave."

"I already did, sir." Archana gave a headshake. "He has not."

"I see." Ravinder made up his mind. "Let's give him a little more time. Meanwhile I'll have a word with the NIA director." Picking up his mobile he dialed. Realizing everyone's attention was on him he stepped out as Kurup answered and briefed him.

"Are you sure?" Kurup asked when he had finished.

"There is no doubt." Ravinder was relieved Kurup took the news in his stride. "They were the only two at NIA who had complete access to everything sent in by MI6."

"And me," Kurup pointed out. "Am I also on your list?"

Ravinder chose not to answer that. "I plan to bring both men in for questioning."

"Do what has to be done." Again, Ravinder was surprised at Kurup's lack of reaction; he had expected fireworks. "What about the four on your team, Ravinder?"

It was a fair question and Ravinder had been wondering what he should do about that. "If both your guys are in the clear, then I suppose you had better keep a fresh team ready to replace the STF."

"Do you have time to get a new team in place?"

"No, but can you think of anything else?"

Kurup could not. Obviously. Just when Ravinder thought they had run out of things to say, Kurup asked. "And why do you assume it has to be an either-or situation? Perhaps there is a mole in both places."

That thought was even more unsettling.

"Ravinder, we *have* to find that mole."

Ravinder knew Kurup was right.

*The mole . . . or moles would lead us to Leon. That is the only way I will get my hands on him.*

"We can consider putting all the STF officers under surveillance." It was not the most judicious of suggestions, but Ravinder could think of nothing else at the moment.

"Let me think about that," Kurup mused. "The manpower issue can be overcome, but we do need to think of the effect on their morale. They are trained officers and it is almost a given they will pick up on the surveillance." The silence this time lingered longer. "But it is worth considering . . . let me think about it."

Ravinder was glad he did not have to make that call. But by the time he put down the phone, most of his equanimity had been shattered. Whatever little remained went flying out the window when he reentered the office.

"You had better see this, sir." Archana was staring at her computer screen. She looked dumbfounded, her face drained of color.

Displayed on her screen was a police report that had just come in, from the Station House Officer, Munirka Police Station, to the NIA. *Deputy Director Sikander Ali and his wife had been found dead at their home.* The maid who came in to clean daily had discovered their bodies.

"Oh, damn!" Philip, peering at the screen over Ravinder's shoulder, cursed.

"Let's go, Philip." Ravinder grabbed his mobile and car keys. "You come with us, too," he told Vishal. "Chance, please hold the fort with Archana." Having a foreign secret agent around on the scene of a crime was not a good idea; there was bound to be media present.

The three of them ran out.

Vishal had done this several times already and *knew* he had left no clues behind that could connect him with the Ali double homicide, but could not stop himself from doing it again. His worry escalated with every passing minute.

# EIGHT

Leon saw how the diversionary attack could be launched, or faked, the minute he entered Ferozeshah Kotla stadium.

He had entered from Gate 1, straight into the West Hill stand—four sections of twenty-five rows, each with fifty seats.

On his right, beyond a well-cordoned three-meter-wide passage, was the Old Club House stand, also divided into four sections, but these were lounges, more luxuriously appointed, and would hold another fifteen hundred people collectively.

The VIP box was right on top, in the upper section of the corporate sponsors box, dominating the stadium. It looked big enough to accommodate thirty or forty people. Leon could not see the bulletproof glass, but knew it would be there, all around and thick enough to stop even a .50-caliber heavy machine gun bullet. He wanted to take a closer look, but knew he would draw attention; there were people working in the VIP box, under the watchful eyes of a couple of uniformed cops.

Shelving that idea he began scanning the stadium, pinpointing four sniper positions and four for the bombs, though he needed only two of each.

The bomb positions were obvious—the upper midsections of the West Hill stand. Also of the East Hill stand, on the other side of the Old Club House stand. Leon saw the layout of the East Side was identical to the West Side stand.

However, Leon realized the best bomb positions would be the corporate sponsors box, directly below the VIP box. Leon surveyed it, using his camera's range finder to assess the distance. He knew a powerful bomb placed in the corporate sponsors box would be enough to damage the bulletproof glass, enough to render the VIP box vulnerable to a high-caliber sniper rifle. At the very least it would activate security protocol and drive the VIPs out of the box. Either would suffice.

Satisfied, he focused on the sniper positions. Most logical would be any suitable position in the North Stand across the stadium grounds. Next would be the West or East Stands on either side of it, though the angle implied increased range and a more oblique, thus more difficult shot.

The three stands were also divided into four sections each, packed with rows of seats. From his research, Leon already knew each stand could take in 19,500 people. All he needed was a quiet nook that offered a clear line of sight to the VIP box.

"Hey! Hullo!" Leon realized the khaki-clad cop was talking to him. "What's with the camera? Don't you know photography is not allowed?"

"Oh! Sorry, I didn't realize that." Leon kept his cool. There were many people in the stadium, most of them working on something or the other, but only a few Caucasians.

"Let's see some ID." The cop came closer, clicking his fingers. "What exactly are you doing here?"

"I'm with *Weekly News*. Cameraman." Leon held out a press card. "Just checking out angles and positions." Leon was confident his fake press card, identifying him as a cameraman, would get him through in a pinch. But he didn't want to push his luck any more than required.

"Don't bother." The cop returned the card after a brief glance. Leon knew security was at low key right now. But in another day, two at best, soon as the preparatory work was over, they would clamp down, if not seal the stadium. That's when the scanners and sniffer dogs would be out in full force. "Media locations are fixed. Go to the control room and get the details." He pointed out a room at the other end of the East Hill stand.

"Thanks. I didn't know that." Leon was shaken because he hadn't even seen the cop coming.

*Wake up, old man.* He admonished himself.

Moving off in the direction indicated by the cop, Leon began to short-list sniper positions. But now he was in a hurry, unwilling to get noticed again, especially by the same policeman.

Tactically, the most obvious sniper positions would be watched; hence the less obvious ones were of greater use to him. However, smart security people knew that and thus always considered the least obvious ones as the more dangerous. *Or not.* Leon knew that ultimately it was a matter of bluff and double bluff; whoever managed to achieve tactical surprise would invariably win.

The solution struck him as he crossed the stand: the giant scoreboards. Electronic, thus unmanned. Huge and colorful; thus perfect for a properly camouflaged sniper. Lastly, they dominated the stadium; line of sight would be no issue. Checking the cop wasn't looking at him, he used the laser range finder to reconfirm the range. Doable. Leon was satisfied and now keen to get out of there. After another glance to see the cop was still not looking at him, Leon headed for the exit.

*Now to get hold of sniper rifles and at least two improvised explosive devices.*

Then get them past security into the stadium.

*That shouldn't be a problem.*

Leon knew Vishal was aching to prove himself. He had every intention of giving him the opportunity. Though not the way Vishal would have hoped for.

Leon allowed himself a satisfied smile; things were falling into place.

*Now if only Baxter comes through with the info and Nitin with the weapons. Then all I need is to motivate Vishal to take on the diversionary attack . . . of course, he will not know it is only a diversion.*

*Won't he?*

*Vishal is a smart cookie.*

*What if he finds out?*

That stalled him; Leon had already gauged that Vishal was devious.

*Not someone to take lightly or for granted.*

Worry returned.

Then he spotted Fatima, sauntering up toward the stadium.

*What on earth is wrong with this woman?*

Worry escalated.

*Does she think this is a holiday tour?*

Leon had taken considerable effort to try out another disguise, the Professor Naug look: brown hair, worn relatively shorter, just over the ears, blue eyes and clean-shaven. It was unrelated to the two he was using for Sarita Vihar and Jorbagh *and* gave him the opportunity to check it out. Leon had, however, deliberately omitted the rimless spectacles. There were too many photos of Naug floating around for comfort, part of the conference publicity materials. He was confident Fatima wouldn't recognize him and eager to test that.

But he was boiling as he headed toward her. Determined to send her off with an earful. Aware the only thing worse than a smart enemy was a dumb associate . . . or client, in this case.

*This woman needs to go back to London . . . or wherever the hell she wants to go. She is going to be the death of me.*

"What on earth are you doing here?" Mindful of the people around, Leon kept his tone low, but there was no mistaking his anger.

To his satisfaction Fatima did a double take at his appearance, but she obviously recognized his voice.

"I thought I would find you here," Fatima replied cheerily, trying to ignore his anger. "I was wondering if I could be of any help."

"Did I not make it clear to you? The only help I want from you is to make yourself scarce," Leon grated. "Do you realize that if you're caught I will abort? Why do you think I told you to order your group's leaders to lie low till this was over?"

"But . . ." Fatima was flustered now.

"No buts!" Leon made no effort to curb his fury. "If you want me to do this, you will have to go to ground and stay there till it's over. Right now you're the weakest link in the chain . . . and I have enough to worry about. Get it?"

# NINE

Fatima was shaking with rage by the time Leon finished telling her off. Coming on top of Vishal's rude brush-off the previous night, Leon's outburst proved to be the last straw. The need to hurt both of them was so strong that only her desire to see the mission to its conclusion prevented her from slapping him.

*Wait till you finish this mission, Leon Binder!*

For the first time she looked forward to telling him she'd run out of money to pay him with anticipation rather than fear.

*As for Vishal . . . I wish I had a gun.*

A seething mass of emotions, Fatima spun around and headed away from the stadium for the cabstand in the distance, across the ninety-foot-wide road. It was only when she'd gotten inside the battered-looking black-and-yellow Maruti van that she realized she didn't know where to go. The mere thought of returning to her hotel room made her feel claustrophobic.

*And I don't want to be alone.*

But Fatima realized there was no one she could seek out. To assuage her loneliness she pulled out her mobile to call her son, but, worried she would infect Zaki with her anxiety, she dropped it back in her bag.

"Maurya Sheraton," she told the cabbie in a resigned tone.

He was a talkative type and, realizing she was a Pakistani, left no stone unturned in explaining to Fatima why Pakistan needed to focus on her own problems, rather than worry about the plight of Muslims all over the world. Even worse, he was the type who read the editorials every day and was keen to discuss them.

"I believe that in Pakistan, unemployment and inflation, both are around 25 percent. Is that right, jee?"

"I have no idea. I live in London." Fatima had no desire to engage with him, yet in her present mood did not mind the lack of silence.

"That's what I read in the papers, jee." His enthusiasm was undampened by her obvious lack of interest. "And that's the point I am trying to make. Since independence Pakistan has fought so many wars with India." He gave a *that's-ridiculous* wave. "Just imagine what Pakistan would be like today if they had focused on their own problems. Not only did they lose every single war, they also lost half their country when Bangladesh became independent. And even worse, today their economy is in such an awful mess." He paused, waited for his passenger to respond, and when he heard nothing forthcoming, resumed. "And see what's happening in Pakistan today . . . all these terror attacks and bomb blasts every day . . . how many hundreds are dying, and all for what? Just because your army has been aiding these terrorist groups. No?"

Luckily they reached the hotel and Fatima was saved the need to answer. However, her mood was even lower now. She carried the loneliness and anger back to her room. Despite the early hour, she opened the minibar.

*Thank God they've replenished the minibar. Life should be like that . . . all good things should be replenished daily.*

Emptying a whiskey miniature into a glass, she grabbed a can of Coke and headed for the bed, flicking on the television as she threw herself down on it.

The BBC news was on. There had been another bomb blast in Pakistan, this time in a crowded marketplace in Karachi.

Fatima grimaced. It had been many years since she'd visited Karachi, but the market looked familiar. So, for that matter, did the shattered glass, demolished cars, and battered bodies lying around on the television screen. These days it seemed to have become a familiar sight whenever Pakistan was in the news.

*Perhaps that cabbie was right, after all. Perhaps it's time for Pakistan to put its terror-sponsoring days behind and focus on things like education, health care, and its economy.*

Feeling even more depressed, Fatima changed channels.

On the next one, a rerun of *Breaking Bad* was on. It seemed appropriate given her current Heisenberg mood. She popped the Coke can, added a dash to the whiskey, and took a long swig. It warmed her, but the crappy feeling refused to go away.

# TEN

Ravinder leaned in for a closer look at the entry wounds. The bodies hadn't been moved. And, possibly due to the heating, decay had accelerated. The stench was horrifying. The handkerchief on his nose did little to mask it.

"The powder burns are consistent with a contact shot." The inspector from the crime team pointed out.

Typical when the firearm is fired while in contact with the body, the powder burns were in a tiny area; confined to a bluish ring around the entry wound.

*But . . .* Ravinder leaned in closer, unsure. *What is that?*

It must have caught Philip's eye, too; he pulled out a torch and leaning in close, examined the tattooing. It was more prominent on Sikander than on his wife.

"Look at the powder burn; notice the tattooing. Seems a silencer was used, sir."

The inspector took a closer look, and looked sheepish for having missed that. "I'll look into it."

"If a silencer was used . . ." Ravinder trailed off. *There was no silencer on the weapon cradled in Ali's hands.* The implications were obvious; someone had known Ali was under suspicion and due to be hauled in for questioning. That meant . . .

*There is another mole . . . in the Special Task Force . . . since we haven't yet shared our suspicions with anyone.*

Ravinder examined the two men on either side.

*One of these two? Archana? Or Saina?*

"You'd better listen to this." A sub-inspector burst into the room. Trailing behind, looking apprehensive and uncomfortable, was a middle-aged woman. She seemed to have been hauled out of her kitchen; traces of flour were all over her blue cotton sari. The sub-inspector noticed three strangers in the room and stopped, confused.

"It's okay," the crime team inspector told him. "These gentlemen are from NIA. His department." He indicated the dead man. "What do I need to listen to?"

"Sister, tell them what you told me." The cop nudged the woman he was towing. "She lives in the apartment below."

# ELEVEN

Vishal felt a shock wave of panic smash at him. He was already spooked by the speed with which Ravinder had identified the powder burn and homed in on the fact that a silencer had been used.

*Had this damn woman spotted me?*

Instinctively he shrank back, trying to make himself invisible. And his hand inched closer to his pistol, preparing to shoot his way out if she fingered him.

"Last night we had guests over for dinner." The woman seemed oblivious of him. "After they left . . . it must have been around eleven, I was out on the balcony with my husband."

"In this cold?" Vishal cut in, unsure where she was going with this, but keen to fluster her. Though her mention of the time reassured him; he had been at home at eleven.

"My husband wanted to smoke and I don't allow that in the house . . . stinks everything up."

"Go on." Ravinder encouraged her.

"We were in the balcony when we heard Sikander fighting . . . more like arguing with someone. He sounded angry." She looked sheepish. "We didn't *want* to hear, but he was very loud."

"What were they saying? Could you make out with whom? Could it have been his wife?"

"Not really. Just the occasional word when his voice rose." She actually looked sorry about that. It would have been amusing if not for the bodies. "I don't think it was his wife." She saw the expressions of her audience and clarified. "Shama . . . his wife, was not the shouting type." Then, perhaps feeling that did not show the wife in a favorable light, added, "She was very soft-spoken. And the Alis didn't fight like that. They have lived here over ten years and I never heard them fight. Lastly, it was only him we could hear. That's why I am sure he was on the phone."

Vishal could see Ravinder process that as the others began to question her. It was soon obvious that she had nothing else relevant to add.

*Thank God!*

Vishal, petrified there had been an eyewitness, was breathing easier. Then he saw Ravinder gesture and followed him out with Philip.

# TWELVE

Leon took much longer than expected to get rid of Fatima. Perhaps it was her womanly need to expend her daily quota of twenty thousand words, or her fervent desire to see the mission succeed. Either way Leon was considerably irritated by the time he got her into a cab.

*Now for Nitin the Nerd. Let's see what he has to offer.*

Leon was apprehensive; though the Delhi-based weapons fabricator had come highly recommended from a reliable contact in Congo, he was still an unknown. For this mission, Leon was dealing with completely unknown people.

*And too bloody many of them.*

His unsettled feeling mounted, putting him on edge. Though Leon didn't mind that, aware the edge would keep him alive. But it was tiring. And his stomach was acting up again. He popped another couple of pills, but knew he had to find a toilet and unload before meeting Nitin.

*Shitting my pants wouldn't exactly convey the right impression.*

Leon grinned, but it was a grim grin.

# THIRTEEN

Ravinder felt the pressure escalating; time was running short and events moving too fast; before he could wrap his head around one thing, something else happened. He pulled himself together, aware losing his head meant losing the game.

"Philip, I want a list of all calls made to or by Ali yesterday," he ordered as soon as they were in the car. A beat later, he added, "His mobile *and* the home phone." Another beat later. "And his wife's mobile . . . just in case."

"On it, sir." Philip got his mobile out and passed on the instructions to Archana.

"I have a feeling we are getting close," Ravinder murmured, in think-aloud mode. "Why else would Ali have been taken out?"

"You're certain he was murdered?" It was not really a question. And there was a strange note in Vishal's tone.

Ravinder was trying to put his finger on it when Philip entered the conversation, distracting him. "Whether Ali committed suicide or was murdered, in either case, it's safe to assume that he and Binder have been warned. No other reason for Ali's death."

Ravinder could see the STF duo watching him carefully; he sensed his leadership was again being tested. That very thought had been nagging him since he had noticed the strange gunshot tattoo consistent with a silencer-fitted weapon.

*It has to be someone in the task force. No one else knew who all were on Archana's list. Unless Kurup . . . the director himself . . .*

Ravinder let that thought go unsaid; it was too farfetched. Aloud he said, "I'm willing to bet a silencer was used. Why would a man about to kill his wife and himself bother with one? And even if he did, where is the silencer now?" He got no response from either STF officer. "I want that weapon traced. I want to know where the hell it came from."

"The locals are already on it," Philip responded. "I have taken the inspector's contacts and told him to keep us in the loop."

"Should not be too hard." Ravinder pointed out. "The N99 is not a popular model and an old one at that."

Silence now joined them in the car as Jagjit Singh navigated down the Outer Ring Road, back toward Nehru Place.

# FOURTEEN

Leon made it to the rendezvous ahead of schedule, despite the time he'd lost finding a toilet. Not as early as he liked to be, but early enough to check if the venue was secure.

Green Park market was as crowded as it had been during his earlier drive through, but Leon was lucky enough to get an empty parking slot opposite the venue. Remaining inside the car, he surveyed Evergreen Sweet House. Located in the middle of the market, it was a two-story building occupying a large part of the market. The sweetshop occupied most of the ground floor. On the first was primarily a restaurant.

Leon noted with satisfaction that it was teeming with crowds, the perfect meeting point. However, spooked by his recent, nearly fatal encounter with Batra, Leon decided to change the venue.

Two minutes past the appointed time, a Tata Safari SUV navigated into a vacant parking slot in front of Evergreen. A huge man got out. Leon checked the photo on his phone provided by his contact in Nigeria. Leon knew Nitin the Nerd had arrived.

*Looks like Batra's little brother.*

The similarity amused Leon.

*Everyone here seems to be gigantic . . . Om Chandra, Batra, his henchmen, and now Nitin. I may as well be in America.*

The weapons specialist was as tall as Leon, but twice the girth. It was obviously his owlish horn-rimmed spectacles that had gotten him the sobriquet of Nitin the Nerd; they housed *thick* lens and gave him a scholarly but also somewhat comical air.

Locking up and double-checking the doors, Nitin rushed toward Evergreen. As much as a man his size could rush. Leon saw him halt near the door and scan the restaurant. Giving him a minute to see what he would do next, Leon called his mobile.

"Hullo, Mr. B?" The first time they'd spoken, Leon could have sworn he was talking to a woman; Nitin sounded so effeminate.

"Come out. Turn left and start walking," Leon instructed.

"Walking?" Nitin sounded confused. "Where to?"

"Just turn left and keep walking. I'll find you." Leon watched Nitin come out, peer around, confused. Then he started walking toward the left. "And don't cut the call . . . . . stay online." Leon did not want Nitin to call or text anyone.

Shifting focus Leon began to check if anyone was following Nitin. The crowd was heavy and it was hard to be certain, but Leon could not spot anyone. He kept watching till Nitin was a hundred feet away and then followed, still watching for a tail.

"Am I going in the right direction?" Nitin asked. Leon noticed he seemed calmer now, though breathing heavily, obviously unused to the exercise.

"Yep. Keep moving."

By the time Nitin had crossed over to the other half of the market Leon was sure he was alone. Lengthening his stride Leon caught up with the fat man easily.

"I needed to check if you were alone," he said as he fell in beside him.

"I see." Nitin gave a bland look. "Never hurts to be cautious, I guess. Satisfied?"

Leon saw no point responding to that. "Let's go in here," he said instead, steering him toward the McDonald's.

Giving a mischievous grin Nitin held up his mobile. "May I cut the call now? I promise not to call anyone."

Leon couldn't help smiling; Nitin the Nerd was sharp. And an easy man to like.

They headed toward the counter to order. Nitin's mobile began to ring; the volume had been turned down, but it was unmistakably his. Leon moved into red alert instantly; swiveling, he began to check the room.

"Relax. I have no idea who it is and no intention of answering it." Nitin tapped his arm. "Would you feel better if I handed it over to you?"

"Best if you remove the battery."

"I could do that." Nitin waited till it stopped ringing and then removed the battery.

Five minutes later they were at a corner table on the first floor. Nitin, a Big Mac Meal arrayed before him, upsized naturally, looked happy. Leon, his stomach still queasy, had bought only a Coke.

"This is what I need you to do." Leon unfolded a paper and handed it over. "Ensure you buy one presentation clicker of each of the brands shown here and three Apple display adaptors for the MacBook."

"Three adaptors? I'm guessing one each for VGA, DVI, and HDMI."

"That's right."

"And I'm guessing you want one clicker of each brand because you are not sure which one you would have to use."

"Right again." Leon saw why Nitin had a formidable reputation; he was admirably quick on the uptake.

"I see." Nitin paused to dig into his burger; just three bites and the Big Mac did not look big anymore. "How much aerosol do you have?"

"Two cans of one hundred milliliters each."

"For how many targets?" Nitin had reduced the decibel level.

"Just the one."

"More than enough then." Nitin calculated on the fly. "I suggest we also get a couple of cordless microphones and package them, too. They would blend in with the other items and may come in handy, especially if you need to enhance the kill radius." Leon was pondering that when he added, "I think I can do three . . . perhaps even four."

"You are sure the quantity will still be enough to do the job?"

"Is it still the same stuff you'd mentioned when we first spoke?" Leon nodded. Nitin gave a soft laugh. "Then it definitely will, unless you're planning to go elephant hunting . . . actually even if you're going elephant hunting . . . that is deadly stuff." ·

"Sounds good. Then go for it." Leon was relieved, sure he had made the right choice with Nitin. "I need them tomorrow." He could have taken delivery the day after, too, but Leon preferred to keep some cushion.

"Not a problem." Nitin swallowed the last of his French fries and washed it down with a large swig of lemon iced tea. "But check with me in the morning, and you will need to come to my place to take delivery. This"—he waved at the restaurant—"may not be the most suitable."

"No problem. I'll coordinate with you tomorrow." Leon now passed over the two cans of deodorant he had collected from Batra.

Nitin noticed the brand on the spray cans, "The AXE effect." He guffawed. "Most appropriate."

*Sharp and witty.* Leon smiled. "Do ensure this stays between us." He kept the tone light, using his eyes to put steel into the warning.

"But of course." Nitin shrugged. "Not exactly a service I would advertise on my website."

"Talking of service . . . how much will this cost me?"

"Fifty thousand," Nitin replied after a little thought.

"Indian rupees?"

"Thank God you didn't say Indonesian Rupiah." Nitin's laugh was infectious. "American dollars, my friend."

Leon knew that was reasonable; he was paying as much for discretion and reliability as for the technical expertise. Extracting an envelope from his jacket, Leon slid it across the table. "That's twenty grand on account. The rest when the job is done."

Nitin pocketed the envelope without bothering to glance inside. Leon liked that. And he wondered if Nitin knew he would probably not live long enough to enjoy that money.

*Pity! Seems like a nice guy.* But it wasn't tactically or strategically prudent to leave behind people who'd seen him and could identify him. *So be it.* "Give me five minutes before you leave." Leon left.

Now he was in a hurry to get back to Jorbagh and rest. Also to go through Naug's dossier; he needed to be familiar with the man he was going to impersonate.

# FIFTEEN

Ravinder went straight to Archana's table when they entered the office. "Archana, have you gotten the list of calls made to and from Ali's phones?"

"I will have it soon, sir." She was a little taken aback at his brusque tone.

"Everyone here, please. Team huddle." Ravinder went straight to the conference table. "Vishal and Chance, I'd like the two of you to search this half of the office." He indicated the left section, which seated Philip, Archana, and Saina. "Philip, you, Archana, and Saina take the other half." That was the bigger section, occupied by the rest.

Then Ravinder realized Saina was not there. "Where is Saina? Hasn't she come in yet?" He got blank looks in response. Flipping open his mobile Ravinder dialed her number. It rang a long time before going to voice mail. Irritated, and a little worried considering what had happened to Goel, Ravinder was about to redial when Vishal asked, "What are we looking for, sir?"

"Bugs. What else?" Ravinder realized he was almost snapping. He willed himself to calm down, but sensed this was not the time to pussyfoot around. "Either our office has been bugged . . . or one of us is batting for the other team. There is no one else who knew we were going to pick up Ali and Verma."

That went through the room like a shock of ice water. Having the suspicion stated aloud made it so much more real. And distasteful.

Half an hour later, it was obvious the latter was true: one of the STF officers had been turned.

"This half is clear," Vishal called out.

"This half, too," Philip added a few minutes later.

The words hung in the silence of the room.

"Right." Ravinder rang for Gyan. "First, let's ensure it stays bug free." When Gyan entered, "Till further orders I want this office under guard twenty-four seven. Two men in the office at all times. And I mean *in*." He stressed the last word. "Both will remain inside . . . one at either end, ensuring they can keep an eye on each other also . . . and everyone else. Got it?"

Gyan nodded. If he was surprised he didn't show it. "And no external cleaners, repairmen, telephone men . . . *No one* will enter without my *specific* permission. Clear?"

Another stoic nod from Gyan. Ravinder noticed the others looked uneasy. He was thinking of the next steps when the fax hummed to life. Being closest, he picked up the sheet that rolled out. It was a list of numbers with the timings noted opposite for three separate phone numbers: Ali's home phone, his mobile, and his wife's.

"Good job, Archana." He held up the list. "The list of calls for Ali." She joined him as he scanned the list. His eyes stopped at the same number as her well-manicured nail.

"Thirty-four minutes." She tapped the time of incoming call to Ali's mobile. "That's a long call." The call had started at fifty-eight minutes past ten the previous night.

"That's the time Ali's neighbor mentioned," Ravinder added, his excitement mounting. "That she had heard Ali around eleven."

Reaching for the phone by the fax machine, Ravinder dialed the number the call to Ali's mobile had been made from—also a mobile, and it looked familiar. He had keyed in the last number when the door opened and Saina entered. Though his attention was mostly on the phone Ravinder noticed she seemed out of sorts. Then the phone held to his ear began to ring. From one corner of his mind Ravinder saw Saina reach into her handbag. Then the ringing in his ear ended. Ravinder realized the call had been answered. And Saina was holding her mobile to her ear.

"Hullo." They both spoke simultaneously.

Realization hit. Hard.

"*You?*" Ravinder was stunned. So was Archana. The others were riveted, too, staring first at Ravinder, then at Saina.

# SIXTEEN

Vishal spotted the opportunity and reacted fast, aware he would be hard-pressed to find a better chance to shatter team morale, derail the investigation, and have them looking in the wrong direction. "You treacherous bitch!" His words cut through the room, stunning everyone.

"What do you mean?" Saina looked more confused than enraged.

"It's over, Saina. We know you warned Ali. Were you the one who killed him, too?" Vishal drew his pistol and leveled it at her. "Put down your handbag. *Slowly.*" The harsh snick, as he clicked off the safety, rang out like a pistol shot.

"Killed him?" Saina sagged. "Sikander is dead?" She spotted the confirmation in the faces ringed around. Her face crumpled.

Vishal saw her disintegrate. "Lose the drama . . ."

Ravinder hove into his gunsight, coming between Saina and him.

"Holster your weapon, Vishal."

"But . . ."

"*Now.*" There was steel in Ravinder's tone.

For a moment Vishal hoped that Saina would do something. Anything that would give him even a remotely plausible reason to fire. Also, the desire to gun Ravinder down nearly overwhelmed him. But realizing this was a dumb idea he lowered the pistol, slid the safety back on, and holstered it.

Ravinder noted Vishal's hand was still on the butt of his weapon and gave him a filthy look. But he turned to Saina. "Why? Why did you warn Ali?"

"Is he really dead?" She looked dazed.

Ravinder nodded.

"Sikander is . . . was my brother-in-law."

Vishal could see her falling apart. He also sensed the opportunity had just gotten better for him. "Is that why you warned the bloody traitor?" he interjected.

Saina's reaction stunned Vishal. She drew herself together and yelled back, "Sikander was *not* a traitor." Suddenly she seemed bigger, even taller.

"Then why did you call him?" Vishal shot back.

"I was shocked when I saw his name on Archana's list of suspects." Saina shrank again. "I only wanted to check if . . ."

"So you also thought he was the traitor." Vishal cut her off triumphantly.

# SEVENTEEN

Ravinder saw the situation deteriorating and knew he had to take charge.

"*Stop that.* Both of you." He held up his hands, warding them both off. "Sit down, Saina." He tensed as he saw her right hand head for her handbag. And he noticed he was not the only one. Gyan, standing directly behind Saina, had his hand on his service revolver. So did Cherian on her left. Vishal's hand was still resting on the butt of his weapon. Archana had backed off. Ravinder knew the slightest misstep on Saina's part could unleash hell. But she was only returning her mobile to her bag.

Ravinder breathed easier when she put down her handbag and sat . . . more like collapsed into a chair. She seemed on the verge of a breakdown.

"Why didn't you tell us, Saina?"

"I didn't know what to say," Saina whispered. "I have known Sikander all my life. I know he was not a traitor." She was crying now, but soundlessly. Just a steady trickle of tears down both cheeks. No sobs, no sniffs.

"Are you saying he was murdered?" Much to Ravinder's irritation Vishal hijacked the conversation again.

"There is no way he would kill Shama. Or himself." Saina seemed to be on surer ground now. "They loved each other and were happy. Just last week they were talking about adopting a child." She looked away, not bothering to wipe her tears. "I *know* they were happy."

"So why would anyone murder them? Unless he was . . ."

"That I don't know, but he was not a traitor." Interrupting Vishal, she turned to Ravinder. "He swore by Allah he was not."

"Do ask Allah to pass that on to Goel." Vishal's tone was bitingly sarcastic. "That would be such a comfort to him."

"Don't go there, Vishal." Ravinder was angry now. He needed to concentrate; Vishal's incendiary behavior and these distractions were not helping.

*If what Saina is saying was true, then . . .* Ravinder turned to Philip. "Take someone and bring the other deputy—Ashok Verma—in. If Saina is right . . ."—he altered direction—"no harm having a chat with him."

"Let me first check where he is." Archana reached for her phone; she seemed relieved to have something to do. A moment later: "Verma has already left the office." She checked his address on her laptop. "So I am guessing he would be home in about an hour . . . max an hour and a half, depending on traffic."

"Where does he stay?"

"Malviya Nagar. Not far, actually, but South Block to Malviya Nagar at this time of the evening would be madness."

"But Malviya Nagar is not far from here," Philip pointed out.

"True." Ravinder nodded. "We could pick him up from his house."

Ravinder's mobile buzzed; a text from Jasmine.

*We are en route. Pick you up in twenty. Max twenty-five. Okay?*

Ravinder remembered he was to dine with Rekha and her parents.

*Damn!*

He was sure Jasmine would be disappointed if he bailed, but also knew he could not sit this one out; Ashok Verma could well be the key to catching Leon. The odds had certainly narrowed.

*Best I explain to her in person when she reaches here.*

Texting her that he would meet them at the gate, he refocused on Philip. "Why don't you bring him back here and we have a chat with him?"

"Sounds good."

"I will go with him," Vishal volunteered.

"And me," Saina added grimly.

"Fine." Ravinder knew that denying her the opportunity to go along would imply he did not trust her. That did not seem fair, not in light of recent events. "Let's get this show on the road."

"Get ready, guys." Philip checked his watch. "We leave in twenty. That should easily get us to his house before him."

They scattered to organize.

# EIGHTEEN

Vishal was seething. He had not expected his ruse to fall apart so fast; thanks to Saina, all the risk he'd taken to knock off Ali had gone to waste. Vishal knew he was skating on thin ice again and needed to do something quickly, before the game spiraled out of control.

*What the hell is Kapil Choudhary doing? Why hasn't he* . . . Vishal fretted, hoping the trucker hadn't lost his nerve.

"I forgot my wallet in the car," he told Philip, and ran out. His mobile was out and dialing when he slid into his Ford Fiesta. Parked on the far side of Ravinder's BMW it was masked from the office.

"Where the hell are you?" Vishal asked when Kapil Choudhary, the truck driver, answered.

"Right behind the women you wanted me to attend to." Kapil's voice was faint, as though he was on a headset.

"Why haven't you done what you were supposed to?" Vishal hissed.

"I couldn't. They drove down this morning to a spa in Vasant Vihar. Traffic was so heavy that I could barely keep up with them." Kapil sounded peeved. "It's only now they have left Vasant Vihar."

"*They?* Which one are you following?"

"Both of them; the wife and the daughter. They are in the same car. The younger one is driving. They are coming down the Outer Ring Road, toward Nehru Place."

"Oh." Vishal was momentarily confused.

*One or two, who cares?*

"Excellent."

*The more the merrier. Ravinder will be so fucking devastated that Binder and the investigation will be the last thing on his mind.*

Then something struck him. "How the hell are you driving around in a truck inside the city? Isn't this the no-entry time for heavy vehicles?"

"Of course it is." Kapil sounded exasperated. "That's why I'm using the smaller one . . . one-tonners are allowed."

"Is it enough for the job?"

"More than enough."

"Fine. Then do it now."

"Now?"

"As soon as you can, but be careful . . . and *don't* fucking get caught." That done, he dialed Leon. But the call went unanswered. Stressed and eager to find a solution to the Verma dilemma, he dialed again. And then again. Still no response.

*Is that bastard ignoring me?*

Vishal hated that thought. He checked the time. Twelve minutes had already elapsed. Aware he had to get back, Vishal tried once more and then returned to the office, his anxiety escalating with every step.

*I cannot allow Verma to be taken alive. If he talks, I am . . . No!*

Unwilling to even countenance the possibility, Vishal struggled to spot a solution.

*Perhaps I can goad Verma into making a run for it . . . that will give me an opportunity to gun him down.*

He was glad he had volunteered to go with Philip. Not so glad Saina was going with them too, aware that with two pairs of eyes on him, he would find it harder to pull something off. Also, he knew Saina would be desperate to prove Ali innocent. And for that she needed Verma alive and talking.

# NINETEEN

Leon settled himself on the bed with his iPad and opened the file Hakon had sent on Naug—five pages and about twice that many photos of Naug and his family. He paused at one with Naug in the middle, his wife, a platinum blond as tall as him and two equally blond eight-year-old girls, twins, one on either side. There was even one of his parents and his in-laws. Leon was pleased; Hakon had done an excellent job. He was halfway through the first page when unwittingly he turned and his weight landed on the hurt elbow. Leon gasped; the pain was searing.

*Must be worse than I thought.*

He took another look. The area around his right elbow was bright red and had ballooned to twice its size. The slightest movement made him wince.

Leon realized he could not ignore it any longer.

*Kak!*

He didn't realize he had lapsed into Afrikaans till he said it aloud. Not that he minded; *kak* sounded so much more elegant than shit.

*Better not risk it. I need both my hands in working order.*

Flipping open a new Safari window on his iPad, Leon began looking for a hospital. His previous visits to the Indian subcontinent had taught him that a government hospital would afford him the most anonymity; due to the sheer number of patients, paperwork in them was almost nonexistent, unlike private hospitals. And some money delivered into the right palms would get him past those endless queues common at most Asian hospitals.

Google informed him that the All India Institute of Medical Sciences was closest to Jorbagh. That sorted, he decided to use yet another identity for this hospital visit. Moving gingerly, ensuring he put no weight on his right hand, from the spare passports in his bag Leon picked that of Colm Honan, an Irish businessman. The change in appearance from the British identity he was using for Jorbagh was the easiest, and Leon knew he could stop somewhere and do it in the car.

Popping another Combiflam to ease the pain, he headed out. Stopped a mile away to switch disguises. But with his right hand almost out of commission, it took much longer. Even the slightest movement made him wince.

# TWENTY

Ravinder was watching his team check their weapons when his mobile buzzed.

"We are almost there, Dad."

"I'll be at the gate, Princess." He walked out with the others. Philip gave him a questioning look, as though to ask if he was coming with them, too. "No. Just need to talk with my daughter," Ravinder explained. "My wife and she are passing by."

His back was turned, so Ravinder did not see the strange look that crossed Vishal's face.

Then he saw Jasmine's car pull up outside the gate, but she was on the other side, across the road.

"Best of luck, guys," he called out to the team. "I will be waiting here for you."

Waving to Jasmine he began to cross the road, afflicted by the fuzzy feeling that the sight of the two lovely ladies in his life evoked. And he was thinking hard.

*How do I break it to them nicely? Jasmine will be very disappointed. And Simran miffed at having to go alone . . . again.*

Rekha's parents were good people, but even in the best of times could not be accused of being good conversationalists or entertaining company; dinner with them always meant excellent food and plenty of silent time to ensure one could chew each mouthful thoroughly.

# TWENTY-ONE

Jasmine had insisted they travel in her car—a silver Maruti SX4 that her parents had gotten her as a graduation present when she had completed law school last month.

Having missed the turn off for the STF office, she was forced to go around the block and found herself on the wrong side of the road. There was no median physically dividing the road, so she waited for a break in traffic to cut across into the STF office compound. That is when she saw Ravinder wave out to her. Relieved at not having to cross the busy road she pulled over to the side and watched him start toward them.

Jasmine was feeling really excited and happy. The day had gone well. Both Rekha and she had gotten confirmation for the Master of Laws program from Duke University School of Law in North Carolina, which was their first choice, and they were thrilled about it.

"What do you say, BFF, should we wait for the formal invitation letter or should we tell them?" Jasmine smiled, remembering Rekha's naughty grin and her reply.

"Let's tell them today during dinner, Jas. May as well give them more time to get the college fees ready."

*And* this was the start of Simran's fiftieth-birthday celebrations. She smiled, knowing how delighted both their parents would be at the news, and tried to visualize their expressions when Rekha sprang the surprise; a dozen of Simran's closest friends were going to be at Rekha's house to ring in Simran's fiftieth.

*"Alagamun-lah, weh, wakun, heya."* Jasmine's smile broadened as Psy's K-Pop song "Gentlemen" burst out of the car radio. The peppy beat went perfectly with her mood. She turned up the volume.

"Good Lord." Beside her Simran groaned. "I have no idea what you see in such music." Pop music, Korean or otherwise, was clearly not high on her list of favorites. Jasmine, head bobbing to the music, responded with another happy grin. Throwing her hands in the air, Simran unbuckled her seat belt and reached for the door handle. "I better go back and let your dad sit up front with you."

Suddenly the revving of an engine overpowered the music. Jasmine turned to see what was causing the annoyingly loud sound. Her mouth fell open as she saw a one-tonner truck bearing down on them. A scream began to form in her mind. Before it could reach her lips Jasmine felt a massive blow strike the rear of her car. The sound of metal tearing apart sundered her mind. Then there was an explosion of glass. And suddenly Simran was no longer by her side.

Her seat belt locked, snapping Jasmine back against the seat. And the airbag exploded, cocooning her in white.

She blacked out.

# TWENTY-TWO

Ravinder was waiting for the green man guarding the pedestrian crossing to light up when the unusually loud revving of an engine made him look up.

At first the sight of the one-ton type truck rushing toward Jasmine's car didn't register. Then, horrifyingly, everything seemed to slow down and speed up simultaneously.

Slow enough for him to see the yellow lemons tied to the front of the truck with a black ribbon. To see the garish orange and black stripes painted on its front, radiating away from the bonnet, like a tiger's snarl. Faded, patchy, but visible. And the bearded driver hunched behind the wheel. His face caught in a tight scowl. Tense. Concentrating madly.

Yet so fast that Ravinder had barely taken a couple of strides when the truck smashed into Jasmine's car. Lifting it up and bashing it forward several feet.

His mouth caught open in a soundless scream, Ravinder stood rooted to the ground as he watched Simran hurtle through the windscreen. Even from across the road Ravinder could see shattered parts of the windscreen spray out, like killer graffiti. He blanched as Simran hit the ground. Hard. In his head Ravinder heard the soggy thud. Simran lay still. Then, miraculously, she swayed to her feet. Ravinder saw her turn toward the car. She took a couple of steps. The first two, tentative. The next two, firmer. Then, deflating, like a leaking balloon, she slowly collapsed in a heap.

Ravinder wanted to run forward, but his legs seemed to have frozen.

There was a blood-curdling screech of metal tearing. Ravinder saw the truck reverse, shaking itself free from the shattered remains of Jasmine's car.

That shattered his inertia, jolting him into action. Ravinder's hand raced for his shoulder holster, for the weapon that should have been there. It came away empty. Regardless he ran toward the truck. Which by now had broken free. With another burst of horsepower it roared down the road.

"Shoot!" Ravinder screamed at Vishal. "Shoot him!" He pointed at the fleeing truck.

Vishal drew his gun but shook his head. "Too many people around." Vishal's yell reached Ravinder as though from very far away.

By now the killer truck had bulldozed its way around the corner two hundred feet ahead.

"Get him!" Ravinder yelled back as he raced frantically across the road. Aching to get to Simran and Jasmine. Yet dreading what he would find.

Galvanized, Saina and Vishal ran toward his car. Philip followed Ravinder across the road. Archana was on the phone, calling for an ambulance.

Minutes later, with a wailing of sirens, an ambulance from All India Institute of Medical Sciences arrived.

By now, Ravinder had cut away the seat belt, freed her from the airbag and pulled Jasmine from the wrecked car. Fearful the leaking petrol tank might explode, Ravinder had carried her several feet away. Then with Philip's help he moved Simran and gently laid her down beside Jasmine, who by now had begun to stir.

The ambulance doors flew open as it screeched to a halt. Then the paramedics were upon them. Within minutes they had checked both and loaded them into the ambulance.

"I'm not leaving you alone, sir." Philip was ready to jump into the ambulance.

But Ravinder desperately wanted to be alone with his family. Simran lay lifeless on the stretcher. Jasmine looked dazed, but was sitting up. She seemed to have escaped unscathed, barring the odd nick here and scrape there; the airbag had taken the brunt.

"No need, Philip." Ravinder stalled him. "I'd rather you keep things on track here . . . find that bastard who did this . . . whatever it takes. I want to take him apart . . . how could he . . ." He broke off, looking helplessly at Simran, watching the paramedics work on her.

Philip halted uncertainly, half in and half out of the ambulance. "I will, sir. I promise you we will find the man who did this."

"I'm banking on you, Philip. You *have to* take charge. There is little time left," Ravinder urged, and goading him out, closed the ambulance door. With a scream of sirens it sped away. But Ravinder didn't hear it; the screaming in his head was much louder. He wanted to find the man at the wheel of the truck and punch him . . . and punch him . . . and . . . With a shudder he controlled himself. Aware that Simran and Jasmine needed him to be at his strongest, he held himself together.

"Don't worry, Jasmine." He tousled her hair, cocooning her in his arms. "Everything is going to be fine." But he could not sound as convincing as he wanted to. And a part of him still wanted to run out and chase the truck and dismember the man who'd been at the wheel.

# TWENTY-THREE

Vishal smacked the palm of his hand with an angry fist. "The bugger got away," he told Philip, pretending to be furious. However, Vishal was pleased with the way his get-Ravinder-off-the-case operation had panned out.

"He wouldn't have if you had driven faster." Saina, trailing a few feet behind, scowled fiercely.

"I don't know what your problem is." Vishal rounded on her. "What did you want me to do? Fly over the traffic?"

"It was not *that* bad." Saina faced him down. "We almost had him at the traffic island. We would have, too, if you hadn't stopped."

"I did *not* stop; the bloody car stalled. Anyway, who is to argue with you?" Shrugging, Vishal turned to Philip, who was watching the exchange, his expression disturbingly curious; it shattered some of Vishal's composure. Ignoring that, Vishal asked, "How is Ravinder's family?"

"They have reached the hospital." Philip's tone turned businesslike. "Meanwhile we continue."

"Shouldn't we go to the hospital to support Ravinder?"

"No." Philip seemed in no mood to relent. "The best thing we can do right now is keep the investigation on track and free him from this worry."

Vishal saw he was determined.

"Whoever is behind that"—Philip waved toward the gate, where Jasmine's battered car still lay—"is out to derail us. Obviously the same people who murdered Goel. It has to be Leon and his henchmen. We have to stop them."

Philip then turned to Saina. "Put some cops on the job. I want the bastard who was driving that truck." She headed for the phone.

"Tell them to report to me every hour till they find him. Then come with us to bring Ashok Verma in. Let us find out if you were right about your brother-in-law."

The sudden gleam in Saina's eyes drove Vishal's dismay deeper. He desperately hoped Leon had received his warning and would do something about Verma.

*But what? What the hell can Leon do?*

That was haunting him as Saina finished her call; the three of them got in to Cherian's car and headed for Verma's house.

*I hope Verma panics and makes a break for it.*

That buoyed him. He began to develop the idea.

*Perhaps Verma would panic enough to try and shoot his way out. Maybe even take that silly bitch Saina with him.*

Not likely, though.

*Perhaps I can induce the panic.*

Vishal liked that better.

"Vishal . . ."—Philip's voice tugged at him—"you secure the rear of the house. Saina and I will go in from the front door. No guns," he stressed. "Absolutely no guns . . . unless he comes out shooting. We just want to talk to Verma. Okay?"

Vishal acknowledged that with a mute nod.

*How can I stampede Verma into coming out shooting? And if he manages to take out Philip, the Special Task Force is as good as dead in a ditch.*

Vishal started to reach for his mobile but stopped; Saina beside him did not miss a thing.

*And Kapil Choudhary, the truck driver? Do I need to stress about him?*

Vishal considered that.

*Nah! Even if they catch him, what can he tell them? That a cop gave him the contract? So what? They already know there is a mole.*

That gave him some solace, but then worry about Verma destroyed that.

# TWENTY-FOUR

Ravinder was dreading the doctor's reply. "When is she likely to recover consciousness?"

"Hard to say, sir. It could . . . we cannot be sure." Mandeep faltered. Though a competent surgeon, Mandeep had not yet been hardened and was trying hard to sound reassuring. It did not help that he'd spent the day in back-to-back surgeries and been on his way home when the doctor in charge of emergencies had called him back. He was exhausted and it showed. That he looked younger than his thirty years did not help either. Not with Ravinder.

"Don't you think we should have a specialist check her? Someone . . . err . . . more senior." Ravinder vocalized his concern.

"Sir, Dr. Mandeep *is* a specialist." The doctor from emergency, who had requested Mandeep, felt compelled to justify. "Your wife is in safe hands."

But Ravinder wasn't reassured. "I don't want to be rude, but I'd like a second opinion."

"I understand your concern," Mandeep replied before the other doctor could. "Let me call in our HOD." Giving the nurse some instructions, they left the ICU as Jasmine came in.

Ravinder was relieved to see Jasmine seemed better; her wounds had been cleaned up and bandaged. A hospital gown covered her dress, which was dirty and ripped.

She took his hand and they stood beside Simran, who looked so out of place on the large hospital bed, with dozens of wires leading to a bewildering bank of monitors and an intravenous drip plugged to her. Simran seemed depleted.

One of the monitors kept beeping, a rhythmic and jarring sound. It seared through Ravinder, making him want to scream. But he kept a tight leash on himself, aware that Jasmine needed him to be strong *and* he wanted to find the man who'd done this to them.

*This has to be Leon's handiwork . . . and that of his mole . . . bastards want to cripple the Special Task Force, but to stoop so low . . . wonder if Leon knows I'm heading up the task force . . . of course he must . . . his mole must have updated him. Is* that *why Leon did this?* Ravinder pushed away the urge to rush out and join the hunt for the truck driver. *Simran and Jasmine need me more.* But having to see Simran in this sorry state pained him.

So he glared at the monitor instead. *Philips* was written in bold black letters prominently in the middle of the white lower panel and *IntelliVue MP90* on the top right. A thin green line traveled across the screen, vanishing to the right and then starting all over again from the left. On the top right, a bold green dot pulsed in sync with the beeping.

Ravinder knew the sound would stay with him to his grave. But he clung to it, aware it meant Simran was alive. Anger at the man who had done this to her battled with fear for her life.

*Binder, you bastard, you should have left my family out of this.*

Rage gnawed at him. Then it struck him that Leon and the dead seemed to go hand in hand. His blood ran cold.

# TWENTY-FIVE

Jasmine could see Ravinder's lips move in silent prayer. And his fists clench and unclench, the veins standing out, stark statements of pent-up fury. She took his hands in her own.

"Dad, don't worry, Mom will be fine."

"Yes, Princess." But Ravinder's gaze stayed riveted on Simran and his fists continued to flex, in tandem with the rhythmic beep of the monitor. "She has to." Ravinder was desperate to reassure her and himself, but could not think of anything else to say. "Tomorrow is the twenty-fifth . . . her birthday. She will be fifty." He blurted.

His pain seared Jasmine. And scared her. Only once before had Jasmine seen him like this, so helpless. That was the day they had gone to consign Ruby's ashes to the Ganges. The memory was still fresh; that day she'd feared they would lose him, that he would do something to himself. Today the same fear was back. She clutched his hand tight, her nails breaking skin.

If Ravinder felt it, he did not show a thing. Immobile, he sat by Simran's bed, within touching distance. His unblinking eyes were riveted on Simran, as though she would stay alive as long as he did not take his eyes off her.

"Why?" Jasmine's voice tugged at him from far away. "And do you know who did this to us? Does it have something to do with the case you're working on?"

"Yes." Ravinder felt guilty, as though he'd personally rammed the truck into their car. "It couldn't be anything else."

"So if you hadn't taken on this . . ." Jasmine bit her tongue when she saw the devastation on Ravinder's face, like someone had plunged a dagger in his heart. "Sorry, Dad. I didn't mean it like that."

He didn't reply. "Don't let them get away, Dad." Flustered, she blurted out, "Make them pay for hurting Mom."

"I will," Ravinder promised. But she could see he was desperately close to tears.

*Perhaps Mom was right . . . perhaps I should not have supported him in taking on this assignment.*

Guilt compounded the conflict and pain seething inside her.

# TWENTY-SIX

Vishal felt his unease escalate as he reached the mouth of the alley behind Verma's house. It was a three-story building set amidst a long line of dissimilar houses behind Malviya Nagar market, overlooking the Shivalik main road. Most of the buildings on this road had gone commercial since the courts had permitted mixed land use; right across the road from Verma's house was a Liberty Shoes showroom. And beside that, a clothes shop, with a blackboard that read MENZ. Philip had parked in front of it.

As he entered the alley he saw Saina and Philip emerge from their car and head for the front. Before he had taken three steps his mobile was dialing; he *had* to stampede Verma and make him come out shooting. That would ensure either Philip or Saina would take him down. And if he got lucky, perhaps Verma would get one of them.

He waited for the phone to ring, but it did not. Instead an engaged tone assaulted his ears.

*Which moron doesn't have call waiting?*

He cut the connection and furiously dialed again.

Still engaged.

*What the . . .* He was about to dial a third time when his mobile vibrated—an incoming call.

His heart plunged; it was from Philip.

"Yes?"

"Come back to the car. Mr. Verma is with us."

Now in turmoil Vishal headed back, dreading being confronted by Verma. He wondered if he would be better off making a break. But he decided to see how things were panning out. Sucking in a large dose of oxygen he forced himself to calm down.

Flicking on the safety, Vishal holstered his weapon and headed back. However, he did not eject the round from the chamber so he could bring it into action instantly should the need arise.

*If Verma gives me away I am going to gun all three of them down.*

The thought of pumping bullets in Saina and Philip, especially Saina, felt so good he nearly drew his weapon out again.

# TWENTY-SEVEN

Ravinder knew something had changed, but took a moment to place it; the monitor was beeping faster. Alarmed, unsure what it signified, he rang for the nurse. But she had already heard it and was heading over.

"You are not happy to see me awake?" Simran was barely audible over the beeping, but the sound of her voice electrified Ravinder and Jasmine.

*"Mom!"* Leaving his hand Jasmine grabbed Simran's and began to cry. He felt like crying, too, but Ravinder knew it was his watch now; they both needed him.

"You have to stop scaring us like that, Simran." He wanted to hug them both. Instead he simply laid his hands over theirs.

Simran smiled. A weak smile. "Me? She has to stop driving like that." Jasmine looked horrified. "What happened back there? All I remember is we were waiting outside your office and then . . ."

The doors of the ICU swung open and Mandeep strode in, with the duty medical officer in tow. "Wonderful to see you awake, ma'am." He examined her. "How are you feeling now?"

"Trying to remember how I got here," Simran replied with a weak smile. "How am I doing?"

"Remarkably well, given the circumstances." Mandeep gave his most reassuring smile. Ravinder sensed his relief at seeing her conscious. "Let me get hold of the rest of your reports and come back to you. Meanwhile I want you to rest. And I mean *really* rest." Mandeep looked at Jasmine. "Make sure your mother rests."

He got a determined nod in return.

Beckoning Ravinder to follow him, Mandeep headed out. "It is wonderful that she has recovered consciousness. A really good sign, sir." However, Ravinder did not miss that Mandeep looked somber. "Her visual reflexes seem good. But we are not out of the woods yet. The x-ray shows a skull fracture, luckily hairline. But there is internal bleeding." Ravinder realized his panic was obvious when Mandeep hastily added, "Please don't worry, sir. I want you to have the complete picture. This is common in such cases."

"What are you really saying?" Ravinder was confused and alarmed.

"Just that it's a good sign she's conscious." Mandeep replied. "We will be doing more tests, and if the internal bleeding doesn't stop we may need to operate on her." That alarmed Ravinder. Mandeep held up a hand to forestall any outburst. "Please keep her spirits up and ensure she rests. I will be back with our HOD."

Ravinder was so relieved he almost ran back in.

"Isn't the doctor cute? And Sikh, too," Simran was saying when he reached their side. "Do you think he is single?"

*"Mom!"* Jasmine threw her a mortified look, to check no one had overheard. "Give it a break. You never give up. Even from a hospital bed, you want to marry me off to every sardar you see."

"Not *every* sardar. Just the cute ones." Simran had a glint in her eyes. "And he seems to be from a good family."

"I think it was a lot better when you were knocked out." Jasmine rolled her eyes at Simran, but she was smiling.

Ravinder was so relieved to hear their banter that he nearly broke into tears.

The ICU doors swung open again and Rekha peeped in. Behind her was Simran's elder sister, Harmala.

"I came as fast as I could," Rekha stage-whispered.

"Me too," Harmala added from over Rekha's shoulder. But her stage whisper was more a stentorian bellow. Though Harmala was one of her peskiest aunts, Jasmine was relieved, knowing Simran was close to her and would be delighted.

The nurse sternly shushed them and informed Ravinder only one person per patient was allowed in the ICU.

"That will be me," Harmala replied officiously. "You take Jasmine home and ensure she gets some rest," she ordered Ravinder.

He was reluctant to leave Simran, but knew Harmala was right; Jasmine was looking beat. Still he hesitated.

Simran noticed his indecision. "She's right, Ravinder. Please take Jasmine home. She needs to rest. You do, too. We cannot have you also falling ill."

Ravinder's mobile vibrated briefly, an incoming message. Before he could read it Mandeep returned with a sheaf of x-rays and reports.

"We're taking her for a CT scan," he told Ravinder. "Looks like we will have to operate; the internal bleeding needs to be stopped."

"Now?" Ravinder felt anxious.

"No. We will wait and watch for a few hours . . . perhaps till morning. That will give her time to recover her strength also."

"Do you think it's okay for me to go home today?"

"Of course. Take your daughter home and see she rests, too." Mandeep gave an encouraging smile. "Don't worry about Mrs. Gill. We will take good care of her."

"Thank you, Doctor." Ravinder now felt more comfortable with the idea of going home. "I'll be back first thing in the morning."

"Don't worry, Ravinder." Simran gave a reassuring smile. "I'll be right as rain by then."

"Of course you will." Mandeep joined in cheerily.

"I like this doctor," Harmala told Simran, again in what she considered a whisper. Both nurses giggled. Ravinder saw Mandeep go red. Jasmine gave an embarrassed smile. If Harmala noticed she was unfazed. "Are you married, Doctor?"

Ravinder saw him go beetroot red. Jasmine, too. The nurses were trying hard to not laugh.

"No, ma'am." Mandeep finally found his voice. Completely flustered he buried his face in Simran's medical charts.

Jasmine gave Simran a hurried peck and rushed out with a murmured *"Oh, God."*

"That's nice. Neither is my niece, Jasmine." Harmala's unabashed comment followed Ravinder to the door. Knowing his sister-in-law, he did not envy Mandeep.

His mobile vibrated again, reminding him about the unread text. He was about to take it out when Jasmine grabbed his arm. "What do I do with aunty Harmala? She is *so* embarrassing, Dad," she lamented.

Still laughing, but now flush with relief, Ravinder put his arm around her and they headed for the car park.

"But you will admit, the doctor *is* cute." A fresh burst of laughter blew their fears and worries away. For the moment.

# TWENTY-EIGHT

Leon noticed the missed calls from Vishal as he exited the Orthopedic Department of AIIMS (All India Institute of Medical Services) and headed for the parking lot, all the way across the emergency ward and out from the lobby. The technician had made him switch off his mobile for the x-ray. He thought of calling back, but first he wanted to get back to Jorbagh, unload, and lie down.

The visit to AIIMS had not proven to be such a good idea. The paperwork was as lax as he'd hoped it would be, but the attendant on duty proved to be a surprise. Not only did he *not* take bribes, he was so offended at being offered one, he made Leon wait. In the jam-packed, unheated waiting area, surrounded by people suffering from all kinds of injuries and disease proved to be nearly as painful as his elbow. The stench of disinfectant, which seemed to be the hallmark of hospitals worldwide, overwhelmed him. For the past twenty minutes, to add to his misery, Leon's stomach had been acting up and he ached to take a dump. He *had* tried using the public toilet at the end of the corridor, but his courage failed at the sight and smell of the overloaded bathroom. Now the pressure was dangerously high.

In his hurry, coping with that, worried Vishal was trying to reach him, *and* simultaneously trying to locate his car in the irregular street lighting, Leon failed to notice Ravinder and Jasmine, as they also exited the emergency ward a few feet ahead of him and headed for the parking lot.

Neither was aware the man they sought to destroy was scant feet away.

There was only one car between them as they exited the AIIMS gate. Both turned left and headed down Aurobindo Marg. Half a mile ahead Leon took the U-turn and headed back toward Jorbagh, while Ravinder continued ahead toward Chhatarpur.

# TWENTY-NINE

Vishal was gripping the pistol so tightly his hand hurt. He tried to relax, himself and his grip. But it was hard. He was on edge as he headed for the front of Verma's house, aware that one false glance or misplaced word from Verma could blow the lid off his life.

Then he turned the corner.

Verma was sandwiched between Philip and Saina. They were leading him to their car. Though they had not cuffed him, it was obvious they viewed him as a prisoner and a potential flight risk. Both had their right hands out of sight; Philip's in his coat pocket and Saina's in her bag.

Verma looked severely agitated. "I can assure you that my boss will . . . you guys have a lot to answer for."

Vishal noted that Verma looked shaken but seemed to be holding up so far. He breathed a sigh of relief. As long as Verma held out and denied all involvement, Vishal knew the STF would be hard-pressed to prove anything. That was now his only hope.

That and the gun in his hand. Though he hoped he would not have to use it, not till he had collected his money from Fatima. He'd received only fifty thousand dollars; the balance of one hundred and fifty thousand he'd been promised would be enough to give him a decent head start. That and the money now promised by Leon; Vishal again wondered how much it would be.

# THIRTY

Ravinder noticed Philip's text only when he had tucked Jasmine in and retired to his room. Though he was exhausted, guilt at abandoning his team and such a critical task compelled him to call Philip.

"How are both of them now, sir?"

"Much better, thank you, Philip. Jasmine is back home with me already. Simran is still at the hospital, but improving."

"Thank God. The news here is good, too." Ravinder picked up on his satisfaction. "We have Ashok Verma in custody and I already started the interrogation. So far nothing, but he *is* a veteran. I didn't think he would break so easily."

"Hold him in solitary and try sleep deprivation," Ravinder suggested.

"That's what I have done, sir. White room, bright lights, and complete silence. The full works. By tomorrow he should be aching to talk."

"Excellent." Ravinder felt better that things were in hand. "Soon as Simran is out of the woods, I'll be back. Hold down the fort till then, Philip."

"No worries, sir. You focus on her." Philip's confidence bolstered Ravinder. "I wanted you to look at the options Archana has come up with . . . she has aged Binder's photos. If you could let us know which ones you think would be the most likely, I could have variants done and the APB issued."

"Now?"

"I can email all five variants to you."

"WhatsApp them instead and I will let you know right away."

A moment later Ravinder was studying five photos on his iPad, correlating them with the Leon he had shared an apartment with.

It was not an easy choice; thirty years is a long time, but Archana had done an excellent job with all of them. Finally making up his mind he called Philip back. "I would suggest numbers two and five."

Number two had shoulder-length hair left loose. Ravinder remembered the time Leon had gone hippie—grown his hair and a goatee.

*Throw in the gray and some wrinkles, add a few kilograms, and that's how he should look now.*

And the fifth simulation also had long hair, but neatly tied in a pony. And oval horn-rimmed spectacles.

*That's like the time Leon had gone arty.*

Right down to zero power glasses.

*Yes! Archana has gone a great job.*

"Two and five it is, sir. I'll have the APB out right away. Apprehend or shoot on sight? Dead or alive?"

"Yes. And emphasize the approach-with-caution bit. We don't want overenthusiastic cops getting killed. Okay?"

"Sir, what about informing the Pakis? Should I do that or will you?"

"Neither. For now, have the NIA Liaison Officer send it to them as a general nonspecific threat. You know . . . we have received intel there is a threat to their PM and are investigating . . . blah blah." Ravinder preempted Philip's next question. "Let's keep it there till we have some more. If we get Binder in time, no need for the Pakis to know at all. If we find things getting out of hand, then we will warn them. The NIA director told me that is how the politicos want it. Okay?"

"Roger that, sir." Philip rang off. Only to ring back a moment later, excitedly. "We have found the truck, sir."

Ravinder shot upright. "What about the driver?"

"Not yet."

"Oh!" Ravinder felt terribly disappointed. "Find that bastard, Philip."

"We will, sir. Don't worry. Saina is personally handling this and I'll keep you posted."

Just the thought of getting his hands on the driver made Ravinder's blood pound. Then his thoughts drifted toward the man who had tasked the truck driver.

*Who is the mole?*

*Verma?* The desire to rush to the office and hammer the truth out of him gripped Ravinder, but he knew it was not practical—not at this late hour and certainly not in the condition he was in.

*Philip?* Instinct told him it did not seem probable, but for once, Ravinder did not want to trust his instincts; this time he needed each man to prove himself innocent.

*Vishal?* Ravinder paused, dwelling on it; there was something about Vishal that he had not been able to put a finger on. Yet his track record was good, perhaps too impeccable.

*Archana?* He found it hard to believe it could be her. *She seems so sweet and helpful.* But Ravinder knew looks could be deceptive. Hers would be the perfect cover for a mole.

*Saina?* Her association with and call to Sikander were damning. But the fact she was spearheading the hunt for the truck driver and had already found the truck made him wonder. *Or is that a ploy to throw off suspicion?*

That left him more confused.

*Quis custodiet ipsos custodes? Who indeed would guard the guards themselves? Had he sent the killer to catch the killer?*

Then Leon's photographs on his iPad caught Ravinder's eye. They seemed to be staring at him.

*Archana has done a terrific job with the mug shots.*

The likeness to the Leon he had known three decades back was so startling that Ravinder could almost *see* Leon, especially photograph number five. The arty, pony-tailed, spectacled man had that same look of fierce concentration Ravinder remembered so well; he could visualize Leon studying or playing chess.

*Always that expression.*

As though hypnotized, Ravinder could not look away.

His attention was still riveted on the iPad as his eyes glazed over. Ravinder's tired mind shot him back into the past.

Ravinder was shocked when face number five on his iPad screen came alive.

Leaping out of the iPad, Leon strode up to Ravinder with that familiar athletic stride and jabbed him, a stiff finger in the solar plexus.

"You fucked me, Ravinder." Leon's betrayed look cut to the bone. "You fucked me nice and proper, old chap."

"I didn't. You did. You reaped what you sowed," Ravinder re-torted. "You should have left Farah alone. She was Edward's fiancée, for God's sake. How *could* you, Leon?"

"We were drunk, Ravinder. I have no idea how it happened, but I didn't plan it . . . neither did I force myself on her. And. You. Know. That." The last four words were punctuated with four more deliber-ate jabs from the same finger, this time on Ravinder's arm. "You know Farah Fairfowler was a wild one. For all you know, she may have been fucking the whole form."

"You can say what you want now. Farah isn't here to defend her-self. You raped and killed her, Leon."

"*I* raped her? I didn't need to. She was the fucking village bicy-cle . . . anyone who wanted to was mounting her." Leon's eyes were angry slits. "And I did *not* kill her. *You* did." Ravinder flinched. "And you know that."

"That's bullshit," Ravinder shouted back. "I was trying to save her."

"*You* brought the poker into the fight, Mr. Ravinder Singh Gill." Leon was relentless. Ruthless. "Don't you remember?"

"So?" Words eluded Ravinder.

"If you hadn't done that, she might still be alive."

"Screw you," Ravinder fired back furiously. "You'd gone wild and I was only defending myself. And I didn't ask you to hit her with it."

Leon overrode him. "I'm not saying you *wanted* to kill her. Or *planned* to, but you did. It happened." Leon jabbed Ravinder's arm again. "Just as I did not *plan* to have sex with her. It happened. It just happened, bro."

Ravinder found his voice. "Don't you dare . . . you murderous bastard." He was shouting now, the veins on his neck bulging, his face red. "Don't try to pass on your misdeeds to me."

"You *don't* remember," Leon's tone hadn't altered. Nor had his gaze strayed from Ravinder's face. "Or you don't *want* to remember."

"Shut the fuck up, Leon."

"Why?" Still the same flat, soft tone. "Why are you afraid to con-front what you did? Why don't you admit you were wrong? You and your fucking righteous anger! You testified against me just because of Edward. For the sake of his so-called honor, you made *me* pay the price. *You* destroyed my life . . . *You* are the reason my parents died of shame and heartbreak. You and Edward killed them as sure as you had put the gun to their heads." Leon was breathing hard now, spitting out the words angrily. "*You* are the buggers who put me on this path. You think *this* is what I aspired to? If it hadn't been for you and that high-and-mighty prick Kingsley, I could have become whatever I wanted to." The same stiff finger pointed at Ravinder's face. "But you see, old chap, life is like a restaurant named Karma. Here we all are served *only* what we deserve." The finger was pointed straight between Ravinder's eyes. Like a pistol.

"That's true, Leon. And you should wonder why it served you this," Ravinder retorted.

"I have come to pay you back, Ravinder. I'll bring you down and destroy you."

Ravinder's anger broke free. "Fuck you, Leon Binder. Don't try to mess with my head." Grabbing Leon's finger, apoplectic, he lashed out with all his might. "You murderous bastard. You got what you deserved."

Dad! *Dad!*" Jasmine shook Ravinder awake. He was clutching her hand. Hard. But if she felt the pain, she didn't show it.

It took a moment for reality to return. For Ravinder's breathing to subside. For his heartbeat to settle. A bit. Only a bit.

"I must have been having a bad dream." Fighting for control, he released her hand. Noticed she began to massage it and was filled with remorse. "Sorry, Princess, did I hurt you?"

"Only when I see you hurting yourself, Dad."

As he took the glass of water she held out, Ravinder noticed how calm she was. That made him proud.

"You have to let go, Dad. Whatever it is . . . out there, in the past . . . it is over and done with. Nothing you do can change that."

"You see . . ."

"I don't, Dad." Jasmine cut him off. "And I don't wish to either. Raking up the past never got anyone anywhere. Let it go," she repeated, more insistently now.

"You are right, Princess. I have to let it go. I will." Ravinder could see she was tired. "Let us get some sleep. We have to be at the hospital early."

"That's right. I want you to sleep now. Would you like me to give you a pill?"

"Don't worry, Princess. I will be fine."

"Of course you will, Dad."

Ravinder saw her determination.

"Remember what you used to tell me whenever I was upset about something?" Jasmine did not wait for a reply. "'Don't worry, Princess. Nothing will happen. Not on my watch.'" He smiled. "Well, it's my watch now, Dad." She caressed his brow. "Sleep."

Ravinder felt another surge of pride; in the past two days Jasmine had displayed more maturity and steel than ever before.

*Yes. Indeed our baby has grown, Simran.*

His mobile chimed; it was a WhatsApp from Archana on the Task Force's group chat that the APB for Leon had been issued. She had also attached a copy of it with the message. He felt better, his doubts assuaged. Jasmine took away his mobile and put it on the bedside table.

"Please sleep, Dad." She stroked his brow tenderly.

He did.

This time no ghosts from the past or worries about the present came to haunt him.

# THIRTY-ONE

Leon stared at the images on his mobile, forwarded to him by Vishal. Despite the screen size the photos were sharp. He was dismayed at how strong the likeness to both the personas used by him at Sarita Vihar and Jorbagh was. He knew neither of these disguises would now hold up to a careful scrutiny.

"They've done a good job," he admitted to Vishal, who was still on the line.

"Yes, Archana, the woman on our task force who does this, is very good." Vishal sounded uneasy. "Now you need to be extra careful when you move around."

"I don't plan to. Much," Leon replied.

"I'd hoped to slow them down once Ravinder was out of commission, but that bastard Cherian is keeping things on track."

"You cannot keep knocking them all off, Vishal."

"No, we cannot," Vishal admitted, though reluctantly; it was obvious he would have loved to kill Cherian.

"Let's focus on what we *can* do instead. I like your idea of striking both targets simultaneously."

"Really?" Vishal warmed at the praise. "Are you going for it?"

"Only if you're ready to help. No way I can do that alone." Leon phrased it in the way he sensed it would appeal most to Vishal.

"I'd be happy to," Vishal replied immediately. "But only if I am paid more."

"Obviously." Leon was delighted his ploy was working; at best he might get both targets, and in the worst case he would have an excellent diversion: one that would embarrass the hell out of Ravinder and make him look like a fool, even if it failed. *What could be more embarrassing than an officer of the Special Task Force trying to assassinate a visiting head of state?* "How much are you expecting, Vishal?"

"That depends on what you want me to do."

"Hmm . . . that sounds reasonable. Let's both give it some thought and talk about that tomorrow, shall we?" When Vishal concurred, Leon added. "Meanwhile, could you get hold of two sniper rifles and two improvised explosive devices?"

"I could." Vishal was on surer ground now. "For the right kind of money, anything is possible."

"Of course." Leon kept his tone even, careful not to let his satisfaction show. "Obviously, nothing comes free. I'll leave it to you to negotiate a good price." But unwilling to give Vishal carte blanche, Leon added, "Never forget, the less you dish out to others the more we will have for ourselves."

It was Leon's usage of the word *us* that turned the trick; Vishal was pleased Leon considered him a part of the inner circle. "Absolutely. For the rifles, any preference?"

"Not really, Vishal. I'm comfortable with most. You decide if you have a preference. You'll be using one of them." Leon sensed that would also appeal to Vishal's ego.

It did. Hugely. "Let me figure it out then. Where and when do we need them?"

"Ideally, we should get them into the stadium after the last security sweep and just before the final shift comes on duty . . . say, the twenty-sixth at night."

"So you *are* planning to hit Masharrat yourself. That's why you want me to take out Zardosi." Vishal sounded pleased. "I thought you would go after Masharrat."

Ignoring that, Leon said, "If we take them in too soon there is a chance they will be discovered. And if we leave it too late we may not be able to get them in . . . the final security shift is generally the most alert."

"Leave that to me," Vishal said confidently. "I know how to make that happen. Just tell me what you need the bombs to do."

"I want them to give us the diversion we need."

Once again, Leon's use of the word *us* did not escape Vishal's attention.

"You want them to be found or to go off?"

"Interesting." Leon marveled at Vishal's deviousness; that had not struck him. "How about one of each?"

"Nice." Vishal smiled. "So if the one placed more strategically is found, they will assume the threat has been blunted. Then when the next goes off it will throw them in disarray. And *that* is when we can strike. Very nice."

On that note the call ended.

And Leon was alone again, with the APB photos Vishal had sent him.

Though he had kept his tone light, unwilling to share his fears with the hired help, Leon was uneasy when he lay down, aware the odds had just gone up. All the photos were good, but one was uncannily similar to the American disguise he'd used while renting the Sarita Vihar apartment *and* with Nitin. Leon, now worried Om Chandra would recognize him, decided he would no longer use the Sarita Vihar safe house. Also, Leon sensed Vishal, though useful, was a dangerous addition; extra danger was something he could do without.

The photos and the APB stayed in his head as he fell asleep. He knew his freedom of movement had been strongly curtailed. And it was time to abandon both these identities.

# THIRTY-TWO

Vishal was feeling good after the call. But the one dark patch on his horizon was Verma blabbing. If he could put that to bed, he was sure he would come out of this winning. Eager to find out the score on that front, he called Philip.

Vishal sensed his tiredness when the STF second-in-command answered. "Would you like me to help with Verma's interrogation tomorrow? I can be there first thing."

"Thank you, Vishal, but I want to handle that myself."

"Cool." Vishal masked his disappointment. "How is it going?"

"Not as well as it should." Philip's sigh was audible. "I sometimes worry we might be barking up the wrong tree." He made a humming sound, like a mental shrug. "Though everything tells me Verma is our man . . . perhaps because Sikander has already been ruled out and I am not sure if anyone on our team . . ." Philip must have realized he was sharing more than he wished to and broke off. "Anyway, thanks for the offer. I'll call you if I need help."

Tossing the phone on his bed, Vishal did a happy jig around it. If the first call had left him happy, this one made him ecstatic. Verma should be able to hold out another couple of days.

*The bugger has as much to lose as I have.*

*More, actually. Verma has a wife and kids.*

Also, with the decision to become a professional like Leon now clearer, Vishal did not dread being blown as much. The additional money promised by Leon had ignited many dreams; he could now see himself living in Europe or America.

*Maybe not. I need to check which countries have no extradition treaty with India . . . and no death penalty.*

But most important, knowing Leon would now have to rely on him more due to the APB, made Vishal feel more secure.

For the first night since the start of this operation, Vishal slept soundly.

# DECEMBER
## 25

# ONE

Ravinder was in two minds about leaving the safe confines of his bed. Despite his eagerness to be back by Simran's side, trapped in a discordant patchwork of thoughts, he lay huddled there. However, eventually the deathly quiet gripping the house began to close in on him. It felt claustrophobic. As though the house was mourning Simran's absence. The intercom buzzed, startling him. Ravinder threw off the quilt and reached for it.

"Good morning, Dad. Should we meet for breakfast in half an hour?"

Ravinder noticed Jasmine sounded deeply tired. He sensed from her soggy tone that she had been crying. "Are you okay?"

"Of course."

But Ravinder could tell that the lightness in her voice was forced. Promising himself to support her by keeping a firm grasp on things, he got ready and headed down. The mail on the dining room sideboard caught his eye. Mingled with a stack of bills was a letter from Duke University School of Law in North Carolina, addressed to Jasmine. Ravinder knew Jasmine had been awaiting admission results from US universities and handed it to her when she entered. Suddenly animated, Jasmine ripped it open, then squealed with delight.

"I'm in, Dad. Duke has accepted me for the Master of Laws program *and* I have a twenty-five percent tuition waiver."

Ravinder laughed as she punched the air and did a victory dance. "I knew they would." He felt proud and equally delighted. "Your mother is going to be thrilled . . . how many people manage to win a tuition waiver?"

"I can't wait to tell her."

That reminded them Simran was waiting. Rushing through

breakfast they headed for the hospital. They were driving out of the gate when Jasmine remembered. She smacked her forehead. "Dad! It's Mom's fiftieth birthday today. How on earth could I have forgotten?"

"I had forgotten, too." Ravinder felt sheepish, but knew how tumultuous things had been. "I guess . . ." He left it there. And then, unwilling to let the gloom return, patted her hand. "No worries. We will have a gala celebration the day she gets back from the hospital."

Jasmine smiled. Ravinder didn't want to dampen her joy by telling her that, but he was aching to have Simran back home so he could focus on finding the man who'd ordered the attack on them.

# TWO

Vishal realized what a shitty feeling it was, not being able to put a finger on what he was missing. And he *knew* something was amiss; that feeling had nagged him since morning.

Verma's being in custody and the fear he would spill the beans *was* bothering him despite Philip's admission that they were not making any headway on that front. Vishal was aching to get to the office and find out what was happening. If possible give moral support to Verma by letting him know the STF had nothing concrete on him; killing him in custody was an option he had explored and discarded.

*For the moment, at least.*

Other than that, the morning had gone blazingly well. He was up at the crack of dawn, fresh and raring to go. Eager to prove a point to Leon, Vishal had gotten cracking on the rifles and bombs.

Aware that finding preassembled bombs was unlikely, he concentrated his hunt on bombmakers. It took him two hours to find one who was not in jail, had access to explosives, *and* was willing to do a rush job. Unwilling to reveal his identity to the bombmaker he called in a favor and got a constable to do it, one he had bailed out of a messy and suspicious shootout. Vishal was confident he would have the bombs by midnight.

With the sniper rifles he had been luckier; finding a factory-sealed box of three, complete with sniperscopes, at the Kapashera police station evidence room. They had been recovered from an arms dealer who made the mistake of crossing the wrong people and consequently was now pushing up the daisies. With him gone it was unlikely the guns would be called into court, hence would not be missed. Getting them out of the evidence room had meant cashing in some more chips with another willing-to-bend cop in that police station. Vishal was sure that the guns, too, would be in his hands by nightfall. He also knew that he was calling in too many markers for this mission. Too many for his own good.

"There is no way I can remain in India once this goes down," he told Leon when he called to update him. "I will need to get out of the country for sure." At Leon's noncommittal *uh-huh* he added, "I have given this a lot of thought. That's why I think it's only fair that you pay me at least a million dollars for helping you complete the project."

The silence this time stretched so long that Vishal thought the call had been dropped. "You there?" he asked.

"Yes," Leon responded finally. "Fine. I see your point, but a million is too much. I can do half that."

"It's not too much. Not if you want me to take on an active role," Vishal countered. "I'll be exposed to the same risk as you."

Some haggling eventually got them to agree on seven hundred thousand.

"Half now and half later?" Vishal asked, happy at the bargain he had struck. With that kind of money he actually looked forward to getting out of the country and starting afresh.

"Give me till tomorrow," Leon replied. "I can transfer the money to whichever account you want."

"I will send you the account details, but I'd like some in cash."

"Let's meet tomorrow then. I will message you when I have the cash ready."

But Vishal was increasingly uneasy after the call ended.

He was entering the office when the reason hit him.

"I would like to point out that not once in all his years as an assassin has Binder ever used an accomplice for anything other than support tasks." Ravinder's caution of two days ago echoed in his memory. "Even the few he used never saw him. The ones that laid eyes on him never lived to tell any tales."

The recollection sliced through Vishal like a hot knife through butter.

*Would Leon dare do that? When he needs me so much?*

Vishal pondered that.

*Nah! There is no way he can pull off the stadium job without me . . . He won't even be able to get hold of the rifles and bombs at such short notice.*

He felt better. But his mind seemed in no mood to relent.

*What if he doesn't really need me? What if he is stringing me along? What if I am just the fall guy?*

Philip emerged from the rear room where Ashok Verma was being held. He looked smug, as though he had cracked something, and Vishal's worry escalated even further.

# THREE

Leon was uneasy. Instinct warned him something was not kosher. Parked across the road, he again surveyed the house where he was to meet Nitin. It was a large, old-style bungalow, set toward the back of a large garden, which had not met the business end of a lawn mower for a while now. And the whole place had an air of disuse. It stood out like a sore thumb amidst the plush spacious houses lining both sides of Model Town, the kind of property builders acquire and convert into a garish glass-and-cement high-rise.

*Nitin the Nerd is sitting on some prime real estate. So why is it in such crappy condition?*

Only the twelve-foot-high boundary wall had been freshly painted. Then Leon spied the notice: large white letters painted on a black metal sheet, stuck to the top right of the metallic gate, informing the world the property was disputed in court.

*That's as good an explanation as any.*

But there was not a soul in sight.

"Strange." Leon muttered. *Nitin should be expecting me. We spoke barely an hour ago.* He rechecked his watch. *Perhaps because I am a bit early.*

But it still didn't feel right. Perhaps it was the knowledge that an APB was out for him; Leon had been on edge ever since Vishal's call last night. He surveyed the street again. Barring half a dozen cars parked sporadically, and the two security guards outside the house at the far end, the street was strangely devoid of life. Leon scanned the parked cars one by one.

*Empty.*

Still uneasy, he got out and headed for the gate. Alert. Ready to swing into action instantly. He was reaching for the doorbell when the gate clicked and began to swing open on well-oiled hinges. That's when Leon noticed the cameras, two of them. Well concealed. Leon guessed there were more. But Leon assessed even these two would cover the house frontage.

The front door cracked open and Nitin peered out, waving him on. Leon's grip on his pistol remained firm as he stepped up the pace.

"Any problem finding the place?"

"Not really." Leon shivered; it was even colder inside. A layer of dust covered everything; the living room hadn't been used in a while.

*The damn place looks like the set of a Hollywood horror movie.*

Nitin noticed his scrutiny. "No one comes here. Not since I put up that property in dispute notice." He jerked his thumb downward. "Let's go to the basement . . . my workplace."

Leon followed him past the dining room into what once would have been the wine cellar. Immediately the landscape altered; starting with the wooden stairs everything had been scrubbed clean. The wine racks had been replaced by long workstation type tables along the two longer sides of a brightly lit basement. Along the third wall, facing the door, was a study table; on it were a half-open Sony laptop, a printer-cum-scanner, a couple of mobile phones, and some newspapers. On the left of the door was a water dispenser and to the right a tea/coffeemaker. Leon automatically absorbed the surroundings.

*Nothing out of sync.*

But his unease declined to dissipate and he kept a tight grip on the pistol in his pocket. "Is my stuff ready?"

"All done." Nitin pointed at the workstation; neatly arranged on it were four sets of cordless microphones, Mac adaptors, and presentation clickers, all of different, popular brands. "All four sets have been paired." He picked up one set of all three items as Leon approached the table. "For easy identification all paired sets have been marked with these stickers." Nitin showed a circular cent-sized green sticker affixed to all three: the microphone, VGA adaptor, and presentation clicker. "All four sets have different color stickers. I've painted a dot with the same color on the flip side of all three items, just in case the sticker drops off." He showed those, too.

Leon nodded, reassured he would not kill himself because some stupid sticker manufacturer had decided to skimp on the adhesive.

"The sarin is in sealed glass vials placed inside the adaptors and the microphones."

"Safe to carry them around?"

"Very safe. The vials are thin enough to shatter when triggered, but thick enough to withstand routine handling." Nitin held up a microphone and shook it hard. "Though I wouldn't drop them on a hard floor if I were you." He gave a cheeky grin.

"Right!" Leon liked his sense of humor. However, his grip on the pistol stayed fast; something did not feel right.

*Or am I just being paranoid?*

Leon sensed the Batra incident had shaken him, but . . .

*Better to be paranoid and safe than sorry and six feet under.*

"Do they still work? I mean, as microphones and adaptors."

"Of course." Nitin tutted, giving him a pained *do-you-think-I'm-an-idiot?* look. "They will function normally till you arm the clicker and switch it to the weapon mode."

"Just asked." Leon smiled. "How do I switch modes?"

"To switch to weapon mode, turn off the clicker and hold down the pointer button for five seconds. To revert back to the normal presenter mode, slide the on/off button to on position. This way there will be no chance of an accident."

"Sounds great. How much gas in each?"

"Obviously the microphones are twice as large as the adaptors, so have bigger vials, but even the adaptors contain enough to do the job over five feet. The microphone would cover almost twice that distance."

Leon knew that would be enough.

"How does the clicker trigger them?"

"Once armed, the button to move slides forward and triggers the paired microphone." Nitin pointed it out. "And the slide-back button triggers the matching adaptor."

"At what range?"

"I have used the same radio receiver the clicker uses to pair with the laptop so it will definitely work up to sixty feet. Here . . . this is a dummy set . . . try it out. You can go to that corner." Completely engrossed in demonstrating his prowess, Nitin handed him a clicker. "This is already armed. To show you it works I have loaded a harmless green gas in both of these." He stooped to retrieve a microphone and adaptor from a toolbox kept under the table.

As Nitin was bending down to reach into his toolbox, Leon pocketed one of the other four clickers kept on the table and headed for the other end of the basement, about twenty-five feet away. While walking across he flicked it to off position and held down the pointer button for five seconds, ensuring it was armed.

Still focused on the test, Nitin asked, "Ready?"

"Ready." Nitin held up the trial set of adaptor and microphone, one in either hand. "Hit it."

Arming the trial clicker now, Leon used the slide-back button to trigger the adaptor. A ball of green gas exploded out of it. The gas hung like a cloud around Nitin's head for approximately a minute. Allowing it to dissipate Leon pressed the slide-forward button, triggering the microphone. The green cloud was bigger this time.

"You will notice this trial gas I've used also dissipates within a minute." Nitin tossed both expended items back in the toolbox; he looked as pleased and proud as though he had given birth. "That's how long sarin also takes. Enough to do the job."

"You are sure?" Leon had decided to use Sarin-AXR after considerable research, but he was also aware the Americans had decided against using this variant on the battlefield because of its limited effective time; the cost of weaponizing, storing, transporting, and delivering it to the target did not make Sarin-AXR a cost-effective tactical weapon.

"Very sure," Nitin replied confidently. "I tried it earlier on a dog. Even in the open air, it worked fine. Should be far more effective indoors."

Leon was putting the trial clicker on the study table when the newspaper on it caught his eye. On the bottom right corner of the front page were four photos; the ones Vishal had WhatsApp-ed him last night. Above them, in large bold letters were the words WANTED— EXTREMELY DANGEROUS. Below them was the reward amount. There seemed to be plenty of zeros in it.

*Enough to ignite greed in even the stoutest.*

Knowing an APB had been issued and seeing it are two different things; Leon felt a shock wave of anxiety.

*Has Nitin seen it?*

The paper was neatly folded over. But it looked like it had been opened. Leon couldn't be sure; his paranoia was in the driver's seat now.

*Will he call the cops?*

*Has he already done so?*

Leon paused, trying to turn a dozen contradictory factors into a decision.

*Does it matter?*

Leon realized it did not; it was too risky. Nitin had seen him and was the only one who could give away his target; the weapon made it obvious Masharrat had drawn the short straw. But Leon needed to know whether Nitin had already sold him out. And if the cops knew about the weaponized sarin.

Nitin sensed the change and tensed.

"I have seen that." Nitin pointed at the newspaper and made a dismissive gesture. "I know they're looking for you. But you should know I don't care."

"Have you called the cops yet?"

"Yet? *No!*" Nitin's tone was shrill with fear. "And I don't plan to either." He placed a hand on his heart. "I swear I have not. Why should I? It has nothing to do with me."

Leon liked the fat man and didn't want to kill him . . . *or anybody . . .* unless operationally unavoidable.

*But leaving him alive is too big a risk.*

Leon kept staring at him.

That unnerved Nitin. "Really. I don't care who you are or what you plan to do." He was pleading now. "I'm a professional, boss. You need something done and I do it. You pay me and I forget I ever met you."

Leon's indecision and Nitin's fear held both immobile.

"Look." Nitin was very anxious by now and sweating profusely. "Just take your stuff and go. Please don't pay me if you don't want to." Leon could hear Nitin's nervousness brim over; the words were tumbling out of him at hyperspeed. "I will forget I ever saw you."

"Sorry, old man." And Leon was; he *had* taken a liking to the fat, jovial man.

"Please," Nitin pleaded again, but a look of resignation had started to settle on his face. Then he sagged. *"Please."* Suddenly tearful. "I have three kids."

"I'm too close to the end. Cannot take a chance . . . you are the only one who . . ." Leon realized it did not matter; nothing he said would make it any different or easier for Nitin. Holding his breath, he hit the slide-forward button of the weaponized clicker.

Leon had no idea which of the microphones on the table it triggered off, but the impact on Nitin was dramatically spectacular. He first clutched his throat, as though suddenly short of breath. Then grabbed his heart with both hands, clawing at it. It must have stopped beating because, face contorted in pain, Nitin sagged and toppled over, hitting the ground with a loud crash.

With a handkerchief clapped to his nose Leon hung back and watched, mouthing the numbers as he counted off the seconds. But his eyes were riveted on Nitin, evaluating the impact of the chemical agent. As the count hit sixty, Leon noted with satisfaction that Nitin had behaved like someone having a heart attack. That was important; by time they figured out it wasn't one, Leon would have exited the venue and be safely on his way.

Leon kept counting till he hit two hundred and fifty. Now sure the sarin would have dissipated he removed the handkerchief from his nose, but his first breath was still tentative. Another two minutes elapsed before he could bring himself to approach the table. Carefully stepping past Nitin's body, Leon collected all the adaptors, microphones, and clickers, even the used one, and made his way out. He kept the used set separate; it would find its way to whichever dustbin or gutter he came across first. Leon did not want to leave any clues behind, either to his identity or those that could provide any insight into his plans.

# FOUR

Ravinder was happy to see Simran sitting up and talking to Mandeep when he entered the ICU.

"Happy birthday, Mom." Eagerly shouldering past him, Jasmine gave Simran a careful hug, mindful of the wires and tubes hooked into her.

"Thank you, sweetheart." Simran was putting on a brave front, but Ravinder noticed she was pale and looked drained. Even the doctor looked pensive. Jasmine also now picked that up; Ravinder saw her smile waver.

"How are you, Mom? You are looking tired. Didn't you sleep well?"

Simran's reply was lost to Ravinder since Mandeep accosted him. "Good morning, Mr. Gill. I was about to call you. We need to take her into surgery right away." His tone dropped. "The internal damage seems worse than we had thought."

"Oh!" Ravinder tensed.

"Don't worry about it, Ravinder," Simran chipped in. "Dr. Mandeep has already explained it all to me. It is nothing major. He has promised I will be home in a day or so. Right, Doctor?"

"That's right, ma'am." Mandeep gave her an encouraging smile. "And now if you will come with me, Mr. Gill, there is some paperwork we need to do."

"Dad, you spend some time with Mom. Let me take care of the paperwork." Jasmine accompanied Mandeep out.

Ravinder sat down beside her and took her hand when his mobile beeped. He turned it to silent, then checked; it was a text from Philip. He was about to return it to his pocket when Simran said, "I don't want you to stop what you are doing, Ravinder. I know how important this assignment is . . . for our country . . . and you." She gave his hand a squeeze. "And I *do* understand why you had to take it on." She must have noticed his look, because she added, "I really do, Ravinder. It is just that I worry for you . . . more so since Ruby's death." Perhaps Simran had wanted to say this out loud for a long time, because Ravinder saw her take a deep breath and plunge ahead. "But you do understand that we worry for you. We need you more than you can ever imagine . . . especially Jasmine. I have no idea what she would do if something happened to you. That girl dotes on you. Always has."

"Nothing will happen to me. Please don't worry, Simran." Ravinder gripped her hand tighter. "And Jasmine is a very brave girl."

"You think?" Simran gave a wan smile. "Don't get fooled by that tough act she puts on. She is a softie at heart. Watch out for her, Ravinder."

"Of course I will. But right now it is you we are both worried about."

"Whoever did this could try again. Right?"

Ravinder knew that was true, but didn't know how to say it. He simply nodded.

"You have to find them and stop them before they hurt our baby," Simran said insistently.

"I promise. Nothing will happen to her. Or you." Ravinder took her hand in both his own. "For now, please focus on getting better. You're looking tired. I want you to close your eyes and get some rest."

Simran must have been more tired than she was letting on, because she closed her eyes without demur. They sat in silence, within touching reach. Simran's hand felt warm in his. Ravinder felt a sudden urge to kiss her. Mindful of the nurses around, he settled for caressing her brow. His touch made her smile.

"Talk to me, Ravinder," Simran murmured, her eyes still shut.

"What about?"

"Anything. Whatever is on your mind . . . even the assignment if you want . . . if you can . . . it doesn't matter . . . I just want to hear you. Recently we have not being doing enough of that. I miss that a lot."

"I thought I was the one who liked listening and you the talking." Her eyes still shut, Simran smiled.

"This assignment is a real pain." Ravinder was surprised how badly he wanted to talk about it. "Honestly, I am not sure how I feel about protecting these two Pakis. I detest them at a visceral level . . . they have both done so much harm to our country." Ravinder was surprised that this was the first thing that came out of him; he realized how deeply that had been bothering him.

"Will that stop you from what you need to do?"

"No," Ravinder replied firmly. "India will suffer a lot if something happens to them while they're here. At the very least, our reputation will be shot to hell. And in the worst case . . . there could be a war." That brought a short silence between them. "But the more crucial problem is time. It is too short, much too short. Especially when we are up against someone as sharp as Leon Binder."

"So that's who he is." Simran opened her eyes. "The other night, you spoke his name several times when you were asleep."

"I knew him . . . back from when we were in college in London. The three of us had been best friends . . . Edward, Leon, and I."

"So how did he end up doing this kind of dirty work?"

"Leon?" Ravinder mulled, wondering how much he could share. And whether he could really explain what had happened back then. How Edward had gone berserk when Farah died. "It's a long story."

"I see. But that must make it tough."

Something in her tone made him look up. He suddenly felt unsure. "Did I say anything else in my sleep?"

"You did take another name." He saw Simran search her memory. "Farah. I think. Yes, it was Farah. Who is she?"

"Edward, Leon, and I shared an apartment when we were in college. Farah was Edward's fiancée." The urge to unburden his misgivings ripped at him.

"Was?"

"She's dead . . . died many years ago."

"Oh!"

Unsure, he paused, saw the query in Simran's eyes, and felt he could not stop now. "One day I returned home early and caught Leon raping Farah. I intervened. We had a big fight, during which Farah was killed."

"Oh," Simran repeated. She was listening with wide-eyed attention now. "Then?"

"It was my testimony that got Leon convicted. He got life."

"Well, he got what he deserved. Rape is unspeakable, and what could be worse than murder? No excuse for either."

"It is not that simple . . ." Ravinder was bursting, aching to share his confusion. Ravinder's dilemma was even deeper since he was the one who'd brought the poker into the fight, though he was pretty sure it was Leon who'd snatched it from him and lashed out. In fact, he was not even sure if there was anything for him to be guilty about. Just that nagging doubt, which all these years had not been able to wash away. "Later, after the case was over, too many stories about Farah surfaced . . . I'm not sure if Leon had actually been raping her . . . perhaps they had been having consensual sex."

"Oh. I see." Simran looked momentarily confused. "Even so, how would that condone his killing her?"

*But Leon kept insisting he didn't kill her.*

*But what else would he say? Every damn criminal believes he's innocent.*

Ravinder's defense mechanism sprang into the battle, valiantly pushing back his doubts. And he was suddenly worried, insecure what Simran would think of him. The very idea that she would think less of him was agonizing; it pulverized Ravinder. "But you see . . ."

Simran sensed his confusion. "You are not sure if you did the right thing by testifying?" she asked gently, sensing his turmoil and eager to help.

"Simran, I don't know how to explain it to you." Ravinder's courage was depleting rapidly, but he sensed that if he stopped now he would never be able to unburden and rid himself of this doubt. "Edward and his family really put a lot of pressure on me . . . I know I did the right thing, but . . . yet . . . I feel guilty."

"Understandably so. Like Edward, Leon was also your friend. It is perfectly normal to feel bad." Simran nodded sympathetically. "But I do want you to know this . . . I know you well, Ravinder. I know you will always do the right thing. Just trust your instincts. Always."

Simran's words struck Ravinder like hammer blows. He remembered the last time she had said that to him—just a few months ago, hours before Ruby had attacked the Peace Summit. And he'd had to shoot Ruby down . . . his daughter . . . his own flesh and blood . . . someone he would have died to protect.

*That did not end well, Simran.*

He wanted to tell her.

*I did trust my instincts that time, too.*

264 | MUKUL DEVA

Now almost tearful.

*But it did not end well at all.*

"I don't know, Simran." The words jerked out, a fractured whisper. "I don't know at all. I am not even sure I want to continue this assignment. Not after all this." Ravinder waved at the tubes and wires plugged into her. "I don't know if I can focus on it . . . not with you like this . . . and Jasmine also hurting so badly."

"See it through, Ravinder." Generations of the martial blood that coursed through Simran's veins now manifested itself in her voice. "You not only have to see it through, but show them your metal. Win."

The tone, more than the words, reinforced him. Her eyes held his, steeling him. Ravinder nodded, tentatively at first. Then with increasing confidence. When he finally spoke, there was no longer any doubt in his voice. "I will, Simran."

Her fingers tightened on his. That drove away the last of his fears. He knew he wanted to unburden; he could no longer bear the thought of carrying this guilt . . . this *doubt* . . . on his own.

"Simran, I feel guilty about Leon . . . especially since Edward's call the other night . . . I feel I may have wronged him." His tongue thickened, almost halting him, but he plowed on. "I have always tried to avoid thinking about that day. I don't think I would have if Leon hadn't resurfaced. But . . ." He faltered. Simran's hand squeeze bolstered his courage again. ". . . sometimes I am not sure whose blow actually killed Farah." The silence between them was now complete. Only the beeping of the monitors strewn around the ICU intervened. Ravinder could not bring himself to meet Simran's eyes, to even look at her. "Leon kept insisting he had not been the one . . ."

Then Ravinder realized that one of the monitors had begun to screech, a never-ending high-pitched whine that made the hairs in his ears dance. He realized it was the one attached to Simran only when two nurses rushed up.

"Please move back, sir." One of them pushed him back, none too gently.

Horrified, Ravinder looked up at the monitor and saw that the wavy line on the screen was now a long flat one. Before he could process that, the ICU doors swung open and Mandeep raced in. Another doctor followed, Jasmine behind them. She froze at the door. The expression on her face brought home the message to Ravinder. His mind noticed and acknowledged the message. His heart rejected the implication immediately.

As though from far away he watched the doctors first shock Simran and then try to revive her with an injection to her heart. But Simran did not stir. He was not sure how much time had elapsed, but suddenly realized the monitor was no longer screaming out its alarm. It had been disconnected and was now blank. Dark. Lifeless.

He swayed.

Felt Jasmine by his side, clutching his arm.

The last thing he saw was the worry on her face and the tears in her eyes.

Then he entered the heart of darkness.

# FIVE

Leon was driving near the ITO Building when he remembered the CCTV cameras at Nitin's house.

*Damn!*

He felt like kicking himself. But he knew there was no option; he had to go back and get rid of the recordings, if any.

*Otherwise the next APB the cops put out would have a far more easily identifiable photo.*

Cursing, he U-turned at the next traffic island and headed back, aware this slip would cost him two hours at least. And revisiting a crime scene was as asinine an idea as any.

*Would anyone else have come around by now? Had the body been found? Would the cops already be there? What if they had found the CCTV tapes . . . what then?*

The questions and his anxiety mounted as Nitin's house came closer.

# SIX

Vishal was thrilled when Philip asked him to help interrogate Ashok Verma, confident he would now get the opportunity to bolster Ashok up.

They were heading for the cell where Verma was being held when Archana called out. "Guys, we need to get to the hospital immediately." She looked tearful. "Boss has lost his wife."

That halted Philip in mid-stride. Vishal realized he needed to show empathy when he saw Philip's expression. Even Saina, at the other end of the room, looked stricken. Pulling a matching expression on his face, he said, "Oh, that's terrible."

"Archana, I want you to hold the fort with Gyan." Philip took charge decisively. "The rest of us will go to the hospital."

"I would like to come with you, sir." Gyan spoke as softly as always; however, Vishal saw from his expression that he would not take no for an answer. "I have been with Mr. Gill for years. I want to go."

Philip did not hesitate. "Put two of your best men to guard him." He chucked his chin toward Verma's cell.

Five minutes later, bundled into the office minivan, they were headed for the hospital. Gyan, at the wheel, had the siren going full blast and kept his huge foot pressed on the accelerator.

Behind him, Vishal wondered how he should pass on the news to Leon. And how Leon would react. Then he remembered the APB was out.

*I hope the bugger is careful. If he gets caught, I get screwed.*

Aware that Archana had done a remarkable job on the APB photos, Vishal knew Leon would have a challenge moving about now; every cop they could spare was on the lookout.

*Who will pay me if he gets caught? Fatima? Not bloody likely!*

That thought depressed him even more.

Then the minivan screeched to a halt in the AIIMS parking lot and they ran into the VIP ward. The first thing Vishal noticed was the TV in the lobby. It was running a special bulletin. Plastered all over was Leon's face, in all four variants that Archana had generated.

*Even a blind fuck will not have a problem recognizing him.*

Vishal mumbled an excuse and veered toward the bathroom, the urge to call Leon irresistible. However, once in the toilet, unwilling to run the risk of being overheard, Vishal sent Leon a text.

*Ravinder's wife is dead. We need to talk. Will let you know soon as it is safe to speak.*

He was about to rejoin the others when it struck him that it would be smart to collect his money soonest, in case Leon was captured or killed. So he sent another text asking if they could meet that evening to collect his cash instead of the next day as they had planned earlier.

# SEVEN

Jasmine felt her father go limp. The sudden weight as he blacked out staggered her. She would have fallen if Mandeep hadn't rushed forward and caught Ravinder. With the help of a nurse they laid him on an empty bed adjacent to Simran's. The sight of both her parents laying there, one lifeless and the other nearly so, terrified Jasmine. She wanted to scream, to cry, to wring her hands and tear her hair. Anything. Instead she turned to Mandeep. "He will be okay." She delivered that flatly, as a statement, not a question.

"Yes." Mandeep was looking at her strangely, perhaps because she seemed in complete control of herself. "He is in shock."

She absorbed that. Nodded.

"I will need to sedate him," Mandeep added. "If you are okay with that."

"Please do whatever is required." Jasmine could not take her eyes off Simran. "My father relied on her totally . . . I am not sure if even he knew how much."

Mandeep wasn't sure she was talking to him, but he nodded, worried she, too, was in shock. "I think you should sit down. Perhaps lie down for a bit."

Again, it was a while before she answered, as though it was taking time for his words to reach wherever she had gone. "No. Not yet." Pause. "As Dad would say, this is my watch now."

Crossing over, she pulled a chair between her parents and sat down, reaching out and taking one hand each of theirs in her own. She watched expressionlessly as Mandeep gave Ravinder a sedative and then stood beside her, unsure if he should leave her alone. Then the nurse came up to cover Simran's face.

"Let it be, Sister." Jasmine's tone was firm and sharp, making it clear she would not allow that. "I will do that. Later."

The nurse backed away as though she had been stung.

Mandeep made a placating gesture.

For a long moment silence reigned.

Mandeep shifted from one foot to the other, awkward and unsure if his presence was an intrusion. Jasmine seemed oblivious to him. In fact, to everything around her. But when he made to leave, Jasmine's voice stopped him. Though she was still looking at her mother when she spoke.

"Doctor, my mother wanted her organs to be donated . . . whatever could be of use. Could you? Please."

"Of course." Again Mandeep seemed struck by her icy control. "But are you sure?" She nodded curtly, eyes still on Simran. "We will need all the paperwork."

"We have the paperwork. I am the one who drafted her will." She halted suddenly. "Mom always said there is no point in having a lawyer in the family if one can't get a free will." Her voice faltered. Mandeep thought her poise would shatter. He hoped it would, aware Jasmine needed the release. But it did not. "I will give you a copy of her bequest and sign whatever release is required."

"I will take care of it right away, then."

"And please don't allow anyone to disturb my father. He needs to rest." With that, Jasmine got up and left the ICU. She moved stiffly, as though recovering from a spinal injury.

It was only when she was safely locked inside one of the toilet cubicles that she allowed herself to cry. But silently. Aware it was her watch now. And Ravinder needed her. So did Simran. There was much to be done. Her father had to be looked after; she knew how hard he had been hit. Her mother's funeral. And handling all those relatives.

By time she came out of the bathroom she was ready to take it all on.

# EIGHT

Leon carried out two passes of the Nitin bungalow before he was satisfied it was as he had left it.

*Perhaps not so surprising—Nitin* had *mentioned no one ever came here*.

Nonetheless, hand on pistol and senses on red alert, he went through the gates and into the house; the horror movie set feel was now much stronger. Pushing it aside, he went down to the basement.

Nitin lay where he had fallen.

Leon was unable to stop himself from looking at the body. It suddenly struck him that never once, in all these years, had he ever had to revisit one of his victims. Till now, barring catching glimpses of them on the television, life had never brought him face-to-face with those he had sent to their deaths.

Strangely, death did not seem to have deflated Nitin. Barring his face, which was still twisted in a grimace with a faint trickle of saliva down one side of his half-open mouth, he could well have been asleep. Possibly because of the cold, he had not yet started to smell. Not badly, anyway.

*Just a faint whiff of . . . What? What* does *death smell like?*

Leon realized he was about to take a deep sniff. He shivered. As though someone had dragged sharp nails down his back. Shook himself, trying hard to push away the ghostly feeling, which threatened to unseat him. Failed. Tried again harder, and finally managed to look away.

Ensuring he did not look at Nitin again, Leon surveyed the room. There was no obvious wiring to indicate where the cameras were sending in their feed. However, Leon knew it had to be displayed on some monitor, and the laptop on the study table was the only available option. Leon flipped open the half-closed lid and tapped the keyboard. It emerged from sleep mode. The main gate and garden sprang sharply into focus. Both lay still. As Leon watched, a crow alighted on the grass and pecked at something. Everything outside looked so serene, so normal.

With a start Leon realized that he was losing time. Opening the finder he began to scan the files. Knowing he was looking for large video files made the task easier, and it took only a couple of minutes to find where the feed was stored. Shutting off the cameras, Leon deleted the files and emptied the trash can. He was about to close the laptop but was uneasy, unsure if the data could still be recovered. Disconnecting the power cord he took the laptop with him. Still keeping his eyes averted from Nitin's body he made his way back to the car and hit the road again.

He was halted at the traffic light near Tis Hazari when his mobile informed him a text had been received.

*Ravinder's wife is dead. We need to talk. Will let you know soon as it is safe to speak.*

Vishal's message stared at him. Leon realized the traffic light had turned green only when the car behind honked, a long impatient blast. With a start Leon drove ahead, his mind in a whirl, surprised he did not feel the satisfaction he had assumed he would.

Spotting a break in traffic Leon pulled off the road and looked at Vishal's text again.

*Nothing!*

He tried to imagine the pain Ravinder was feeling. That brought him *some* satisfaction, but just a teeny bit and only fleetingly. For some silly reason that he was unable to rationalize, Leon could not get rid of the feeling that what he had done was cheap. Unwarriorlike. Unmanly.

*Not cricket, old chap.*

That is when Leon realized this was also the first time he had ordered a woman's death. And that too many people had been killed on this mission. Usually Leon ensured the target was the first, and more often than not, the only one to die. Too many deaths always attracted undue attention, something Leon avoided at all costs.

*But this time?*

*Too many bloody firsts on this mission.*

Leon cursed.

*I should not have taken on this assignment.*

His mobile beeped again, a second text from Vishal asking if they could meet later at night and if he could get some cash. Leon sensed Vishal's anxiety even in the bland message.

*And I should not have given Vishal such a free rein. The slimeball is hedging his bets . . . in case I am taken.*

That angered him.

*I will not be stopped. Or taken down. Not this time. And definitely not by Ravinder the Cloth Head or Edward the Anal.*

Their nicknames, from all those years ago, came back effortlessly. Then they had been used in jest. Now they were spiked with hatred.

The admixture of anger and hatred blew away his doubts and misgivings, egging him on.

# NINE

Jasmine, now more composed and having cleaned up as best she could, ran into the task force officers as she was heading back to the ICU. Barring Chance, whom she had met briefly a few months ago, the others were strangers. Chance and she exchanged strained nods. Jasmine wanted them to go away, to leave her father alone, but knew they were here to show their support. She was wondering what to say when the man to Chance's right stepped forward.

"Hullo, miss. I am Philip Cherian. We all work with your father." He waved at the others. "Deeply sorry about your loss."

Jasmine nodded, not trusting herself to speak.

"Please tell me how we can help."

Jasmine's mind was still blank; she could think of nothing to say.

"Perhaps we can help with the funeral arrangements," Philip suggested gently.

It was the word funeral that broke Jasmine's inertia. "Thank you very much, Mr. Cherian. I . . . *we* really appreciate that, but my aunt is already here and others from our family are on the way." The awkwardness returned with the silence. "I am sure my father would be most grateful if you all kept the work going." Jasmine was fidgeting, now keen to get back to Ravinder. "I understand you all are working on something very important . . . perhaps it would be best if you took care of that."

Philip sensed her discomfort and anguish; however, before he could respond, his mobile vibrated. He saw the call was from the NIA director. "Please tell your father we will do our best," Philip promised her. "And please don't hesitate to reach out if there is anything we can do. Anything at all." Excusing himself, he rushed out to take Kurup's call.

Giving the others an awkward nod, Jasmine headed back in, not looking forward to what awaited her there, but aware she needed to take charge. She was at the door when she turned back and said to them, "Please find the person responsible for killing my mother." But the request was delivered very gently, without any heat or drama. As blandly as though she were asking one of them to pass the salt.

She saw them staring at her. Finally one of the women, Saina, nodded. "We will. I promise you that."

Jasmine thanked her and resumed her journey back in to the ICU.

# TEN

Suresh was not sure what bothered him more, Ravinder's personal loss or that the Special Task Force was again leaderless and he had run out of options on that count. He was aware that with barely forty-eight hours left for both targets to reach Delhi, there was no time to bring in a new man.

"You will have to take charge, Philip. I will personally support you every step of the way."

"Thank you, sir." Suresh sensed Philip's unease; Philip was a competent man, but he had never been in independent charge yet, especially not in such a high-stakes operation. "I will do my best, sir."

"That's all I want, Philip. Give it your best shot."

"Roger, sir." Philip sounded a tad more confident.

"Update me. Where exactly are we?"

"We have gotten an APB out for Leon Binder."

"Yes, I saw that. Good work," Suresh encouraged him.

"Ashok Verma is in custody. He hasn't said anything yet, but we are working on him. If he is the mole then we should be able to get some tangible leads to Binder."

"Would you like me to come down and talk to him?"

"Not yet, sir. Give me a little more time."

*That is exactly what we don't have,* Kurup wanted to tell him, but realizing Philip was already shaky, he held back on that. Instead he asked, "Anything on Fatima Basheer?"

"Basheer?" Philip was nonplussed. "I was not aware we were looking for her. Is she here? In India?"

"Oh! But the alert was issued from your office." Suresh checked. "It has been signed off by Archana."

"Ravinder must have briefed her directly." Philip realized Ravinder had forgotten to brief him. "Give me a minute, sir." Suresh heard him call out to Archana and then talk. "Archana confirms we have checked almost seventy percent of the hotels. Those remaining will be done today, sir."

"Okay. Keep me posted. What else?"

"Nothing on the Goel case yet, but we have come up with some leads on the truck that was involved in the hit-and-run on Mr. Gill's family."

"That's good. He may lead us to Binder." But Suresh did not sound hopeful, aware it was too long a shot; Leon would not have exposed himself that way.

Perhaps that came across more strongly than he realized. Feeling pressured and keen to exhibit some progress, Philip added, "Our team has also reevaluated the security plans and the threat perception. Mr. Gill wanted to send them to you. We believe they would help identify weaknesses that Binder could exploit."

"That's useful. Send them right away, Philip. Keep me posted on the progress . . . at least twice a day . . . and if something comes up, no matter what the time."

# ELEVEN

Philip felt even more pressured when the call ended, aware he had very little time left.

"Anything wrong?"

Philip became aware his team was ringed around him. Everyone looked tense. Vishal, who had asked the question, looked most anxious.

"That was the NIA director." Philip used his most reassuring tone, desperate to show he was in control. Failed. "He wanted to know where we were in terms of finding Binder."

"What was that about Fatima Basheer? Anything on her?"

Again, Philip noted that Vishal looked unduly stressed.

"Why didn't you tell me that Mr. Gill had asked you to put an alert out for Basheer?" Philip confronted Archana, peeved. "We all need to be on the same page. I did not even know she was in Delhi."

"Sorry. I assumed Mr. Gill had briefed you all."

"Fine." Philip saw it was a pointless discussion. "Let us leave it here. Please ensure they finish searching all the hotels today."

"I just rechecked with the cops. They have only a few hotels left now."

"Good. If that woman is here I want her found. Alive."

# TWELVE

Vishal felt as though he was caught in an inexorably tightening vise: Verma in custody, the APB out for Leon, insecurity about Leon's intentions, and now the noose tightening on Fatima.

*How much worse could it get?*

He had already given up on the idea of being able to stay on in India after this mission. However, with Leon and Fatima both under threat of capture, there was now a big question mark on the payment he was to receive from them.

*Without that I am screwed. Without that payout there is no way I can get out of this shit hole.*

Suddenly, the tunnel had become a lot darker. Then he realized Philip was addressing him.

"Vishal, we need to break Verma. I've been talking to Saina and she's certain Sikander Ali was not the mole."

"Hardly surprising. They were related."

"No. His death doesn't jell, and she is willing to stake her life on it."

But Vishal noticed he did not sound very sure. Eager to fan this spark of doubt, Vishal made a moue, but kept silent.

Philip continued, "I tend to agree with her. Assuming *that* is true, then Verma has to be the mole. And if he is . . . the bastard has a lot to pay for."

Vishal noted the STF second-in-command's determination and his despair deepened; he cursed Saina silently.

Then Philip inadvertently threw him a lifeline. "You want to help me with Verma's interrogation?"

Vishal clutched at the sudden lifeline with both hands. "Sure. Let me at him." He felt charged up. "I will kill the bastard if he doesn't talk."

"No killing." But Philip's smile was bleak; he was clearly feeling the pressure. "We still don't know for sure if he is the mole."

"Let us find out then, shall we?"

In his excitement, Vishal forgot to send Fatima the warning he had wanted to.

# THIRTEEN

Fatima was going stir-crazy. She was fed up with hanging around her hotel room. The wait was frustrating. Even more aggravating was that neither Vishal nor Leon was keeping her in the loop.

Despite repeated reminders and threats Vishal had given her nothing tangible, though he did call in. She had contemplated confronting him, but their altercation on the first night had left her with no appetite for a repeat performance.

Likewise, the rude manner in which Leon had warned her to steer clear had really upset her. Unwilling to spook him again, she had stayed away.

That left her with little to do. Several times in the past two days she had considered joining the other SOB leaders in Dubai; however, her hunger for witnessing the results of her vendetta firsthand kept her in Delhi.

Bored stiff, she threw on a T-shirt, jeans, and sneakers and headed down from her suite on the fourth floor.

*Shopping is always therapeutic.*

She was crossing the lobby when she saw one of the ladies at the front desk point her out. It was done discreetly and Fatima would probably not have noticed if her attention had not been drawn to the two men talking to the receptionist; their demeanor gave them away faster than any uniform could. They reminded her of the way Vishal carried himself: with that same authority, arrogance, and assurance. Intuition warned her they were cops. Panic seized Fatima when the duo left the reception and purposefully advanced on her. One of them waved to her. "Madam, could we have a word with you?"

Without further thought she turned and ran.

Surprise gave her a head start and fear lent her wings.

This was the sixteenth hotel these two cops were visiting since morning and about the fiftieth since yesterday. At each one, they had been pointed to one or two probable Fatima Basheers. Each lead had to be investigated. So far, all had proven false. By now both were bored stiff and expecting to draw another blank. They watched openmouthed as Fatima fled through the lobby.

By the time they got over their surprise Fatima had already cleared the entrance and was racing toward the road. They gave chase.

Like most luxury hotels, the entrance to the main lobby of the Maurya Sheraton was set at a distance from the main road, linked to it by a C-shaped drive.

Bursting past the surprised doorman and the valet parking attendants, Fatima fled toward the main road. She had not yet given thought to where she was headed, just that she needed to put the maximum distance possible between herself and the cops.

Hitting the main road she raced across it, keen to get to the other side, aware that would automatically put any vehicle bound pursuit at a disadvantage.

The traffic light half a mile down the road was red, so she got a clear run to the median bisecting the road. However, there was no traffic light on the other side, and traffic coming down the Dhaula Kuan overpass tends to move fast.

Despite her panicked run, Fatima cleared the first three cars as she navigated the first of the three lanes in that half of the road. It was the fourth car that struck her, a glancing blow. Fatima staggered, almost fell, but managed to regain her footing and continued her mad dash, straight into the fifth car that was close behind the fourth.

The impact picked her up and propelled her forward. Her own momentum kept her going toward the other end of the road. Consequently, she landed almost plumb in the middle of the third lane, the bus lane, just a few feet from the edge of the road, and safety. But it was a few feet too far.

The incoming bus could not have stopped even if it had wanted to; the startled driver had no warning. In all fairness he tried, slamming down and almost standing on the brakes. But it was too little, too late.

The bus mowed her down. By the time the brakes locked down the wheels, more than half the bus had crossed over Fatima. She was still alive when the huge, bulbous differential struck her head, literally pulping it.

# FOURTEEN

Vishal was not sure whether he was relieved that Fatima Basheer would not be telling any tales or depressed that he would not be getting paid the promised extra for acting as her eyes and ears.

"Are they sure, Philip?" he could not help asking. "Is she really dead?"

"What's there to be sure about?" Philip sounded tired and frustrated. "There is nothing left of her head."

"Just asked." Vishal pretended to mirror his exasperation. "If she had been alive we could have questioned her and gotten somewhere."

"If . . . " Philip sighed. "We are simply not getting any breaks."

"We will." Vishal forced an encouraging smile. "Soon."

"Let's hope so." Then Philip turned to Saina in the rear seat. "Get to the hotel and go through her room. Take it apart. There has to be something there. Everyone leaves a clue."

"Why can't I help to interrogate Verma instead of Vishal?" Saina replied defiantly. "He can go search her room."

"Because you are taking this too personally." Philip said sharply. A tense silence held till they drew up outside the office. As they were getting out, Philip said to her, "Don't worry, Saina, if Verma is guilty, we will find out. I promise you that. And then we will also find out who killed your brother-in-law. Okay?"

"Okay." But she still looked sullen as she drove away.

"Phew!" Vishal tried to dissipate the tension. "She is taking it badly."

"So would you, Vishal, if it had been your brother-in-law." Archana threw him a look of distaste as she walked away.

Vishal felt a surge of anger, but aware Philip was watching him, checked it. "Damn! What's with them today? Both seem to be PMS-ing."

Ignoring that, Philip led the way in. "Let's get cracking. We have just hours left before this spins completely out of control."

So anxious was he to find out how Verma was faring that Vishal completely forgot to let Leon know that Fatima had been knocked out of the game.

# FIFTEEN

Jasmine walked up to the ICU to see a cluster of aunts and uncles by the door, held at bay by a stern-faced nurse. Jasmine had expected them and knew they meant well, but she had no idea how to deal with them.

"You poor child." The aunt, a distant cousin of her mother's who spotted her first, descended upon her like a falcon. "How are you doing?"

*What a dumb question! Given the circumstances, how could I be doing?*

Jasmine had no idea what to say. Luckily she did not need to say anything; her relatives fussed around, doing it for her.

Soon Jasmine could not stand it any longer; she needed time with her father and, though she did not realize how badly, time to process her own grief. Because she felt the need to be strong for Ravinder, her sorrow was still trapped in her head, aching to be allowed access to her heart.

Just then two more aunts and uncles arrived, her father's brothers and their spouses. She saw them headed her way and seized the opportunity.

"Thank God you are here. I need your help with the funeral arrangements."

"Leave them to us." The elder uncle manfully took charge.

"I will take care of everything at the gurudwara sahib," said the second.

"Thank you." Jasmine felt a weight lift off her. "Then I will go and see how Dad is faring."

"Take it easy. You are not alone, Jasmine." Aunty Harmala's tender touch almost shattered Jasmine's composure. Fighting back her tears she ran in and threw herself into the chair by Ravinder's bed.

She did not realize she was sitting ramrod straight. Alert. Like a goalkeeper preparing to stop a penalty shootout.

# SIXTEEN

Vishal followed Philip to the cell where Verma was being held. He was again worried that Verma, in his current state, might let slip something that could give him away. Vishal was also not sure whether to pretend he did not know Ashok Verma or let on that he did.

*It is bound to come out sooner rather than later.* In fact, Vishal was surprised it had not already come to the notice of the Special Task Force or the National Intelligence Agency.

Deciding to stay as close to the truth as possible, he confronted Verma as soon as they entered the interrogation room. "How could you of all the people get involved in this nonsense?"

"I have no idea what the hell you are talking about, Vishal," Verma retorted angrily. "And I demand to speak to my director. Mr. Kurup will have your balls for breakfast when he learns about this. How dare you people . . ."

"Mr. Kurup is already aware you are in custody," Philip added calmly. "And I suggest you stop kidding yourself and start talking. It will be better for you if you help us find Binder. We have enough proof of . . ."

"*Proof?* You have proof?" Verma exploded.

Vishal was relieved that Verma did not fall for that. He was aching to give him some kind of reassurance, but with Gyan standing watchfully in one corner and Philip beside him, dared not.

"Show me the proof, then. And while you are at it, get me my lawyer. I am going to make all of you pay for this . . . especially you, Cherian." Verma shot them both an indignant glare.

But looking past Verma's bluster, Vishal sensed he was shaken; sleep deprivation and the nonstop questioning had started having an impact him. As Philip went at him, gentle but firm and relentless, Vishal again wondered how long Verma would last.

*He will talk. Everybody does. It is just a matter of time.*

Vishal did not need to check his watch, keenly aware forty-eight hours from now it would all be over. If luck held he would be on his way out of the country by then. An anti-terrorism veteran, Vishal did not need much time or effort to plan his getaway; either Nepal or Sri Lanka would provide him the anonymity he would need to lie low till things cooled off.

*I should be fine as long as I ensure Leon passes me some serious cash tomorrow.*

That reminded Vishal he needed to check on the sniper rifles and the bombs. He had to get them into the stadium before first light tomorrow; after that, the stadium would be sealed off.

"Would you like some tea?" Vishal heard Philip ask. When Verma nodded, Philip gestured to Gyan, who stepped out. "Look, Mr. Verma, we don't have a problem with you," Philip continued in that reasonable tone, which went well with the good-cop position he had adopted for this interrogation. "It is Leon Binder we are after. Help us find him and . . ."

Verma cut him off brusquely. "Binder? I have never set eyes on him. All I know is what MI6 passed on to us."

"Come on . . ."

Verma again interrupted aggressively. "You can keep asking me till you are hoarse, but I have no idea where he is."

Then Philip's mobile buzzed. He checked the calling number, mouthed "the director" to Vishal, and stepped out to take the call.

Double-checking that they were alone and already aware the room was bug-free, Vishal seized the opportunity. "Stay calm and keep your head," he hissed to Verma.

"Easy for you to say that," Verma shot back angrily.

"Keep it down, for fuck's sake." Alarmed, Vishal hushed him. "They have nothing on you. You are safe as long as you keep your mouth shut."

"I know they have nothing on me." Verma lowered his tone. "Get me out of here."

"I am trying to figure out how. Just give me a little more time."

"Hurry up, you . . ."

Vishal heard the door opening. "Don't think we will give up." He cut Verma off. "If you help us find Binder, it will go easy on you."

Gyan came in and put down a cup of tea in front of Verma.

Two hours later, Philip was still patiently plugging away at Verma when Saina joined them.

"Nothing that I could find in Fatima's hotel room except a camera . . . unfortunately one of those older models that uses film. But Archana is working on it right now," she murmured to Philip as she pulled up a chair beside him. "The mobile is clean, but we are tracking all calls made and received on it."

*Shit!* Vishal almost cursed aloud, remembering his second mobile number would be amongst those found on Fatima's phone. It was a backup phone, one of several he'd procured at the start of this operation, but . . . *I need to get rid of it immediately.*

He was about to make an excuse and leave the room to do so when Saina lit into Verma.

"That Paki bitch who was paying you is dead," she yelled at Verma, obviously hoping to shock him. "Soon you will be too."

Bolstered by Vishal's reassurances, Verma, who had just started showing signs of stability, blanched. He managed to hold his tongue, but Vishal sensed he was struggling.

Realizing it was too stressful and depressing to watch this, Vishal decided to leave. He had hoped Verma would stay calm and steady after he had pepped him up, but watching Saina tearing him a new arsehole, he was not sure anymore.

# SEVENTEEN

Leon was trying Baxter's phone for the fifth time when the television news came on. The TV was tuned to NDTV News.

Pakistanis killed in suspicious circumstances in India always generate a lot of media attention. Fatima Basheer getting her head pulped in broad daylight on a heavily trafficked road while fleeing the police was a surefire headline item. It had set loose a storm of speculation, from ISI agents running rampant in the national capital planning more terror attacks to Paki drug peddlers trying to corrupt Indian youth.

Leon upped the volume and watched footage of Fatima's nearly headless body being carried away on a blood-soaked stretcher as an excited female reporter breathlessly narrated, "Identified as Fatima Basheer, a Pakistani national who had entered India on a fake passport, she had been fleeing the police when . . ."

Leon snapped off the television with a curse.

*Heck! This mission was jinxed right from the start. I should never have gotten involved. How the hell do I get paid now?*

But he was surprised that a hint of sadness laced the irritation coursing through him. So surprised it took him a moment to become aware of it, and another, much longer moment to acknowledge it. That disturbed him more than the emotion.

*Not too late even now. Perhaps I should just pull out.*

He rapidly reviewed that option; an hour to the airport and he could take the first flight out using the emergency set of documents.

*And give up this opportunity to get back at Ravinder and Edward?*

That stalled him.

*Revenge is a dish best eaten cold.*

*It's been almost thirty years. Any colder and it will be indigestible.*

He grinned. An icy, mirthless grin. Almost a grimace. Leon's mind urged him to make a run for the border. His heart egged him to stay on and see this mission through.

*Would life ever present such an opportunity again?*

*Unlikely.*

That turned the tide in favor of his heart.

*Besides, it is now only a matter of hours. Ravinder is out of the game. Vishal and Verma, both are dispensable. The weapon is ready with me. Even if Vishal fails to get the rifles and bombs into the stadium, I can bring down one target. All I need are the flight and hotel details from Baxter.*

His mind now made up, Leon reached for his mobile, removed the SIM card he had been using to communicate with Fatima and flushed it down the toilet. Inserting a fresh SIM card he dialed Baxter.

Leon was so surprised when Baxter answered on the very first ring that for a moment he didn't say anything.

"Hello," Baxter said for the third time, irritably.

"Where the hell have you been, Baxter?" Leon found his voice. "I have been trying you for *days.*"

"Sorry, guv. I got myself in a bit of a mess with the rent." Baxter cleared his throat sheepishly. "Bleeding landlord tossed me out. But don't worry, I did the work you asked me to. Would have called you, too, but your number was at home and I only just got back in."

"Give me the details." Leon felt relief flow through him, as though the gods had sent him a signal, telling him to go ahead. He jotted down the details of Professor Naug's flight into Delhi and the hotel he would check into.

*That's it. Now what could possibly go wrong?*

"And guv? Do you mind sending me a few bob soon?" Baxter asked unabashedly. "Things are a bit tight these days."

"When aren't they, Baxter?" It was a lot more than a few bob, but Leon was okay with that; for all his idiosyncrasies Baxter had been useful many times and could be again in the future. "Twenty-four hours tops. Usual way. Okay? Take care now."

But Leon was pensive when he sat down by the window and idly watched the world go by, on the road in front and the market across. Prominently visible was The Meat Locker's signboard. The light behind the M had failed, so it read THE EAT LOCKER now.

*Soon as I get clear from India I need to track down the other SOB leaders and get my money from them. And they had better bloody well pay . . . if they know what is good for them. But let me worry about that later.*

Throwing himself on the bed, Leon began to sift through the likely contingencies that could arise from now till the time he cleared Indian airspace. Darkness deepened, slowly engulfing the room around him. One by one, as he worked his way past every contingency he could think of, his confidence escalated. And Leon felt better than he ever had since he had set foot in Delhi. Then he realized he'd not yet been through Naug's file. Pulling it up on his iPad again he began to pore through it, memorizing relevant details.

# EIGHTEEN

Jasmine watched Ravinder sleep, scared to leave him alone.
*Or am I the one who is scared to be alone?*

Confused, she tried to blank her mind out. In vain.

Then Ravinder cried out in his sleep. And then again. She felt his anguish and held her own at bay. She realized Mandeep was by her side only when he tapped her shoulder lightly.

"Oh!" She started.

"Sorry. I didn't mean to startle you." The long day had taken its toll on Mandeep also. "I wanted you to know we've done everything as per your mother's wishes. Every usable organ has been removed. We already have a recipient for her heart and kidneys. And they're matching for the liver now."

"That's good." But Jasmine wasn't sure she really meant that; her heart was still refusing to feel.

"Her body is ready for . . . err . . . for tomorrow."

"May I see her?"

Perhaps it was her lifeless tone. Perhaps her lack of emotion. But Mandeep gave her a worried look. Jasmine noticed. "Are you sure you are okay?" he asked.

She nodded. Though she wanted to say, *No! I'm not okay. I'd like to lie down and sleep . . . and then wake up and find all this was only a bad dream.* Instead she nodded and asked again, "May I see my mother? Please."

"Why not wait for your father to wake up," Mandeep suggested, trying to let her know it wasn't a great idea. "I'm sure he would like to see her, too."

"I'd like to see her now." Jasmine glared, daring him.

"Okay." Realizing he wouldn't be able to dissuade her, Mandeep reluctantly led the way to the mortuary.

Barring the echo of their footsteps, nothing accompanied them down the narrow stone-paved corridor that led to the rear of the hospital. It was late, but the mortuary lights were on and several groups of people in various stages of bereavement flocked in and around it.

*Obviously death does not maintain any office hours.*

Jasmine felt an insane urge to laugh. But that vanished as they entered the icy cold room. She followed Mandeep to the long steel table at the far end. Her hands were steady as she peeled back the bedsheet covering Simran's face.

Jasmine saw they had cleaned her up. Mandeep seemed to have done an excellent job; it was hard to tell Simran's organs had been removed. But for the cotton swabs plugging her nostrils, she could have been sleeping.

*Why do they do that? Why plug the nostrils?*

Jasmine felt her mind wander.

*What is there left . . . to go in . . . or come out?*

She gave one final look, but could not see any traces of her mother in that cold, lifeless body. Covering Simran's face she turned to Mandeep. "Thank you. I'd like to go back to my dad now. I want to take him home when he wakes up."

She sensed Mandeep's scrutiny. He was obviously struggling to think of something to say. Giving up, he led her back to the ICU. There she sat down beside Ravinder and waited for him to wake up. Wanting him to wake up and be with her again, yet dreading how he would cope.

And Jasmine was sharply aware of Mandeep's presence. Glad he was there, so she was not alone, yet somewhat resentful of the intrusion on her space.

# NINETEEN

Leon was so deep in thought, nearly asleep, that for a long time he did not realize his mobile was ringing. Immediately on answering the phone, he heard the panic in Vishal's voice.

"I doubt Verma is going to last another day." Fear was audible in Vishal's high-pitched tone. "You should have seen the way Saina went for him. *Man!* She is one tough bitch . . . and she's out for blood . . . wants to prove Sikander was innocent."

"Calm down," Leon said sharply. "It's all over if you lose your head now."

That seemed to get through. Leon heard Vishal draw a deep breath. Then a rustling sound, as though he was shifting the phone to his other hand.

"You're right. That's exactly what I told Verma." Vishal sounded calmer, but Leon sensed it was a momentary respite. Vishal seemed to have hit the end of his tether.

*I need to keep him going a little longer. At least till he gets the rifles and the bombs into the stadium.*

"And that's just what you too need to do, Vishal," Leon said encouragingly. "Let us focus on the practicalities. That's always the best way to deal with such situations. I'm confident we can find a solution to Verma if we put our heads together."

"What could we possibly do?"

"Should we get the other stuff out of the way first?" But Leon didn't wait for a reply. "What is the status on the rifles and bombs?"

"My man has collected both." Vishal sounded smug. "They will be inside within the next few hours. Definitely before the stadium is sealed."

"Excellent, Vishal. That's amazing." Aware Vishal relished it, Leon was lavish with the praise.

"It *was* tough, but without them our plan would have stalled." Leon sensed Vishal was preening.

"True. I'm sure you have told them to let you know when the job is done."

"Of course. I'll message you soon as I get their confirmation."

"That's great. Well done, Vishal."

"Thanks. Now what about Verma? And my money?"

"I should have the money by morning." Leon had decided he was not going to hand over a dime to Vishal till the rifles and guns were inside the stadium.

"Even with Fatima out of the picture?"

"Fatima was representing the client organization," Leon lied. "There are others besides her. Our money is going nowhere." Leon had every intention of reaching out to the SOB as soon as he was done here in India.

Leon heard the intermittent beep of another incoming call. "I have another call coming in. Let me call you back." Wondering who was calling him at this ungodly hour, he accepted the new call.

"Sir ji, imagine my surprise when I saw you on television."

The caller sounded familiar, but Leon couldn't place him. "Who is this, please?"

"It is I, Om Chandra. The owner of the service apartment in Sarita Vihar."

Leon knew the shit had hit the fan. Hard.

"I was saying, sir ji, I was *so* surprised to see you on television."

"I have no idea what you mean," Leon tried, though doubtful the bluff would work. It did not.

"Let's not play games, Mr. Berman. Or should I say Mr. Binder?" Om's tone hardened. "We both know the police alert is for you."

Leon did not respond.

"Now the question is, why does the police want you badly enough to pay a million rupees." Om paused dramatically. "And the *bigger* question is, how much would *you* pay for them not to find you?"

Leon waited him out, trying hard to think of the best way out of this.

*I don't need to go back to that apartment again. And I can dump the bugger's car someplace where it will not be found for a couple of days.*

Leon's relief was short-lived.

"I know you must be thinking, why bother to pay anything?" Om Chandra continued, driving the final nail in the coffin, "so I thought I'd help you see the big picture. You see, that car you are driving is expensive. And given the number of car thefts in Delhi, it is fitted with a GPS tracker. That tracker tells me you are right now parked in Jorbagh and in the very same place as you were last night." Om Chandra gave him a moment to assimilate that. "I'm not sure of the exact location, since I am a simple man and not very good with sophisticated technology, but then, I don't really need to be, do I? I'm sure the police will figure it out."

Leon knew Om Chandra had him by the short hairs; he needed Om to stay silent, at least till be was out of India. "What do you want?" he asked.

"What could I want, sir?" Om Chandra reverted to his oily tone. "I'm a simple man, with simple needs. But you know how children are . . . so expensive . . . always wanting this and that. And the school fees . . . don't even remind me of them." Chandra snickered. "Perhaps you'd like to make a small donation, which can help me take care of their needs?"

"How much?"

"Well, the cops are ready to pay a million rupees. Would two million not be a reasonable amount for me to look the other way?"

*Two million rupees . . . about thirty thousand dollars.*

Leon rapidly did the math. Doable. But he countered, "I don't think I could raise that kind of money,"

"I would if I were you, sir ji." Om's tone was no longer pleasant. "I have no idea what you are up to, but it cannot be small change, not with that kind of reward."

"I will need time." Leon hedged, trying to buy some whilst he wrapped his head around this.

"Of course. I'm a reasonable man. You have till tomorrow eleven o'clock."

Again Om's tone brooked no discussion. Leon realized fighting the deadline would not be a smart idea. "Okay. Meet me tomorrow at . . ."

"At the apartment in Sarita Vihar," Om Chandra completed his sentence. "Come alone. No hanky-panky, sahib. I promise you there will be no trouble as long as I get my money."

But Leon suspected there would be trouble. There always was.

*Damn!*

Now he had two issues to resolve, Vishal Bhardwaj and Om Chandra.

*Just when I thought I was out of the woods. This damn mission* is *jinxed.*

Ten minutes later, with a plan clearer in his head, Leon called Vishal and told him he'd have his money ready by noon. "Why don't you meet me at about thirteen hundred tomorrow?"

"Same place?"

"Same place."

"That's great." Vishal sounded happy. "Oh! I'd like most of it in dollars."

"I will do the best I can," Leon answered noncommittally.

"And what about Verma? Given any thought to that?"

"Frankly, no. But let me sleep over it. I am sure we can find a solution."

"I see." But the worry was back in Vishal's voice. Leon sensed he was on the verge of panic. "Don't sleep on it too long. I don't think he will hold out much longer. They haven't allowed him to sleep a wink and someone is always at him." Leon clicked his tongue moodily. "I am screwed if he talks."

"Don't worry. We *will* find a solution." Leon murmured reassuringly. "Another thirty hours and it will all be over." But even over the phone Leon could sense Vishal's jumpiness. It transferred; Leon was equally uneasy when the call ended.

# DECEMBER
# 26

# ONE

Ravinder was unable to suppress a pang of guilt when he saw Kurup's number flashing on his mobile, aware he had lost track of the assignment. Reluctantly he took the call.

"Deepest condolences, Ravinder. Really sorry about your wife." Ravinder noticed this was the first time Kurup had used his first name and was touched. "I called yesterday, too, but your daughter said you were not to be disturbed."

"Oh! I was . . ." Ravinder trailed off, not sure how to respond.

"I understand." Kurup sounded concerned. "Please let us know if there is anything we can do to help."

"I will. Thank you."

An awkward silence followed. Ravinder was relieved when the call came to an end. He was also feeling terribly guilty. Though Kurup had not brought up the investigation, Ravinder was aware time had almost run out for the home team and of the possibly catastrophic consequences if Leon succeeded. Yet grief held him inert; he could not contemplate going back to the assignment that had claimed Simran's life. The fact she had been dead against it made him feel worse.

There was a soft knock and Jasmine peeped in. "You up, Dad?"

"Come in, please." Ravinder sat up.

"I thought I heard you talking. All well?"

Ravinder saw she was worried. He nodded. "That was Kurup, the NIA director."

"And?" She looked even more worried.

"And nothing." He shrugged, unwilling to share the guilt he was suffering; strangely it made him feel disloyal to Simran.

"How're you feeling now?" She sat beside him, studying him closely.

"Better, thank you."

"Good." She gave him a hug. "Why don't you get ready then? We need to go to the gurudwara sahib for the *antim sanskar*."

Ravinder was marveling at Jasmine's composure as he showered. He'd never seen her so collected before; it filled him with pride. Also sorrow that she had had to learn this lesson at such a terrible cost.

Emerging from the bath he headed for the bedroom to get dressed and then realized Simran was no longer there to lay out his clothes, something she had done every day for the twenty-eight years of their togetherness. Wiping away the tears that suddenly clouded his vision, Ravinder turned heavily to his cupboard and dug out a black turban, white sherwani, and churidar pajama. It took him a while; he had paid scant attention to his cupboards once he had surrendered them to Simran when they got married. Usually not big on early morning conversation, Ravinder now missed Simran's chatter.

Twenty minutes later he stood before the full-length mirror and checked everything was in order.

Turban. He tucked in an errant hair. *Check.*

Sherwani. He smoothened out the front. *Check.*

Pajama. *Check.*

Juttis. *Check.*

Wallet. He confirmed it had his credit cards and enough cash. *Check.*

All good.

*Good. Jasmine needs me to be strong.*

Taking a deep breath he headed out. His hand was raised to push open his bedroom door when the thought struck him.

*There should be a checklist for people, too.*

*Heart. Strong and happy. Check.*

*Head. Clear and focused. Check.*

He faltered, squeezing his eyes tightly to push back the sudden flash flood of tears. But it was a while before he felt in control enough to open the door.

Jasmine emerged from her room on cue. She took his arm and headed down. He could feel the tremor in her hands and knew she was on the brink, too.

# TWO

Leon took stock of himself. Though a large, dark red welt remained on his right arm, the pain was almost gone. His stomach was feeling more settled, too; time, gallons of water, and the Norflox seemed to have done the trick. He flexed, taking deep breaths, and stretching his body. Barring that tight knot of tension in the pit of his stomach and the fact that he had not exercised the past few days, he felt fighting fit.

Then he took out the bag containing the three remaining sets of microphones, adaptors, and clickers that Nitin had weaponized for him. He transferred two sets to a well-worn, brown leather Hidesign wheelie bag, the kind professional speakers use: as ubiquitous at conferences as the black carry-on bags air crew use at airports.

From the final set he placed the clicker in his jacket pocket and the microphone and adaptor in a smaller Nike sling bag, which was already half filled with money.

Finally Leon packed all his belongings, barring the clothes he had worn when he had gone to rent the Sarita Vihar service apartment. Checking that he had gotten everything, he then donned a pair of surgical gloves and began to scrub the Jorbagh apartment clean. In the unlikely event the cops managed to get this far, Leon had no intention of gifting them with a set of his fingerprints. He was almost done when the text from Vishal came in.

*All items have been correctly delivered.*

Brimming with energy, Leon finished cleaning; things were falling into place nicely.

# THREE

Vishal was surprised when Philip called.

"Please make sure Archana and you are in time for Mrs. Gill's funeral." He sounded rushed. "I may be slightly late and Saina is busy interrogating Verma. I want him constantly under pressure."

"Sure, but . . ."

Philip cut him off. "Sorry, man, got to rush now. I think we finally have a break."

"What kind of break?" Vishal was suddenly anxious.

But Philip rang off with a hurried "I will tell you when we meet."

Vishal was fretting as he got ready.

*What had Philip managed to get his hands on?*

That bit about Saina keeping the heat on Verma also gnawed at him; he wondered how Verma was faring. Vishal wished he could rush to the office and give Verma a covert morale boost, but knew it was a terrible idea, and also there was no time. Texting Archana to meet him outside the Nanakpura gurudwara, he headed there.

# FOUR

Jasmine felt Ravinder slow down as they left the car and walked into the Nanakpura gurudwara sahib. They were the first to arrive; but for the sewadars, (the helpers), there was no one else about. She was filled with reluctance; as though going through with the ceremony would make Simran's death final. No longer deniable.

*Jyot milee sang jyot reh-i-aa qhaal-daa.*

(My light merges with the Supreme light, and my labors are over.)

The hymn rolling out of the gurudwara sahib, suffusing the area with its haunting beauty, greeted them as they entered the compound.

"Do you know why we Sikhs call it *antim sanskar*?" Jasmine noted the quaver in her father's voice. She saw he was struggling to compose himself and needed to talk. "It is the celebration of the completion of life's journey." He seemed to be searching for words. "It is the merging of the soul with the Divine." Another pause. "Death is our final destination. We should not lament or mourn it."

"You are right, Dad. We should not. Mom is always going to be with us . . . in our hearts and our thoughts." She saw him grow more morose and tightened her grip on his hands. "No. Don't forget you're on my watch now." Jasmine tried to force a smile. Nearly succeeded.

"But of course, Princess."

Jasmine felt her heart break as she saw him struggle to return her smile. "We have to be strong. Mom would have wanted that."

Ravinder looked away. Silent. Finally looked back at her, nodded, and then gave her a long hug. So long Jasmine wished it would never end and she could stay safely hidden in his arms forever.

Then several cars drove up in quick succession. Soon a sea of relatives had surrounded them. Within no time the prayer hall was full; also flush with the soft but pervasive scent of incense and the melody of hymns, washing over them like balm.

Jasmine watched as the ceremony progressed and they bid farewell to Simran.

Friends. Relatives. Colleagues. Neighbors. People she had not met in years. Some not at all. But today they had all come together. To stand by them.

Jasmine felt as though she was hovering near the ceiling, breathing in the incense that wafted up. And she was watching everyone from up there, listening to them sing, seeing some cry and some remain stoic. Aunt Harmala, right in front, nearly hysterical; Jasmine knew how close the sisters had been. Her husband, looking distressed and somewhat embarrassed, was consoling her, without much success. Across the room were a string of Simran's cousins and their spouses, all suitably somber. One of them, Jasmine struggled to remember his name, kept eying his watch. Rekha stood beside her, deeply concerned.

Jasmine felt her anxiety. She wished she could tell Rekha she would be okay. But she could not; Jasmine didn't know if she would.

And despite everything Jasmine could not cry. She wanted to but could not. Frozen, she watched the ceremony slide by in slow motion. Acutely clear yet bereft of feelings.

Jasmine realized the ceremony was over only when people started drifting out of the prayer hall into the courtyard. Jasmine knew they would wait outside in the gurudwara sahib courtyard, to offer condolences to Ravinder and her.

When the prayer hall was empty she took Ravinder's arm and led him outside, Rekha on his other arm. He moved as though catatonic, but his face was composed. Barring a murmured automatic response, when people came up and offered their condolences, Ravinder seemed oblivious.

Then a Mahindra Bolero jeep pulled up at the gate, an official vehicle complete with a red light on top and the Delhi Police logo on either side: WITH YOU, FOR YOU, ALWAYS. A familiar-looking man alighted. It took Jasmine a moment to place him: Philip Cherian, the task force officer who had spoken to her at the hospital.

She saw Philip halt, poised on the periphery. He surveyed the crowd, spotted Ravinder, and began to walk toward them. His purposeful stride was at odds with the solemnity of the occasion and serene ambience of the gurudwara sahib. Jasmine felt a pulse of alarm; she *knew* Philip was not here to offer condolences, but for something else. She also knew that whatever it was, she did not want her father to hear it.

*Enough. He's done enough and given enough. I don't want Dad upset any more.*

She was trying to decide whether to confront and stop Philip from speaking to her father or warn Ravinder to ignore him when she felt a tap on her arm.

"Jas, my parents want to talk to you," Rekha murmured solicitously.

Though she did not want to leave Ravinder's side, Jasmine reluctantly allowed Rekha to lead her to them. Rekha was not just her best friend, she was almost a sister, and Jasmine knew Rekha's parents cared for her, too. Checking her impatience, Jasmine distractedly heard them out. Condolences. Meaningless words that did nothing to alleviate the pain. Yet needed to be said. Perhaps more by the person saying them than by the one they were said to.

A moment later, when she turned toward her father again, Philip was by his side. And Ravinder looked like death. Alarmed, she rushed to his side.

"They have caught the truck driver, a repeat offender called Kapil Choudhary." Ravinder said to her, his voice a monotone. "He had been paid to hit your car."

Jasmine felt as though someone had punched the air out of her lungs.

"Paid by a cop." Ravinder's face was a death mask. It stunned her. She had never seen him like this. "A damn cop! How could a cop stoop so low?"

"Dad." He was scaring her.

"I'm going to find out who paid him." She now felt the façade that had been holding him up crumble and his rage begin to peak. "And when I do . . ."

Jasmine felt death whisper past. *"Dad!"* She clutched his angrily flailing hand. The thought that Ravinder was getting back into the game terrified her. This deadly mission had already taken her mother's life. The very thought that something could happen to her dad also was too awful to contemplate. *"Please*, Dad. Let it go."

Jasmine felt her nail snap as it pressed into the metal band of Ravinder's Rolex. But she felt no pain. Nothing.

# FIVE

Leon was really irritated by the time he drew up outside the Sarita Vihar apartment. He had wanted to be early, but the traffic proved impossible and it was almost half past eleven. His dismay deepened when he let himself in and saw Om Chandra waiting for him inside the apartment. The first thing he noticed was the weapon in Om Chandra's hand.

"Don't mind this." Om held up the country-made 12-gauge with the barrel sawn off. At that range, in the close confines of the living room, Leon knew it could cut him in half. "Just insurance, sir ji. You have nothing to worry about as long as you don't try anything smart. All I want is my money."

"I don't want any trouble either." Leon held up the black bag like a peace offering. "Here's your money."

"Put it on the dining table and open it." When Leon had done that, Om waved him away with the shotgun. "Back off . . . to that end of the room." Keeping him covered Om went through the bag one-handed. He first counted the bundles of money, seemed surprised they were correct, and then suspiciously began to rifle through the bundles, checking if they were real currency notes. Still not satisfied, he overturned the bag. "What's this?" Om asked as a Mac adaptor and then a microphone fell out.

"I didn't realize they were there. Sorry. May I have them back, please?" Leon held out his left hand, palming the clicker into his right and arming it as he did so.

"But what are they for?" Om suspiciously held up the Mac VGA adaptor.

"Nothing really," Leon replied, depressing the slide-back button on the clicker, activating the adaptor. Despite being well out of the danger area Leon could not help holding his breath. Triggering the sarin, he began to count down.

Leon had hit the count of five when Om's expression changed. Puzzlement. Then concern as his breath ran short. Panic followed. Perhaps he realized Leon had tricked him because Om tried to raise the gun, but was unable to. His eyes bulged. Dropping the gun, his hands desperately clutched first at his throat and then his chest.

By the time Leon hit the count of twenty-three, Om was dead.

Though assailed by a sense of urgency Leon waited till the count had hit a hundred and fifty before he moved. He had no idea whom Om had told about him and that he was coming here, but Leon knew he needed to get the body out of sight and get clear of this apartment as soon as he had dealt with Vishal.

*Then I will worry about anything else.*

Kicking the sawn-off shotgun under the living room sofa and replacing the money and used Mac adaptor into the Nike sling bag, he caught the dead landlord and dragged him into the master bedroom.

In his hurry Leon missed the microphone and one of the bundles of cash.

# SIX

Ravinder was staring at Jasmine's broken nail with sightless eyes. "Does that hurt?" He was aware she'd replied, but her words failed to register. He felt her shake his arm hard. Then harder still.

"Dad! *Dad!*" Jasmine's voice finally reached him, through the fog of anger enveloping him. "Please don't do this. Nothing will bring Mom back." He now saw tears streaming down her cheeks. "If something happened to you, I would . . ."

But he was feeling disoriented. Her face kept swimming in and out of focus, sometimes Simran and sometimes Jasmine. And Simran's voice kept tugging at him.

"I know you well, Ravinder. I know you will always do the right thing. Just trust your instincts." Simran was insistent. Refusing to stay quiet. Drowning out whatever Jasmine was saying

Then, as though divinely ordained, the hymn singers inside the gurudwara began to laud the glory of Shakti.

*Deh siva bar mohe eh-hey subh karman te kabhu na taro.*

*Na daro arr seo jab jaye laro nischey kar apni jeet karo.*

The hymn echoed through the courtyard, swamping out everything else from Ravinder's mind. The passage of years had done nothing to dim the hymn's powerful appeal. Even today it was brimming with the magic it'd had the day its composer, Guru Gobind Singh, the tenth Sikh guru, had appealed to Lord Shiva, the Liberator.

*O Lord, grant me the boon that I may never deviate from doing a good deed.*

*That I shall not fear when I go into battle, and with determination I will be victorious.*

The magic of those words and the transcendental beauty of the music erased all vestiges of doubt from Ravinder and jerked him back to the present. When he turned to Jasmine he felt renewed. All his confusion and fears had been jettisoned.

"I have to do this, Jasmine. The man who took your mother from us is almost certainly the same one helping Binder. I have to find both and make them pay."

Jasmine did not know whether to be happy the father she'd always admired and adored was back or scared she might lose him. She also saw Ravinder was now beyond faltering. The steel in his eyes stiffened her resolve. Reconciling to this new reality, she nodded. "Make sure you get them, Dad. And come back in one piece. I need you."

Ravinder gave her a hug, then turned to Cherian. "Philip, get the team back to the office." Ravinder checked his watch: half past eleven.

*Twenty-four hours. Twenty-five at best. That is the maximum we can hope for.*

"I'll be with you in a moment, Philip." Ravinder headed back into the gurudwara sahib and knelt before the *palkhi* on which the Guru Granth Sahib was kept. And he prayed as he'd never prayed before.

When he got up everything had been laid to rest: guilt, fears, anger, hate, and self-doubt. All that remained was the stony calm and steely resolve required to take the battle to the enemy. And the hymn was now echoing in his soul.

*Deh siva bar mohe eh-hey subh karman te kabhu na taro.*
*Na daro arr seo jab jaye laro nischey kar apni jeet karo.*

Ravinder headed out, eager for battle.

He knew he would not falter.

Not this time.

# SEVEN

Jasmine noticed Ravinder's back was straight and his chin jutted forward in that determined manner so familiar to her. He erupted purposefully from the gurudwara sahib, moving fast, heading for the car park.

"Take care, Dad," she called out as Ravinder crossed her.

"I will." He had taken two more steps when Ravinder halted and spun on her. "Where's the gun I gave you before the peace summit?"

"With me at home." Though she hated guns, Jasmine had kept it safely in her bedroom locker. It was precious to her; her half sister Ruby had used it to save the family when Lashkar-e-Toiba terrorists had attacked their house earlier that October. "Why?"

"I want you to keep it close," Ravinder said tersely. "Whoever did this to us obviously wanted me off this case. They could try again once they find out that I am back in the game."

"Fine, Dad. If you think there is danger I will do so." Jasmine nodded. "But only if you agree to carry one yourself."

Jasmine saw him flinch. As though he had been slapped. But she held his gaze resolutely. Finally, seeing her determined, he nodded.

"Promise?" she persisted, knowing that if he did, he would.

"Promise." Ravinder spun around again and headed for the car.

Philip followed. At a signal from him, Jasmine saw Vishal and Archana also peel away from the crowd and follow them.

# EIGHT

Vishal knew something had changed. He had been bursting with curiosity since he had seen Philip come in.

"What happened, Philip?"

"We caught the truck driver who killed Ravinder's wife."

"Oh!" Vishal managed to keep the shock off his face, but his heart plummeted. He recovered fast. "That's great news. Did he confess?"

"I got him to," Philip muttered grimly. "He has admitted he was paid by a cop to do that hit-and-run."

*Thank God that bugger cannot point a finger at me.*

But Vishal's heart was in his mouth. "A cop? Really?" Philip nodded. "Does he know who?"

"Unfortunately he doesn't." Philip's frustration showed.

Vishal felt some of his anxiety lift.

"But says he might be able to recognize the cop's voice."

Vishal's hope crashed and burned again.

"That's not much of a help."

"I agree. But that's the best we have."

"Where are we going now?" Vishal felt sudden dread that he would be asked to confront Kapil Choudhary.

*Would the bugger really be able to recognize my voice?*

"Boss wants us all back in the office. Now. He is taking charge of things again."

Vishal was stunned. Already struggling to find a solution for Verma, suddenly being told that his truck-driver henchman was now in custody and then, to cap it all off, that Ravinder was back in the game dashed his hopes, demoralizing him completely. It took him a moment to realize Ravinder had halted near his car and was speaking to them.

"Do any of you know of a good security agency?"

"Why?" Vishal heard Philip ask.

"I want some security guards at my house. To ensure Jasmine is safe."

"Let me send a couple of constables," Philip offered.

"No. No cops." Ravinder gave a firm headshake. "Not till we know who the mole is. I prefer private security guards."

"I do, sir." Vishal leaped at the opportunity. "My cousin runs an agency."

"Good one? Reliable?"

"Very." Vishal fought to contain a smile, realizing Jasmine as a hostage could be an invaluable bargaining chip if things went out of kilter.

"Please get them to deploy four men at my farmhouse 'round the clock. Immediately."

"I'll take care of it right away." Vishal added to Philip, "Let me get this done and catch up with you guys at the office."

"Thanks." Ravinder looked at Archana and Philip and indicated his car. "Are either of you coming with me? I want to get my hands on that trucker . . . and Verma."

Vishal noticed his determination and his anxiety deepened. He sensed Ravinder would be unstoppable in his present mood.

*The trucker is no direct threat, but Verma . . .*

Vishal knew he could not allow Verma to talk. He ran for his car.

*I have to find a way or get the hell out of Dodge.*

The dashboard clock told him it was twenty-three minutes to noon.

*Enough time to call the security agency, brief his cousin, and get to Sarita Vihar.*

The need to collect his getaway money from Leon and be ready to make a run for it now overrode everything else. Clipping on a Bluetooth headset he dialed his cousin as he gunned the car onto the Ring Road. Taking the first U-turn he headed for Sarita Vihar.

# NINE

Leon was breathing hard and the pain in his elbow was back. Om Chandra was a big man; lugging his body into the bathtub of the master bathroom turned out to be harder than he had thought and did his elbow no good. It took him a moment to realize the doorbell had rung.

*Damn!*

*So Om Chandra had told others he was here.*

The doorbell rang again, more insistently this time.

*Who? How many?*

He pondered as he cat-footed toward the front door.

*Get them inside without a fuss, and then deal with them? Or cut and run?*

Holding the pistol ready for instant action he peered out through the spy hole.

Vishal was raising his hand to ring the bell again.

*What the hell is he doing here so early? He was supposed to come at one.*

With a quick look to ensure everything was in order, Leon pushed the pistol back into his waistband and opened the door.

"Thank god you're here." Vishal's rapid staccato tone betrayed his anxiety. "All hell has broken loose. You're not going to . . ."

"Want to catch your breath first?" Leon asked with a disarming smile, wanting Vishal with his guard down. "Let me get you a drink." Leon headed for the refrigerator by the dining table.

It worked. Vishal followed, and pulling out a dining chair, threw himself into it. "Ravinder has the truck driver in custody and has gone to the office to interrogate him." He gave a low whistle; Leon saw he was badly shaken. "Man! I have *never* seen anyone so angry. I am *pretty* sure he will break Verma down today. Then it's curtains for me."

At that precise moment Leon made up his mind; he could not let Vishal walk out of this room alive. Verma and the truck driver were of no consequence to Leon; Vishal was the only one who had seen him.

The bundle of cash on the dining table, partly covered by the Nike sling bag, caught Vishal's eye. He perked up. "Ah. You have my money."

"Of course. I told you I would."

"How much is it?" Vishal eyed the bag greedily. "I hope it is enough for me to . . ." He broke off.

"Why don't you count it while I get you a drink?" Leon picked up that Vishal was trying to hide something. Ignoring that since he knew, it did not matter anymore, Leon crossed over to the fridge at the far end of the room. "Coke or Sprite?"

"Coke." But Vishal was not really paying attention. He had reached across the dining table and pulled the bag closer, opening it. "What is this?" he asked as the microphone rolled free from under the bag. He looked at it, perplexed, and then, shrugging, put it down next to the bag and opened it. "Oh!" Leon heard his dismay. "It is all in rupees. I thought you would give me dollars."

Vishal must also have done a rapid count because he looked up sharply. Leon saw he was steaming. "This is only two million rupees . . . thirty thousand dollars. *That's it?*" An angry thump on the table. "What the fuck do you think I am? A bloody beggar?" He glared at Leon aggressively, as though ready to jump him.

"Cool it, man." About to pop the Coke can, Leon paused, convinced it was time to end this. He contemplated dropping the Coke can and going for the pistol in his right pocket.

*Or the clicker in his other one?*

Luckily, both were armed. He mulled, trying to decide between the two. "Vishal, I got hold of whatever I could arrange in this short time. More is on the way and *that's* in dollars."

Perhaps he didn't sound convincing enough, or something in Leon's eyes gave away the game.

# TEN

Vishal sensed Leon's tension; evident in the way Leon's eyes narrowed and his hand tightened on the Coke can. The pistol in his shoulder holster suddenly seemed too inaccessible for Vishal's liking.

*"I would like to point out that not once in all his years as an assassin has Binder ever used an accomplice for anything other than support tasks."* Vishal again remembered what Ravinder had told them. *"Even the few he used never saw him. The ones that laid eyes on him never lived to tell any tales."*

The first pang of fear hit Vishal. Still not sure why, but Vishal sensed Leon had no intention of letting him walk out of this apartment alive. There was a moment of doubt, more like wishful thinking, then sudden clarity.

Pushing off the dining table Vishal shot to his feet and went for his pistol. Driven by desperation, he was moving fast.

# ELEVEN

Leon saw Vishal's brow unfurrow and knew the jig was up.
   Then Vishal moved incredibly fast, shocking Leon.

Deciding with equal rapidity, Leon dug into his coat pocket for the clicker. He got hold of it immediately. But it caught in his pocket.

Leon fumbled, trying to tug it free.

He saw Vishal had gotten hold of his pistol and was hauling it out; it had already cleared the holster and was coming level fast.

Leon yanked the clicker free.

# TWELVE

Vishal saw Leon reach into his pocket and believed he, too, was going for a gun.

Stunned by his speed, Vishal knew he would never get his gun out in time.

Desperate to distract Leon and slow him down, Vishal grabbed the microphone on the table with his left hand and chucked it at Leon.

It was an awkward throw, but the microphone didn't have to travel very far. It cartwheeled through the air, headed straight for Leon's face.

# THIRTEEN

Ravinder threw open the cell door. It crashed into the opposite wall with a loud bang. Kapil Choudhary, who'd been huddled in one corner, shot up, shocked. Ravinder went straight for the jugular. Striding up to Choudhary, he grabbed his collar, hauled him up, and began to rain blows on him.

Choudhary was so stunned by the sudden assault that he was reduced to a whimpering wreck by the time Ravinder threw him back into the chair. The push was so violent that the chair broke.

"You're dead if you don't tell me who hired you." Ravinder, his eyes murderous slits, towered over the hapless man groveling on the floor.

"I promise you, sahib, I don't know."

Without another word Ravinder went to work on him again, hands and feet beating a deadly tattoo. The stench of fear mingled hotly with that of sweat in the stuffy cell. If Ravinder heard the truck driver's screams at all, they had no impact.

"I will ask you once more." Ravinder was breathing hard when he pushed Choudhary down again.

"I swear on my children, sahib. I never met him. Just spoke to him on the phone."

Grabbing hold of his collar Ravinder stared deep into his eyes for a long time. He sensed Choudhary was telling the truth. With a snarl of contempt Ravinder pushed him away and headed out. Pausing near the door he asked Gyan, "Men such as this deserve to be executed."

Gyan nodded.

"Pity that our courts take so much time."

Another nod and a scowl of disgust from Gyan.

"And sometimes these monsters get away because of scumbag lawyers."

"I don't think this man will survive long in the jail," Gyan replied softly, but loud enough for Kapil Choudhary to hear. "I hear they don't much like woman killers."

The implication got through fast enough to the trucker. Kapil Choudhary began to whimper.

His fear-laden whimpers were like balm to Ravinder.

"I will not spare any of them, Simran," he muttered harshly as he headed for the next cell, where Ashok Verma was being held.

# FOURTEEN

Leon caught himself from depressing the trigger button on the clicker just in time. A fraction of a second later, and he would have released the sarin just as the microphone reached him. Dropping the Coke can, Leon caught the mike in midair and threw it back toward Vishal in the same motion. That is when he realized Vishal's pistol was level and he was readying to fire.

Leon sensed he was already too late. That fleeting moment of indecision, deciding whether to use his pistol or the Sarin, had lasted too long. But Leon also knew he could not give up.

*I* cannot *lose. Not to this arrogant upstart.*

He dropped to the ground, pulling the refrigerator door open as a shield just as Vishal's aim settled on him.

# FIFTEEN

Vishal was about to fire when he saw Leon vanish behind the fridge door.

That unsettled him.

The incoming microphone distracted Vishal further; swaying to the left he swatted it aside.

Then, pistol extended in a classic shooter's stance, he started to move around the dining table, seeking a clear shot. Confident he now had his man.

# SIXTEEN

L eon heard Vishal shuffle to the right. He was unable to see the microphone now but heard a sharp metallic thud and guessed Vishal had used his pistol to swat it aside.

Leon triggered the clicker from behind the safety of the refrigerator door.

Sarin exploded out of the microphone a moment after Vishal had smashed it aside with his pistol.

Vishal took the brunt of the gas directly in the face. There was a muted yell, then a terrible choking sound. Then Vishal crashed to the ground, striking the dining table en route. Two of the chairs overbalanced and landed in a heap around him. The rasping chokes continued for a few more seconds, and then there was silence.

# SEVENTEEN

Ravinder knew Ashok Verma was his last resort; if he failed to break him . . .

*Or if he is innocent, then I am up the creek without a paddle.*

That desperation spurred him on.

Saina, who had not witnessed the short, sharp, and surgical interrogation of Kapil Choudhary, was aghast when Ravinder sailed into Verma. Even Philip, who had been present for the Choudhary interrogation, was surprised.

On Ashok Verma, the impact of a huge, murderously angry Sikh was devastating. Neither Philip nor Saina had resorted to anything other than relentless questioning; Ravinder slammed into him like a trigger-happy prizefighter.

Also, Verma had been buoyed by the hope held out by Vishal the previous evening. Already edgy and confused by the sleep deprivation, Verma was shattered when his hopes were dashed. He broke within minutes.

"Vishal," Verma mumbled through bloodied lips. "He's working for Binder."

"*What?*" Ravinder was stunned.

"I knew there was something wrong with that man," Saina hissed angrily.

Philip looked murderous; the betrayal cut deeply.

"Vishal is the one you want," Verma repeated. "He's in touch with Binder and Basheer."

"That bastard." Ravinder felt Philip's anger break bounds.

Then Ravinder remembered with horror that he'd entrusted Vishal with Jasmine's security. Ravinder felt his heart plummet. Grabbing his mobile he ran for the door. "I need to get Jasmine to a safe place," he yelled at Philip as he hit speed dial. "Find out where Vishal is. Saina, warn the others, too."

Jasmine answered on the first ring. "Dad! Are you okay?" She sounded frantic with worry.

"Where are you?"

"Still here at the gurudwara sahib. Waiting for the guests to leave."

"Thank God!" Ravinder felt relief hiss through him. "Whatever you do, don't go home."

"Why?"

Ravinder rapidly briefed her, now in a tearing hurry to track down Vishal, aware they could be close to catching Binder. But he needed to ensure Jasmine was safe.

"Don't let him get away, Dad." Ravinder heard her anger.

"He won't," Ravinder promised. "Meanwhile, I want you to go back with Rekha to her house. You will be safer there. Don't step out till I call you."

"I'll do that, Dad," Jasmine promised without demur.

Now certain that Jasmine was safe, Ravinder ran out into the main office. Philip had just put down the phone. "We have traced his mobile. Vishal is at Sarita Vihar. They're triangulating his location."

"Let's go." Ravinder paused briefly near his desk, pulling out the pistol he had been issued when he'd joined the task force. It was a standard service issue, 9mm Beretta. Checking it was loaded, he pocketed both the spare clips, chambered a round, flicked on the safety, and shoved it in his coat pocket.

"Philip and I will bring him in. Chance and Saina, you two back us up."

All four headed for the door.

"I want him alive," Ravinder added grimly. "He will lead us to Binder . . . I want both of them to rot in jail for the rest of their stinking lives."

"That he will." Philip's anger was fearsome.

# EIGHTEEN

Leon drew a deep shuddering breath. The close encounter and holding his breath till the sarin lost potency had left him shaken. Leon knew he was lucky to be alive. Just one tiny sliver of time more and Vishal would have gunned him down.

*The blighter would have come out of this a hero.*

Pushing the refrigerator door shut Leon got up and surveyed the room.

Barring Vishal's body slumped by the dining table and two overturned dining chairs, it was in surprisingly good shape. It was hard to believe two people had forfeited their lives here in the past hour. But Leon knew he now needed to get clear as fast as possible.

*Only a matter of time before someone comes looking for one of these blokes.*

Quickly wiping down the areas he had touched, Leon threw the money back into the black bag and headed out.

Like the safe house, the car rented from Om Chandra was no longer safe. Parking it at the opposite end of the colony, tucked in behind an Innova that looked like it hadn't been moved in a while, Leon cut through the housing blocks on foot.

At the colony market he avoided the auto rickshaw stand, preferring instead to hail one passing by on the main road. Soon he was on his way back to Jorbagh.

En route Leon opened his mobile cover, removed the SIM card he had been using to communicate with Vishal, and tossed it out the window.

*One person, one SIM card . . . first Verma when he'd been captured, then Fatima, and now Vishal.*

Leon found the thought depressing.

*Is that all that remains?*

*Wonder how many will replace their SIM cards when I go down?*

It took Leon only a moment to realize there was no one.

*No one that matters.*

That depressed him even more. Shrugging off the horrible sinking feeling that threatened to swamp him, he inserted his last unused SIM card into the mobile.

Blown by the wind and passing cars the discarded SIM card was soon tossing its way down the road.

Back in the Sarita Vihar apartment, Vishal's mobile began to ring.

# NINETEEN

Ravinder looked down at Vishal's body and suppressed the urge to scream out his frustration. Instead he began to examine the room minutely.

"Gloves, please, everyone," he cautioned the others. "And get the crime team here ASAP, Saina."

"Already on the way, sir."

The can of Coke lying near the fridge caught Ravinder's attention. The can had rolled halfway under it and was still sweating; obviously it hadn't been out of the fridge too long.

"Whoever it was with Vishal, looks like we just missed him by a whisper," Ravinder said ruefully.

They had lost valuable minutes trying to identify the apartment, though cell triangulation had delivered them to the right block of apartments. If it had not been for the old lady in the adjacent apartment, they would still have been going door to door.

*Even so, too late.*

Ravinder made a moue.

"Bag that Coke can," he ordered Saina. "Run it for prints."

"We have another body here," Philip called out from inside.

Ravinder went running. *Could it be Binder?*

He saw it was Indian. *Obviously not Leon.*

Om Chandra had been bundled into the bathtub, again obviously in a hurry; he was half in and half out.

"Who the heck is that?" Ravinder was perplexed; yet another loose end. He leaned in for a closer look. "Strange that neither of them have any marks. What did they die of?"

"Poison?" Saina hazarded a guess, but she looked dubious; most poisons leave *some* traces.

"Guess we'll have to wait for the autopsy. This body is still warm." Philip checked. "So he, too, was killed recently."

Ravinder returned to Vishal's body and checked. "This one, too."

He now noticed the microphone near Vishal's outstretched hand; it had rolled to the other side of the dining table. "What have we here?" The microphone puzzled him; not the sort of thing one expected to find in a house. "Bag that too, Saina."

Then the crime scene people arrived. Soon a trio of men was sifting through the apartment.

"Seems to have been wiped clean," one of them commented.

"Doesn't matter, keep going," Ravinder ordered. "I want every inch of this apartment done. There are bound to be some prints. And those items Saina has bagged. Rush it. Do whatever you have to, but I want the report yesterday."

They were on their way out when it struck Ravinder. "Get Vishal's mobile and check his pockets, Philip. There might be something to point us to Leon."

They were waiting for Philip to do that when the chess set in the living room again caught Ravinder's eye; some of the pieces were in play. The set bothered him. However, they were almost a mile away when it struck him.

"Leon." He did not realize he had spoken aloud; saw the others give him curious looks and explained, "That chess set back in the apartment; Binder was crazy about chess." Not sure why he was so certain, Ravinder added, "I'm sure it was him." He smashed his fist on the seat. "Damn! We missed him by so little." There was silence in the car. "Wonder where he is right now?"

# TWENTY

Leon did not want the landlady at Jorbagh to raise an alarm. That is why he decided not to vanish without warning.

"It is most unfortunate, Mrs. Kapoor"—he gave her his saddest face—"but my brother has taken ill and I need to fly back to London today." He noted her disappointment and added, "But you have been very kind to me and I would like to pay for the full week that I had spoken to you about initially."

That perked her up. She even sent up tea and sandwiches for him as he gathered his stuff. Leon had already packed and was ready to go, but still had some time to kill. Careful not to touch anything with ungloved hands, he allowed an hour to pass before calling a cab.

Unwilling to take even the slightest chance, he got the cab to drop him off near Sarojini Nagar market. Crossing to the other side of the market, he got another from the cabstand.

Traffic was unusually heavy, and the portly Sikh driver equally eager to please his foreign passenger; he kept up a running commentary, pointing out trivia that a tourist would have enjoyed. Leon was in no mood for trivia, but he was unwilling to make himself memorable by telling the driver to shut up, so he stayed silent. It took fifteen minutes for the cabbie to take the hint and finally keep quiet.

An hour later Leon walked into the Leela Palace, a luxury hotel located in Chanakyapuri, the heart of Delhi's diplomatic area. The lobby was crowded. Leon spotted several familiar faces and realized he had seen them on the conference posters. He guessed most of the speakers for the New India Times Summit were staying here.

Getting a room on the fifth floor was harder, and Leon managed that only when he agreed to upgrade to a suite. With that final piece in place, Leon settled down to wait for his quarry to come to him. Like most other not-at-risk conference speakers, Professor Naug was booked on the same floor, though at the far end.

# TWENTY-ONE

Ravinder saw Philip was bursting with excitement.

"Most of the recent calls to and from Vishal's mobile have been to three prepaid numbers. Two of these have been in service for a while now, but one was purchased just five days ago."

"Any luck on the owners?" Philip's excitement infected Ravinder.

"Bogus." Philip made a face. "Names and addresses were false. Right now all of them are switched off . . . can't even trace the damn things. No breaks there. But that does confirm all three are up to no good."

Ravinder felt let down, but did not want Philip to feel demoralized. "I'm guessing the new mobile number points at Leon?"

"That's what the timing suggests, since he, too, came to Delhi at that time, but even that's switched off." Philip brightened. "However, equally important, since yesterday three calls were made to Vishal's mobile from a public booth outside Ferozeshah Kotla."

"From near the stadium? Damn it, man." Ravinder jumped up. "You should have told me right away. This means that . . ."

"Most probably Zardosi is the target," Philip completed.

"Are we trying to identify the caller?"

"Already on it, sir. Saina has gotten the locals to put a dozen men on the job."

"Excellent work, guys." Ravinder was delighted. "I must call the director. We need to lock down the stadium and search it from top to bottom. And circulate copies of the Binder APB to every cop on duty at the stadium."

"The lock-down is already in place, sir," Saina chipped in. "As per the security SOP it began an hour ago. Also, the APB copy is being issued to every single man on duty there even as we speak. But I agree about the search. We should send in a fresh team for that."

"Precisely. We have no idea who and how many Vishal managed to subvert."

"Scrutinize every man on duty there this past week," Ravinder tasked Archana. "I want everything . . . bank records, property purchases . . . any signs of sudden unexplained wealth. You know, the usual stuff."

"Already on it, sir, but there are almost two hundred people." Archana looked doubtful. "We won't be able to complete it in time."

"I agree." Ravinder knew she was right. "Put a small team on it nevertheless and run oversight. We may get lucky . . . or not. Either way, we have to find him . . . or them . . . eventually."

He was picking up the phone to call the director when Philip asked, "Do we take it as a given Binder is targeting Zardosi?"

"Yes. All things considered I think that would be our best bet," Ravinder replied after some thought, but an errant thought kept nagging him.

*What have I missed?*

"Logical, too," Archana concurred, temporarily submerging that worry. "Taking out a head of state in his own country would always be tougher. And I would not want to go to Pakistan if I was Binder. It's crazy out there."

"True. We go with Zardosi, but let's hedge our bets." Unable to dispel the nagging doubt, Ravinder made up his mind. "Archana and Chance will go with me to the stadium to keep an eye on Zardosi. Philip, I want you and Saina to be at Siri Fort. Make sure you don't let that bugger Masharrat out of sight." He saw both of them scowl and explained, "What if we are wrong, Philip? What if Leon is going for Masharrat? We cannot ignore that possibility. That's why I want both of you there. We *have* to cover all bases."

That seemed to mollify Philip, but Saina still looked unhappy.

Realizing there was nothing more he could do about that, Ravinder called Kurup.

# TWENTY-TWO

Jasmine was terribly uneasy and feeling lost . . . adrift; Simran had been her anchor. And Jasmine knew she wouldn't be able to sleep a wink knowing Ravinder was also alone. Despite the best efforts of Rekha and her parents to keep her engaged, Jasmine grew restless as evening fell. Unable to stand it any longer she called Ravinder.

"I'm not staying here, Dad. Safe or not, I want to be home. I want to be with you when you get home."

Unaware the threat from Vishal had been blunted, she was surprised when Ravinder acquiesced. "Sure, I understand. Pick me up from the office, please."

"Now?"

"Whenever you are ready." Jasmine sensed he, too, was happy about not being home alone.

"I'm on my way." Jasmine was so keen to be with her father again, she could not wait to get moving. It was only as she neared the Special Task Force office that she realized what she had let herself in for. A sense of dread seized her as the site of the accident drew closer. Caught in a web of thoughts she missed the first turnoff and again found herself on the opposite side of the road.

Jasmine felt a wave of nausea as she turned the corner and Ravinder's office hove into view. Her nausea heightened. An agonized scream began to build up in her head as she came up to the same spot, directly across the STF complex gate, where she had parked the last time, three days ago.

*Was it only three days?*

So much had happened since.

She tried hard, but was unable to look away from the spot where the truck had smashed into her car. By now she was almost parallel. Even in the rapidly gathering darkness, she could see bits and pieces of her car scattered on the berm. Pieces of shattered windscreen. A tiny triangle ripped from her car bumper. A few shards of reflective glass from the tail lamps. They littered the accident site. Glittering intermittently as they caught errant strands of light.

*Like tiny tombstones.*

By now the scream in her head had built up into a heart-rending roar. Jasmine felt her head was about to explode. Suddenly galvanized and unable to be there a second longer, she accelerated, plunging back into the traffic, aching to flee as far from that horrid place as possible.

There was a horrific screeching as the vehicles behind her braked or swerved to avoid hitting her car. The driver immediately behind leaned out his window and shouted an obscenity as he swerved past.

As she raced away, Jasmine heard neither the screech of rubber on the road nor the profanity. Nor did she see the trail of near accidents she left in her wake. She was desperately trying to leave her memories behind.

# TWENTY-THREE

Ravinder was at the office gate when, across the road, he saw Jasmine drive up and slow down. He started, horrified, when he saw her car suddenly jump back on to the road and race madly into the traffic.

Stunned he watched her speed away. He was worriedly dialing her mobile when he saw her car's tail lamps light up brightly in the distance. Then the reverse lights came on. A moment later she was driving up to him.

"What happened, Jasmine?" Ravinder saw her face was covered with sweat and she was shivering, as though running a high fever.

"I . . ." Jasmine gave up trying to speak, fighting to get a grip on herself, suddenly ashamed.

Ravinder noticed she was sitting stiffly, as though trying to avoid looking anywhere but straight ahead. Suddenly he understood and felt like kicking himself for making her come back to the accident site. "I'm sorry, Princess. I did not realize . . . I shouldn't have asked you to come back here."

Contrite and feeling horrible he'd been so insensitive Ravinder took the wheel from her and they headed home. Neither brought up Simran, but she was with them in the car all the way back to the farmhouse. Like the treacly silence.

Barring the security lights and those in the kitchen, the farmhouse was in darkness when they drove in, as though mourning for Simran.

They were getting out of the car when Ravinder saw Jasmine suddenly sway and then double up over the flowerbed. With an awful retching sound she threw up. Again. And again. Till there was nothing left to throw up.

He rushed around the car to her side as the emotions she had bottled up over the past two days surged up. He saw her fighting off tears when she finally stopped retching and straightened up.

"Must have been something I ate," Jasmine mumbled. She was working her mouth, as though trying to get rid of the foul taste.

Ravinder knew it wasn't that. "You're sure you are okay?"

But she didn't reply. Nodding wordlessly, she hurried up to her room. Ravinder watched her go, helpless. He didn't know what he wanted to do: run after her and console her, or bend over the flowerbeds and puke.

His mobile chirruped to life. Desperate for the distraction, Ravinder hurriedly took the call. "Yes, Saina."

"Sir, I have managed to get ten men from Delhi Police. They will be at the stadium within the hour."

"Only ten? They will take forever to sweep the stadium."

"Even ten took a lot of effort." Ravinder sensed her tiredness and frustration. "With two major events happening simultaneously and the festive season in full swing, manpower is stretched thin."

"Thanks, Saina. I know. You've done a great job." Ravinder realized nothing was going to be easy, not for this operation.

*So be it.*

"Please keep me posted." Ravinder wished she would keep talking, but Saina hung up.

# TWENTY-FOUR

L eon hated making himself so visible. Though he had already switched to his third, getaway identity, he had been forced to stay with the photograph on the passport he had presented while checking in at the hotel. This photo was, unfortunately, not remarkably different from one of those generated by Archana and picked by Ravinder; they had gotten very lucky with the APB.

The Leela Palace has a broad, sweeping lobby, high ceilings, marble floors, and exquisite cornices. The reception desk lies to the left as one enters; almost directly opposite is a bank of elevators. Between the two is an open seating area, and to the left a 24-hour coffee shop.

Probably because of its central location, the hotel was usually full. Today it was packed because it was hosting most of the New India Times Summit speakers and conference delegates.

When Leon came down from his room the lobby was flush with people. Avoiding the crowded seating area between the reception desk and the elevators, Leon headed for the coffee shop. Selecting a corner table where he could keep an eye on the entrance and the reception desk, he ordered tea. A moment later, a young waitress was offering him a selection of teas. Leon picked a Korean organic green tea with brown rice. It was mild, with almost no aroma but with a soothing, earthy flavor. Relishing it, he pulled out an iPad, and mindful of possible watchers, launched the Kindle app and pretended to read a book; aware the human mind tends to gloss over people engaged in such mundane activities as reading and surfing the net. But all the while Leon's attention was on the main entrance, huge glass doors manned by a ceremoniously dressed doorman.

Twenty minutes later Professor Naug entered and went up to the reception desk. Leon used the photograph on his iPad screen to double-check.

Tall, about the same height as Leon, equally fair, with brown hair worn just over the ears, and rectangular, rimless spectacles. Going by the surveillance photos sent to him by Hakon, the professor was wearing what he usually did: a turtleneck pullover, slightly faded cords, a heavy tweed-ish coat, and dark brown slip-ons. He was wheeling along a well-worn, brown leather bag. It was also a Hide-sign, like the one Leon had checked in with earlier. Unlike most academics, or rather, unlike the public perception of academics, Naug looked fit and moved with an easy gait, someone who worked out regularly.

Leon felt a huge weight lift off; Naug's arrival in Delhi was an-other key factor in this already messy mission over which he'd had absolutely no control. And Naug's presence was critical for Leon to get within striking range of the target.

Watching Naug check in, Leon felt his spirits lift; he was now confident he would succeed.

Charging the tea to his room, Leon was already in the elevator whilst Naug was still checking in. Returning to his room, Leon left his door slightly ajar and kept a close eye on the corridor. After a few minutes, he saw Naug emerge from the elevator and walk down the hall to his room. Another two minutes later the bellhop arrived with Naug's luggage—one big suitcase.

Allowing another twenty minutes to elapse, for the professor to settle down and hopefully call his wife, Leon donned surgical gloves, crossed over, and knocked. It was a while before he heard a rustle at the other end. When the door opened, Leon led with the stiletto. He drove the eight-inch-long blade straight into the scien-tist's jugular.

The attack was so sudden and swift that Naug did not even have time to be surprised. As the stiletto punctured the windpipe, his scream of pain ended in a gurgling, soapy whimper, which died away even before it could properly get started.

Pushing Naug back with the palm of his hand, Leon entered swiftly and heeled the door shut behind him. Now safe from prying eyes Leon aimed carefully and delivered a second blow to the heart. The stiletto slid between the ribs and punched a hole in Naug's heart. Soon it stopped fluttering and Naug lay still.

Moving swiftly, Leon first stanched the blood to ensure nothing spilled on the carpet; even if any housekeeping staff came in, they should find nothing to alarm them.

*Not unless they go to the bathroom.*

Leon then hauled the body to the bathtub, washed off the blood that had gotten onto his hands, placed a DO NOT DISTURB sign on the door, and then lowered the room temperature to eighteen degrees, the lowest it would go. The colder the room, the slower the rate of decomposition; Leon knew he needed to contain the smell as best and as long as he could.

Mindful of security cameras, he checked the corridor was empty of housekeeping staff and then went across to his room. He returned a minute later with his bag.

Back in Naug's room he transferred the clickers, microphones, and adaptors to the professor's capacious brown bag.

Already present in Naug's bag was a nifty 11-inch MacBook Air, a power cord, an assortment of pens, and a sheaf of papers on a variety of incomprehensible scientific topics—the kinds of things one would expect to find in an academic's bag.

Peering out from behind the plastic business-card holder was the photograph of a smiling blond woman in her mid-thirties, with two equally blond and cheerful eight-year-old girls. From the dossier complied by Hakon, Leon recognized them as Naug's family. The picture made Leon pause; he wondered what they were doing.

*Hopefully not expecting Naug to call any time soon.*

Leon needed to ensure Naug's body was not discovered till four p.m. the next day. By then he would have cleared Indian airspace. But he knew several factors were beyond his control. The operation had now entered the terminal stage and he would have to act and react as the situation evolved. Much as one would want it otherwise, as in every battle, chance would now play a significant and increasing role in the proceedings. Now even an overzealous housekeeper who ignored the DO NOT DISTURB sign on the door could tilt the balance against him. Leon knew he needed to be extra alert now; the smallest slip could cost his life.

Without meaning to, Leon glanced at his watch: a little past ten. He did not need to calculate; in a few hours both his targets would be in town. In sixteen hours Masharrat would be down and Leon would be clear of this mess.

*Or dead.*

*No way. No damn way.*

*This time I will not fail. I cannot.*

But the words rang hollow. A strange sense of foreboding swamped him. Leon tried hard, but was unable to get rid of it.

*Those bastards, Ravinder and Edward, must pay for everything they did to me.*

A cold smile fled across his face.

*Whether Benazir's vendetta brought satisfaction to Fatima's crowd or not, it would certainly appease mine. They'd look like fools when I cut down the target from right under their nose.*

The long pent-up hate was still simmering in his head as he threw himself on the bed and tried to catch a nap. But sleep refused to oblige. Whether he looked forward or backward, it was riddled with restlessness. Conflicted and filled with doubt, Leon tossed and turned.

# TWENTY-FIVE

Ravinder was unable to sleep, though emotionally drained and physically exhausted. This was the first time he had been alone since morning and he welcomed the solitude. For the first time he was able to put away the mask, not worry about being strong for anyone and allow himself to feel. His grief and pain begged for release, yet lay trapped inside, like a piece of meat trapped in the windpipe, choking him. Ravinder *wanted* to cry but could not.

*Perhaps later . . . after all this is over. Right now I need to focus and ensure Leon doesn't succeed . . . or get away. He needs to pay for Simran and Goel.*

For the umpteenth time he wondered where Leon was and what he was up to. Also if they were right about the target he would strike at.

*Is it really Zardosi?*

Ravinder weighed the evidence again and again.

*I can't afford to be wrong.*

He was worrying about that when he heard Jasmine come out of her bedroom and head down, her slippered feet making a soft slapping sound on the stairs. Then he heard her moving around in the living room, the sound echoing dully through the huge empty bungalow.

*She has held herself together so well.*

He again felt a surge of pride at the way she had taken charge.

Then Simran's caution tugged at him. "Don't get fooled by that tough act she puts on. Jasmine is a softie at heart. Watch out for her, Ravinder."

Worry returned. So did the thought that he was not living up to his promise.

He got up to go downstairs and check on her, but sensing she, too, needed to be alone, he lay down again, paralyzed by an admixture of grief, worry, and the need to give her space.

Some time later he heard her come up the stairs and return to her room.

Then silence returned to the house.

Sleep followed a while later. With it came the nightmares.

Yet again Ravinder heard the truck engine revving loudly and saw it bearing down on Jasmine's car. He felt the shock as it struck and saw Jasmine's car being thrown forward. And Simran smash through the windscreen, fly over the hood, and hit the road. He saw her rise shakily and then with gathering strength walk back toward the shattered car. Midway she crumpled.

As she fell, she turned her bloodied face toward Ravinder and looked at him beseechingly. And Ravinder realized with horror that it was not Simran at all. It was Farah Fairfowler. And she was glaring at him.

*Angry?*

*Pleading for help?*

*Accusingly?*

Then, engine revving madly, the truck sped past. But now Leon was at the wheel, sneering and shaking a fist at Ravinder as he drove past.

And the ICU monitor flat-lined; its irritating but comforting beep mutating into a horrible whine of protest.

Ravinder's heart was pounding when he jerked awake. Thereafter he could not fall asleep again. Not properly. He lay there spent, dropping in and out of an uneasy sleep, watching the sky outside darken till the darkness was complete. Then slowly, uneasily, it began to lighten up again.

# DECEMBER
## 27

# ONE

Leon was not sure what woke him—probably the icy room temperature and that he had kicked off the comforter while sleeping. He was shivering with cold and bursting to pee.

The bedside clock showed 3:43 a.m.

Groggy with sleep, he stumbled into the bathroom and was unzipping when he spotted Naug's body in the bathtub. The dead man's face had collapsed and he looked deflated. And he seemed to be staring at Leon. Plaintively.

Reality returned with the abruptness of a 440-volt jolt to his nervous system. Unable to relieve himself Leon rushed out of the bathroom. But his bladder was killing him. And the surgical gloves he had fallen asleep wearing were itching. Resisting the urge to remove them he threw on Naug's coat, which he had readied for the next day, and hurried across to his room at the end of the corridor.

Still half asleep, Leon forgot he was wearing the disguise he'd used whilst renting the Sarita Vihar apartment: photograph number two on the APB. He'd meant to change out of it last night, into the Naug persona, but had drifted off.

The bigger mistake was to forget about the security cameras that monitor every nook and cranny of most hotels.

Pramod Jha, the supervisor manning the security control room, could not have failed to spot Leon; he was the only guest moving about at that unearthly hour. Not only did he see him, but Pramod also noticed his resemblance to the APB, which had been circulated by the Delhi Police to all security personnel of all hotels, and was now taped to the wall above the bank of CCTV monitors.

But luck was still riding pillion with Leon. At that late hour, watching over a slumbering hotel, Pramod was sluggish with sleep and the camera image was fleeting enough to preclude certain identification. Perhaps, like most human beings, Pramod was also not expecting trouble, not in *his* hotel and certainly not on *his* watch. Even when he saw Leon make his way back a few minutes later Pramod failed to make the connection between the man on the monitor and the APB stuck above it.

Blissfully ignorant of his mistake and the lucky break he had caught, Leon made his way back to Naug's bed and tumbled into it. Aware that he had a long day ahead of him and needed to be on top of his game, he fell asleep again.

# TWO

Ravinder could not stay in bed any longer, even though he knew he needed the rest. Feeling sluggish and unrested, but simmering with anticipation, he got out of bed when the grandfather clock struck six.

It was a typical Delhi winter morning: still dark outside; a leaden gray fog shrouding everything, reducing visibility to a few feet.

A stinging hot shower coaxed life back into his tired limbs. Forcing himself not to think of Simran as he got dressed, Ravinder headed down to the living room. The haunting fragrance of incense greeted him. He was about to ring for the maid to get him breakfast when his eye fell upon Simran's portrait mounted in the center of the family vanity wall.

*So that's what Jasmine was doing last night.*

Done a few months ago, during their last trip to Punjab, it was a good painting; the artist had captured her mood. Simran looked content and at peace.

Ravinder realized he was crying when he felt a tear trickle down his jawline.

"Isn't Mom looking lovely?"

Ravinder started; he had not heard Jasmine enter. "Yes. Yes, she is." He did not turn to face Jasmine, unwilling to let her see his tears.

But she came up and gave him a hug. "We are so busy being strong for each other . . . both of us need to let go." Jasmine began sobbing. "I miss Mom."

Ravinder felt the dam within burst. All the pain he had been damming up came hurtling out. They clung to each other and were still crying when the maid entered several minutes later. She stumbled to an embarrassed halt and hurried out, but both had sensed her presence and their moment of shared pain and release evaporated.

By the time they reached the breakfast table, both were back in control. Ravinder wasn't hungry, but he was aware that he had a long day ahead and would be plagued by headaches if he didn't eat, so he forced down an orange juice, some scrambled egg, bacon, and toast. Jasmine picked at her food, but she was at the door when he was leaving. And she seemed resolute again.

"You planning to step out anywhere today?" Jasmine's headshake brought him relief. "Excellent. Get some rest."

"I will." She forced a smile. "And you make sure you get back . . . as soon as you can."

"That's a promise, Princess."

"I'll hold you to that. And Dad, make them pay." Her request, almost a command, followed him out to the Bimmer.

Resolve reinforced, Ravinder told the driver, "Ferozeshah Kotla stadium. Go via the office. We have to pick up Archana and Chance."

Without meaning to, he touched the pistol in his coat pocket. He carried it because he'd promised Jasmine, but he was not sure he wanted it to see action.

# THREE

Leon reached for the phone out of habit. He had already picked up the call when he realized he was in Naug's room, not his own. A robotic voice informed him it was time to wake up. He did. And this time, despite his distaste, he used the bathroom to get ready. But it was eerie; even after closing the shower curtain to hide away Naug, Leon felt the dead man's stare. It compounded his unease.

Forcing himself to blank out everything, he focused on the makeup, using Naug's photo to ensure he got the details right. That took the better part of an hour. He was almost done when the phone began to ring. Leon knew he could not ignore it though it could be someone known to Naug, his wife, or it could also be the conference organizers. Hoping it was the latter, Leon answered.

*"Hei. Du ikke ringe?"* Leon had no idea what she meant, but guessed from her plaintive tone the woman was complaining about something in Norwegian.

"Hello," he answered. "The professor has already left for the conference."

"Oh. I see." The caller switched, her English fluent, with only a slight accent. "Please let him know his wife called."

"I'll do that, ma'am."

"And ask him to call me back, please," she added before ringing off.

Leon was about to breathe easy when the phone rang again.

"Good morning, Professor. This is Amit from New India Times Summit. I wanted to check if you would be joining us for breakfast at the auditorium, or would you prefer to come in later?"

"Later, please." Leon copied the tone and pitch he had heard Naug use during a TV interview and a TEDx talk he had pulled off the

Internet. The hours of practice paid off; Leon was happy with the ease with which he lapsed into Naug's voice. "I am tired from the flight and will come later."

"That is perfectly fine, sir. Your car will be waiting. Please ask the valet to page it when you're ready."

"Thank you."

Now Leon knew there was one final hurdle to cross before he left the hotel. Rechecking his makeup, he got dressed in Naug's suit, reviewed the equipment he had packed in Naug's conference bag, and settled down to wait for the housekeeping staff. He had to ensure they would not enter the room, at least not till evening.

# FOUR

Ravinder was surprised at the crowd thronging the Ferozeshah Kotla stadium. Despite the early hour there was a mile-long queue at the entrance and cars were backed up bumper to bumper for twice as many miles. It was going to be a full house.

Entering from Gate No. 1, they headed for the security control room, located at the far end of the East Hill stand.

"Good Lord!" Chance looked around, overwhelmed. Though the match was due to start only a couple of hours later, the stadium was already jam-packed. Bollywood music was blaring and cheerleaders of both teams, mostly young Caucasian women, could be seen practicing at opposite ends of the stadium. Cries of hawkers selling soft drinks, snacks, Indian flags of all sizes, and an assortment of trumpets and drums filled the air. "And I thought it was only we Brits who were so crazy about cricket."

"Seriously? Well, just FYI, we have two primary religions in India: cricket and Bollywood." Beside him, Archana laughed. "And when it is an India-Pakistan match"—she gave a wolf whistle—"it is nothing short of war."

"What's with you guys and Pakistan? Don't you think it's time to let bygones be bygones?" Ravinder heard Chance murmur; he was still surveying the teeming stadium.

"Right!" Archana gave him her sweetest smile. "Just like you Brits and the Irish have done?" Chance smiled at her sarcasm. "Besides, we Indians don't have a problem with Pakistan, as long as they stay out of our hair," Archana continued. "Most Indians don't give a damn what happens in Pakistan, we would rather focus on our economic development, but for Pakistan, it's a different story. You must understand, Chance, that Pakistan is possibly the only country that came into being based on the rejection of another state. The powers that be in Pakistan, their army and intelligence service, will never allow peace between the two countries because that would reduce their importance and thus their hold over Pakistani society and politics. That's why they have never allowed Indo-Pak relations to stabilize . . . not in the last sixty years . . . even at the cost of using terrorism as a weapon of state policy, even though that's tearing their own country apart now. All the crap that's going on in Pakistan now is merely a result of their own stupidity. But it suits the generals in power."

"Guys, can we have this lesson in international relations and geo-politics later? We have a job to do." Ravinder cut in, surveying the packed stadium. Though he had been expecting something like this, the full extent of the challenge they faced in stopping Leon struck Ravinder only now. He was overwhelmed.

Picking his way through the crowds he led them to the security control room.

It took them a while to find Aditya Trivedi, the stadium security chief. And he did not look too happy at being found. Obviously the last few days had been trying; Trivedi looked harried and frazzled. "Yes, Mr. Kurup told me to expect you." He was surly, just short of hostile. "What can I do for you?"

"Could we begin with a security update, please?" Ravinder asked.

"Seriously? You want me to brief you? *Now?* With a match about to start?" Aditya growled. "I have been looking after the security of this stadium for two years." He wagged an impertinent finger in Ravinder's face. "Nineteen international matches without the smallest incident and now you barge in here and . . ."

"Perhaps you would like to talk to Mr. Kurup again?" Nostrils flared, Archana jumped in before Ravinder could respond.

That worked like a Molotov cocktail tossed in a smoldering gas station; Ravinder saw Trivedi's face go bright red, as though he was having a seizure. Being threatened by newcomers in the heart of his domain was bad enough. That an upstart female about half his age had done it irked him no end.

"Sure, missy," Trivedi grated. "Why don't you do that? I have better things to do right now."

Ravinder realized the situation had escalated needlessly. "Calm down, everybody." He stepped in between them. "Let's all calm down."

"I *am* calm," Trivedi shot back. "Tell the lady here to relax." He glowered. "Do you realize I have a match—an *Indo-Pak* match—starting in less than two hours? *And* I have the Pakistani PM in attendance, along with God knows who else."

"That's precisely why we are here." Ravinder forced himself to stay calm; there was too much at stake and too little time left.

Just then an inspector rushed in. "They have found a bomb in East Hill stand."

"What?" Trivedi looked as though it had exploded between his legs.

# FIVE

Leon got rid of the housekeeping lady after making it clear his room was not to be disturbed in his absence, then called room service and ordered breakfast.

Twenty minutes later he was working his way through a bowl of muesli with cold milk, followed by a plate of cheese, ham, and turkey sandwiches. By the time he had downed the coffee Leon felt fortified and the misgivings he'd woken up with had receded. But he felt his nerves getting tauter, normal in the terminal stages of every operation. Today, for some reason, they seemed drawn tighter. The chocolates in the welcome pack by his bedside looked appealing; two of them gave him the sugar rush he craved.

A sudden burst of sound from the television caught his attention. It showed a long shot of the Ferozeshah Kotla stadium. The morning fog had lifted. Almost gone except for some errant wisps hovering over the pitch. Half a dozen teams with rollers were working briskly, smoothening and drying out the ground. The stands were awash with colors. Banners fluttered in the brisk breeze. Also visible were scores of dungaree-clad, gun-toting security men. They were everywhere. And they looked alert.

Leon knew the sheer numbers looked awesome and posed a credible psychological deterrence, but not a foolproof obstacle to a professional.

*Have they found either of the sniper rifles or the bombs yet?*

He hoped they had and wondered if Ravinder had taken the bait.

*Where are you, Ravinder? Stadium or auditorium? Zardosi or Masharrat?*

The clock on the stadium's giant scoreboard reminded him of the time.

*0957.*

*Time to move.*

He could start out a bit later, but in the past week had realized how unpredictable Delhi traffic could be. The thought of failing to finish the job because he had been stuck in a traffic jam made him smile. Almost.

After a final check to ensure he had everything he needed for the strike and had left no clues behind, Leon shouldered Naug's brown leather wheelie bag, caught hold of the food trolley, and pulled open the door.

As he parked the food trolley along the wall outside his door, he surveyed the corridor. In the distance past the elevator bank, he could see the housekeeping cart and three women heading for the elevator, one in hotel livery. The other two, leotard-clad, looked like they were headed for the gym. The woman in the pink and purple leotard certainly needed gym time, about ten kilos of it.

*But nothing else.*

No sign of anything out of the ordinary.

Confirming the DO NOT DISTURB sign was still in place, Leon watched the door click shut, double-checked it, and then headed for the elevators.

Leon was waiting in the porch for his car, which the valet had paged, when Pramod Jha, the supervisor who had been manning the control room during the night shift, emerged from the staff entrance.

# SIX

Pramod Jha was crossing over to the two-wheeler parking area where he had left his motorcycle when he spotted Leon. It was the coat that caught his eye—the same coat Leon had worn when he had gone to the toilet last night.

Memory synapses fired, and Pramod recalled not just when he had seen that coat, but also the man who had been wearing it. The APB photographs, lingering on the periphery of his memory, surged to the forefront. But before he could make the connection, one of the night-shift security guards, also going off duty, called out to him.

"Heading home, Boss? Can you give me a lift?"

"Sure, Naresh. Come along." Pramod knew Naresh lived en route.

"Thanks, Boss. I hope we can get back in time to watch the cricket match."

Pramod checked the time. "It's about to begin. But we should be able to catch the bulk of it."

"Hopefully."

The two got busy chatting as Pramod started the bike and Naresh hopped on. The coat and the man in the corridor early that morning both faded from Pramod's memory.

# SEVEN

Leon felt Pramod's gaze linger on him; his senses sent up a flare. But by the time he turned, all he saw was two hotel security men in casual conversation. Then the car sent for him by the conference organizers, a swanky gunmetal-colored Lexus, pulled up beside him. And he lost interest in them.

Nerves now as taut as piano wires, Leon got in; aware that from this point on the danger would escalate geometrically. Caught up in a multitude of thoughts, incessantly playing and replaying dozens of contingencies in his head, Leon hardly noticed the city passing him by as they hit the Ring Road and turned left toward Siri Fort auditorium.

"We will be there very soon, sir," the smart white-liveried chauffeur commented, startling Leon. That is when he noticed there was hardly any traffic.

"How come there is no traffic today?" Based on his experience of Delhi traffic the past week, he'd factored in forty-five minutes for this drive.

"It's the cricket match, sir. India and Pakistan are playing a one-day cricket match today." He saw the driver's grin, wider in the rearview mirror.

"I see." He didn't, though.

"Is cricket popular in your country?"

"Not really." Leon wasn't quite sure which country the driver was referring to and chose the safer answer to avoid conversation.

"We Indians love cricket." His grin was broader now. "An Indo-Pak match is a big deal. This one more so because it's the first time we have allowed their team into India since they carried out the terrorist attack on Mumbai. Many people will have taken leave today."

From the bare roads Leon saw it was a lot more than many people. They were making very good time. Inwardly he grimaced; now he would arrive much earlier than planned. Every additional minute onsite exposed him to more people and enhanced the chances of exposure. The unnecessary risk worried him.

# EIGHT

Ravinder could see Trivedi was badly shaken by the discovery of the bomb.

"How's that possible?" Trivedi confronted the inspector. "Every stand was swept yesterday and the stadium has been locked down since. No way a bomb could have gotten in."

Realizing this could be a blessing in disguise, Ravinder tapped Trivedi on the arm. "May I have a word with you? In private."

Trivedi seemed too dazed to object. Ravinder led him away from the others.

"That's what I wanted to tell you," Ravinder continued when they were out of earshot of the others. "We have evidence some of your men have sold out."

"But that is not . . ."

"Please, Mr. Trivedi," Ravinder cut him off. "We don't have time. There is going to be an assassination attempt on Zardosi and some of your men have been subverted or compromised. That much is certain. As you yourself pointed out, how could the bombs have gotten in otherwise?"

"One of my men is a traitor?" Trivedi looked devastated. "I'm going to kill him when I find him."

"Be my guest. But right now let's focus on keeping the Paki PM alive."

That sank in; Trivedi nodded.

"We need to work together, Mr. Trivedi. That's the only way we can beat this."

Trivedi nodded again, more vehemently now. "You have my assurance. Please tell me what you know."

Ravinder gave him a succinct summary.

"Bloody hell!" Trivedi was shocked. "So what do you suggest?"

"Let's do another sweep. Dogs, detectors . . . the full works."

"It'll be hellish." Trivedi surveyed the stands; they were chockablock. Drums and music rocked the stadium. Madly gyrating, skimpily clad cheerleaders were busy hyping up the crowd. "It's a fucking *tamasha* out there. If we set off a panic, hundreds could die in the stampede."

*Even more if a bomb goes off in the crowd.*

But Ravinder sensed he didn't need to say that; the thought must have struck Trivedi, too; he looked grave.

"But it has to be done, so let's do it as discreetly as possible . . . and the sooner we start the better," Ravinder emphasized. "I suggest we start with the VIP stands and work outward."

On more certain ground, now that the action required was clear, Trivedi walked back to his lieutenants and began barking out orders. They in turn got onto their radio sets. Soon Ravinder saw teams of khaki-clad men converging on the VIP box.

"How long before the match starts?"

Trivedi checked his watch. "Ninety-five minutes, but the VIPs will be here in an hour . . . . . at the latest. There's the opening ceremony and the toss; forty-five minutes before the match."

"Damn!" Ravinder swore. "That's cutting it too fine. We need to move fast." He turned to Chance and Archana. "Keeping the VIP box as the target, why don't you two work out possible sniper positions and help Mr. Trivedi's men search them."

"We've done that already, but I think it's a good idea to double-check." All traces of hostility had evaporated. Trivedi seemed relieved someone else had taken charge. "Let me give you some men." He called four constables from the control room.

Then Ravinder saw Kurup enter from Gate No. 1 and wave him over. He walked over and together they started toward the VIP box. Ravinder could not help notice how closely the director was scrutinizing him.

# NINE

Kurup was aware heads would roll if they failed to stop Leon from assassinating either target; his one of them. And he was unsure about Ravinder's stability; only natural considering the man had just lost his wife. Vishal's betrayal and Verma's complicity had shaken them all.

*Lousy bastards! I wish we had taken Vishal alive.*

"Trivedi's men found a bomb." Kurup jolted as Ravinder dropped that bombshell in his lap.

"*What?* Where?"

"That stand." Ravinder indicated East Hill stand, to the right of the VIP box.

"How on earth did it get in? I thought the stadium had been swept and sealed off last night."

"Looks like the handiwork of the blighters in cahoots with Vishal."

"Any idea who?"

Ravinder shook his head. "We're working on it. But my immediate worry is Leon." Kurup nodded agreement. "By my reckoning he should already be in the stadium." Pause. "I would, if I were executing something like this. I would be right out there"—Ravinder swept an arc around the VIP box—"somewhere in striking range."

Kurup saw doubt on Ravinder's face as he surveyed the teeming, pulsating crowd. The stadium was packed to full capacity and the crowd seemed in the mood to party.

As though to reinforce that, a roar exploded through the stadium. Everyone was cheering. Many were pointing and waving at the gigantic projection screens on all four sides of the stadium. On screen, Kurup saw a knot of colorfully clad people making their way toward the VIP box: Bollywood stars. A couple were waving and smiling at the crowds, exciting them further.

"Damn!" Kurup heard Ravinder mutter. "I hope they don't plan to put Zardosi's journey across the stadium on display." He slammed an irate fist on the VIP box wall. "We may as well gift-wrap Zardosi and hand him over to Leon."

"I agree." Kurup realized they had overlooked that. "Let's ensure that doesn't happen."

Both started at a rapid trot toward the control room. They had gone a dozen feet when another roar broke out; the picture on the screens changed. Surrounded by dozens of Black Cat commandos, the Indian prime minister could be seen walking alongside Zardosi. They had entered from Gate No. 1 and were making their way across to the VIP stand.

"I had no idea our PM would also be here." Ravinder was surprised.

"Neither did I," Kurup mumbled. He looked like he was going into cardiac arrest; as director of the NIA, he expected to be informed when the PM decided to gallivant in public. *Especially* when there was a clear and present threat. "This is just not done," he muttered under his breath. Then louder, "Must be some buffoon's idea of cricket diplomacy . . . silly twits."

"Look at the brighter side," Ravinder consoled, "we will have twice the security now. Hopefully it will make things harder for Leon."

"Yeah. Maybe he will abort." Kurup made no attempt to mask his sarcasm. "Twice the bloody risk, too. Now Binder has a hit-one-get-one-free offer going . . . especially if he's planning to use a bomb."

The prime ministerial entourage came up the stairs, turned left, and began to walk toward the VIP box two hundred feet away.

Kurup realized he was holding his breath.

Beside him Ravinder appeared equally tense.

If ever there was a sniper moment, this was it.

# TEN

Leon steadied his breathing as his target hove into view. Despite his telling the driver to take it easy, they had arrived at the Siri Fort auditorium in fifteen minutes.

*Half a mile now.*

A sudden wave of dread swept through Leon. As though something deadly awaited him beyond the auditorium gates.

*Quarter of a mile.*

His heart plummeted; Leon knew he should go no further. An eerie premonition screamed at him. Warning him. He *knew* if he went through those gates he would not come out alive.

*Five hundred feet.*

Leon leaned forward to tell the driver to turn back. Before he could speak, a motorcyclist cut across the front forcing the driver to brake suddenly.

"Stupid sardar," the driver muttered under his breath at the Sikh motorcyclist, who sped away, weaving through traffic without a care in the world.

It reminded Leon that Ravinder could be waiting for him past those gates.

*Unless the decoys I got Vishal to deploy at Ferozeshah Kotla stadium have fooled him.*

Leon was not sure how he felt about that; the professional within hoped Ravinder would have taken the bait, but the man did not; angry, he *wanted* to confront Ravinder. To force Ravinder to confess *he* had killed Farah Fairfowler. To make him beg for mercy. And *then* kill him.

*Two hundred feet.*

Fortified by hate, Leon leaned back; he would *not* avoid this tryst with destiny. If life had brought him thus far, it would see him through to the end.

*Ravinder's end.*

Leon longed to see that hated face in his gunsight.

The Lexus rapidly chewed up the final hundred feet and pulled up at the Siri Fort auditorium gate.

"This is as far as I can go, sir. No cars are allowed beyond this point," the driver said apologetically as he held the door open for Leon and handed him over to the waiting liaison officer.

"Good morning, sir. I am Deepa Pandey and will be assisting you today."

"Good morning, Deepa." Leon scrutinized the petite young lady as they shook—a college student, he guessed; conference organizers the world over tended to hire them by the dozen.

*Good! Not security trained and eager to please. What more could one want?*

Deepa Pandey was dressed in a black blouse, printed maroon sari with a matching black border, and fashionably high heels. She was giving her best smile, blissfully unaware that after today life would never again be the same for her.

"Thank you for helping me, Deepa."

"My pleasure, sir. This way, please." She ushered him toward the arsenal of men and machines securing the auditorium gate.

Leon took a moment to review the layout, trying to spot changes from the time he'd carried out the last recon.

There were three security lanes, cordoned off from each other by lines of flowerpots and orange traffic cones. A red runner—a twenty-feet-long strip of red carpet, about two feet wide—depicted each lane. The runner passed through a doorframe metal detector manned by two security guards, one male and one female, both armed with the usual complement of handguns and batons.

To the right of each doorframe metal detector was a baggage-screening machine, the kind used by airport security; each was manned by a guard at both ends and a third man keeping an eye on the monitor on which baggage passing through was displayed.

*Rapiscan 620DV.* Leon identified it immediately. He knew its dual-view multi-energy high-resolution x-ray technology and material analysis software made it virtually foolproof, capable of detecting even liquid explosives. Leon was relieved he was not carrying any obvious weapons.

Standing farther back from the gate, safe from any immediate assault and with a wider view of the gates, were another set of guards, two per lane, armed with 5.56mm INSAS semiautomatic rifles. Further away, behind sandbags, was the final line of defense, also armed with semiautomatic rifles. Leon counted four sandbagged fortifications with two men each. Everyone alert.

His mind auto-calculated: nine handguns and sixteen semiautomatic rifles, at the very least. Leon knew there would be plenty more, at the other gates and on patrol around the auditorium. Not to mention the snipers on the roof and, of course, the reserves standing by in neighborhood police stations.

*Nothing short of a full-scale attack by an infantry company would even make a dent.*

He had expected nothing less.

The third security lane, the one on Leon's left, was marked "Speakers Only"; Deepa guided him toward it.

The guards were alert and knew the drill. However, the ones manning the speakers' lane had been told to handle their guests with care. Also, they had just been told by Deepa to expect Professor Naug, and human beings tend to see what they expect to. Leon passed the identity check with barely a glance.

The items in the bag were inspected thoroughly, first by the Rapiscan and then at the other end of the security lane manually by a polite but conscientious guard. However, most speakers carry clickers, connectors, and the like, so the things in Leon's bag excited no alarm. The guard did find the microphones a bit odd, but not to the point of making an issue. Hustled on by the liaison officer, he allowed the professor to pass.

Every operation has a point of no return. The point when critical mass is obtained and the mission takes on a life of its own.

Leon knew this point had been crossed as he stepped past the doorframe metal detector, collected his bag from the Rapiscan, and followed Deepa toward the auditorium. Exactly as had happened every time when the final security barrier had been breached, he felt his anxiety bleed away and his nerves start to settle down.

Soon he was in the zone; everything except the target and the kill faded from his mind.

# ELEVEN

Ravinder felt a wave of relief as the two prime ministers vanished into the VIP box. The cocoon of bulletproof glass and triple layer of men would keep them safe, at least for the moment. He scanned the stadium again, wondering how and when Leon would strike.

*Where are you hiding, Leon Binder?*

The roar of the crowd escalated; Ravinder saw both team captains were out in the middle. Standing between them was another veteran cricketer, Sunil Gavaskar, a legend who had captained the Indian team for many years and was now a commentator. Facing him was a tall Caucasian man with a full head of gray hair.

"We are now ready for the toss." Gavaskar spoke with the pumped-up enthusiasm commentators display so effortlessly. "Both the captains are here and so is Michael Hobbs, the match referee." He turned to the gray-haired Caucasian. "Looking forward to an exciting day of cricket, are we?" He got a smile in return. "And who has the coin?"

The Indian captain, Mahender Singh Dhoni, held it above his head, showing it to the crowd, before tossing it up in the air.

"Heads is the call from the Pakistani captain." Gavaskar's excited voice rang out as the high-speed camera caught the spinning coin glinting in the air.

Hobbs leaned in as the coin hit the ground.

"Heads!"

"And the Pakistani captain has made the right call. Heads it is."

"We will bat." The Pakistani captain told his Indian counterpart as they shook.

Ravinder tuned out as Gavaskar spoke to both team captains. He switched his attention back to the crowd, trying to figure out where Leon could be. Ravinder could see the search teams making their way through the stands, but progress was excruciatingly slow; so far not even the stands around the VIP box had been cleared.

The teams would soon be emerging from the dressing rooms; a Mexican wave splashed over the stadium. Anticipation was escalating, like artillery fire softening up the target before an infantry attack.

# TWELVE

Leon hit the second security barrier as they entered the stadium. But by now his nerves had iced over; he was in the eye of the hurricane.

"Sorry about all these security checks, sir." Deepa's smile was sheepish. "But you know how it is."

"I understand." Leon returned a polite smile and waited patiently as the guard rifled through the bag.

Once again it did not take long. Unwittingly, Deepa Pandey did her bit to help things along.

Then they were in.

A thrill raced through Leon as he shouldered his bag and followed Deepa. She walked briskly, turning back every now and then to confirm he was behind her. Cutting through the crowd in the auditorium lobby, she led to the left. At the end of the lobby they reached a corridor barricaded off with a long table manned by four guards, two men and two women. All four with sidearms.

CONFERENCE SPEAKERS ONLY announced the sign on the table. To the left there was an arrow indicating GREEN ROOM. And to the right was another that said RED ROOM. Deepa waited till the security man had checked both their conference tags and then led Leon toward the Green Room.

"What is that?" Leon pointed at the RED ROOM sign.

"That's for speakers believed to be facing additional security threats."

Leon looked back and noticed there was another cluster of guards at the end of the corridor, this lot armed with automatics.

*So that is where Masharrat is likely to be.*

Absorbing the layout he followed Deepa into the Green Room. It was empty, barring an elegant elderly Indian lady in a Temple silk sari; she was immersed in her laptop and looked up only briefly to give a vague smile.

It was a large room with thick maroon carpeting, deep, matching sofa chairs, and a massive glass chandelier. Several miniature paintings from the Mughal period adorned the walls. The curtains had been drawn, held back by tasseled cords at either end; a large dose of sunlight lit up the room. At the far end was a long buffet table laden with snacks, tea, coffee, and juices.

"May I get you something to drink, sir?"

"No, thank you, Deepa. Please don't worry about me. I think I will also go through my speech." Indicating the lady with the laptop, Leon headed for the opposite corner, as far from her and the coffee table as possible.

"Sure, sir. You will not be disturbed here. The morning speakers have already gone for their sessions and the afternoon ones will come in only around lunch. We still have half an hour before they start arriving."

That suited Leon; the less people he was exposed to the better. Opening Naug's laptop he began browsing through it to kill time; Leon had only one task left before he pulled the plug on his target.

# THIRTEEN

Ravinder felt the energy in the stadium escalate as the Indian team jogged into the middle. The crowd roared as they fanned out to take position.

"*Sachin! Sachin!*" The Little Master, Sachin Tendulkar, acknowledged the accolades with a smile, which was captured by the large screens, as he moved to take position at the slip. This was his final match before he hung up his pads, and his fans were looking forward to some stellar fielding and then a blistering knock from him.

"*Dhoni! Captain Cool! Pack off the Pakis!*" began the second, louder chant. "*Pack off the Pakis.*" The chant gathered momentum.

Then the two Pakistani opening batsmen emerged from their dressing room and began to walk out into the middle, swinging their bats to free their arms. The cheer this time was muted and restricted to a smaller corner of the North stand, directly across from the VIP stand, where the Pakistani supporters were huddled. Ravinder could see some Pakistani flags being waved there. Predictably there were some boos and hisses, too, from the other stands. Understandably so, this was the first time since the Pak-sponsored terrorist attack on Mumbai that their team had been allowed to play in India, and not everyone favored this decision. The recent beheading of an Indian soldier by the Pakistani army on the Kashmir border had added much heat.

Fighting to avoid these distractions, Ravinder focused on the VIP box. He saw both prime ministers waving and smiling for the cameras, which were right now focused on them. Ravinder knew that would last only till the first ball was bowled.

Kurup's mobile must have rung because he put it to his right ear, closing the other one with his left hand as he tried to converse about the roar of the crowd.

"The PM wants me," Kurup muttered darkly after the call was over. "Ravinder, I'm banking on you to keep that Paki bugger alive." He chucked his chin at Zardosi.

"I will do my best." Ravinder wished he felt as confident as he sounded. He was more than a little overwhelmed by the sea of humanity. Leon could be anywhere and no one would be wiser.

*All Leon needs is one tiny window of opportunity.*

Ravinder grimaced, aware it was impossible to protect anyone all the time. Luckily, the saving grace was that Leon was a professional and not one of those suicidal jihadis.

*He will want to get away, too.*

That was the one major chink in Leon's armor Ravinder knew he could exploit. But he had to do that *before* Leon could carry out his strike. If Leon managed to assassinate Zardosi, then capturing him would provide scant solace.

Kurup picked up on his apprehensions; Ravinder saw him frown as he peeled off and headed for the VIP box.

"What the hell are you guys doing?" Ravinder heard Trivedi, beside him, growl into his radio. "You morons are supposed to be looking *out*, at the audience, and not at the damn game."

That had the desired effect; security men around the stadium stopped gawking at the players and straightened up, aware their chief was watching them. But Ravinder realized again how easily people could get distracted, even when they knew the importance of their tasks. Weaknesses such as this were what assassins like Leon exploited.

There was a bitter taste in his mouth as Ravinder scanned the stadium again; the men checking the stands around the VIP box had progressed. Barring the group working the section below the VIP box, the other two had moved on to the next sections.

Ravinder knew they needed a break. Badly.

Unbeknownst to him, the God of War had just switched sides.

# FOURTEEN

Pramod snapped out of autopilot when there was a sharp bang and his motorcycle developed a life of its own. He fought the handlebars and brought it to a stop.

"It's a puncture." Naresh, the security guard riding pillion, peered down.

"I figured, genius." Getting off, they examined the front tire; there was a long bent nail protruding from it.

"There is a puncture repair shop around the corner." The guard with the high IQ pointed it out and then helped wheel the bike. "Hope it's open, though." An understandable fear, since Indo-Pak cricket matches were notorious for keeping people home glued to their television sets.

The shop was open, but devoid of customers. The owner was huddled in one corner with an electric stove to stave off the cold and a portable television, an ancient model, to catch the match. He did not look pleased when he saw the punctured motorcycle.

"Give me a minute." He pointed at the television set. "The match is about to start. I don't want to miss the first over."

The motorcycle was forgotten as the guard and his supervisor both joined the huddle in front of the television.

"Pity your television set is so small," Pramod commented.

That earned him a dirty look from the puncture man. "I will get a big flat-screen high-definition one too, as soon as misers like you start paying a hundred bucks for a puncture instead of a measly fifty."

An excited roar from the TV distracted the duelists.

"Captain Dhoni has given the ball to Ishant Sharma, one of the

374 |

spearheads of the Indian pace battery," the commentator said excitedly.

"Pack off the Pakis." The chant escalated to a crescendo as
Ishant, rubbing the ball on his pant leg, measured off his long run
up. Then Ishant turned to face the opening batsmen.

At the other end Saeed Anwar, the Pakistani opener, tightened
his helmet strap, adjusted his pads, and settled down to meet the
bowl.

Between the two, the Stadium end umpire slowly swung around
to check everything was in order. Then, aware of the significance of
the match, walked out of the bowler's line, dropped his hand dramatically, and called out loudly, "Let's play."

A hush descended on the stadium as Ishant Sharma came steaming
down his amazingly long run up, gathering speed with every stride.

Saeed Anwar stood stock-still; eyes unblinking, mouth slightly
open and bat poised an inch above the ground.

Ishant Sharma hit the final stride with a loud *umph* and released
the bowl at the highest end of its trajectory.

Traveling at 149 kilometers per hour, the ball slashed forward, a
blur of white. It hit the pitch inches short of the crease and shot forward, staying low.

Anwar's bat came down, right in line with the ball, but a tad too
late.

*"My god! What an amazing ball."* The commentator's excited voice
erupted out of the television set. "Anwar was almost done in by the
lack of bounce."

A hiss went through the crowd.

Ishant's expression changed from excitement to frustration as he
realized he had beaten the bat but missed the wicket.

Anwar looked shaken, but gathered himself and, swinging his
arms to free them up, took guard again.

The puncture man and his audience looked equally tense as the
ball made its way back from Dhoni, the wicket keeper, to Rohit
Sharma at silly mid-off and thence to Ishant at the other end.

Again, Ishant ferociously delivered the second ball, a fuller-length
delivery.

Anwar, aware he needed to assert himself or risk being cowed by
the bowler, stepped forward and swung. A solid well-timed swing.
There was a satisfying thud as he connected.

"Saeed Anwar has picked that one up nicely. On the up." The commentator loved this. "And it has gone high in the air." It was impossible to see the ball on the grainy television. "Will it clear the distance?"

The puncture man was looking sick.

"*Yes! It does.* And nicely, too. Into the crowd."

"*Bhenchod* Paki!" The puncture man broke the silence around the television set. He looked ready to murder someone.

Miles away, in the stadium, the duel between bat and ball continued as Ishant Sharma ran in again.

There was another meaty thwack as bat and ball collided.

"Anwar does it again. Much flatter this time, but it will clear the ropes easily. More runs on the board for Pakistan. Their prime minister must be delighted with this start."

On cue the camera cut to the VIP box, where Zardosi was beaming. The Indian PM did not look happy, but aware of the cameras he had on the smile that tired hookers and slimy politicians use with uncanny ease.

"I don't know what the hell Dhoni is doing. Why did he have to give the new ball to Ishant Sharma?" The puncture man gave his captive audience an all-knowing look. "I would have asked Umesh Yadav to bowl."

Pramod, who worshiped Dhoni, looked irritated, but held his peace, unwilling to rock the boat till the puncture was fixed.

On screen, Ishant Sharma was racing in again, looking as determined as before. There was again that *umph* sound when he released the ball.

The third one stayed low and came in much faster, at 152 kilometers per hour according to the ball speed counter on the screen. It slipped past before the bat had descended fully. This time the line was flawless.

CRACK! The outer wicket went cartwheeling into the air.

"*Bowled him!*" The commentator was beside himself.

The crowd in the stadium exploded.

Anwar looked stunned. Then, shouldering his bat, he began the long walk back to the pavilion.

Ishant, who had been shaken by two successive sixers, was aggressively pointing at Anwar, showing him the way out, whilst an exuberant Indian team ran up and thumped him on the back. A wicket in the first over is always a massive morale boost.

"I knew that would happen." The puncture man-cum-cricket sage remarked. "It always does when the batsman becomes too confident." Then, deciding he had not done justice to the event, he felt the need to insult Anwar's sisters again. *"Bhenchod* Pakis."

"Why don't you start fixing the puncture while the new man comes out?" Pramod, who by now had had enough of his side commentary, asked sourly.

"Let me know when they start again." The puncture man reluctantly went out to the bike.

On the screen, the cameras cut for the commercial break that happens whenever a wicket falls. However, instead of the usual soap and soda sales spiel, the APB for Leon Binder came on. Archana had played it smart; aware Indo-Pak matches attract millions of eyeballs, she had ensured the APB would be run during commercial breaks. Considering the commercial value of such prime viewing slots, it had taken a lot of arm-twisting, but it is hard for any television channel to refuse a request that has the full weight of the NIA behind it.

For twenty seconds, the four photos of Leon, generated by Archana, occupied the screen in Technicolor glory. Splashed across the photos was the reward amount, a million rupees.

"I know this guy." Pramod stared at the screen, eyes shifting between the photos and the reward money, trying hard to jog his memory. "I have seen him . . . somewhere . . . just recently."

The APB vanished, replaced by a slick anorexic woman sashaying across the lobby of a fancy mall, telling the world SK-II had restored her youth. However, she failed to impress Pramod, who was racking his brains. The anorexic lady was followed by a swish-looking man in an equally swish light brown coat, who strode up to a gleaming black and red motorcycle and said, "If it is a 100 cc bike you're looking for, look no further."

It was the coat that flicked the switch in Pramod's head.

"It was the guy in the corridor." He turned excitedly to Naresh. "That guy last night." Naresh looked bewildered. "On the fifth floor of the hotel." Now excited, aware of all he could do with a million rupees, Pramod hauled out his mobile and headed out of earshot; he had no intention of sharing the reward money with anyone.

By the time the second Pakistani batsman arrived at the crease and Ishant Sharma completed his over, giving away only one more run, Pramod was connected to the Police Control Room.

"You are certain I'll get the reward?" Pramod inquired suspiciously when asked which hotel he had spotted the wanted man in. "Why can't you connect me with someone senior?"

By the time the officer in charge of the Police Control Room came on and Pramod finished telling his story, Umesh Yadav had bowled the second over.

# FIFTEEN

Ravinder saw Trivedi wave frantically from near the control room. He was hurrying over when he heard the commentator announce that Ishant Sharma would be bowling the third over, again from the Stadium end.

"We've found another bomb!" Trivedi was breathless with anxiety.

"Where?" Ravinder was shocked.

"In the West Hill stand . . . to the right of the previous one."

"To the right? That means further away from the VIP box?" Ravinder was surprised.

"Yes." Trivedi pointed. "There."

"Defused it yet?"

"Not yet. There are so many people about. There will be a panic."

"Even more if it goes off," Ravinder retorted. "Get your best men there. Now!"

"I already have." His mobile rang. Trivedi clicked on his Bluetooth headset. "What? *Really?* Are you sure? Oh, excellent." He ended the call and told Ravinder excitedly, "They've defused it."

"That fast?"

"I know. Great, isn't it? My man said it was a crude device."

"What do you mean?" Ravinder's surprise escalated. "Ask him for details. Could you please get him to talk to me?" Trivedi got him on the line and handed Ravinder the mobile. "What kind of device is it?" Ravinder asked. Then added hastily, "In plain English, please. Spare me the technicalities."

"Very basic device, sir." The bomb disposal man was obviously used to briefing people who didn't know a bomb from a blond. "Some explosive, a handful of nails and ball bearings, a detonator, and an improvised timer. No cutouts, no bypasses, no trips. Nothing."

"When you say *some explosive,* what kind of damage are you talking about?"

"Oh, it would have done damage, for sure. Seeing how packed the stands are, we're talking fifteen to twenty people at the very least." He went on: "But it was a crudely assembled bomb. A professional would have used some more explosive, a lot more shrapnel, and ensured it wasn't so easy to disarm. This was a poor, hastily put together job."

"I see." But Ravinder did not. He was lost in thought when he handed the mobile back to Trivedi. Then his mobile buzzed. Ravinder took the call with alacrity. "Yes, Chance?"

"We have found a sniper rifle."

"*What?* Where?" Now the alarm bells were clanging louder in Ravinder's head.

"Eleven o'clock from the VIP box." Ravinder faced that way. "Do you see the rafters? Just above the top edge of the scoreboard."

"Remove the rifle's bolt or firing pin and leave it there. Put two men in the vicinity to keep an eye on it. Discreetly. They should nab anyone who comes for it."

"Will do," Chance said briskly.

"Then continue the search, Chance. We're not out of the woods yet." Ravinder ended the call and turned to Trivedi. "Did your people search that area?" He pointed. Trivedi followed his finger, then nodded. "Yes, we did. I can even tell you when and who searched it. We have logs." He looked really worried. "Why?"

"They found a sniper rifle there." Ravinder was so lost in his thoughts that Trivedi's shock barely registered.

*This is too weird . . . too easy.*

The feeling that something was wrong began tightening its grip on him. Ravinder sensed he was missing a vital clue. He began to run through everything, right from the get-go, trying hard to spot the missing link.

# SIXTEEN

Leon took in the trio, two men and a woman, who entered the speakers' waiting room and headed for the buffet. He returned to his laptop, pretending he was busy. Then the door swung open again and another group of four entered. Then, a couple of minutes later, another larger group. Deepa was with the last lot.

"Time for lunch, sir." She came up to him, smiling brightly.

"Quite so." Leon shut the laptop. "I was about to look for you. Would it be possible for me to test my Mac connections to the projector?"

"That will not be a problem, sir. Everything has been checked and rechecked. You don't need to worry at all."

"But I would prefer to check for myself," Leon said a little more insistently.

Deepa shrugged. "If that will make you feel better, certainly, sir. May I go and check if the room is free now?"

"Thank you." Leon was relieved; this would be the only opportunity for him to plant the equipment since Masharrat's speech was right after lunch, just before Naug's talk.

"Meanwhile, why don't you have some lunch?"

Leon had no desire to mingle with the other speakers clustered around the lunch table. Deepa noticed his hesitation. Mistaking it for shyness or the nervousness that many speakers suffer, she added, "Please allow me to get some for you."

Brushing aside his protests she went off, returning a few minutes later with a loaded plate. "I got a selection of items since I was not sure what you would prefer. And mostly nonspicy things." Then she headed out.

Leon had managed a few bites of the delicious Tunde kebabs

when Deepa returned. "Sorry, sir, but they're having a special session for some dignitaries in that room right now. That will end in only twenty minutes. However, I have checked with the technical officer and he has assured me you will have no problems connecting your Mac."

Leon let his disappointment show. Deepa noticed, mistook it for pretalk jitters again, and added, "But you're welcome to check if you still wish to, after that session." She checked the time. "We will still have about ten minutes before General Masharrat's keynote."

"That's fine, then." Leon hid his relief; ten minutes was more than he needed to switch the items on the lectern with his own.

"Would you like to attend the general's keynote, sir?"

"That would be wonderful." If she hadn't asked, Leon would have.

"Excellent. The first row is reserved for speakers, so you'll have a great seat."

Leon had studied every word of the speakers' invitations and was aware of that. Though he had also planned for the eventuality where he'd have to trigger the weapon from a distance.

He checked his watch; only five minutes had elapsed.

*Fifteen more to go.*

His mind began to race ahead, planning each step of the journey: switching the microphone and adaptor, triggering the sarin, use the ensuing confusion to exit and get to the airport. There were no major roadblocks he could visualize.

Splashing some mint sauce on the Tunde kebab, he helped himself to another piece, wondering where Ravinder was.

# SEVENTEEN

Ravinder was so deeply immersed in thought he realized Kurup was by his side only when he felt the tap on his shoulder.

"We have a sighting." Kurup looked animated. "Leon was seen at the Leela Palace early this morning."

Kurup's enthusiasm infected Ravinder as the NIA director brought him up to speed.

"The hotel's security supervisor does not remember the room numbers, but he is confident he can point them out. He should be back at the hotel soon. Then we will know which room Leon was spotted coming out from, the one he went to, and who they both are registered to."

"Brilliant!" Ravinder was excited.

A roar filled the stadium. The crowd was on its feet as another Pakistani wicket fell. Again Ravinder was reminded Leon could be somewhere out there, in the seventy thousand people crammed into the stadium, biding his time, and waiting for the right moment to strike.

*And we still don't know how . . . those bombs and that sniper rifle don't jell . . . something is wrong . . . what was he doing at the Leela?*

His unease affected Kurup. "I know what you're thinking, Ravinder." The director was equally somber. "Binder could be out there right now. Moving in for the kill."

Ravinder nodded. "And we still don't know which of Trivedi's men have been compromised . . . or how Leon plans to use them."

"What have we here?" The excited voice of the commentator tugged at his attention. "It looks like Dhoni is keen to exploit these early wickets and is going for the kill. He has given the ball to Ashwin."

*Ashwin! Ashwin!*

*Bluffmaster! Bluffmaster!*
*Pack off the Pakis!*
*Send them home, Bluffmaster!*

The crowd was up on its feet now. With only a hundred and eleven runs on the board and six wickets down, the Pakistani tail had been exposed. Another one or two quick wickets and the game was pretty much lost; with the Indian batsmen in form, anything below two hundred runs on the board was certain hara-kiri. Pakistan needed at least two-fifty to pose a credible challenge.

Still preoccupied, trying to pinpoint what he'd missed, Ravinder watched Ashwin run up to the wicket; it was a short, almost lazy run-up. Ashwin released the ball with a gentle flick. Ravinder watched it hit the ground just before the batsman and then spin, arcing wildly in the air. The bat missed it by a mile. There was a collective intake of breath as it snicked past the wicket, missing off-stump by a whisker.

Dhoni had a wicked smile on his face as he collected the ball behind the wicket and tossed it to Tendulkar, who in turn threw it back to Ashwin. Understandably so—Ashwin was known for his uncanny ability to outthink and outmaneuver even the most seasoned batsmen.

The Pakistani tail-ender was feeling the pressure, though he forced a smile when his compatriot at the other end, the only top-ranking batsmen who had survived thus far, said something to him.

The Indian players did not need to guess he had told the tail-ender to take a single and get to the non-striker's end; they closed in on the batsman, adding to the pressure.

*Bluffmaster. Bluffmaster. Pack off the Pakis.*

The crowd egged Ashwin back to his starting point.

Ravinder saw Ashwin swivel slowly, surveying the field. Then he gave the batsman a smile, the sort a python gives to a rabbit before devouring it.

Despite the tension about Leon, Ravinder could not take his eyes off the players.

Ashwin knew the batsman was wondering where the ball would land—full or short; flighted or flat—and which way it would spin, or if it would spin at all. Both knew the better part of the game was played in the head; that's where matches are lost and won.

*And I own the head. Even yours*, Ashwin's smile seemed to be saying.

Watching him on the giant screen, gently rotating the ball in his hand whilst he smiled the batsman to death, Ravinder got a sense why Ashwin had such a deadly reputation.

Then Ashwin moved. Again that leisurely run-up and gentle flick as the ball shot out of his hand. It flew across, deceptively slow, landed well short of the batsman and then shot forward, but hugging the ground. The hapless tail-ender had no chance; it was the sort of ball that would have left far better batsmen gasping; he watched it crash into the center wicket.

"*Bowled him,*" the commentator roared. "That one rattled his cage."

The crowd was on its feet again.

Tendulkar did a victory jig.

Dhoni pumped the air.

Ashwin smiled; again that soft, barely discernible, deceptively lazy smile.

*Pack off the Pakis.*

*Give us another one, Bluffmaster.*

Head down, the Pakistani tail-ender began the long walk back to the pavilion. The batsmen at the order end banged his bat on the ground to vent his frustration.

And Ashwin kept smiling. No theatrics. No dramatics. Just that beatific smile.

It was Ashwin's smile that turned the trick. Ravinder knew where he had seen such a smile before: it had been Leon's trademark, whenever he bested anyone at chess.

And Ravinder *knew* he had been duped. Outplayed. Outmaneuvered.

# EIGHTEEN

Leon checked his watch again; it seemed to be crawling. Fifteen of the twenty minutes promised by Deepa had elapsed. But it seemed much longer.

By now Leon's nerves were stretched to the max. He craved action. Forcing himself to calm down, he fought the urge to get moving.

Across the room he could see Deepa in a cluster of other similarly clad liaison officers. He threw several mental barbs at her, willing her to turn and look at him. But Deepa was engrossed with her colleagues and the plates of food between them. Aching with impatience, but unwilling to attract attention, he decided to wait another few minutes.

# ΠΙΠΕΤΕΕΠ

Ravinder was momentarily stunned by the realization that Leon might have bested him.

*I'm in the wrong place.*

*No! It cannot be.*

But, from all those years ago, the sight of Edward and Leon huddled over the chessboard, by the fireplace of their London apartment, kept rebounding to the forefront of his memory. Of Edward smacking his forehead with his palm as Leon checkmated him. And Leon smiling that inimitable smile. Just like Ashwin had been giving the Pakistani batsmen.

*Bluff and counterbluff. Leon never did the obvious.*

"Which was the hotel again?" Ravinder spun around on Kurup. "Where they spotted Leon."

"The Leela Palace. Why?"

This time the name clicked. "Isn't that where most of the conference delegates are staying?"

"Yes. *Damn!*" Kurup's brow unfurrowed. "*Masharrat.*" He looked thunderstruck. "Binder is going for Masharrat?"

It was not really a question, but Ravinder nodded. "Why else would he go to that particular hotel? I'm guessing he plans to enter the conference disguised as a delegate. Perhaps one of the delegates is helping him out."

"That's possible. Give me a second." Kurup brought his mobile into action. Three quick calls. The third caller put him on hold. Minutes began to tick away. Agonizingly.

Ravinder could hear Kurup cracking his knuckles against his thigh. Despite the cold, Kurup was sweating. Ravinder checked the urge to start wearing out the floor; instead he used his smartphone to access the schedules and details of both targets and venues; Archana had stored them on his Dropbox.

The caller must have returned; Ravinder heard Kurup bark, "Are you sure?" Ravinder wished he could hear the other half of the conversation. "Damn sure? Okay. Fine. Go find him."

When Kurup put down the phone he looked shaken. "Bloody hell! That room Leon was spotted coming out from belongs to Professor Naug, a scientist who is scheduled to . . ."

"Speak after Masharrat," Ravinder completed, reconfirming it from the conference schedule. "Where's the professor now?"

"Last seen leaving the hotel in a car sent by the conference organizers."

"So we assume he is either a willing accomplice or Leon has duped him into cooperating. Either way we need to find him."

"I'll tell them to do so right away."

"And the other room?"

"Registered in the name of one Noel Rednib, a British national."

"Noel Rednib." Ravinder thoughtfully repeated the name a couple of times; it seemed familiar. "Bloody hell! The gall of the man. That's Leon Binder spelt backwards." He smashed his fist on the seat back; it was as though Leon was taunting them, challenging Ravinder to find him. "We have him now."

Kurup's mobile sprang to life again. "They saw him leave? What about . . . okay. I understand. Get hold of a warrant, then, and search that room, too." He turned to Ravinder. "The hotel staff saw the professor leave and Leon's room is empty." Kurup looked morose. "They want a warrant before they let us search the professor's room."

"How did they let them search Leon's without one?"

"My men got lucky; it was already open and housekeeping was cleaning it. But Naug's has a 'Do Not Disturb' sign on it and the professor specifically told housekeeping not to clean it till he got back."

"A warrant should not take long."

"No, it won't." Kurup looked really upset. "But by now I'm sure Leon is inside Siri Fort already or will be soon."

"I think so, too." Ravinder felt his excitement peak; they finally had the break they desperately needed. "We have to ensure he doesn't leave Siri Fort alive."

"I get that, but I will not allow Masharrat to get on the stage. I cannot take any chances with that," Kurup said resolutely.

"I agree." Ravinder knew the director was right. Ravinder was equally reluctant to tempt fate. "Though, knowing Leon, I am not sure how safe Masharrat would be even otherwise, with Leon loose inside the auditorium."

"I think so, too. I plan to move him out right away. To somewhere safer."

"Unplanned transit protection is always dicey," Ravinder pointed out. "Till we can plan a properly secured exit, it might be better to hold him in a secure room, double the guard, and ensure nothing gets in or out. Also, if I were you, I'd move that bugger straight to the airport and send him back to whatever hole he crawled out of."

"I wish." Despite the tension Kurup grinned. "But I agree with the need for a planned exit." He reached for his mobile to put things in motion.

"Please make sure they keep it quiet," Ravinder cautioned. "We don't want to spook Binder . . . I want that bastard alive."

"Easy, Ravinder. Don't take this personally, we have to . . ."

"We have to find him and bring him in." Ravinder grated back. "That bastard killed my wife. It does *not* get any more personal."

Kurup made to speak, but Ravinder cut him off with a raised palm. "Please. I got into this because of you." Kurup reluctantly subsided. "What time is Masharrat scheduled to go onstage? One thirty, right?"

"One thirty." Kurup nodded. "Right after lunch."

Ravinder's eyes flicked to his watch. Twelve-forty.

"Mothball Masharrat for all I care, but tell them to keep it real quiet."

"I am not going to put him at risk, Ravinder," Kurup reiterated.

"Don't! I don't care. From my side you can tie him to a stone and throw him in the ocean. But give me a fighting chance to get Leon." Ravinder glared at him. "You owe me that."

Reluctantly, Kurup nodded. "Go get him, then."

Spinning around, mentally plotting the route to Siri Fort auditorium, Ravinder ran toward the exit as Kurup got on the phone.

*Mathura Road, Zakir Hussain Marg, Bhishma Pitamah Marg, and then August Kranti Marg.* Ravinder knew that would be the best route to take.

*Pack off the Pakis.*

*Bluffmaster, give us another one, just like the other one.*

*Pack off the Pakis.*

The chant followed Ravinder to the car park. Despite the tension, the irony of the moment struck him.

*That is precisely what Leon wants to do. But he won't. Not on my watch.*

Ravinder's determination took a hit as he emerged from the stadium and the sight of a thousand cars clogging the car park assaulted his eyes.

*Getting out of here will be a bloody nightmare.*

And he knew time was at a premium. No matter how good the protection, every target was vulnerable. With a hunter as wily as Leon, Ravinder knew the smallest slip on the part of the security team and Masharrat would be playing the harp with Benazir.

Till Leon was knocked out of the game, hunting season on Masharrat was open. Personally appealing though it was, shelving the thought, Ravinder ran for his car.

# TWENTY

Leon was about to get up and fetch Deepa when he saw her answer her mobile. Then she got up and walked toward him.

"I'm sorry, sir, but it is going to be a few more minutes before we can access the main conference hall." She looked apologetic.

"What happened?" Leon felt a stirring of alarm.

"Nothing. The special session is not yet over." She held up her mobile. "I'd requested the general's liaison officer to call me when the hall was free. The general also insists on checking his slides." Then she realized that might not have sounded nice and added hastily, "His session is right after lunch . . . just before yours."

"Will the general come personally?"

"I'm not sure." Deepa looked confused. "I think so. Why?"

"It would be exciting to meet him." Leon forced a smile.

"I'll check and let you know. Perhaps we can go at the same time." She gave a mischievous smile. "I'd like to meet him, too."

Leon could have hugged her; the unexpected break thrilled him.

*If I can get the general within sixty feet, it will all be over but for the cheering.*

Leon knew it did not matter how many guards there were around him; they would not even see the hit coming. By the time they figured it was not a heart attack, he planned to be several air miles out of Delhi.

# TWENTY-ONE

Ravinder wished he had been riding a tank; he would have bludgeoned everything in the car park out of the way. Aware that losing his cool would only increase his handicap, he forced himself to sit patiently as the driver navigated through the untidily parked cars. Despite his best efforts it took twelve minutes before they broke free from the parking lot.

"Good man." Ravinder breathed a sigh of relief as they got onto the road. "Now hit it, Jagjit. We needed to be there an hour ago."

Activating the siren, Jagjit Singh complied. Soon they were tearing down Mathura Road. The road was blissfully devoid of traffic and they made good time.

Ravinder remembered he had not yet warned his team. He speed-dialed Cherian, but got a busy tone. Then Saina. She answered immediately.

"The target is Masharrat, not Zardosi."

"Really?" Saina was shocked. Then excited. "Are you sure?"

"Seems certain. I'm unable to get hold of Cherian. Find him and brief him. Tell him to stick to Masharrat and ensure no one gets near him. You meet me at the gate. I don't want to be held up by security."

"Not to worry, sir." Saina had perked up; one moment she had been guarding the dark-horse target and now, in the blink of an eye, she was in the eye of the storm. "How long before you get here?"

Ravinder checked with Jagjit. "Ten . . . max fifteen minutes."

"Roger, sir. I'll inform Philip and then wait for you at the gate."

# TWENTY-TWO

Leon controlled his eagerness as he replaced his laptop in the carry bag and got up to follow Deepa.

"Unfortunately General Masharrat will not be coming to test his slides," Deepa said as they made their way to the door. "He's sending his assistant instead."

"That's a pity." Leon masked his disappointment at the lost opportunity.

"It is, isn't it? I would have loved to meet him, too. I have seen a Pakistani general before, but never an ex-dictator," Deepa said glumly. "Some security issue," she added as she held the door open for the man she thought was Professor Naug.

"What security issue?" Leon felt a stirring of alarm.

"I'm not sure, but my friend, the general's liaison officer, tells me they have chucked everyone out of his room and doubled the guards."

The alarm in Leon's head was louder now, too loud to ignore.

"Oh! That's disturbing." His mind moved into rapid-process mode. "I hope there is nothing for *us* to worry about." Then he added, "You know, what with all these terrorist attacks."

"Oh no, sir." Deepa seemed anxious to alleviate his concern. "I'm sure we are safe. If there'd been any problem I'm sure we would have been warned." Then, as an afterthought, she added, "The new security measures are only for General Masharrat."

And with that, Leon *knew* he had been blown. "Why do you mean?"

"When my friend told me about the increase in General Masharrat's security I asked if the other speakers were also affected. I even checked with our manager. But the alert is only for the general." Thinking he was worried, Deepa reassured him, "We're fine."

There was no further doubt. Leon's mind spun into action, absorbing the new reality and adapting.

*First things first, I need to get out of here immediately.*

Leon knew they would begin clamp down any time, if they had not done so already. But now there was no panic or fear; he knew that would get him killed more surely than any cop's bullet. He had been in tight corners before and knew he needed to be at his best if he was to survive.

*Who are they looking for? Me? Or Naug?*

*How could they know about Naug?*

Lulled by the APB, Leon discounted that. *Possible, but not likely.*

His mind kicked into high gear and began to sift through the various contingency plans he had deliberated in the days past.

"Give me a minute, please, Deepa." Leon vanished into the toilet adjoining the Green Room. Safe from prying eyes, in the solitary confines of the toilet cubicle, he marshaled his thoughts, worked through the most likely contingencies and how he would counter them.

*Should I get rid of the Naug disguise?*

Leon was confident he could alter it sufficiently to beat a casual scrutiny.

*But what about Deepa? She would know something's wrong.*

He briefly contemplated getting rid of her with some excuse, but sensed that she would not leave him alone for long, and killing her was not a viable option; there were too many people about.

*Besides, I need her to get me out of the auditorium.*

*And I have to do it without arousing her suspicion.*

Leon sensed she was naïve but far from stupid. He didn't want to do anything to arouse her suspicions.

*In the worst case, she could also be useful as a hostage.*

He made up his mind; best to go through the motions of checking his Mac and then claim he had forgotten something in the car.

*That should get me out.*

Leon weighed that; seemed logical and workable.

*I also need to be ready to fight my way out.*

Leon longed for the comforting feel of a pistol, but realized it would be of little use against dozens of armed guards. Opening Naug's bag he took out the heaviest microphone and put it in his right pocket, along with the matching adaptor. The paired clicker went into his left pocket; but Leon did not arm it, worried it might be checked at the gate; he did not relish the idea of someone triggering it off by mistake.

He now joined Deepa, who'd been waiting outside, doing what most people her age did when they have a moment, texting.

"Sorry for making you wait, Deepa."

They resumed their journey toward the conference hall, Deepa half a step ahead.

A minute later Leon was on the podium, hooking up the Mac with practiced ease. Soon Naug's Mac screen was displayed on the projector.

Leon pretended to root through his carry bag. "Oh!" He smacked his forehead in exasperation. "I think I left my thumb drive in the car. Would you please help me get it?"

"Sure, sir." Deepa was Help Incarnate. "If you want, I can go and get it for you from the car."

"Perhaps it would be best if I came along. We may need to search for it. I remember taking it out on the way down, but I am not sure where I left it." Leon saw she was about to suggest something else, so he added. "Would it be okay to leave my Mac connected . . . till we get back? So that I can test my slides."

The distraction worked; most people respond to a question instinctively. "Sure, sir. I will brief the staff to take care." She crossed the stage and spoke to the two men in the wings. A moment later she was back. "Should we go, sir?"

Leon grabbed his bag as they went; his passport and the weaponized items were in it and Leon did not want to leave those unattended.

With Deepa again leading the way, they headed for the main gate.

# TWENTY-THREE

Ravinder heard the call-waiting tone even as Saina hung up. He switched to the new call.

"That's it, then." The relief in Kurup's voice was tangible. "We have locked Masharrat down. He was playing general and kicking up a fuss till I gave him a gist of the possibilities." Kurup laughed, not a pleasant one. "That shut him up really fast. He is now behaving like a very good boy. I have a dozen well-armed men nursing him."

"Pity!" Ravinder could not help himself. "Considering what the blighter did when he was the president of Pakistan, it would have been fun to see him fry."

"Now, now, Ravinder," Kurup chided.

Ravinder noted Kurup seemed much more settled now that he had Masharrat under lock and key. "Have they started looking for Leon?"

"Done that! They already had copies of the APB. I told them to hand out copies to every available man."

"And Professor Naug's photo?"

"Crap!" Some of Kurup's composure evaporated. "Masharrat exasperated me so much that completely slipped my mind. Let me do that right away."

"They can take Naug's photos from the conference organizers and distribute them to security."

"Good thinking. Let me get them on it." About to ring off, Kurup asked, "Where are you now?"

"Almost there," Ravinder told him.

"Keep me posted." Before putting down the phone he added, "And best of luck, Ravinder."

Dropping back the mobile in his pocket Ravinder silently egged the driver on. He was aching to get started.

Instinct told him Leon was within his grasp.

# SHOWDOWN

Leon felt acutely alive, like an infantry soldier infiltrating through enemy lines; the kind of alive that's second cousin to fear and danger; the kind that sends adrenaline coursing through the veins and puts an edge on all human faculties.

The click-clack of Deepa's heels, walking before him, leading the way to the gate and safety beyond, became sharper as they transited from the carpeted corridor to the marble lobby floor. The abrupt glow of the mobile in her left hand as it received yet another text. The faint clinking of bangles on her right hand. The murmur of people standing around the lobby in clusters. Fleeting strands of conversation. An occasional burst of laughter. The rustle of paper. The white-and-black-liveried waiters, moving around with glasses of water, Coke, and Sprite. The occasional flash of light as it reflected off some jewelry. Name cards changing hands. The confusing mass of aftershave lotions, colognes, and perfumes. Errant dust mites rising up in columns, visible wherever stray rays of the winter sun pierced through the skylights.

Leon registered everything; eyes seeking anything out of the ordinary; body primed to leap into action at the first sign of trouble; mind on DEFCON ONE, sifting through the possible scenarios that could play out. He knew he was now in a zero tolerance zone, with absolutely no margin for even the slightest error.

*Not if I want to get out alive.*

They were halfway across the cavernous central lobby when he spotted the first sign of danger: six men dressed in the distinctive black suits of security officers, telltale earpieces, half-folded papers in their left hands, the right ones hovering near the handguns holstered under their coats. They were strung out in a line, five or six feet apart, moving through the crowded lobby, scanning each face as they went past. Like a line of beaters working the jungle, intent on spooking the game and driving it out into the open, to the waiting guns.

Leon tensed, faltered, almost broke step, and then, realizing there was no way out but forward, continued.

*Trust the disguise. Stay calm. Look confident.*

Leon knew security people were trained to watch out for nervousness; he forced himself to relax. But his hand was gripping the microphone in his coat pocket tightly. Realizing it was useless and looked suspicious, he drew his hand out of his pocket.

Deepa's mobile buzzed to life. He heard it above the noise of the crowded lobby. He even sensed its vibration as keenly as if it had been in his own hand. From the corner of his eyes Leon saw her take the call, though his primary focus was still on the hunters.

They had almost drawn level when Deepa got off the phone and turned to him. "My friend tells me the general's talk is likely to be canceled."

"What happened?" Leon was convinced he had made the right call; Ravinder was onto him. He wondered what had happened at the stadium.

*Why had they not taken the bait?*

*Why had the sniper rifles and bombs failed to create the required diversion?*

"It seems he has taken ill." Leon realized Deepa was speaking. "They are planning to take him back to his hotel."

The line of hunters was abreast of them now.

Leon saw the closest one focus on Deepa, who was still speaking. Realizing how beautifully she was distracting the hunter's attention, Leon continued the conversation, keeping his eyes on her and tone chatty.

Then Leon felt the hunter's gaze settle on his face. It lingered. His face burned and his body tensed, ready to leap into action. But ignoring the hunter, Leon responded to Deepa. "I see. That is such a pity. I would have loved to hear him speak."

"Me too, sir."

The hunter lost interest, perhaps distracted by the sight of two people engaged in an apparently normal conversation. His gaze moved on.

Leon noticed the paper in the nearest cop's hand as they passed;

it was a copy of the APB, with all four of Leon's photos on the portion facing up.

*So they still have not made the connection to Naug.*

*Strange?*

Leon sensed that would not last long.

Then they were out of the lobby, down the seven steps to the porch.

Ahead of him, a bare fifty steps away, lay the gate.

Leon again took in the three security lanes at the gate. Most of the guards were facing outward and had their backs to him.

The security lane for conference speakers was now to his right; that's where Deepa was headed. Now that was all that lay between him and safety.

"Why don't you wait here while I get my thumb drive from the car?" he told Deepa as they walked up to the security lane and he placed his bag on the Rapiscan.

"Are you sure, sir?" Deepa made a dubious moue, obviously unwilling to let her charge loose in the big, bad city.

"Of course. I will be back in a moment."

The Rapiscan whined into action and his bag began to inch forward into the machine. Leon started forward toward the doorframe metal detector.

The screech of tires on tarmac made him look up. Leon saw a Bimmer come careening around the corner and shriek to a halt across the road. Even before it came to a stop, the rear door flew open and Ravinder leaped out.

Leon froze.

Ravinder spotted Saina waiting by the gate as he leaped out of the Bimmer; she was standing by the security channel on the extreme left, the one designated Conference Speakers Only. Waving to her, he changed direction, speeding up. He was now in a tearing rush to get inside the auditorium and find Leon, aware Leon would lose no time in getting clear once he learned Masharrat's talk had been canceled.

Leon felt as though a mule had kicked him right between the legs. He froze as he saw Ravinder wave out from across the road and run toward him. For one frantic moment, he thought Ravinder had made him. Then he realized Ravinder was waving out to someone behind him. Relief flooded through him. Leon contemplated turning back, but realized he could not. The Rapiscan had already swallowed his bag, and he was now hardly ten feet from the doorframe metal detector. Deepa, beside him, was giving him an odd look; or so he thought.

Ravinder was greeted by an angry blast of horn as he stepped in the path of a car. He jerked to a halt and stepped back off the road, apologetically waving it on.

Shaking an angry fist, the irate driver accelerated past.

Three more cars and then a bunch of two-wheelers followed closely behind it, forcing Ravinder to stay put.

By now Ravinder was skipping with impatience, shifting his weight irritably from one foot to the other, waiting for a break in traffic. With his quarry now almost in his clutches, he was raring to go.

Leon took in the tall erect figure across the road. Ravinder still looked fit, with no hint of flab, barring a slight thickening at the waist. Leon sensed his impatience.

*The cloth head hasn't changed much.*

He was dressed pretty much as Leon would have expected him to, expensively but not flashily. Leon remembered, even during their college days, unlike most other students, Ravinder, like Edward, had always had money to burn.

*Why not? They were the privileged bastards. Always had it easy.*

Without knowing it, he grimaced.

*I'm the one who got screwed.*

An admixture of anger and fear slashed through Leon. He *knew* if he had been packing right now, he would have drawn and fired, consequences be damned. The urge to see Ravinder go down in a welter of blood overwhelmed Leon. So strong he wanted to run across the road and beat Ravinder to death with his bare fists. Leon almost succumbed to the insane urge, but at the last minute, caught himself.

*Not now! Not here!*

Leon knew even if he managed to kill Ravinder, he would go down, too.

*Not acceptable. I'll not be brought down again . . . not because of this son of a bitch. Not ever again.*

Leon contemplated retreating into the auditorium, for the moment at least, but knew turning back was not an option, not without attracting unwarranted attention. Also, now that the manhunt was under way, he'd be in danger as long as he stayed on the premises. Sooner or later the hunters would find him.

*Get clear of this trap first.*

Steeling his nerves, Leon resolved he would live to fight another day.

*Trust the disguise.* He reminded himself.

Now the doorframe metal detector was just a couple of feet ahead. And the man he hated another fifteen feet beyond that.

Leon started forward.

In tandem, as though the gods were orchestrating this personally, there was a break in traffic and Ravinder also darted forward.

*Will Ravinder recognize me?*

Leon tensed.

*I did. I recognized him immediately.*

His tension escalated.

*But then, I'd been expecting him.*

*So is he!*

Leon cautioned himself to act confident; nervousness was a surefire attention magnet.

*Just a few more steps and . . .*

Something fluttered over Leon's shoulder from behind. It was so sudden and so unexpected it nearly gave him a heart attack.

Ravinder saw Saina was holding up a security pass for him.

"Toss it across," he mouthed and made a throwing gesture, as he jogged purposefully across the road, toward the gate.

She must have got the drift; wrapping its bright yellow ribbon around the pass, Saina tossed it up, along the security channel, toward Ravinder. But she misjudged the throw; instead of going over the gate it barely cleared the shoulder of the man navigating the security channel and struck the inner edge of the doorframe metal detector.

---

Leon, senses still operating at their zenith, followed its flight down, from the edge of the metal detector to the carpet. It was a conference card wrapped in its ribbon. Whoever was waiting for Ravinder had tossed it to him, not too accurately, as it turned out. The security pass landed plumb in the middle of the metal detector, just a few feet ahead of Leon. Heart in his mouth, thumping madly, Leon watched Ravinder speed up and stoop to retrieve it.

Ravinder had noticed the tall, nerdy-looking man accompanied by a young lady—obviously conference staff, judging by her outfit—halt by the metal detector. He saw them speak briefly, noticed she'd stopped on the other side, and then began to check something on her phone.

However, Ravinder was so intent on getting to Saina, briefing her, and joining the search for Leon, that neither they nor the other people at the gate really registered.

The security pass tossed by Saina distracted him further. Ravinder saw it fall onto the red carpet. He sped up to get to it. The nerdy-looking man coming through stopped as Ravinder stooped to retrieve it.

*There was something about him that* . . . but Ravinder was in a terrific hurry.

"Sorry about that." Ravinder murmured as he grabbed up the security card, cleared the doorframe metal detector, and then stepped aside to let him pass.

The channel was narrow, and the two men brushed as they crossed.

Leon was shaken, but the momentary respite as Ravinder stooped to pick up the security pass, fleeting though it was, gave him the chance to compose himself. By the time Ravinder had straightened up, Leon was ready, his face immobile.

Knowing his eyes could give him away, Leon focused on keeping recognition out of them.

"I'm sorry," Ravinder murmured as their eyes met briefly; then he turned sideways to let Leon pass down the narrow lane.

Ignoring him, not trusting himself to speak, Leon kept moving. And then they were crossing, not even inches apart. Instinct warned Leon to turn away from Ravinder as they brushed past. The desire to see his enemy up close made him want to turn toward Ravinder.

Desire won.

Leon knew he should not stare; that always draws attention, but he was unable to look away. He soaked in every wrinkle on that hated face as they slid past each other. The mustache arched up. The beard neatly fixed down. Every fold of the turban pulled taut with military precision, beads of sweat glinting on the forehead, despite the winter chill. Face taut with tension. Breath coming slightly fast, possibly due to exertion.

*Or was it excitement?*

And Leon could not mistake the aftershave, Hugo Boss Bottled.

Just the sort of cologne Ravinder had always favored: male, strong, and dominant. The flame of almost forgotten familiarity flared up. So strong and stark it nearly overwhelmed Leon.

Leon was only able to start breathing again as he stepped away from the man he would have loved to kill.

The metal detector beeped, breaking the spell. Leon cursed himself, realizing the items in his pocket had set off the detector. He made to take them out and show them to the guard; however, the man waved him on, not too perturbed by what the professor was taking out of the auditorium; his mandate was to keep bad stuff out. But that sudden beeping flustered Leon further.

Still dominated by the need to get away, and controlling the urge to speed up or break into a run, Leon kept going at a steady pace toward the car park across the road. He could see the Lexus parked a few cars from the exit.

Leon had gone a few steps past Ravinder when he heard the guard manning the Rapiscan call out.

"Excuse me, Professor. You forgot your bag."

Then louder, since the guard thought Leon had not heard him.

"*Professor. Sir.* You forgot your bag."

Ravinder, acutely aware that time was critically short, was aching to bring Saina up to speed and get started with the search for Leon when the gate guard called out.

The security man's actual words bounced off Ravinder's mind, but he turned, thinking the guard was addressing him. Seeing the guard was talking to the man who had just passed him in the security channel a moment ago, Ravinder lost interest and turned back to Saina.

Then the guard called out again, louder this time.

It was the word *professor,* that caught Ravinder's attention. Though, when he turned around again, he had still not processed the thought, hence was not sure why it seemed significant.

Ravinder saw the man who had just passed him in the security lane also turn around and head back toward the Rapiscan.

Leon felt sudden alarm when the guard called out even louder the second time. Desperate not to draw attention to himself and cursing himself for having forgotten the bag, Leon swiveled to head back and grab the bag off the Rapiscan.

He saw Ravinder had also turned. Without meaning to, Leon looked at him.

Their eyes met again.

This time, even more unsettled by the guard's sudden call, Leon flinched.

There was momentary puzzlement on Ravinder's face. Then Leon saw his eyes widen. Recognition flared. And Leon *knew* Ravinder had made him.

For a moment both men froze, stunned.

Ravinder's mobile began to ring.

Ravinder was so shocked he could not move. Then he saw Leon reach into his coat pocket and assumed he was reaching for a gun.

The hiatus ended.

Galvanized, Ravinder went for his gun, whilst at the same time rushing forward to tackle the assassin. But even as he started forward, Ravinder sensed he was too late; the distraction caused by his mobile, though fleeting, and that moment of shocked inaction was going to cost him. Ravinder saw Leon's hand emerge from his pocket, holding something black and tubular, like a pistol barrel.

Leon caught hold of the microphone in his coat pocket on the very first try. Whipping it out, he took two quick steps forward and lashed out at Ravinder's head. Powered by rage and desperation, the blow was delivered with all the force he could muster. But Leon was in motion and the blow was hastily aimed. And Ravinder was also rushing forward. The blow landed around Ravinder's left ear, blunted mostly by his turban. However, it landed with enough power to give him a nasty gash and send him reeling.

Ravinder felt a jolt of pain as the metallic bulb of the microphone landed on his cheekbone, just short of his left ear. Blood spurted, a large dollop of it into his eye, half blinding him. The shock of the blow drove Ravinder back and down. That proved to be the saving grace.

Leon was now in a tearing hurry to drop Ravinder and make a run for it: aware he would have a fighting chance of escaping if he could get to the car park. There were enough people milling around and they would provide him the distraction he needed, as well as make it hard for Ravinder or any of the guards to open fire indiscriminately. He saw the gate guards had taken note of the scuffle. They seemed undecided between intervening and holding their positions. But Leon knew this was at best a temporary respite.

Driven by his desperate need to get away, Leon swung again with all his might. However, reeling from the first blow, Ravinder had been pushed backward and down. The second blow missed completely, its momentum throwing Leon off-balance.

Realizing he had missed the window of opportunity surprise had won for him, Leon cursed, swiveled, and ran. A few quick strides and he was across the road. A look over his shoulder and he saw Ravinder was rising; though one hand was pressed to his left cheek and he looked dazed. The need to keep Ravinder down a while longer mated with his desire to destroy him.

Leon threw the microphone at him, simultaneously reaching for the clicker in his left coat pocket, trying to arm it *and* at the same time trying to increase the distance between them.

But he was trying to do too many things at the same time; everything slowed down. To make it worse, the clicker snagged in his pocket.

Ravinder sensed more than saw the microphone fly at him. He could not make out what it was, but instinct made him drop the pistol and reach out with both hands to catch the incoming projectile and stop it from striking him.

Fired from hardly ten feet away, the heavy microphone came in fast, cartwheeling through the air. There was a meaty thwack as it slammed into the palm of Ravinder's hands. It was a catch that would have made the Indian team captain proud. It also caught one of Ravinder's fingers awkwardly, sending pain shooting through him.

Leon saw Ravinder catch the microphone and knew half his job was done. The microphone was now inches from Ravinder's face. Another few seconds and the man who had condemned him to this bloody life would be dead.

But the clicker was still caught in his coat pocket.

With a furious snarl, Leon tore it free. The pocket ripped out with it; the piece of cloth was trapped between the clicker buttons and his fingers.

Ravinder realized what it was the minute he caught it. The microphone he had found near Vishal's body leaped into his mind. He did not know the relationship between the two, but his instincts were screaming, warning him that the microphone did not just happen to be with Leon . . . *that the microphone was bad news*.

Without thinking, Ravinder flung it back in the same motion, straight at Leon, who had pulled something out of his coat pocket. Ravinder lunged forward.

Leon lost another vital second to toss off the torn pocket, flick the on switch of the presenter, and then depress the pointer button to arm it.

*One, two, three . . .*

Five seconds had never seemed so long to Leon before.

*Five.*

Finally.

His thumb fumbled to locate the slide-forward button on the clicker, to trigger the microphone.

*Found it!*

Leon was thumbing down the button when he saw Ravinder fling the microphone back at him. He managed to stop himself from triggering the sarin, but was unable to duck out of the flight path. The microphone hit him hard below the chin, smack on his Adam's apple.

The blow was hard enough to stagger him and left him winded. By time he recovered, Ravinder was upon him.

Ravinder closed in on Leon as he staggered back and lashed out with a flurry of savage blows. Only two connected properly, but both had been delivered with the pent-up fury of a man out to avenge his wife.

The first blow struck Leon on the side of his chin, almost knocking him out. The second landed a trifle higher, half on Leon's cheekbone and half on his eye.

"Got you! You filthy bastard." Ravinder did not realize he was screaming.

Cursing that he had dropped his pistol, Ravinder raised his fists to strike again.

Leon, though now down on the ground, was still very much in the game. He was aware the game was tilting against him very fast. If he didn't break free, the gate guards would be upon him in no time. Rallying, he retaliated with a sharp, well-aimed kick.

Ravinder felt a sharp jab of pain as Leon's kick landed on his shin. Then a second one, a little higher, on his kneecap. The pain was pulverizing and this kick hard enough to fell him. Ravinder felt himself falling backward.

He spun sideways to try and break the fall.

That is when Leon's third strike landed. Another powerful kick, delivered with all the desperation and hatred swirling through Leon. It destroyed Ravinder's attempt to break his fall.

Ravinder fell badly, hitting the road hard. He was stunned by the impact.

---

L eon saw Ravinder go down, falling backward, away from him. Simultaneously he saw the guards at the gate rush forward, guns drawn, and realized he would not get away alive.

*Not this time.*

Leon was seething, that his hated enemy had bested him again. The desperate urge to get even energized him.

*I will not go down alone.*

Leon was beyond pain now. Anger and despair had coalesced into a confused, furious mass. His finger again located the trigger button on the clicker. Raising it high, with a final, scornful look, Leon triggered the Sarin.

R avinder was trying to scramble up when he saw Leon's face twist into a smile that reeked of scorn and hatred. For a moment, Ravinder thought Leon was going to say something. Instead, raising the presentation clicker in his hand mockingly, like a champagne flute offered in disdainful toast, Leon pressed one of its buttons.

Unseen by either man, sarin exploded out of the microphone lying on the road between them. It fanned out in a deadly cloud.

L eon, three feet away, felt his lungs constrict. A gigantic wave of pain smashed at him. His lungs screamed as oxygen vanished. A tsunami of pain blanked out everything else.

R avinder had fallen backward and thus was farther from the microphone, about seven feet away. He was almost out of the effective range of the gas. Almost.

He felt a wave of nausea and was suddenly short of oxygen. Pain began to numb his brain.

His last sight was of Leon's face contorted in agony.

Then a massive wall of pain slammed down on Ravinder's chest. And the lights went out, as though someone had turned off the mains.

# EPILOGUE

Jasmine sensed Ravinder was conscious before she felt him stir. Before she could decide whether to ring for the nurse or reach for him, Ravinder's eyes flickered open. He checked her out. Satisfied she was okay, he took in the rest of the room.

"It's good to see you smiling, Princess." He sounded scratchy.

"Is your throat hurting?" Delighted he was coherent, Jasmine grabbed his arm with both hands. She was beaming with relief.

"A bit"—he looked at his arm and smiled, a wicked smile—"but not as much as my arm."

"Oh!" Releasing it with a start, Jasmine jumped up and rang for the nurse. "I'm so happy to see you up and about." A cloud passed over her face. "They kept telling me . . ." She broke off, suddenly tearful.

"How long have I been unconscious?"

"Five days." Tears were now welling up in her eyes, threatening to brim over. "Five *horrible* days, Dad."

"Oh, well. That's behind us now." Ravinder tried to sit up. Abandoned the attempt as a wave of nausea racked him. "I'll be fine soon."

"Thank God," Jasmine exclaimed, putting on her bravest face.

"What about Leon Binder?" Ravinder was unable to stem his curiosity any longer. "Did he . . ."

Jasmine shook her head, suddenly somber. "No. He is dead. I don't know the details, but . . ."

*So I did not fail.*

Ravinder felt a wave of relief swirl through him; suddenly everything seemed so much lighter and brighter.

The door opened and Mandeep hurried in, with a couple of nurses in tow.

Ravinder saw Jasmine suddenly perk up. She smoothed out her

clothes and quickly hand-combed her hair. And she was smiling broadly. Her behavior seemed . . . *strange* . . .

Ravinder had never seen Jasmine like this. He studied both of them as Mandeep and the nurse fussed over him, one checking the monitors and the other him.

"Your vital signs seem stable, sir," Mandeep commented. "How're you feeling?"

"A bit queasy, but not too bad." But Ravinder could not get his mind away from Jasmine.

"Dad, I can't tell you how helpful Dr. Mandeep has been the last few days." Jasmine gave him a tender look, realized Ravinder was watching her, started and stuttered on, "He looked after you personally and kept my morale up."

Realization kicked in. "Thank you very much, Doctor," Ravinder murmured, feeling mischievous.

"You're very welcome, sir. You were really lucky."

"What was it that put me down?"

"Sarin," Edward Kingsley said from the door as Kurup and he entered. "God knows how the blighter managed to get hold of it."

"It was a variant the Americans had tried to develop for tactical use," Kurup added. "But all that is behind us now. You pulled it off, Ravinder, against all odds."

"All a team effort." But Ravinder flushed with pleasure.

"You're too modest." Kurup pulled up a chair. "I really think you should consider coming to work for NIA full-time."

"No way." Jasmine leaped in like a tigress defending her cub. "Not today, not ever. You're so not going back to any kind of police work, Dad."

She was so vehement that everyone laughed. Everyone except Mandeep.

"Not a good idea," Mandeep elaborated solemnly. "Your nearly fatal exposure to sarin will have some permanent effects like nausea and headaches. They are liable to occur without warning and especially if you are stressed. Oh, and they can be severe. Whenever you feel them coming on, lie down and rest."

"Seems like they have to put you out to pasture, old chap," Kingsley chipped in with a grin.

"I don't know about that," Mandeep rewarded him with a severe look, "but you will certainly be coming in for checkups every week till you're stable."

"I will ensure he does." Jasmine had the familiar, determined, Simran-like scowl. "To ensure that, I'm going to stay home and take care of you, Dad."

"You're going to America to study, Princess."

"I can do that next year, Dad. It's not as though they are shutting down law schools any time soon."

"Unfortunately, no." Ravinder grinned.

"Very funny." But Jasmine looked delighted to see him smiling.

"But you will not put your studies on hold, hon. I can look after myself."

"I agree with Mr. Gill. I think you should go. Not everyone gets admission to Duke University School of Law," Mandeep added. "I promise to keep an eye on your dad."

"Do you now?" Ravinder murmured.

"But of course, sir."

"Yes. I have a feeling we will be seeing a lot more of you, Doc," Ravinder said softly, but his gaze was riveted on Jasmine. "And I'm wondering how much of it will be professional," he added with an impish smile.

Jasmine went bright pink as she caught his drift. Mandeep now got it, too. He suddenly found something noteworthy in the medical charts.

Neither Kurup nor Kingsley missed a thing; both spymasters were grinning.

Ravinder reached out and gave Jasmine's hand a squeeze. Their eyes met.

"He's nice," Ravinder whispered.

Both smiled.

"I wish Mom were here," Jasmine whispered back. "It would have been perfect."

Ravinder knew Simran would have been delighted. He also realized how badly he was missing her.

*But Simran has completed her life's journey.*

Ravinder pushed away the pangs of melancholy threatening to overwhelm him.

"I cannot wait to get home, Princess." Ravinder caught Jasmine's hand and smiled. He was incredibly sad Simran was gone. Yet he felt at peace after a very long time.